# The Blue Feather

*B*

BADGER BLISS BOOKS

# DEDICATION

Eight years ago, my heart was broken into countless pieces and scattered to the winds. I never knew being in love could hurt so much. I spent the next two years following the trade winds in a desperate attempt to collect the shards of my heart. I searched far and wide with some success, but try as I might, I was unable to locate the final piece that would make the healing complete. Then, on June 6, 2007, while helping my publisher set up tables in the lobby of the Sheraton Midtown Hotel in Atlanta, Georgia, I looked up and there on the stairs leading into the lobby was the final shard, cradled lovingly in the hand of the most amazing woman I have ever met. Five years later, we were married, surrounded by our sons, grandchildren, and countless friends and family. I never thought I would be thankful for a broken heart, but had it not happened, I would not be where I am today, in the arms of the most perfect soul mate and in love with all life has to offer. I dedicate this book to my wonderful wife, Barb. Thank you for protecting the final shard, while I was searching to make myself whole once more, and for delivering it to me in person.

ALSO WRITTEN BY KAREN D. BADGER AND
AVAILABLE FROM BADGER BLISS BOOKS:


ON A WING AND A PRAYER
YESTERDAY ONCE MORE
THE BLUE FEATHER
ALL MY TOMORROWS
1140 RUE ROYALE

The Billie/Cat Commitment Series:
  IN A FAMILY WAY
  UNCHAINED MEMORIES
  HAPPY CAMPERS
  COLLECTIVE IDENTITY
  SWEET ANGEL
  RELATIVE-LY SPEAKING

www.badgerblissbooks.com

# *The Blue Feather*

## *B*

## A BADGER BLISS BOOK

## By

# *Karen D. Badger*

This is a work of fiction. All characters, locales and events are either products of the author's imagination or are used fictitiously.

THE BLUE FEATHER

Cover design by Ann Phillips

A Badger Bliss Book
Published by Badger Bliss Books
Georgia, VT 05468

www.badgerblissbooks.com

ISBN 13: 978-1-945761-04-1
ISBN 10: 1-945761-04-0

1st Edition published by Blue Feather Books, Ltd, June, 2013
2nd Edition, published by Badger Bliss Books, September 2015
3rd Edition published by Badger Blis Books, August, 2016

Printed in the United States of America and in the United Kingdom

# ACKNOWLEDGMENTS

It is with full awareness that I admit I would look like a total idiot if not for my beta readers: Ellie Atherton (my mom), Sheri Barnett (aka Big Guy), Donna Brown, Daisy Delarm, and of course, my wife, Barb Sawyer (aka Bliss). You all provide an invaluable service—finding errors, inconsistencies, and guffaws, but mostly providing feedback that allows me to improve my craft. I sincerely appreciate your contributions and your efforts, not only toward making this book the best that it can be, but also for helping me become the best writer I can be. Many thanks as well to Nann Dunne, my editor and dear, dear friend. You rock, Nann. Thank you so much for your guidance and for being my friend. Finally, many thanks to Emily Reed, who has consistently shown her support and confidence in my ability to produce a good story and who worked very hard to get this book out in record time… thanks, Em!

# Foreword

## by Nann Dunne, editor

Some events in The Blue Feather are set in England in the early 1600s. This time frame falls within the Early Modern English period, when the English language was in transition. People still used the second person singular "thou" and "thee" with their "-st" and "-est" verb endings ("hast" and "needest," for example). The use of the plural "ye," however, had given way to "you." The third person and plural use of the verb endings "-th" and "-eth" ("doth" and "speaketh," for example) was phasing out but could still be heard occasionally. After a lot of research, author Karen Badger and I did our best to stick to speech that was authentic to the times. If you notice any inconsistencies, that's understandable, because the speech itself was going through a time of inconsistent growth. I, for one, am grateful that English has become simpler to speak, to read, and to edit.

# Chapter 1

## 1613—North Yorkshire, England

Jenna led Hadley to the edge of the forest where Caleb and Maura were waiting with the children.

"Thou must take the wee ones and go, right quickly. The king's men will be here anon. Thou must save them. I fear I won't escape this time. Pray do as I say. The babes cannot be harmed."

"But they have nothing on thee, Jenna."

"They know who we are, Hadley. Thou knowest they won't rest until we are all dead. After the massacre in Lancashire, no one is safe."

The thunder of hooves could be heard in the distance. "Great Goddess, they are near. Thou must go."

Jenna removed Hadley's white cloak and wrapped a long, dark, hooded cloak around her. She clasped it closed with Hadley's blue feather brooch. Hadley reached for Jenna's arm. "Where shall I go? What shall I do?"

"Go to the clan in Scotland. They will care for thee."

"I won't leave thee. I cannot. Pray don't make me go."

Jenna took Hadley's face between her hands. "If I can, I will join thee in a fortnight. If not by then, know that I love thee. Forever, thou wilt live in my heart."

"Come with us, pray."

Jenna kissed Hadley tenderly and touched her forehead to hers. "I cannot. The babes must be saved. Thou knowest how important that is. Thou knowest what is at stake here. I will give thee time to escape. I must lead them away—at any cost."

"Nay!"

"Aye. The Mother Goddess will protect thee on thy

journey. Go with thee, now. Caleb shall see to thine escape. I shall hold them at bay for as long as I can."

With tears in her eyes, Hadley climbed into the back of the wagon and pulled the blanket over her and the babes.

"Wait. Take these." Jenna retrieved a book, a bag of coins, and something else from the pouch around her neck and pressed them into Hadley's hand. "The Book of Shadows cannot be found. 'Twould mean the end of the family. Pass these on to the children. Future generations shall need them. Now go."

Hadley reached for her one last time. "I love thee, Jenna. I always shall. Pray come to us. Pray."

"I shall try, my love." Jenna kissed the babes' foreheads. "Be good for thy mum, and know I will always love thee." She looked once more into Hadley's eyes. "God speed, Hadley Metcalf. We shall be together again—if not in this life, then in the Summerlands. Blessed be." Jenna nodded to Caleb and ran back toward the clearing.

Hadley felt the jolt of the wagon as it surged forward. She could hear loud voices in the distance.

"Halt! By decree of the king, thou art to be taken into the custody of the court."

"By what charge?" Hadley heard Jenna demand.

"Witchcraft."

Hadley lay beside the babes and pulled the blanket over them. She stifled a sob and clutched the Book of Shadows close to her chest. "May the Goddess be with thee, my love," she whispered. She wrapped the cloak tighter around her and realized, still clutched in her hand, was the object Jenna gave to her for the babes. She opened her hand and revealed Jenna's blue feather brooch, the sister to her own that clasped the cloak she wore. She slipped the brooch into the pocket of her cloak and kept it clasped in her hand. She rode silently into the night with tears in her eyes and fear in her heart.

# Chapter 2

## 2013—Plymouth, Massachusetts

Willow McCord pulled her car up to her rural delivery mailbox and rolled down the window. Sheets of rain invaded the dry comfort of her car as she opened the box and gathered several pieces of mail. She threw them onto the passenger seat, quickly closed the window, steered her car into her driveway, and turned off the ignition.

"Damned rain. Maybe the downpour will let up if I wait long enough." She drummed her fingers on the steering wheel and peered out into the rain. "Come on. Let up just a little. I've got to pee." Her leg bounced up and down as she strained to avoid an accident.

"All right, I can't hold it any longer. Here goes nothing."

She collected her handbag and the mail, grabbed her keys from the ignition, and flung the door open. In a dash, she was out of the car and running toward the porch. Soaked through, she fumbled with her keys while standing cross-legged, trying not to wet herself.

"Oh God, I'm not going to make it," she said out loud as the key slipped into the lock. The mail fell out of her hands and scattered at her feet on the wet porch deck.

"God damn it!" She paused just long enough to realize she would have to retrieve the mail after she silenced her bladder, which was screaming hysterically at her. She ran into the house, threw her handbag on the couch, and made a mad dash to the bathroom. She made quick work of her clothing and sat down.

"Oh, my God. This is better than an orgasm," she said as relief flooded through her. She giggled, "It's a pee-gasm!" She caught sight of herself in the mirror above the vanity. Geesh.

She looked like a drowned rat. Willow's long and curly auburn hair was plastered to her face and neck and her scrubs top was soaked to the point she could see her bra through it. "It'll be great fun running a comb through this mess. I've got to get out of these wet clothes."

She washed her hands and headed toward the stairs in the far corner of the living room that led to the upper story. Then she recalled she'd left the door wide open and the mail scattered on the porch. She retrieved the mail, closed the door, and deposited the damp pieces on the couch beside her handbag as she went to change into dry clothes. She tossed a pair of plaid lounge pants and a T-shirt from her drawer onto the bed and peeled off her wet scrubs. When she opened the hamper, she found it was full. "I guess I'd better do some laundry or I'll be going to work naked tomorrow," she muttered under her breath. She stopped and grinned evilly. That might get Susan's attention. *God knows nothing else has worked.*

Willow enjoyed her job as a dental hygienist. The commute between Plymouth and her job in Boston was sometimes long and tedious, but she loved the idyllic setting of her home on the seashore. Plymouth provided a feel of small town living amidst a rich colonial history and eclectic diversity. She loved quiet walks on the seashore, window-shopping in the tiny stores along Main Street, and wine-tasting at the various vineyards that dotted the edges of countless cranberry bogs. When she felt like a little fun, King Richard's Faire was only a short drive away, and she was within an hour's drive of Provincetown where she always felt at home. Willow's coworkers at the dental practice were pleasant and engaging, especially Susan. She was beautiful and sexy and had a wonderful sense of humor. Willow found herself pining for Susan's attention. Even a simple smile sent her over the moon, and any opportunity she had to assist alongside her had Willow walking on clouds for days. Unfortunately for her, Susan was married—to a man.

As she dressed, she released a resigned sigh. "Okay, Willow, you need to get a handle on this. Straight-girl crushes can only end in disappointment."

She grabbed an armful of clothes from the hamper and headed back down the stairs. When she passed the couch, she glanced at the pile of mail thrown there in haste. "Oh, yeah. I still need to go through the mail."

She went into the kitchen and dropped the laundry on the floor beside the folding doors that concealed the washer and dryer. She opened the doors and loaded the clothes as well as a scoop of detergent into the washing machine. "That should do it," she said and turned it on.

After she got a beer from the refrigerator and carried it to the living room, she twisted off the cap and took a long draw from the bottle. She placed it on the coffee table as she sat on the couch and picked up the mail. "Okay, what do we have here? Bill, junk mail, charity, another charity. Everyone seems to want money these days." When she was finished, she had two piles, one for the trash and the other for bills. "Not too bad. Just two bills out of the whole stack."

Willow stood up to throw the pile of junk mail away and was interrupted by a knock on the front door. She pulled back the curtain and saw a UPS delivery man on her doorstep. She opened the door.

"Hi there," she said.

"Package for Willow McCord."

"I'm Willow McCord."

He scanned the barcode on his handheld device and offered it to Willow. "Sign here, please."

Willow signed her name on the touch screen and handed it back to him. "Okay, Ms. McCord. Here's your package. Have a nice day."

"Thank you. You, too." Willow accepted the medium-sized box, and the man hustled back to his truck. She looked at the return address. "Hawksworth Estates, Newcastle upon Tyne, Northumberland County, England. Who do I know in England?"

She carried the box to the coffee table and grabbed a sharp knife from the kitchen. She carefully cut the tape along the top and side seams and unfolded the flaps, then searched inside the packing peanuts until her hand encountered a rectangular box. Approximately four inches long by three wide and one deep, the box was crudely wrapped in a burlap type material and tied with coarse string. She shook it gently and heard a slight scraping sound.

*What could it be?* She put the box on the table in front of her and untied the string. Folding back the layers of burlap, she exposed an intricately carved wooden box with a pentagram encased in a circle on the cover. "Where have I seen that symbol before?"

A sudden surge of nervous apprehension filled her as she struggled with whether or not to open it. Curiosity won out, and she reached forward and carefully removed the lid.

"Oh, my God!"

Willow jumped to her feet and paced back and forth in front of the coffee table, never taking her eyes from the object. Finally, she ran upstairs to her room and returned a short time later with something clutched in her fist. She sat down and laid it on the table beside the open box. There before her were two brooches—mirror images of each other, each containing a single sapphire blue feather mounted on a silver Celtic cross. One was hers, passed down from her grandmother, and the other came from someone in England.

She retrieved her pin from the table and looked at it closely. "How can this be?" Willow whispered. "Grandmother McCord left this brooch to me in her will. I always thought it was one of a kind." She glanced again at the other brooch still nested in the box. "I wonder who sent it." She looked at the return address on the box once more. Hawksworth Estates. She had no idea who it could be.

She felt around inside the box and pulled out a piece of paper. Her hands shook as she unfolded it and spread it out on the table. She read it out loud.

"Willow McCord. Follow the path of your heritage. The brooch will lead you home." The letter was signed, "S.H."

"What the hell does that mean? 'The brooch will lead you home.' I'm already home. And who is S.H.?"

# Chapter 3

## 1610—North Yorkshire, England

Hadley Metcalf looked up from her sewing as the door to her Tailor Shop swung open.

"Good day to thee, Mistress Metcalf. How art thee this fine day?"

"Master Sheffield, 'tis so good to see thy smiling face. A fine day 'tis. What can I help thee with?"

"It seems I had a bit of a mishap while dressing, and I've managed to put a tear in the sleeve of my shirt. Couldst thou repair it for me?"

Hadley took the garment from her customer and looked at the tear. She glanced at him. "How didst thou tear it?" Hadley watched as a flush rose to his cheeks.

"Ah, I caught it on a nail. Aye, that's it."

"I see." Hadley thought to herself that the tear looked like a clean cut, not ragged as one would expect if caught on a nail. She smiled. "I believe I can fix it up for thee."

Master Sheffield bowed at the waist. "I would forever be in thy debt, kind lady. Allow me to thank thee with dinner at the pub."

Hadley rose to her feet and reached for Master Sheffield's hand. "I look kindly on thy offer, sire, but I have too much work here to consider it."

Before Master Sheffield could respond, the door to the shop opened. Hadley patted his hand and nodded toward the new customer. "As I said, kind sir."

Disappointment crossed his handsome features. "I understand. Perchance another time?"

"Perhaps," she replied.

"Good day to thee, then."

"Good day to thee as well. Thou canst collect thy blouse the day after the morrow."

"Until then."

Master Sheffield left and Hadley turned her attention to her new customer. The man faced away from her while looking at the sturdy leather material on display. From behind, he was tall and slim and wore soft leather trousers, a dingy white shirt, tucked in, and heavy black boots with his pant legs stuffed into them. A strip of leather secured his long brown hair in a tail at the back of his head.

"May I help thee, sir?"

Hadley gasped when the customer turned around and she realized 'he' had breasts. She fumbled with an apology. "I'm so sorry, Mistress. I didn't realize…"

"Not blaming thee one bit. I do look a bit like a lad from the back."

Hadley felt faint as this woman's bright smile radiated to the very core of her being. She couldn't stop staring into the piercing blue eyes that looked back at her.

The customer put her hand on Hadley's shoulder. "Art thou all right?"

Hadley snapped out of her trance and blushed profusely. "Ah, I have the manners of a blacksmith today. 'Tis just that… well, 'tisn't right for a woman to be wearing trousers." She nervously tidied her hair. "'Tis not something one is accustomed to seeing. Thou caughtest me off guard. I beg thy forgiveness." Hadley inhaled deeply to compose herself and curtsied. "Welcome to my shop. My name is Hadley. Hadley Metcalf."

The customer grinned sheepishly and gave a bow. "Jenna Hawksworth. I am honored to meet thee. I am the new blacksmith."

Hadley's eyes opened wider. "I am going to the devil himself. Mama always said my words would cause me pain one day. She was right. I do not mean to disparage your trade, mind thee."

Jenna crossed her arms and laughed. "Think naught of it."

"I ask thy forgiveness for my rude ways, Mistress. Tell me, what can I do to make up for my disrespect?"

"The first thing, thou canst call me Jenna. Next, I am looking at the bolt of leather over there. Need a new apron for smithing, aye? Canst thou oblige?"

"Oblige, I can. When art thou needing this new apron?"

"My need is two days hence."

"Two days it will be. Where shall I deliver this new ware?"

"Dost thou always deliver to thy patrons, Mistress Hadley?"

Hadley smiled coyly. "Not all."

"Here is my offer. Allow me to provide thee with dinner and drink, two days hence at the village tavern. 'Tis there thou canst deliver my wares."

"Two days hence at the village tavern. I accept thy offer."

Jenna bowed and took Hadley's hand in her own. In a show of chivalry, she kissed the back of Hadley's knuckles. "Until then, Mistress Metcalf."

Hadley rushed to the window and watched Jenna saunter across the dry, sandy ground toward the village center. Her heart fluttered, and she thought about their meeting in two days. "I best be getting to that apron."

# Chapter 4

## 2013—Plymouth, Massachusetts

Willow removed the blue feather brooch from the box and laid it on the table beside her own. They looked curiously similar yet different. She picked them up, one in each hand, and weighed them. She turned them over and held them close together. They appeared to be mirror images of each other. Noticing something curious about them, she switched them from one hand to the other and placed them close together again. Just then, the clock struck seven p.m. and began to chime loudly. Willow jumped. "Jesus! That scared me."

She turned her attention back to the brooches. Almost like some magnetic force was pulling them toward each other, the two brooches locked together like puzzle pieces. "Oh, my God. It's like they were made to be together. How could two pieces of jewelry from separate sides of the world be a matched set? This can't be a coincidence."

She picked up the paper that accompanied the brooch and read it again. "'Follow the path of your heritage. The brooch will lead you home.' I don't understand what that means. Grammy's been gone for ten years now. I wonder if Mom or Dad know anything about it." Willow picked up the phone and dialed her mother's number.

"You have reached the home of Sandy and Roger McCord. Leave a message at the beep, and we'll get back to you as soon as we can."

Willow hung up the phone. "Rats. I forgot Mom and Dad are on a cruise."

She put her laundry into the dryer and prepared a light dinner for herself. She placed the connected brooches on the table in front of her while she ate and studied how well they fit together. The brooches were beautiful. She had no idea how old they were, but the dark blue sapphires that made up the feathers were still bold and shiny and the Celtic crosses on which they were mounted were intricately carved in silver, with recesses brushed in black. "They must be worth something. I'll have them checked out by a jeweler in Boston on the way to work tomorrow."

Willow yawned. She glanced at the clock and saw it was nearly nine p.m. "Where does the time go? Long drive to work in the morning. Maybe I'll hit the sheets early tonight." She rinsed and put her dishes in the dishwasher and made her rounds to close windows and lock doors, then returned to the kitchen to retrieve the brooches and headed upstairs to her room. She placed the pins on the bedside table. Minutes later, dressed in a T-shirt and panties, she drifted off to sleep.

* * *

Willow sat up quickly in bed, disoriented, as a low chanting sound reached her ears. She looked around her room. Everything was in place, including the clothing she'd removed and thrown over the chair before climbing into bed. The room had an eerie glow about it that came from outside. The glow flickered as though caused by something afire. She threw aside her blankets and rushed to the window. On her lawn was a large circle surrounding a five-point star, all of which was ablaze. At each point of the star, hooded figures in long, flowing capes chanted an indiscernible mantra. She threw open the window.

"What are you doing?" she yelled. "Get off my lawn."

The chant continued. "Willow, follow the path of your heritage. The brooch will lead you home."

"I'm calling the police," she screamed. She ran to her cell phone she had placed on the bedside table. As she reached for the phone, the interlocked brooches beside it began to glow. She snatched her hand away, and the chant grew louder.

"Follow the path of your heritage. The brooch will lead you

home."

She ran back to the window. "Who are you?"

"The brooch will lead you home. The brooch will…"

"Ahhh!" Willow bolted upright in bed. "Oh, my God!" She looked around the room. Everything was in place. The room was dark, the silence broken only by her labored breathing. "Holy shit!" she said as she tried to calm herself. She threw her blankets aside and went to the window. The lawn outside was empty and dark. She opened the window and listened carefully. The only sound to be heard was the singing of crickets in the distance, and there was no trace of smoke in the air.

Willow returned to her bed and sat down. She ran a hand through her tussled hair. "Was I dreaming?" She lay back down and stared at the ceiling, trying to recall the dream. "It must be the brooch," she mused. "My subconscious mind is playing tricks on me." She turned her head and looked at the interlocked brooches lying innocently on the bedside table. She reached over and picked them up but dropped them immediately. They were hot to the touch.

# Chapter 5

## 1610—North Yorkshire, England

Jenna washed her face and hands at the basin, donned a clean shirt and trousers, and combed and tied back her hair. Next, she slipped on her long duster and picked up her brooch from the table. She caressed it in her hands and felt the warmth generated by her touch. She closed her eyes and thought back to when she smithed the brooches. She worked painstakingly hard to craft them with intricate detail. Each brooch was designed to enhance the innate potential and power of the wearer selected for the repression. In her mind's eye, she could see the ceremony offering the pin to the Goddess and asking for the power to do good in return. She clearly remembered the spell she chanted over and over during the smithing. "Mother Goddess, hear my plea, in this symbol, inhabit thee—all the chosen souls will give, forever in thy essence live—deep inside these stones of blue, together walk the path so true—with thy power fair and just, bar the gates of Tartarus. Mother Goddess, hear my plea—as I will it, so shall it be." She carefully pinned the brooch to her lapel and headed out.

She arrived early at the village tavern and arranged for a table at the back of the room. As usual, the tavern was full of common folk, mostly men, enjoying an evening of mead, the company of friends, and an occasional squeeze of the buxom waitress's bottom. A goat wandered randomly from table to table looking for handouts. Jenna ordered a tankard of mead while she waited for Hadley to arrive.

Jenna had come to town a week earlier. She migrated from Billingham to North Yorkshire looking for work in order to support herself after leaving her father's house. Between her preference for the fairer sex, and her 'ungodly pursuits' as her father put it, she was neither wanted nor accepted in her village. At twenty-four, she was well trained in the art of blacksmithing, having apprenticed with her own village blacksmith for nearly ten years. It was a trade not very many women were good at. They lacked either the physical strength it required or the mental strength to endure the ill favor of male blacksmiths. On the trek from her hometown to North Yorkshire, she was turned down for work no less than six times. Her luck changed when she arrived in this village. The blacksmith had just retired and was yet to be replaced. The people of the village were desperate, and they gave her a chance to prove her worth. Within the week, she completed five projects, all to the satisfaction of her customers, and was offered the job that included lodging.

Two days ago, she visited the tailor, intent on finding suitable leather for a new apron. She found more than she bargained for. When she entered the shop, she nearly walked into a display of fabric, for instead of watching where she was stepping, her gaze was drawn to the shop owner. The auburn-haired beauty took her breath away, and she had to turn her back on the woman to hide the flush on her face caused by her own desires. When she first exchanged words with Hadley, she had all she could do to keep her gaze trained on those piecing green eyes and not on the ample curves that were clearly outlined by her form-fitting smock. And now here she was, waiting to dine with her, and if perchance she was lucky, she may go home with a kiss on her breath.

Jenna was drawn from her daydream by the sounds of a commotion at the door of the tavern. Her gaze leveled on the woman making her way across the room amidst several offers from the gentlemen for her to join them. She smiled. It was her good fortune and not theirs that this lady would grace her table tonight.

She rose from her seat and met Hadley halfway across the room. She offered her arm and looked at the gentlemen vying for her attention. "My apologies, kind sirs, but the lady is here to join me for dinner. Pray excuse us."

Jenna walked Hadley across the room to their table. "Thy chair," Jenna said as she held it out.

Hadley looked over her shoulder and smiled. "Gramercy."

Jenna inhaled deeply to regain control of her rapidly beating heart and sat down opposite Hadley. "Thou lookest beauteous in that dress," she said.

"I must say thou trimmest well thyself. After my earlier guffaw, I wasn't sure whether thou wouldst appear in a dress or men's ware."

Jenna could feel Hadley's gaze run over her. "I have to admit I like to dress up now and then. Working under that sweaty apron all day grows weary, and trousers are more comfortable than dresses. In fact, I don't remember when last I wore a dress."

"Speaking of aprons, I believe this is thine." Hadley handed Jenna the package she was carrying.

"This is my new apron, I surmise. What do I owe thee?"

"Consider it a welcome gift."

"Nay. I insist on paying for it."

"I'll hear naught of it. Now, be quiet with thy wretched self and accept the gift."

Jenna sat back and smiled broadly. "Aye, Mistress. Dost thou always have such fire in thy blood?"

"When the need arises."

"Well, fair lady, thou forever hast my gratitude."

Hadley reached forward and touched the jewelry on Jenna's lapel. "I like this. 'Tis a feather, is it not?"

"'Tis. It has special powers."

"Powers? What exactly dost thou mean?"

A waitress approached with a tankard of mead for Hadley.

Jenna lifted her tankard and held it up toward her. "I took the liberty of having a drink brought to the table for thee. I hope thou dost not mind."

Hadley clinked her tankard with Jenna's. "Not at all."

"So, Hadley Metcalf. Tell us about thyself."

Hadley drank from her mead and placed the tankard in front of her. "What is there to tell? I be all of thirty years old, and a tailor. I've been doing the business for nigh on five years now."

"Thirty years old? Quite an old woman, thou art. Hast thou a husband and babes?"

Hadley slapped Jenna's arm. "How old art thou, Mistress Trouser-wearing Blacksmith?"

Jenna sat back and grinned. "I am teasing, thou dost know. I am all of twenty and four."

"Twenty and four? If I am an old woman, then thou art a child. How is it at twenty and four thou dost strut around like thou dost own the world?"

"I had to grow up in haste. Leave it at that. So I am asking again—hast thou a husband and babes?"

Hadley leaned on her forearms. Jenna couldn't help but notice how it pushed her bosom up into her cleavage. "It is just me, myself."

"How is it that a comely woman like thee isn't spoken for?"

"I prefer to be mine own woman. I answer to no man. And I thank thee truly for thy kind words."

"No thanks necessary. Just speaking the truth."

Hadley drew from her tankard of mead and placed it back on the table. She crossed her arms in front of her. "So, thou art twenty and four and ownest the world, sitting there in thy fancy trousers and that blue feather on thy lapel. So tell me—what powers doth it possess?"

Jenna picked up her tankard, drank from it, and cradled it on the table in front of her. "Power to fulfill thy desires. Power to control thy dreams. Only those who wear it knoweth what it means."

"Dost thou mean there are more of them?"

Jenna became serious as the mischief left her face. She reached for Hadley's hand. "Aye. Many more."

# Chapter 6

## 2013—Newcastle upon Tyne, England

Sawyer Hawksworth glanced at the clock. It was ten p.m. She was having trouble falling asleep. Willow was on her mind. "I wonder if it's arrived." She looked at the clock again. "It's nearly five o'clock where she is." She closed her eyes and thought back to the events of nearly a year ago. She'd just buried her parents after their untimely deaths in an auto accident.

Sawyer knew from an early age that her family was wealthy. She enjoyed the comforts of privilege, but unlike her contemporaries, she resisted the practice of flaunting her wealth to those less fortunate. Sawyer was very different from other girls. Instead of spending her teenage years learning social graces to attract the attention of suitors, she became a master horsewoman. Instead of schooling herself in the latest etiquette of the day, she went to university and earned a degree in economics. Her goal was to be independent: to become a self-made woman in a career that would allow her to support herself and make a difference in the world.

Directly out of university, she was hired as a clerk in a small accounting firm. During the lean years, she stubbornly refused financial help from her parents and insisted on paying them back for four years of university tuition. Ten years later, she was director and CEO of her own financial advising firm. She was wealthy in her own right and made a point of funding projects to improve the economic lives of others.

She never would have imagined returning to her family home after ten years on her own. She especially never imagined having to bury her parents and take over the family estate. For the first two weeks after their deaths, she sat around feeling sorry for herself and avoiding the world. She barely ate the food her housekeeper, Matilda, fixed for her every day, and she refused all calls from friends. Finally, at the urging of the family barrister, she forced herself to go through her parents' belongings.

Sawyer opened her eyes and looked at the clock once more.

"Nearly eleven—six in the evening her time. I wonder what she's doing right now."

Her thoughts drifted back to her discovery a month after her parents died. She spent the day going through her parents' clothing, tagging most of them to be given away to charities. When she was finished, she decided to sort through the contents of her father's desk. An intense feeling of warmth and security filled her when she opened the door to his study. She spent many hours in this room as a child, the walls lined in leather, the smell of tobacco smoke embedded in everything after generations of use. She sat in her father's chair and ran her hands over the top, still shiny and dust free, thanks to Matilda's watchful eye over the cleaning staff.

Sawyer pushed the chair back and dropped to her knees on the floor. She crawled under the desk where she used to hide as a child to scare her father when he came into the room. Sitting cross-legged, she looked out into the room and imagined her father sitting in the chair and suddenly jumping up to exclaim his surprise when she grabbed his trouser cuff and yanked. She would squeal with delight that she managed to pull it off each and every time. As an adult, she now knew his reaction was more for her benefit than in actual alarm. That made her miss him even more.

She shook herself out of her reverie and began to sort through the documents in his desk. Two hours later, she had three neat piles: the first contained business papers; a second contained documents about the estate; and a third contained personal papers, including several birthday cards she made for him as a child. She sighed heavily and wiped the tears from her eyes as she reviewed the last pile in detail. Finally, she placed each set of documents in its own separate file and rose to leave the room. It was then she noticed an envelope had fallen to the floor. The envelope was addressed to her. She opened it, extracted a letter and a key, and read the letter out loud.

My darling daughter,

If you are reading this letter, it most likely means I am no longer with you. I have wanted to say so much to you over the years. I have wanted so much to tell you about your heritage, but your mother thought it best to let sleeping dogs lie, to use her words. You are a gifted woman—more than you realize. Your gift has been handed down through generations of Hawksworths, and now it's time to reveal your heritage to you. There will be much weighing on your shoulders in the very near future, specifically in the year 2013. The key you found in the envelope is to a safe deposit box located in the Newcastle depository. There you will learn your role in the future of our kind. It is time you take your place in the lineage. It will be dangerous and more challenging than you know, but you are strong, Sawyer, strong enough to control the power of your gift and to use it for the common good. Wherever life leads, and whomever you choose to live it with, know that I love you and I will be watching over you.

Your devoted father,
William Hawksworth.

Sawyer sat in her father's chair and stared at the letter. She placed it on the desk and, with a pen, drew a circle with a five-pointed star inside. "Papa, I've known about my gift for many years. Nana Hawksworth told me. She made me swear never to tell until it came time to pass it on to my own children. Nana taught me to use the gift and to do no harm. I made a vow to her and to the Great Goddess to always use it wisely, and now I make that same promise to you. Don't worry, Papa. I know what I have to do. I promise I won't let the family down."

* * *

Sawyer awoke with a start, fully awake. She looked at the

clock—the time flashed midnight. She sat up perfectly still with her back against the headboard. The only sound in the room was the beating of her heart. Suddenly, she stiffened and grabbed two handfuls of bed sheet while slight tremors shook her body. Seconds later, it stopped and she sank down into the sheets. She closed her eyes and smiled. "The feathers have been joined."

# Chapter 7

## 2013—Plymouth, Massachusetts

The events of the previous night spooked Willow. After realizing the brooches were hot, she had run down the stairs and grabbed a potholder and the box the English brooch arrived in. She looked at the entwined jewelry on her bedside table and couldn't for the life of her remember which of the two was hers. She grabbed them both with the potholder and dropped them into the wooden box, which she took downstairs and put on the kitchen table for the remainder of the night. It took forever to fall back to sleep.

When her alarm went off in the morning, she rushed to her bedroom window to see if the daylight would make visible any evidence of burn marks in the grass. When she saw none, she was more convinced than ever that the symbol on the box's cover planted a subliminal message in her subconscious mind and made her have that god-awful nightmare. She sat on the edge of the bed and looked at the spot where the intertwined brooches had been the night before. There on the wooden surface was the letter "H" burned into the wood. "What the hell?" She glanced at the clock. "Damn—it's nearly six-thirty. I better get into the shower."

Willow gazed at the box on the table as she stood at the kitchen counter and stirred her coffee. She drank the last of her coffee and rinsed her cup. She cautiously approached the box, picked it up, and removed the cover. The two brooches nestled inside, still locked together. She tentatively touched them with her fingertip and found they were cold. A little bolder, she picked up the brooches and held them in her palm. "Huh. Maybe I was imagining the temperature thing last night." She turned the intertwined brooches over. The overlapping horizontal bars on the Celtic crosses formed a stylized letter H. "Well, I'll be. I wonder..." She ran upstairs with the brooches and carefully aligned them to the burn mark on her bedside table. They were a perfect fit.

More confused than ever, she returned to the kitchen. "Maybe a jeweler can shed some light on this," she mumbled. She pulled the two brooches apart and put them back into the box. Just then, the grandfather clock in her living room began to chime. "Shit! Seven o'clock. I've got to get on the road if I'm going to have time to drop these off at the jeweler before work."

Willow pulled into the parking lot of a jeweler on the outskirts of Boston. She glanced at the sign above the door before entering: Treasured Memories—specializing in heirloom jewelry. The man behind the counter was slightly balding and middle-aged. "Good morning," Willow said as she approached the counter.

"Good morning, young lady. What can I do for you?" the man replied in a British accent.

Willow put the box on the counter. "I was wondering if you could look at these brooches for me."

"Do they need repair?"

"No. I don't think so. I received one of these in the mail yesterday from England, and it's almost a duplicate of one my grandmother gave to me many years ago. They seem to fit together like puzzle pieces. I thought it was odd that two pieces from distant parts of the world would have so much in common."

"From England? Did a friend send it?"

"No. That's the peculiar part. I have no idea who sent it to me."

"Well, let's take a look."

Willow took the cover off the box and slid it toward the shopkeeper. "They're beautiful, aren't they? Look at how they lock together." She retrieved the brooches from the box and slipped them together.

The man took a step backward. "Put them back into the

box."

Alarmed, Willow separated the brooches and put them into the box. She looked at him while she put the cover back on. He seemed scared. "Is something wrong?"

"No. Nothing's wrong. I don't recognize them. You'll have to take them elsewhere."

"Where? Can you recommend someone?"

"There are many jewelers in Boston. Choose one. I'm sorry, but I'm very busy. Have a good day." The man took Willow's arm and ushered her toward the door.

"Geesh. What was his problem?" Willow slipped the box into her handbag and walked toward her car. She noticed the time on the digital clock across the street. It was almost eight-thirty. Thirty minutes left before she needed to be at work. Should she find another jeweler or get a coffee? She waited a brief moment. "Coffee it is." She pulled out of the parking space and drove to the end of the lot.

Just as she was about to pull into traffic, her car stalled. "What the hell?" She turned the ignition key, and it started up again. "That was odd." She slipped into traffic and stayed in the closest lane. She expected the usual bumper-to-bumper Boston traffic, but this morning, she was hitting all the green lights. Just as the car in front of her passed through the intersection, a car on the cross street ran the red light. The cars collided and spun around. Willow slammed on her brake and narrowly avoided being hit. Everything inside her car became airborne, including her handbag, which emptied onto the passenger-side floor.

She threw the shifter into park and scrambled to reach her cell phone on the floor. She called 911 and reported the accident, then ran to see if there was anything she could do to help. Broken glass was scattered everywhere. When she reached the car, she looked in and nearly lost her breakfast. "Oh, my God." She walked a few feet away. Another motorist stopped and ran to her side.

"Are you okay? Were you in the car?" he asked.

"No. I was behind him. Oh, my God. There's blood everywhere. We need to help him and check the other car."

The motorist looked inside the car. He took Willow's arm and led her away. "There's nothing we can do for him now.

Look, the paramedics just arrived. They'll take care of everyone. We need to get out of their way. Where's your car?"

"Over there." Willow pointed and allowed the stranger to help her to it. He left and she sat inside for what seemed like a very long time, crying and trying to regain control of her emotions. Minutes later, the police arrived and an officer approached her window.

"Ma'am, we need you to get out of your car and stand over there on the sidewalk until the ambulance leaves."

Willow climbed out of her car and followed the officer. "It looks like you were right behind the car that was hit."

"Yes I was."

"Did you see what happened?"

"It happened so fast. He drove into the intersection, and I saw this car coming on really fast from the left. There was this horrible crash, and the car spun around and almost hit my car. He stopped just inches from my bumper. I tried to help, but there was so much blood."

"You're a lucky lady," he said. "Thirty seconds sooner, and it would have been you. Someone was looking out for you." He glanced off to the side, and Willow saw another ambulance near the other car. "Look, I can't allow you to go back to your car until the ambulance crews are finished. I need you to wait here on the sidewalk. Okay?"

Willow nodded, unable to find her voice through her tears.

The police officer touched his hat brim. "Have a good day, ma'am."

Willow called her office to let them know she would be late. She stood on the sidewalk and watched in horror as black body bags from both cars were hefted onto the stretchers. It took nearly an hour before she was allowed back into her car.

She put on her seatbelt, pulled into the nearest parking lot, and turned off the ignition. The police officer's words rang true in her head. "He's right. If my car hadn't stalled in that parking lot, it would have been me in that intersection." She swallowed hard and felt goose bumps rise on her arms. She rested her head against the window until she felt calmer then looked into the rearview mirror.

"God, I look like death warmed over. I've got to do some damage control before going to work." She looked at her makeup and other items that had fallen out of her handbag onto the floor when she slammed on the brakes.

She got out and walked around to the passenger side where she opened the door. She put her handbag on the seat and began returning the spilled items to her bag. The box containing the blue feather brooches had landed upside down on the floor with the cover still on it. The lid fell off when she picked it up, but the box was empty. She turned the box over and looked inside. The brooches were gone! She got down on one knee and felt around under the seat but only found a tube of mascara. "How can that be? The cover was still on the box." She inhaled deeply to calm her rattled nerves, returned to the driver's side, and slipped behind the wheel. Looking in the rearview mirror, she combed her hair and repaired her makeup.

After she drove the rest of the way to work, she shut off the car and reached for her handbag. Something shiny on the seat under the bag caught her eye.

It was the brooches, and they were locked together.

# Chapter 8

## 2013—Newcastle upon Tyne, England

Sawyer looked at her clients who sat opposite her at the table in her office. "Do you have any questions for me before you go?"

They shook their heads. "All right then." She rose and escorted them to the door. "You know how to reach me if something comes to mind." She shook their hands and they left. She closed the door and leaned against it. Her stomach rumbled. No wonder she was hungry; it was twelve-fifteen. Time for lunch. She pushed off the door and walked back toward the table. She reached it just as a wave of dizziness came over her. "Ah. What the devil?" She sat down and held her head between her palms. Suddenly, the dizziness was gone. "Willow," she whispered, "I can't feel you anymore."

Sawyer's stomach growled again. She retrieved a sandwich and a drink from the small refrigerator in the corner of her office then collected a file from her desk and returned to the table. She thumbed through the file as she ate. The name Willow McCord was scrawled across the tab. "Willow McCord, age 30, lives in Plymouth, Massachusetts. She's a dental hygienist. Works in Boston. I remember Boston, although I was only a child when I was there with Daddy and Mum." Sawyer took a bite of her sandwich and turned her attention back to the file. She picked up a picture. "She has auburn hair. I wonder if it's part of her Celtic heritage."

She thought about how much work it had been to locate Willow. After she found the letter from her father, she went to the depository and brought home the contents of the safe deposit box. She sat on the floor in front of the roaring fireplace in her father's office and placed the package in front of her. In the deafening silence of the great mansion, she opened it and methodically arranged the contents around her.

She picked up the athame and examined the intricate symbols engraved in its handle. Beside the dagger was a bolline, or white-handled knife. Her fingertips drifted over the pentacle attached to a delicate silver chain, and the strong odor of incense wafted from the censer she unwrapped from within many layers of tissue paper. Also in tissue paper were a golden chalice and a delicate brass bell. She found a deck of tarot cards enclosed in silk.

A large, rectangular object wrapped in burlap was revealed to be a very old book. Sawyer leafed through the pages and noted several styles of handwriting. Her heart swelled when she realized she was holding in her hands the family Book of Shadows, handed down through generations of Hawksworths. Each had penned, in their own hand, ritual guidelines, magical secrets, spells, runes, poems, and herbal remedies. She closed the book and held it close to her chest to absorb the power of her ancestors. She vowed to read the book cover to cover as she rewrapped her precious treasures.

Finally, she removed the last item from the box—a rectangular object. Approximately four inches long by three wide and one deep, it was crudely wrapped in a burlap type material and tied with a coarse string. She shook it gently and heard a slight scraping sound. She put the box on the floor and untied the string. Folding back the layers of burlap, she exposed an intricately carved wooden box with a pentagram encased in a circle on the cover. Inside was a brooch containing a single sapphire blue feather mounted on a silver Celtic cross.

In the bottom of the box was a letter from her grandmother, the late Melinda Hawksworth. Sawyer knew what the letter contained. Her grandmother had schooled her in secret for most of her life on the responsibilities and consequences of being one of the gifted Hawksworths. Melinda's mother, Richelle Hawksworth, bore the same load, and now it was Sawyer's turn.

Along with the letter was a genealogy chart, or what

Sawyer thought was a genealogy. It contained pairs of names that dated back to England in the early 1600s. Oddly, it stopped abruptly with her grandmother's name and the name Jenny McCord.

For the next several weeks, Sawyer studied the writings within the Book of Shadows. Each new entry, combined with the stories and lessons learned from her Nana, made the meaning of the genealogy chart clearer. She now understood why she was the next in a long line of Hawksworth women to carry the gift... a gift that began several hundred years ago. It wasn't until Jenna Hawksworth and Hadley Metcalf learned how to channel the gift four hundred years earlier that it became imperative to pass it on and to see that it was properly used. The future depended on it.

Once Sawyer understood what she needed to do, she hired a private investigator to help her complete the genealogy and to find the next person in Hadley Metcalf's line. That person turned out to be Willow McCord.

Returning her thoughts to the present, Sawyer closed Willow's folder and inhaled deeply in an attempt to chase away the heavy weight of anxiety that settled on her mind. Instead of easing it, a feeling of dread came over her. Something was wrong, and she needed to find out what.

Sawyer reached for the phone on the table. "Catherine, please reschedule my afternoon appointments. Thank you." Sawyer hung up and crossed the room to her desk to retrieve her Tarot cards from a drawer. She sat at her desk, closed her eyes, and concentrated on Willow. Several moments later, she shuffled the cards and drew seven cards from the top. Starting with the first card on the left, she named each card as she laid it down to form an arc.

"Past. Present. Shrouded factors. Obstacles. Those around her. My action. Final result."

The first thing Sawyer noticed was the abundance of Swords. "This is not good," she whispered. "Swords can indicate misfortune. Maybe that explains the feelings of dread I've been having." She turned each card up and cited its interpretation out loud.

"Past—Wheel of Fortune, inversed. Failure, bad luck, interruption, outside influences, bad fate, and unexpected events.

Present—Nine of Swords, upright. Illness, injury.

Shrouded factors—Chariot, upright. A rushed decision, adversity, turmoil.

Obstacles—Six of Swords, inversed. No way out of present obstacles or difficulties.

Those around her—The Devil, upright. Unexpected failure, controversy, violence, disaster.

My action—Ace of Swords, inversed. Caution when trying to use power to gain an ending.

Final result—Death, inversed. Narrow escape."

Sawyer sat back in her seat and looked at the overall message in the cards. "Great Goddess, she's in trouble. I've got to do something to help her. Everything depends on it."

Sawyer opened the bottom drawer of her desk and retrieved a blue feather, a bottle of water, and four beeswax candles. She took the items to the table, positioned the candles, one at each cardinal direction, and placed a bowl in the center into which she poured some of the water. She placed her palms flat on the table and closed her eyes.

"Mother Goddess, please guide me in this quest."

She dipped her right index finger in the water and touched the candle located in the North position. She repeated the rite for the other three in the order of South, East, and West. Next, she lit the candles in the opposite order. With each candle she lit, she chanted, "With this flame, I call upon the spirits of the North candle," using the correct direction name for the candle being lit. With all candles aglow, she placed the feather in the bowl and stirred clockwise. She stopped and waited for the water to become still then she stirred it counterclockwise. She held the feather above the bowl, closed her eyes, and tilted her face upward.

"Spirits of the winds, I invoke the power of this symbol to watch over Willow who carries the blue feathers in her possession."

Sawyer opened her eyes, and while still holding the feather

over the bowl of water, she extinguished the North candle and followed it with the South, East, and West. She sat back, exhausted, and glanced at the clock. It was one-thirty-five in the afternoon— eight-thirty-five a.m. in Boston, Massachusetts.

# Chapter 9

## 1610—North Yorkshire, England

Hadley reached into her basket and picked up a damp bed sheet. She maneuvered one end of the sheet over the line while being careful not to drag the other end through the dirt. Within moments, she had the sheet draped evenly over the line and secured with carved wooden clothespins. She bent over once more for the next garment and as she stood, she came face-to-face with Jenna Hawksworth who appeared suddenly from behind the sheet. Hadley was so startled she dropped the shirt she was holding, right into the dirt. "Ahhh! Thou art the she-devil herself, Jenna Hawksworth! What wast thou thinking? Now look what thou hast made me do."

Jenna laughed and bent at the waist to pick up the garment. "My apologies, fair lady, but I could not resist." She shook the dirt out of the garment and handed it to Hadley. "Allow me to help."

"Thou hast better help, thou motley-minded harpy."

"Motley-minded harpy, am I?"

"Thou shouldst know better than to go around scaring the stuffing out of a person."

"Stuffing? Is that what I smell?"

Hadley picked up a wet dish towel from the basket and snapped it across Jenna's thighs. "Take that, thou impertinent hedge-born horn-beast."

Jenna tried to jump out of the way, but the end of the towel bit sharply into her leg. "Ow! Not fair. I have no weapon." Jenna ran to the basket and grabbed a towel of her own. "This is more to my liking. En garde, Mistress Hadley Metcalf."

Jenna and Hadley circled each other while trying to land

their marks on the other's person. Jenna's towel hit its mark on Hadley's backside.

"Thou flea-bitten flap-dragon," Hadley yelled as she chased Jenna around the yard.

"Such colorful language," Jenna teased as she jumped beyond the reach of Hadley's towel.

"I will show thee colorful, blacksmith. Thou art naught but a common codpiece kisser."

Jenna circled around behind Hadley and surprised her by wrapping the towel around her waist and pulling her in close, trapping Hadley against her. She whispered into her ear, "I have no desire to kiss a codpiece, Mistress. I would, however, accept a kiss from a certain redheaded temptress."

Hadley held her breath for several long seconds, not sure she'd heard Jenna correctly. She felt the towel around her waist fall away as she turned around to face her, never leaving the circle of her arms. She looked directly into her eyes and all doubt as to Jenna's meaning melted away as the desire she saw there was tangible.

"The fire in thine eyes burns as hot as thy forge, blacksmith."

"Thou hast bewitched me, Hadley Metcalf."

"As thou hast me, Jenna Hawksworth."

Hadley held Jenna's gaze while neither moved. Hadley broke the stalemate. "Wouldst thou kiss me or not, blacksmith?"

Jenna cupped Hadley's face between her palms and lowered her head to meet Hadley's lips. Tentative at first, the kiss was soft and gentle, then it increased in intensity as each fought to explore the other's mouth.

Hadley felt an uncontrollable swell of desire in her abdomen as the urgency of the kiss increased. She reached behind Jenna's head and pulled her closer, deepening the kiss even more.

And then it was over. Jenna pulled her face away and looked into Hadley's eyes. Her breathing was ragged and shallow. "Thou hast cast a spell over me, Hadley Metcalf."

Hadley's hands fell to Jenna's hips when the kiss ended.

"'Tis no escape."

Jenna placed a gentle kiss on Hadley's forehead and stepped away.

"Art thou well, Jenna?" Hadley asked.

Jenna buried her hands deep into her pockets. "Aye, I am fine." She looked down and kicked the dirt around. Finally, she looked at Hadley. "Wouldst thou allow me to provide thee a meal at the tavern? There's something I wish to talk with thee about."

Hadley smiled. "I would love that."

\* \* \*

"What weighs so heavy on thy heart?" Hadley asked as she sat across the table from Jenna.

Jenna cupped the tankard of mead on the table in front of her and stared into the amber liquid. "I am thinking about thee."

"Me? Have I given thee cause for worry, for surely, the look on thy face betrays thee."

"I worry not."

"Then speak thy thoughts, Jenna Hawksworth. What about me doth trouble thee?"

Jenna directed her gaze at Hadley and for long moments said nothing.

Hadley cocked her eyebrow. "Speak, girl," she said impatiently.

"Thou dost things to me... makest me think things I never gave thought to before. Thou makest me feel things foreign to my being."

Hadley stood and placed her knuckles on the table. She leaned toward Jenna. "Art thou asking me to believe thee never had unnatural thoughts about a woman afore? The moment thou didst walk into my shop, I knew who thou wast... knew what thou wast. Don't tell me thou hast never been thought of as a fricatrice before. I shall not countenance that."

Jenna placed her hand over Hadley's. "Pray sit. I fear I am offending thee. I beg thy forgiveness."

Hadley stood her ground. "Thou didst kiss me today. A kiss from someone who knows how to please a woman."

"Thou art right. I am who thou sayest I am. I am also scared out of my wits."

Hadley sat down. "Why art thou scared? I do not understand."

"Hadley Metcalf, I have known thee all of two fortnights, and thou art all I can think about. Thoughts of auburn hair and green eyes have driven me to distraction. I burned myself in the forge today on account of my mind wandering to thee instead of my work."

"Thou hast burned thyself? Where? Showest me."

"I am fine. My point is, thou makest me feel agitated, woman. My innards do flip and flop every which way. I cannot think. I cannot concentrate."

Hadley found it hard to hide a grin. "Art thou always this romantic, Jenna Hawksworth? It sounds like thou art describing a sickness."

Jenna sat back, an expression of dejection on her face.

Hadley leaned forward. "I am sorry. I should not have said that. If it makes thee feel any better, I have caught thine illness, too."

Jenna raised her eyebrows. "Thou speakest the truth?"

"Aye."

"I have never felt like this before. What doth it mean?" Jenna asked.

"If I had to put a name to it, I would say we are falling in love."

"I was afraid thou wouldst say that."

Hadley was on her feet once more, this time with her hands on her hips. "Why is falling in love with me a bad thing?"

"Because I fear if thou knew what I really am, thou wouldst run away and break my heart."

"I don't run from things I want, blacksmith."

"Herein is the problem. I'm not so sure thou wouldst still want me if thou knew the truth."

Tears formed in Hadley's eyes as she sank back into her seat and brushed them away. "Do not tell me thou art already promised to another."

"No. I am not."

"Then what is it about thee I shall find so abhorrent?"

"I am a witch."

# Chapter 10

## 2013—Boston, Massachusetts

"Wow, that's a beautiful brooch," Susan said as she handed it back to Willow.

"Actually, its two brooches… see?" Willow separated the two blue feathers and handed one back to her co-worker.

"It's almost as if they were made to go together," Susan said. "You know, kind of like the friendship necklaces you sometimes see best friends wear."

"Yeah, I thought the same thing, except one of them was given to me by my grandmother, and I received the other one in the mail yesterday from England. They were on separate sides of the earth, so I doubt these two pieces were intentionally made to fit together."

"That's odd. Who sent it to you?"

"Beats the hell out of me. There wasn't even a name on the package—just initials and an address."

"They look very old. I wonder if they're worth anything?"

"Actually, I stopped at a jeweler's this morning to have them appraised."

"And…?"

"Well, the jeweler kind of acted weird about it, almost scared. He wouldn't even touch them and told me to take them elsewhere."

"That's strange. Are you going to do that?"

"Probably after work. I debated about stopping at another jeweler's on my way here, but the accident kind of changed my plans."

"Thank God you weren't hurt. I watched the news coverage in the break room at lunchtime. It looked pretty gruesome."

"If my car hadn't stalled coming out of the parking lot, I'd be in the morgue right now."

Susan handed the brooch back to Willow. "Well, I'm glad someone was watching out for you. This place wouldn't be the same without you. Oops. There's my two o'clock appointment coming through the door."

Willow glanced into the waiting room. "Casanova, huh? Good luck with that one."

"If he makes one more pass at me, I'm going to shove the floss right down his freaking throat," Susan joked.

"I hear you. Look, he's waving to you."

"Grrr," Susan replied as she went to greet her patient.

Willow watched Susan's hips sway back and forth as she walked toward the waiting room. She sighed heavily. "Get a grip, Willow. She doesn't play with girls," she muttered to herself.

\* \* \*

During her break, Willow found an antiquities jeweler on the Internet that was located just a few blocks from her dental offices. She called to make an appointment.

"Heirloom Jewelers, how may I help you?"

"My name is Willow McCord. I have a pair of brooches I'd like to bring in for an appraisal."

"If you can hold for a moment, Ms. McCord, I'll put our appraiser on the line with you."

"Sure. Thank you." Willow listened to the Muzak drone through her earpiece for what seemed like an eternity before a man's voice came on the line.

"Ms. McCord, my name is Stephen Wilkinson and I'm the appraiser here at Heirloom. I understand you have a brooch you would like appraised."

"A pair of brooches, actually," Willow said.

"A pair of brooches?"

"Yes. They can be worn as two separate brooches, or as one. They actually interlock."

"Can you describe these brooches?"

"They're mirror images of each other. Each is a sapphire blue feather mounted on a Celtic cross."

"I see. You said they lock together?"

"Yes. If you kind of tip them toward each other, they lock in place." After nearly thirty seconds of silence, Willow began to be concerned that she had lost the connection. "Mr. Wilkinson, are you still there?"

"Ah, yes. Forgive me, Ms. McCord, I was consulting my colleague. Do you have the brooches with you right now?"

"Yes, I'm holding them in my hand."

"Good. Turn them over, please, and tell me if there's anything printed on the back."

Willow turned the brooches over, one at a time. "There is something, but it's in really small print. Can you hold on a minute, Mr. Wilkinson?"

"Yes, take your time."

Willow put her phone down on the table and went to her work station to get her safety glasses. When she returned to the phone, she slipped the glasses on and flipped the magnifying lenses in place that she normally used while assisting the dentist with minute crown adjustments. She picked up the phone. "Okay, Mr. Wilkinson, I'm back. Now let's see…" Willow held the first brooch up in front of the lenses. "It says, 'Mother, Crane, 13.' No, wait a minute, that's Crone, not Crane."

"Good. Good, Ms. McCord. Now the other brooch?"

Willow frowned at the odd sense of excitement that emanated from the person on the other end of the phone. "Mr. Wilkinson, is there something significant about the writing on this brooch?"

"The other brooch, Ms. McCord. Please, what does it say?"

"Hold on." Willow turned the other brooch over. "It says Maiden, Warrior."

"Hecate!" Mr. Wilkinson said.

"I'm sorry, what did you say?"

"Ms. McCord, please lock the brooches together and look at the back. Are the four words in alignment with one another, like a sentence?"

Willow did as she was asked. "Yes, they line up quite well. Maiden, Warrior, Mother, Crone, 13. What does it mean?"

"Ms. McCord, can you bring the brooches to our shop? I'd like a closer look at them for a more accurate appraisal."

"Yes, of course. Is today okay… maybe around five p.m.?"

"Perfect. I'll see you then."

\* \* \*

Willow watched the jeweler caress her brooches like they were priceless. The sheer expression of awe and joy on the man's face brought her more than a little consternation. "How old are they?" she asked.

Mr. Wilkinson looked up, the magnifying device still positioned over the right lens of his glasses. "I would estimate them to be around four hundred years old."

"Holy— For real?"

"Yes indeed."

"What are they worth?"

"I would need to do a more in-depth inspection, but off the cuff, I would say tens of thousands at the least."

"Tens of thousands? Oh, my God!"

"Their real worth, however, isn't measured in dollars."

"What do you mean?"

"In certain circles, these brooches are professed to have, let's say, special powers."

"Special powers? What kind of special powers?"

Mr. Wilkinson looked at her for several long moments before speaking. "Ms. McCord, if you're the true owner of these brooches, you should already understand their significance. I'm afraid I couldn't do the legend justice. I suggest you do a little digging of your own."

"That's pretty cryptic. Care to elaborate?"

"No, I'll leave that to you. Oh, one more thing. Where did you get the brooches?"

"One of them was given to me by my grandmother, Jenny McCord. The other one arrived in the mail this week from England."

"By chance, did it come from anyone by the name of Hawksworth?"

# Chapter 11

## 1610—North Yorkshire, England

"Thou art a witch?" Hadley asked loudly.

Jenna immediately covered Hadley's mouth with her hand. "Be quiet. Dost thou want to see me burn at the stake?"

Hadley shook her head no.

"I will take my hand away if thou dost promise not to yell again. Do I have thy word?"

Hadley nodded and Jenna immediately removed her hand. "Thou art a witch?" Hadley whispered hoarsely.

"That I am. Thou asked about the blue feather I wore a few nights ago at dinner. 'Tis a symbol of sorts, a way for us to recognize each other."

"Us? Who exactly is us?"

"The others. I did say there were many more."

"Holy mother of God. I'm being sorely tempted by a witch."

Jenna rose to her feet. "I knew this was a bad idea."

"No, wait," Hadley said. "Sit down. Pray don't go." Hadley waited patiently as Jenna sat. "How long hast thou been doing it?"

"Doing it?"

"Aye—doing the witch thing."

"'Tisn't something one chooseth to do. I've always had the gift. For as long as I can remember, 'tis been a part of me."

"Dost thou cast spells on people?"

"I don't follow the forces of dark magic, Hadley. Those who do are evil and destructive. Black magic is used to hurt others and for personal gain. My clan—the Blue Feather Coven—we aim to help people in need. We do cast spells, but only for good reasons. Mostly we work with herbs and potions."

"If your clan performeth only good deeds, why would the king punish you?"

"Because the king is a puppet of the church, and the church is afraid of anything that may take its power away. That, and the fact that all of the clan members either prefer relations with their own kind, or are supporters of such."

Hadley sat back. "Art thou saying all of the clan members are sodomites?"

Jenna smiled and nodded. "Aye. Our clan members are either sodomites or those who support the right to love whom they want."

Jenna reached into her pocket, withdrew two brooches, and placed them on the table between them. Hadley picked one of them up and examined it closely. The brooch flared in her hand. She sat back, startled. "'Tis a beautiful piece. It flashes as if it is alive. What is the stone?"

"Sapphire, and the cross is silver. I smithed them myself. In fact, I've smithed all of the pins."

Jenna picked up the remaining pin. "May I have the pin?" she asked.

Hadley handed over the brooch she was holding, and Jenna held them side by side.

"I made these pins for a special occasion," Jenna said. "They are a set—a matched pair. They are two halves of a whole." In one smooth movement, she interlocked the two halves of the brooch and handed them back to Hadley. "Of all the pins I have made, these are the only two that lock together." Once again, the stones glowed from within.

"Jenna Hawksworth, 'tis amazing." Hadley tried to separate the brooches but could not.

"Here, let me show thee." Jenna placed her hands over Hadley's and tilted the two sides of the brooch toward each other. They came apart easily, and the glow ebbed. Hadley's eyes grew wide as she interlocked and separated the brooches several more times. Each time, the glow intensified when together and faded when apart. "Amazing, I tell thee."

"I would be honored if thou wouldst have one," Jenna said softly.

Hadley became serious and set the brooches on the table between them. "I am not a witch. Besides, 'tis a gift of unspeakable value that should not be given lightly. Thou hast not known me long enough to give such a gift."

"I do not give it lightly, Mistress. My heart speaketh to me with such intensity as I have never known. It leaveth no doubt of the depth of my love for thee. I knew the moment I saw thee in thy shop that our lives were meant to be entwined. The halves of this brooch fitteth together in the same way thy heart fitteth with mine. 'Twas made for you. I beseech thee, take it."

"I say again, blacksmith, I am not a witch."

"Dost thou believe in doing good for thy fellow man?"

"Thou knowest I do."

"And art thou a lover of the fairer sex?"

Hadley blushed. "I cannot deny that thy kiss earlier today left me feeling more than a little faint in the knees."

Jenna picked up one of the brooches and offered it to Hadley. "Then I am honored to welcome thee into the clan, and I ask thee to be one with me, just as these brooches are two halves of a whole."

Hadley took the brooch from Jenna and held it tightly in her fist. "I accept thy gift and thee." Hadley held the brooch out to join it with Jenna's. The pins locked, and the stones on both brooches flared to life, shining brighter than either by itself. "Look, Jenna, there are two women embracing." The outline of the women glowed softly.

"Aye. The Mother Goddess recognizes thee and takes thee for her daughter," Jenna said.

Hadley closed her eyes and mumbled, "Holy mother of God. Truly, I'm going to hell for consorting with a witch."

# Chapter 12

2013—Newcastle upon Tyne, England

Sawyer paced back and forth across her father's study. "Why hasn't she contacted me? It's been four days since the package was verified as delivered."

"Perhaps she doesn't realize the significance of the brooch," her companion replied.

"She's a McCord for Christ's sake. How can she not know?"

"Maybe the tradition wasn't passed down along her line. I don't know why you're making such a big deal of this. You don't really need her anyway."

Sawyer stopped in front of her guest. "Bridgit, you don't seem to understand. The power is strongest when a Hawksworth works with a Metcalf, and since Willow is a descendent of Hadley Metcalf, we need her to assure success."

"Do you really know she's a descendent of Hadley? You told me your Nana's genealogy stopped with Jenny McCord, who we both know is dead now."

"The private detective I hired to find her traced her back to Jenny McCord through Jenny's son, Roger. Jenny McCord was Willow's grandmother, and since we already have documented proof that Jenny McCord was a descendent of Hadley, that makes Willow a descendent of Hadley. It's not rocket science."

"But you've said yourself that the uprising skips every other generation and sometimes two. If that's true, it would not have happened in Jenny McCord's lifetime. Maybe the promise stopped there. Maybe Jenny didn't pass it on."

Sawyer began pacing again. "I can't believe that. Too much

is at stake to simply stop passing the torch. There have been four successful repressions. I will not allow the fifth to fail on my watch."

"Well if you ask me, the note you included in the package was rather cryptic. If she doesn't know about the gift, it will make no sense to her at all. Four hundred years is a very long time to expect a promise to be kept, especially across several generations."

Sawyer stood in front of the window looking out on the courtyard. Her arms were crossed in front of her. Bridgit came up behind her, wrapped her arms around Sawyer's waist, and rested her cheek between Sawyer's shoulder blades. "You don't need her. I can help you with this."

Sawyer stiffened. "I stand a marginal chance of success without her, Bridgit. I don't do marginal. Besides, she now has both the brooches. They play a pivotal role in the ritual. There's no other answer. I need her here—with the brooches."

Bridgit released her hold on Sawyer and walked a few feet away. "If you're intent on getting her here, then I guess you don't need me."

"I need her, Bridgit. There is no way around that."

"And if she doesn't come—what then?"

"Then I will go after her."

* * *

Sawyer lifted the receiver and held it to her ear. "Hello?"

"Ms. Hawksworth?"

"Yes, this is she."

"Ms. Hawksworth, my name is Stephen Wilkinson and I am the appraiser at Heirloom Jewelers here in Boston, Massachusetts."

"Mr. Wilkinson."

"Ms. Hawksworth, I thought you might be interested in a pair of blue feather brooches I had the good fortune of appraising today."

"Go on."

"They were brought into the store by a Ms. Willow McCord. They were very interesting brooches... dark blue sapphire feathers mounted on silver Celtic crosses. Interestingly enough, the brooches seemed like they were made to be a matching pair. Ms. McCord was quite fascinated with how they locked together."

"What is your point, Mr. Wilkinson?"

"I thought you might want to know that she apparently had no knowledge of their value or purpose. As an heirloom jeweler, I am very familiar with what those brooches are worth. They are quite valuable, and I don't mean that in the worldly sense."

"And did you enlighten her, sir?"

"Not exactly. But I could. For a price, that is."

"That won't be necessary, Mr. Wilkinson. Thank you for calling."

"But—"

"Goodbye, Mr. Wilkinson."

Sawyer replaced the receiver on the antique phone on her father's desk and sat back in her chair. *Bridgit was right, Willow didn't know. Why am I surprised? If it wasn't for my Nana, I wouldn't have known until I found the letter my father left for me to read after he died.* Sawyer reached into her jacket pocket for her cell phone. Within moments, she was booked on a flight to Boston, Massachusetts, leaving the next afternoon.

* * *

Sawyer spread her grandmother's genealogy chart out across the table in front of the Council of Thirteen. In the last two boxes, she had penciled in four names: William Hawksworth, Roger McCord, Sawyer Hawksworth, and Willow McCord. She took a step back and allowed the Council to study the chart.

After a time, the high priest spoke. "Explain."

"What you see before you are fifteen generations of Hawksworths and Metcalfs, beginning with Jenna Hawksworth and Hadley Metcalf," Sawyer said. "Across these generations, there have been four successful repressions, sentried by the

Age at the time of the uprising

| 2013 | 1988 | 1963 | 1938 | 1913 | 1888 | 1863 | 1838 | 1813 | 1788 | 1763 | 1738 | 1713 | 1688 | 1663 | 1638 | 1613 | Year |
|---|---|---|---|---|---|---|---|---|---|---|---|---|---|---|---|---|---|
|  |  |  |  |  |  |  |  |  |  |  |  |  |  | 79 | 54 | 27 | **Hadley Metcalf** |
|  |  |  |  |  |  |  |  |  |  |  |  |  |  | 85 | 60 | 33 | **Jenna Hawksworth** |
|  |  |  |  |  |  |  |  |  |  |  |  |  | 75 | 50 | 25 |  | Lachina Hawksworth |
|  |  |  |  |  |  |  |  |  |  |  |  |  | 75 | 50 | 25 |  | Ewain Hawksworth |
|  |  |  |  |  |  |  |  |  |  |  |  | 73 | 48 | 23 |  |  | Evan MacDonald |
|  |  |  |  |  |  |  |  |  |  |  |  | 75 | 50 | 25 |  |  | Ian Hawksworth |
|  |  |  |  |  |  |  |  |  |  |  | 70 | 45 | 20 |  |  |  | **Machara MacDonald** |
|  |  |  |  |  |  |  |  |  |  |  | 68 | 43 | 18 |  |  |  | **Rowena Hawksworth** |
|  |  |  |  |  |  |  |  |  |  | 65 | 40 | 15 |  |  |  |  | Davinia MacDonald |
|  |  |  |  |  |  |  |  |  |  | 67 | 42 | 17 |  |  |  |  | Henry Hawksworth |
|  |  |  |  |  |  |  |  |  | 70 | 45 | 20 |  |  |  |  |  | Elspeth McIntyre |
|  |  |  |  |  |  |  |  |  | 72 | 47 | 22 |  |  |  |  |  | Connor Hawksworth |
|  |  |  |  |  |  |  |  | 75 | 50 | 25 |  |  |  |  |  |  | Shena McIntyre |
|  |  |  |  |  |  |  |  | 72 | 47 | 22 |  |  |  |  |  |  | Samuel Hawksworth |
|  |  |  |  |  |  |  | 76 | 51 | 26 |  |  |  |  |  |  |  | Travis McVicker |
|  |  |  |  |  |  |  | 78 | 53 | 28 |  |  |  |  |  |  |  | Robert Hawksworth |
|  |  |  |  |  |  | 70 | 45 | 20 |  |  |  |  |  |  |  |  | **Keeley McVicker** |
|  |  |  |  |  |  | 70 | 45 | 20 |  |  |  |  |  |  |  |  | **Maeve Hawksworth** |
|  |  |  |  |  | 73 | 48 | 23 |  |  |  |  |  |  |  |  |  | Innes Milne |
|  |  |  |  |  | 75 | 50 | 25 |  |  |  |  |  |  |  |  |  | Edward Hawksworth |
|  |  |  | 72 | 47 | 22 |  |  |  |  |  |  |  |  |  |  |  | Blair Milne |
|  |  |  | 70 | 45 | 20 |  |  |  |  |  |  |  |  |  |  |  | Nicholas Hawksworth |
|  |  | 74 | 49 | 24 |  |  |  |  |  |  |  |  |  |  |  |  | **Maggie McCord** |
|  |  | 71 | 46 | 21 |  |  |  |  |  |  |  |  |  |  |  |  | **Richelle Hawksworth** |
| 88 | 63 | 38 |  |  |  |  |  |  |  |  |  |  |  |  |  |  | Jenny McCord |
| 90 | 65 | 40 |  |  |  |  |  |  |  |  |  |  |  |  |  |  | Melinda Hawksworth |
| 65 | 40 | 15 |  |  |  |  |  |  |  |  |  |  |  |  |  |  | *Roger McCord* |
| 68 | 43 | 18 |  |  |  |  |  |  |  |  |  |  |  |  |  |  | *William Hawksworth* |
| 30 |  |  |  |  |  |  |  |  |  |  |  |  |  |  |  |  | *Willow McCord* |
| 32 |  |  |  |  |  |  |  |  |  |  |  |  |  |  |  |  | *Sawyer Hawksworth* |

names highlighted in bold on the chart."

"Why are you showing this to us?" the high priest asked.

"Because I fear the fifth repression may not be successful."

The Council of Thirteen exchanged uneasy glances.

Sawyer walked over to the genealogy chart and placed her finger on Willow's name. "I have confirmed that the current generation of Metcalfs, in the person of Willow McCord, is unaware of her heritage, the upcoming event, and her role in it. I have also confirmed that she has the brooch that was passed down through the Metcalf line over the years. The last person known to possess that brooch was Willow's great-grandmother, Maggie McCord in 1913. Maggie would have participated in the last repression. Considering Willow has it in her possession now, it has obviously been passed down to her. However, it's apparent through a source in Boston that the significance of the brooch was not passed down with it."

"This is unacceptable," the high priest said. "This Willow McCord is vital to our success. At the very least, we need her brooch to join with yours."

Sawyer looked away uncomfortably.

"Is there something you're not telling us, Sawyer?" the high priest asked.

"I'm afraid there is. You see, Willow has both brooches. I sent mine to her, assuming she knew about the gift."

"This is a very unfortunate turn of events. The uprising will begin less than three months from now—at the end of October. I expect you to make this right."

"My flight to Boston leaves tomorrow."

"Blessed be, Sawyer Hawksworth."

# Chapter 13

## 2013—Boston, Massachusetts

"So, what did the appraiser say?" Susan asked as she transferred the dental implements from the sterilizer to individually sealed plastic bags.

"He said they were around four hundred years old and worth tens of thousands of dollars," Willow replied.

"Are you serious? That's a lot of money."

"That's only part of it. He also said their real value isn't measured in money. They have some sort of power."

"Is that guy for real? I mean, come on, power? So, how much did he offer you for them?"

"Nothing, actually. He suggested if I didn't already know what that power was, I should do some research."

"Research? Like what?"

"For starters, he knew they were sent to me by someone named Hawksworth. I swear I didn't tell him that. He just knew it."

"This is starting to creep me out."

"You don't really think they could possess some sort of power, do you?" Willow asked.

"I guess that depends on whether you believe in stuff like that. There are certain cults and religions that believe idols have power, so why not a brooch?"

"I guess I'm more of a skeptic than you are. Oh, one more thing. Once the brooches are joined, there's some writing on the back that says, 'Maiden, Warrior, Mother, Crone, 13.' I have no idea what that means."

"I took a class in Pagan Religions in college to fill my credit requirements, and if I remember right, Maiden, Warrior,

Mother, and Crone are references in the Wicca religion to the stages of a woman's life. You know, Maiden would be a teenager, Warrior would be a twenty-something woman, Mother is kind of self-explanatory, and Crone is like a grandmother."

"Well that makes sense, except I wonder what the 13 means?"

"Beats the hell out of me. What are you going to do?"

"Like the man said—research. I'm heading to the library after work. Between library resources and the Internet, maybe I can get to the bottom of who sent the brooch to me, and why."

"Let me know if you need any help."

"I will, thanks. Look at the time. Doesn't your break start right about now?"

"Is it ten o'clock already? The morning has really flown by."

"Let me finish that for you. Go take your break," Willow said.

"Thanks."

* * *

Sawyer glanced at the time on her cell phone as she waited for her flight to be boarded. Three p.m. Her trip was about ten hours, so she should land in Boston around eight or nine p.m., including the time difference. Willow would be gone home from work by then. She'd better get online and book a room.

"Now boarding the first class cabin for flight 105 to Boston Logan Airport. Flight 105. First class cabin only."

Sawyer shut off her cell phone, slipped it into her pocket, and stood in line to board.

* * *

Willow sat at the library table surrounded by about a dozen books on antique jewelry. For the past hour, she had painstakingly thumbed through each book and searched for pictures of old jewelry that even remotely resembled her brooches, to no avail. She was gathering the books into a pile when an announcement came over the intercom. "It is four-forty p.m. The library will close in twenty minutes. Please bring any books you wish to check out to the Circulation desk."

"Geesh! Closing time already?" She returned the books to the shelves and headed directly to the reference desk.

"May I help you?" the reference librarian said.

"Yes, Ms. Lawrence," Willow said after looking at the librarian's name plate. "I'm trying to do some research on an antique set of brooches, and I don't seem to be getting anywhere on my own. Do you have any advice?"

"Do you have the brooches with you, Ms...."

"Willow. Please, call me Willow. Yes, they're right here."

Willow took the brooches out of her pocket and handed them to the librarian.

"They're beautiful. You said they're antiques?"

"I've been told they're about four hundred years old."

"My goodness! If you don't mind, I'll photocopy them and have our IT specialist run them through an image recognition program tomorrow. Would that be all right?"

"Yes, of course. I'd like to give you a hand with that if I could. You see, they actually lock together to form one brooch, so maybe we should photograph them both ways."

"Good idea. Come with me."

Ten minutes later, Willow was headed toward home with a promise from the reference librarian to call her the following day.

* * *

"Taxi!" Sawyer called as she towed her luggage to the curb. She handed her bag to the driver who stowed it in the trunk.

"Where are you headed?" he asked.

"Boston Marriott."

"Which one?"

Sawyer looked at her cell phone. "Copley Place."

The cabby reset the meter and pulled into traffic. Fifteen minutes later, he pulled up to the curb of the Marriott. "Here we are. That'll be fourteen fifty."

Sawyer handed the cabby an American twenty dollar bill, got her luggage, and entered the hotel. Moments later, she was in her room where she immediately closed the curtains and stripped off all of her clothing. From her suitcase, she gathered a black candle, a chalice, a small bottle of wine, a censer, and incense. She sat cross-legged and straight-backed on the floor with her items placed before her.

For the next few minutes, she closed her eyes and worked to control her breathing and to suppress the panicky feelings that accompanied her on the trip. When she felt relatively in control, she knelt before her items, lit the black candle, and poured the wine into the chalice.

Sitting back on her heels, she held her hands out to the sides, palms up, and chanted. "Hecate, beautiful Crone of Night, I call you here to put things right. Transform the negative thought and pain, and help my life be whole again." Sawyer repeated this phrase twice more, then lifted the chalice and bowed her head. "Lady of the Dark Moon, share with me this wine. Bring your protection to this life of mine. May the waters of your eternal womb bring change most divine. Lift her eyes and help her see. As I will it, so shall it be."

Sawyer sipped a small amount of wine and felt it flow through her as liquid energy. She lit the incense in the censer and carried it to all four corners of the room. As she did so, she chanted, "Negativity be gone." She returned to her position on the floor and visualized the entire room bathed in a peaceful blue light. Finally, she retraced her steps, counter-clockwise around the room, inviting positive energy into the void vacated by the banished negativity.

Kneeling once more on the floor, she held her hands out and closed her eyes. "Thank you, Hecate, for freeing my life of negative happenings and feelings and for bringing to me the feelings of love, prosperity and happiness. Guided by your warmth and light, know that I will not fail you as I seek the means for a successful repression of the evil that awaits at your gates."

Sawyer opened her eyes and drank the rest of the wine. She blew out the candle and climbed into bed. She lay there for long moments and stared into the darkness, planning her first meeting with Willow McCord.

# Chapter 14

## 1610—North Yorkshire, England

"May I offer thee my arm, Hadley?" Jenna said as they left the tavern.

"Thou mayest, blacksmith. Art thou planning to be my protector this night?" Hadley slipped her hand through the crook of Jenna's elbow.

"Protector?"

"Aye. Will thy magical powers protect me if some scallywag tries to accost us?"

Jenna's gaze met Hadley's, and she frowned when she saw the hint of mischief in Hadley's eyes. "This is not a joking matter. 'Tis part of who I am. If thou canst not take that seriously, perchance we should be rethinking our future together."

Hadley stopped in her tracks and removed her hand from Jenna's arm. "Jenna Hawksworth, if thou thinkest for one moment thou art going to tell me how to behave, thou better thinkest again. Humor has gotten me through some difficult times, and what thou hast told me tonight goes way beyond difficult. 'Tis part of who I am. 'Tis part of whom thou dost profess to love. At least I didn't try to hide that part of me from thee."

Jenna crossed her arms over her chest and narrowed her eyes at Hadley. "I have never met a wench like you before. Thou makest me all crazy inside."

"Wench? I will be showing thee wench, thou surly, motley-minded lout."

"Again with the name calling. Surely thou canst do better than that."

"At this moment, I'm asking myself if I can do better than you."

Jenna ran a hand through her hair and took Hadley by the shoulders. "Look. What I am is important to me. It carries with it more responsibility than thou wilt ever know. I need thee to understand that."

"What I understand is thou art asking me to risk my own life as well as thine. 'Tis bad enough we could be arrested simply for loving each other. What thou art asking me to become involved in could get us killed."

Jenna released Hadley's arms and took a step backward. She clasped her hands behind her back and nodded solemnly. "I understand I ask too much of thee." Jenna walked a few feet away then turned around. "I would be honored if thou wouldst keep the brooch."

Hadley put her hands on her hips. "Thou art damned right I am keeping the brooch, and don't think thou art walking away from me, Jenna Hawksworth. Thou madest a commitment to me not an hour ago, and I plan to hold thee to it."

"But... but thou didst say—"

"I said thou art not about to tell me how to behave. Like it or not, blacksmith, this wench takes not orders from the likes of anyone, including thyself. Now how about thou dost conjure up thy magic and get us home quickly so I can take thee to bed. Call me a wench, wouldst thou? I will be showing thee a wench." Hadley winked at Jenna.

Jenna was stunned into inaction.

Hadley took Jenna's arm. "Push, I say. Woe be it if I have to take care of business myself."

\* \* \*

Hadley pushed Jenna up against the door as soon as they were inside her cottage. Her breath came in deep rasping pants as she fought to control her emotions. Not a word passed between them as their gazes locked, neither one able to look away. Jenna cradled Hadley's face between her hands and gently lowered her lips to hers. Hadley's arms wound around Jenna's waist and pulled her close as Jenna devoured her mouth.

Spasms of delight coursed through Hadley as Jenna's tongue danced in her mouth. She could feel her pulse pounding between her legs as passion flooded her core. Her moans of pleasure only enticed Jenna to go deeper. Hadley pulled Jenna's blouse out of the back of her trousers and ran her hands under the hem and over the skin on Jenna's back.

Jenna broke the grip she had on Hadley's mouth as she moved across her jaw toward her ear and down her neck. Hadley could feel Jenna's legs shake as she dug her nails into her back.

"Sweet Hecate… Hadley, you bewitch me."

"Perchance I'm a witch after all, my love," Hadley replied.

"That thou art. I am under thy spell, and I submit willingly."

"'Tis thou who hast enchanted me, Jenna. Feel what thou hast done to me." Hadley took Jenna's hand in her own, hiked up her skirt, and slipped Jenna's hand into her undergarment. She nearly climaxed as she felt Jenna's fingers slide into the moistened folds. She held on to Jenna's arms for support.

Jenna moaned and closed her eyes and rested her forehead against Hadley's. She cupped Hadley's womanhood and squeezed slightly. "By all that is sacred, I love thee, Hadley Metcalf. I don't know how much longer I can hold out. This beautiful gift thou art

offering me is nearly bringing me to climax as I stand before thee."

"Let me feel thee," Hadley said as she unlaced the front of Jenna's trousers and pushed them off her hips, along with the undergarment. She slid her hand between Jenna's legs. "Holy mother of God," Hadley exclaimed as her fingers encountered a sea of moisture.

Jenna's breathing became labored. "I… I can't…"

"Let it go," Hadley whispered in her ear as she plunged her fingers deep into Jenna, only to feel Jenna return the favor at the same time.

Hadley leaned into Jenna, trapping her between herself and the door—effectively holding them both up as orgasmic spasms ripped through their bodies. Jenna's head slammed into the door as an especially strong spasm shook her, the veins on her neck protruding like tree roots.

When it was over, they slid together to the floor and Jenna cradled Hadley in her arms while they returned to themselves. Jenna kissed the top of Hadley's head. "I love thee more than a summer's day, Hadley Metcalf."

"And I, thee, blacksmith—with all my heart."

"Blessed be, Hadley."

"Blessed be, to thee as well, blacksmith."

\* \* \*

"Art thou sure thou art not a witch?" Jenna asked as she played with Hadley's auburn hair which, was splayed across her own naked chest.

Hadley lifted her head from Jenna's shoulder and placed a delicate kiss on her lips. "Not to my knowledge. Why speakest so?"

"How is it that thou hast captured me in thy spell? I am totally lost."

"Is that such a bad thing, blacksmith? I tend to think not."

"Nay—it's just that I have never been hexed like this before. I cannot get thee off my mind. Methinks about thee every waking moment... and now this," Jenna said, motioning to the two of them lying naked and entwined in Hadley's bed. "Thy gift of loving me is something I will be cherishing for the rest of my life."

"Art thou telling me there's nary a someone thou hast loved before?"

"Not like this. It's like the Goddess has been saving me for this moment."

Hadley rolled over, retrieved the blue feather brooch from her bedside table, and lay on her back beside Jenna. She held the brooch such that the candlelight reflected off the dark blue sapphire gem that formed the feather itself. "'Tis a beautiful piece. Tell me about the clan, Jenna."

Jenna rolled to her side so she was facing Hadley and rested her head on her arm. "What art thou wanting to know?"

"Everything. Who are they? How is it thou becamest part of them?"

Jenna reached forward with her free arm and turned Hadley's face toward her. "Hadley, when thou accepted the brooch, thou became one of us—understand?"

"I do. 'Tis the reason I ask. I will be doing whatever it takes to be part of thy life. 'Tis too late for me to turn back."

"The clan was formed about four years back. I was still living at home and apprenticing with the local blacksmith when they came to town. I was all of twenty years old."

Hadley rolled onto her side to face Jenna, their faces a mere inches apart. "They?"

"A troupe of traveling gypsies, only they really weren't gypsies. If the king's men discovered who they really were, they would have surely been hanged, or worse."

"They were witches?"

"Aye, but like I said before, the clan doth not practice dark magic. These gypsies were healers and herbalists, using spells, incantations and combinations of herbs to treat sickness and chase away evil spirits."

"How didst thou become part of them?"

"They came to the smith one day looking for help to fix a broken wheel on their wagon. I was the only one there. While I was repairing the wheel, the heat from the fire was so intense, I removed my shirt. They noticed the marks on my arms."

"What kind of marks?"

"Whip marks."

"O me, the Gods! How didst thou come by whip marks? Who did that to thee?"

"My father."

Hadley ran her hand gently up and down Jenna's arm. "Hold thy arm near the candle, that I might see."

Jenna obliged and rested her arm on the side table, near the base of the candle holder. Hadley rolled over and lay across Jenna's midsection as she strained to see the scars left by the beating. "I see them now in the glow of the candle, though they are faint. Pray tell, why would a man beat his child so?" she asked as she rolled back onto the bed beside Jenna.

"He caught me in the barn with a bar maiden. I needn't tell thee what we were doing."

"He beat thee for indulging in the favors of a bar maiden? Nay so!"

"That he did. Called it the work of the devil. Called me a fornicator and a sodomite and he vowed to report me to the deacon for practicing unnatural acts if I ever did it again. He convinced himself I was possessed by Satan himself and proceeded to beat the devil out of me… among other things."

Hadley began to softly cry. "How could he do that to thee? His own child." She trailed her fingertips down the side of Jenna's face. "I could never beat a child of my own that way. My heart bleeds for thy twenty-year-old self."

"Like so many of his cronies, Hadley, he was a puppet of the Church. He allowed them to control his mind. He truly believed he was saving me." Jenna wiped the tears from Hadley's face. "It pains my heart to see thee cry. Pray stop."

Hadley nodded. "Pray—go on with thy story."

"So this band of gypsies noticed the whip marks on my arms and implored me to tell what happened. Much to my chagrin, I found myself telling them everything. I know not why I was so free with my story to a group of strangers, but it felt safe. Before they left, they paid me handsomely for my work and invited me to attend a gathering at their campsite two days hence. I went, and my life was forever changed."

Hadley's eyes opened wide. "What happened?"

"There was a large fire, surrounded by a five-pointed star, and around that was a circle. At each point on the star stood a figure cloaked in a robe with the hood pulled down nearly over their faces. Each and every one of them wore a blue feather attached to their robe. Some were dark blue and others were pale blue. There was a rite—a ritual of sorts. They called on the Goddess Hecate to provide good luck and success in the quest to find the 'chosen' one who would help to protect the world from the approaching evil."

"Approaching evil? What meant they?"

"I knew not. What I did know is that I was terrified... and captivated at the same time. I felt goodness in these people. At the end of the rite, they assembled and assigned a charter to all present to go out and help those less fortunate than they. Once the charters were given, the five sentries standing at the points of the star removed their hoods, and I recognized several of them as town folk.

"Before I left, the high priest took me aside and slipped into my hand a jar of salve he said would heal the whip marks. I took that opportunity to ask about the blue feathers. He explained to me that the blue feather was a symbol, worn as an ornament, but possessing a meaning secret to all but clan members."

"Secret meaning? Did he tell thee what the secret was?"

"Not at first. I needed to earn their trust before that secret could be divulged. That knowledge in the hands of the king's men would mean certain death to all who wore it."

"But thou hast already told me the brooches are a way for clan member to recognize each other."

"'Tis true, but there is more. Those who wear the dark blue feather prefer relations with their own kind. Those who wear the light blue feather prefer the opposite sex but support a body's right to love who they want."

"The town folk thou didst meet at the ritual—didst thou befriend them afterwards?"

"No. As thou knowest, engaging in unnatural acts is against the Church's teaching, and anything that disagrees with the Church is a crime in the eyes of the king. Engaging in unnatural acts and witchcraft at the same time is surely a death sentence if found out. So, no, the town folk lived, and still live, quiet lives. Outwardly, they live within the laws of the Church—even those who wear the dark blue feather. 'Tis only through the symbol of the feather and within the clan that they are recognized for what they truly are."

Hadley took Jenna's hand in her own, kissed the palm, and pressed it against her cheek. "It matters not to me if no one knows of my love for thee. If it means keeping thee safe, I can live with that secret."

"Aye. As well can I."

"Thou hast said the members of the clan wore feathers. Real feathers?"

"Aye. But once I became a clan member, I smithed the brooches for the leaders of the other twelve clans in the coven, as well as thy brooch and mine. While crafting them, I asked the Goddess's blessing to choose the wisest and strongest of character within each clan and they have worn them since."

"So that was four years ago. Did the high priest find the one he was looking for?"

"Art thou referring to the 'chosen' one?"

"Aye."

"He did."

"Well—out with it. Who? Is it someone I know?"

"'Tis at that."

"By all that be holy, blacksmith, tell me who?"

"Jenna Hawksworth."

# Chapter 15

## 2013—Plymouth, Massachusetts

Willow shut off the alarm clock, turned onto her back, and rubbed her face. "I hate mornings," she said. "But at least it's Friday." She threw off the covers and sat on the edge of the bed while she rolled her head around in circles. "Why is my neck sore this morning? It must be from looking at so many jewelry books in the library." She shook her head. "Geesh. Now I'm talking to myself. I need to get a cat."

She quickly made her bed and retreated to the adjoining bathroom to shower and dress for work. Twenty minutes later, she stood, coffee in hand, and watched the morning news network on the television in her kitchen. "Chance of rain. Lovely. Guess I'd better grab my umbrella... oh, and let's not forget these." She scooped up the blue feather brooches from the kitchen table and slipped them into her scrubs pocket. "Keys... where are they? Why am I always losing my car keys?" After a short search, Willow found her keys on the side table just inside the entry door in her living room. "I'd lose my head if it wasn't attached." Fresh coffee in hand, she climbed into her car and headed toward Boston.

"Wow, traffic is amazingly light this morning. I think I have time to stop at the jewelers on my way to work." Moments later, she parked her car in the lot of Treasured Memories and entered the shop. The strange little man with the British accent she had talked to earlier in the week was behind the counter. His demeanor changed as soon as he recognized her.

"Miss, I told you I can't help you with your brooches."

Willow looked at his badge. "Mr. Kipling, I took them to another jeweler, and he said my brooches were around four hundred years old."

"I-I know nothing about them."

"He also said they possessed certain powers. Mr. Kipling, I suspect you know more about these than you're saying. I need your help—please."

Mr. Kipling backed up a few steps when Willow offered the brooches to him. "Take them back to the other jeweler you spoke with. I can't help you."

"The other jeweler won't help me."

"And neither will I. Please go."

"But, Mr. Kipling, I need to understand why these brooches are so special. I need to understand if the dream I had was real… and why the brooches were hot enough to burn the letter 'H' into my bedside table?"

Mr. Kipling lunged forward and placed his hands on the counter between himself and Willow. "May the heavens protect us. It's starting," he said, fear evident on his face.

"What's starting? I need to know."

"You will know soon enough. Now go, before I call the police."

Willow slipped the brooches back into her pocket. She took one of Mr. Kipling's business cards from the stand on the counter and fished a pen out of her bag. "I'm leaving my phone number with you in case you change your mind. My name is—"

"Willow McCord. Yes, I know who you are," Mr. Kipling said. "Now go, please."

\* \* \*

Willow pulled out of the parking lot of Treasured Memories and into traffic. "Geesh—I wonder what his problem is. And what did he mean by, it's starting? And oh, by the way, how did he know my name?" She came to a stop at the first traffic light and looked around; a chill ran down her spine. This was the intersection where she almost met her demise earlier in the week. The police officer's words came back to haunt her: someone was looking out for you.

She took a deep breath. "Okay, Willow, don't let your imagination get the better of you. They're just two pieces of jewelry and nothing more. Get a grip."

Willow got to the dental office with five minutes to spare, which gave her time enough to pick up a paper from Pete.

"Good morning, Pete," Willow said as she approached the newspaper stand set up outside her office building.

"'Morning to you, too, Miss Willow. Here's your paper." Pete handed the Boston Herald to Willow and nodded his head toward the curb. "That's a fine looking lady over there if I do say so myself."

Willow took a quick look over her shoulder at the woman leaning against a parked car. She looked back to Pete and handed him a dollar. "Has she been there long?"

"For about the last half hour. She must be waiting for someone."

Willow folded the paper in half, tucked it under her arm, and covertly looked once more at the woman. Pete was right; she was striking, albeit a little odd all dressed in black. "Thanks, Pete. I hope the weather holds out for you today. Forecast says rain."

"No worries, old Pete ain't gonna melt. You have yourself anice day now, Miss Willow."

"You too, Pete."

"Thank you, kindly."

Willow dared one more look at the woman as she pulled the door open and was surprised when the woman looked directly at her and smiled. Willow frowned and entered the building.

*Willow McCord, your picture doesn't do you justice.* Sawyer watched Willow hurry down the street toward the dental office. She hoped her willingness to cooperate was as nice as her appearance. She had watched the interaction between Willow and the newspaper vendor and was encouraged by the kindness that radiated from the woman. Despite Willow's obvious efforts to hide her interest, Sawyer was aware of the covert glances she shot in her direction. She's curious about me—that's good. I need to be careful not to come on too strong. Just before Willow entered the building, their eyes met and Sawyer smiled; although, considering the frown on Willow's face, she wondered if eye contact was smart .

Willow rushed into the building and stepped aside so she was out of view through the door. She peeked around the corner. The woman pulled a cell phone out of her pocket and appeared to be reading something on it.

The clock in the lobby gonged. "Damn—I'm late!" Willow ran to the elevator. As soon as the elevator opened on the fourth floor, she stepped out and rushed to her workstation to store her bag. As luck would have it, her station was on the front side of the building. She stood at the window and looked down. The woman was still on the sidewalk, talking on her phone and walking back and forth.

Suddenly, she stopped and looked directly up toward Willow's window. Willow jumped back, startled.

"Good morning, Willow," Susan said, and Willow jumped once more.

"Oh, my God. You scared the bejesus out of me!" Willow exclaimed.

"I'm sorry. Hey, are you okay?"

"The strangest thing just happened to me."

"What's that?"

"There was this woman watching me this morning as I bought a paper from Pete. Look, she's still down there." Willow pulled Susan toward the window.

Susan scanned the curb in front of the building. "I don't see a woman."

"Of course she's there. Let me look." Willow placed her forehead on the windowpane and intently scanned the area below. "She was there just a moment ago. I swear she was."

Susan crossed her arms and knit her brow together. "What did she look like?"

"She was maybe five-seven or five-eight, short dark-brown hair—almost a boy-cut, nice figure, attractive."

"Of course you'd notice that!" Susan joked.

"Odd thing is, she was dressed totally in black. Black trousers, black blazer, and a black vee-necked shirt. She even wore black shoes."

"If it makes you feel any better, I saw her, too. She was there when I arrived this morning."

"She was? Don't you find that odd?"

"Maybe she was waiting for someone. I wouldn't fret over it. She's gone now."

"You're probably right. Well, I've got to set my station up. My first cleaning is at ten."

"My next appointment should be here in about five minutes," Susan said.

"How did it go with Casanova the other day?"

"Ugh. Please don't remind me. Oops, there's my patient. Catch up with you later!"

Just before noon, a call came into Willow's cell phone, which she had tucked away in her scrubs pocket and set on vibrate. The unexpected buzz caused her to jump. Luckily, she had just finished a dental cleaning and was entering the patient's exit information into the computer. "Okay, Mr. Cross, here's a card for your next cleaning in six months." She pulled a drawer open at the side of her desk. She gathered a small tube of toothpaste, dental floss, and a new toothbrush and handed them to her patient. "Here you go—be sure to throw out your old brush when you get home. We'll see you in six months, then. Have a great rest of your day."

Willow walked her patient back to the waiting room and went directly to the lunch room to check her phone. She had one voicemail.

"Ms. McCord, this is Diana Lawrence, at the library. I have the results of your image recognition matching for your brooches and have uncovered some very interesting matches. Please call me, and we'll set up a time for you to come by for the information."

Willow wrote down the phone number supplied by the librarian. When she returned the call, it went to voicemail.

Willow waited for the beep. "Ms. Lawrence, this is Willow McCord returning your call. I assume you're at lunch. Please call me back when you get a chance. I appreciate it. Thank you."

Susan poked her head into the break room. "Want to run with me to Chang's? I'm collecting takeout orders from the staff."

Willow slipped her phone back into her pocket. "Sure."

Moments later, Willow and Susan stepped onto the sidewalk in front of the dental office and headed toward the Chinese restaurant. Willow looked around uneasily, but to her relief, she saw no strange woman clad in black watching her.

# Chapter 16

## 1610—North Yorkshire, England

Jenna came up from behind Hadley and wrapped her arms around the woman's waist as she stood at the basin. The feel of skin against skin caused a flame to erupt in her belly as Hadley leaned back into her embrace.

"Thou hast said nary a word since last night, Hadley. What is ailing thee, woman? I looked forward to greeting the morn with thee in my arms, but thou wast gone when I awoke."

Hadley turned around in Jenna's embrace. "I fret over what thou toldest me last night. Couldn't sleep and didn't want to wake thee. Thou wast sleeping like a babe."

"Hast thou been up all night, then?"

"Nearly."

Jenna took Hadley's hands in her own. "Come back to bed with me for a spell."

"I cannot. The shop awaits. We can talk more tonight. I need to wash and prepare a bite to eat."

Jenna took the cloth and soap from Hadley. "I shall wash thee."

Jenna liberally rubbed lather into the cloth and ran it over Hadley's back. Hadley moaned in pleasure.

"Hast thou any idea how long it's been since someone washed my back for me? 'Tis heavenly," Hadley said.

Jenna stepped closer and placed a kiss on Hadley's shoulder. "I shall wash thy back for thee any time," she said as she reached around and ran the soapy cloth across Hadley's breasts. Hadley shuddered against her as the cloth brushed her sensitive nipples.

"Jenna Hawksworth, thou art the devil himself with thy wanton ways," Hadley whispered hoarsely. Jenna pressed herself into Hadley's back, the soapy film providing a frictionless coating between them. One arm snaked around Hadley's waist and pulled her closer as Jenna moved the soapy cloth downward.

"Holy mother," Hadley whispered as the cloth slid between her legs.

"Dost thou want me to stop?" Jenna asked.

Hadley turned around and took Jenna's face between her palms. "The shop be damned. Take me to bed."

Sometime later, Hadley and Jenna rushed to wash, dress, and head to their respective jobs.

\* \* \*

Jenna carried a plate of rolls to the table and returned to the hearth to heft the pot of stew off the spit and carry it to the table as well.

"Put it on the trivet, if thou mindest not," Hadley said as she set bowls and utensils out for the two of them.

"It smells heavenly." Jenna sat down and leaned in to inhale the aromas emitting from the pot.

Hadley fetched the ladle from the hearth and returned to the table. "When last hast thou had a home-cooked meal, blacksmith?"

"Since I left home. My mum was a wonderful cook. I miss her and her cooking a lot."

"Well, hand thy bowl over to me. Not saying 'twill be a good as thy mum's stew, but I'm guessing it'll be better than thine own cooking."

"Considering I can't cook, 'twill definitely be better than whatever I fix for myself." Jenna took her bowl from Hadley, scooped up a spoonful, and put it into her mouth. She closed her eyes and tilted her head back. "By all that is sacred, 'tis good," she said.

Hadley smiled and spooned some stew into her own bowl. She sat down opposite Jenna and savored her food. Jenna hungrily inhaled large spoonfuls of the stew, along with two rolls. "Thou art hungry?" she asked.

"The demon in my belly has been growling at me all day. Hadley, this stew is better than my mum's. I thank thee for preparing it."

"Thou art welcome, but slow down or thou wilt make thyself sick. There's plenty more."

The next few minutes were spent in silence as they enjoyed their simple dinner. Hadley looked across the table at Jenna who smiled shyly at her.

"What is thy smile for, blacksmith?"

"I am thanking the Goddess for my good fortune. I still cannot believe I am here with thee."

Hadley reached her hand across the table and accepted Jenna's hand in her own. She squeezed lightly. "The powers that be are truly smiling on us both. When I looked upon thee this morn, sleeping like a babe, my heart flipped in my chest. The feeling was so strong, it almost hurt. I thank thee for coming into my shop, Jenna."

"The Goddess brought me to this town for a reason. I wasn't sure why until I met thee. I am convinced she sent me to thee."

Hadley released Jenna's hand. She rose from the table, collected her dinnerware, and carried it to the basin, where she stood for long moments with her back to Jenna.

Jenna turned around in her seat. "Hadley, art thou all right?"

Hadley faced the table again. "My heart is heavy in my chest, Jenna. I am more than a little worried about this witchcraft thing."

Jenna rose to her feet and collected her own dishes. She placed them in the basin behind Hadley and took her into her arms. Hadley placed her head on Jenna's chest, just below her chin. "I can hear thy heartbeat."

"It beats only for thee. Thank thee for loving me, Hadley Metcalf."

"Jenna, we need to talk about this."

"Aye. 'Tis a fact, we do."

Jenna fed another log into the fireplace and arranged the coals with the poker while Hadley refilled their tankards with mead. Hadley sat back in her chair and waited for Jenna to complete her task before handing her drink to her. Jenna settled on a pillow on the floor between Hadley's legs and kissed the inside of Hadley's knee. She stared at the fire as she sipped her brew.

"Where shall I begin?" Jenna said.

Hadley kissed the top of Jenna's head. "Tell me about being the chosen one."

"It took a long time before any of us realized I was the one," Jenna said. "In the beginning, I was simply new to the clan. I came from a family who swore allegiance to the Church and all that it stood for, including condemnation of the very beliefs the clan stood for. Only, I was different. I loved women, and loving one's own kind in the carnal sense is considered an unnatural act punishable by death in the Church. Hence the beatings at the hands of my father."

"And the rest of thy family—did they stand by and watch thy father beat thee?"

"They had no choice. My younger brother left home because he couldn't bear watching. I know not where he is today, or if he's even alive. My mum was powerless against my father. When she objected, he'd beat her, too."

Hadley cradled Jenna's head and rocked slightly back and forth. "I'm so sorry for thee, my love."

"That's all behind me now. The clan opened their arms and welcomed me, freeing me from the archaic beliefs of my father and his religion. For the first time in my life, I felt accepted for what I am. I continued to work as a blacksmith in my town, but I lived out of the barn behind the smithy's house. The smithy was a kind soul and secretly a member of the clan himself. Once I left my father's house, I vowed never to return."

"How long ago was that, my love?"

"When I met the gypsies."

"Thou wast twenty when that happened. So thou wast on thy own ever since?"

"Pretty much. Yes."

"How didst thou discover thou wast the chosen one?"

"I carry the mark. I was in the clan for two whole years before we discovered it."

"What dost thou mean? I have seen thee in naught but the skin thou wast born in, and I haven't seen a mark. Show it to me."

"'Tis difficult to see in this light."

"Then come closer to the fire. Move thee."

Jenna obediently allowed Hadley to lead her to the fire.

"Off with thy clothes," Hadley said.

Jenna grinned. "I thought thou didst wanted to see the mark, but it appears thou didst want carnal knowledge instead. I will be happy to oblige, but we will need more pillows to lie on."

Hadley whacked Jenna on the arm. "Is that all thou thinkest of, blacksmith?"

"Pretty much."

Hadley tried hard not to laugh. "Thou art enough to drive a sane person crazy, Jenna Hawksworth. Now show me the mark."

"As you wish." Jenna lay on her back in front of the fire and turned her face toward the flame. "Thou needest to get close to see it, and I shall not be able to talk while I show it to thee. Now get down here and take a look."

Hadley knelt down beside Jenna's head. Jenna opened her mouth wide. Hadley just frowned at her. "What art thou doing?"

"Hook," Jenna said.

"Hook? What the devil art thou saying?"

Jenna lifted her head. "I said look. The mark is inside my mouth, on my cheek." She laid her head back down and opened her mouth wide once more.

Hadley tilted Jenna's face more toward the fire and looked into her mouth. "I see three dark blue lines side by side on thy right cheek. How didst thou get these lines?"

Jenna closed her mouth and sat up. "Been there since I was a babe. The clan believes the Goddess Hecate put it there as a sign I was the chosen one for the uprising."

"Hecate? Uprising?"

Jenna extended her hand to Hadley. "Help me up, woman. We have a lot to talk about. What say thou, we get naked and talk in bed?"

Hadley crossed her arms in front of her. "Why do I believe thou hast more than talk on thy mind, blacksmith?"

Jenna grinned ear to ear and extended her hand once more. "So now art thou a mind-reader?"

# Chapter 17

**2013—Boston, Massachusetts**

Willow stepped out of the doorway of her office building and began to walk the two blocks toward the parking garage. She stopped in her tracks as a thought occurred to her. Damn! I forgot to see if the research librarian got back to me. She pulled her cell phone out of her bag and checked her voice messages. She had one new voicemail.

"Ms. McCord, this is Diana Lawrence at the Boston Community Library returning your call. I am available anytime before six p.m. today if you'd like to come in and discuss the results of the image matching on your brooches."

Willow looked at her watch. "Five p.m. I may have just enough time if I hurry." She dropped her cell phone back into her bag and rushed toward the parking garage.

Sawyer spotted Willow leaving her office building from an obscure vantage point inside a storefront across the street. She exited the store in time to see Willow stop short and search for something in her bag. Sawyer halted her pursuit momentarily as Willow appeared to be checking the messages on her cell phone. Before long, Willow dropped her phone back into her bag and quickly moved down the street. "Bugger!" Sawyer said as she picked up her own pace, finally coming to within hailing distance as she entered the parking garage.

"Willow!" Sawyer shouted as Willow reached for her car door handle.

Willow's head whipped around at the sound of her name.

Her eyes bulged out as she recognized her pursuer. Willow walked directly up to Sawyer. "Who are you? I saw you standing outside my office building this morning."

Sawyer put her hands up in front of her. "I can explain."

"It'll have to wait. I have an appointment I can't miss." Willow walked the few feet back to her car and opened the door.

"Willow, please—this is important."

"My appointment is important, too." Willow got into her car. "More important than the lives of thousands of people?" Sawyer yelled.

Willow lowered the window. "Look, I give to my share of charities, okay? So go look for money elsewhere. I have somewhere important to be." Willow raised the window, started the ignition, and pulled out of the parking space.

Sawyer stamped her foot and buried her hands deep into her trouser pockets. "That went well, Sawyer. Why are Americans so damned rude?"

\* \* \*

Willow parked in the lot of the Boston Community Library and hurried into the building. She approached the research librarian's desk. "I'm sorry, Ms. Lawrence. I'm Willow McCord and I just got your message. I hope this is a good time to go over the image- matching search on my brooches."

"Yes, of course, Ms. McCord. Follow me. I think you'll find this very interesting."

Willow followed the librarian into a small room at the back of the office area that held an image projector hooked up to a laptop computer.

"Please have a seat," Ms. Lawrence said.

"Thank you." Willow sat and waited for Ms. Lawrence to set up the slide show.

"Let's begin with a photograph of your brooches, both joined and apart," Ms. Lawrence said.

Willow looked at a magnified version of her brooches on the screen. Their beauty struck her as amazing at that magnified level, and she saw things in the intricate carving that she had never seen before, like the distinctive forms of two naked women, one on each of the brooches, seemingly intertwined when they were locked together. "Ms. Lawrence, is it my imagination, or do you see figures carved into the brooches?"

"Are you referring to the two ladies?"

"Yes. I'm glad you see them, too."

"They are symbolic of the Mother Goddess within the Wicca religion, representing fertilization of the Earth."

"Wicca—as in witchcraft?"

"Be careful how you think of the word witchcraft, Ms. McCord. It can sometimes imply something quite negative, when in fact, most of the earliest witches were women who used semi-medicinal practices such as herbs and extracts to heal the sick, or to cast 'spells' to make people fall in love. Many of them were also midwives. When the general population became dependent on these women as healers, their so-called 'power' began to threaten patriarchal religions. They soon became targets and were identified as witches to be feared."

The next slide was a picture of a five-pointed star surrounded by a circle. "Oh, my God—that's the symbol on the box the brooch arrived in from England... and it's the same symbol I saw in my dream!"

"The symbol came up frequently during the image-matching search," Ms. Lawrence said. "It represents a talisman of sorts and was generally used for protection against evil spirits." She advanced the slide show and displayed the back of the joined brooches. "Maiden, Warrior, Mother, Crone," she read.

"My co-worker thinks this phrase represents the stages of a woman's life," Willow said.

"She's partially right. The phrase refers to a Triple Goddess and exists in both Roman and Greek mythology. Regardless, the Goddess Hecate most often represents the Crone in both lines of mythology."

"Hecate? Where have I heard that before?" Willow muttered.

"Hecate is many things, too numerous to discuss in the

short time we have today. She is most known as the Goddess of the Underworld and is also well known as having dominion over fertility and child bearing. Depending on the school of thought, Hecate is either an evil or a beneficial goddess."

The last slide showed a drawing set in seventeenth century England. Figures in hooded cloaks, with blue feathers pinned to the front, watched a witch burning. The scene disturbed Willow. "This is awful. What does it mean?"

"I wasn't able to determine an interpretation for the picture. Associated with it, however, were the words 'Blue Feather Coven.' As far as I could learn through the search, those words have some association with homosexuality and witchcraft. It's unclear by looking at the drawing whether the people wearing the blue feathers are responsible for the witch burning, or simply bystanders. I will say that in the 1600s in England, homosexuality and witchcraft were both categorized as unnatural acts and punishable by death."

"Seriously? People were executed for being gay?"

"In the 14th and 15th centuries, acts against nature were associated with witchcraft, and homosexuality was considered an act against nature. Some believed that demons and devils would collect semen to make new bodies for themselves. At that time the term 'sodomy' was used to describe a variety of unnatural acts that couldn't lead to procreation, including nocturnal emissions, homosexual behavior, solitary masturbation, mutual masturbation, copulation between the thighs, anal sex, and even heterosexual sex with the woman on top or vaginal penetration from behind. Basically anything but heterosexual vaginal penetration in the missionary position was considered sinful. The Church's position was clear on acts most often referred to as 'wickedness not to the named,' and those who violated it were considered to be carrying out the work of the devil. Punishment often included mutilation, burning at the stake, hanging, or hot pokers inserted into the anus or vagina."

Willow sat back in her seat, stunned. "What does it all mean?"

Ms. Lawrence shut off the projector and turned the lights back on in the room. "That, my dear, is for you to determine with further research, if you are so inclined."

"Yes. Yes, of course." Willow rose and walked toward the door. She stopped and faced the librarian once more. "Is it possible to get a copy of those slides?"

"Yes, indeed. Just give me your email address, and I'll send them to you."

Willow shared her address and Ms. Lawrence wrote it down then extended her hand to the woman. "Thank you, Ms. Lawrence. I sincerely appreciate your help with this."

"You're welcome. Good luck on your quest."

# Chapter 18

## 2013—Plymouth, Massachusetts

Willow pulled into her driveway, turned off the ignition, and ran into the house straight to her computer. She pulled up her favorite search engine and typed the words "Blue Feather Coven" in the search field. She found dozens of sites on the use of feathers in magic, a list of birds with blue feathers, tons of sites about covens in general, and even a lesbian publishing house with 'Blue Feather' in the name, but nothing with the specific combination of words "blue feather coven."

"Damn. Now what? Wait, what was the name of that goddess? Was it Hector… no, that's a guy's name. Hectate? Maybe." Willow typed the word "Hectate" into the search field and the browser returned the message, "Do you mean Hecate?"

"That might be it," Willow said as she clicked on the link.

She sat back and looked through the long list of websites containing information about Hecate. "I can't possibly get through all of this. I wonder what it all means relative to my brooch. Could it really be connected to witchcraft? Grandma Jenny, exactly what were you involved in?"

The rumbling in Willow's stomach reminded her it was dinnertime—significantly beyond it, in fact. She got up from her computer and went into the kitchen in search of dinner fixings. In a few moments, she had ingredients for a salad and some pre-cooked chicken sitting on her kitchen table. She grabbed a cutting board and a sharp knife from the butcher block, and just as she was about to slice the tomato, her doorbell rang.

"Who the hell can that be?" Still holding her knife, she walked through the kitchen and living room to the front door and switched on the porch light. She pulled the curtain aside a bit to see who was calling on her after dark. "What the fuck?" she said as she swung the door open. "Seriously?" she asked. "You seriously followed me home?"

Sawyer saw the knife and immediately took a step back with her hands out in front of her. "I promise I'm not an axe murderer or anything even remotely resembling one."

"I thought I made myself clear. Man! They couldn't pay me enough to track down potential donors at home."

"I don't know what you're talking about," Sawyer said.

"You're not here looking for money?"

"No. No, I'm not."

"Then tell me why I should let you into my house."

"I've come a long way to seek your help with a very delicate matter."

"You need my help. Me. Willow McCord."

"Yes. You are the only one who can."

"I think you need to leave now." Willow began to close the door.

"No. Wait. Let me explain," Sawyer said as the door closed in her face. She raised her voice. "I'm Sawyer Hawksworth."

The door swung open.

"Say that again," Willow said.

Sawyer pulled at the hem of her jacket. "I'm Sawyer Hawksworth. Glad to make your acquaintance," she said as she offered her hand.

Willow took Sawyer's hand, yanked her into the house, and closed the door. "You've got a lot of explaining to do," she said, shaking the knife at her.

"Yes, but trust me, you won't need that knife to get the information you want."

Willow looked at the knife. "Sorry, I was about to make a late dinner when you buzzed. Have you eaten?"

"Actually, no, but you needn't go to any trouble," Sawyer said.

"No trouble at all—especially since you're going to help me make it."

"Ah… All right. If you insist."

"I do. Follow me."

Willow led her guest back into the kitchen and went to the cupboard for another salad dish. "I hope salad is okay. I have this amazing homemade Asian dressing."

"Salad is fine. I appreciate the invitation," Sawyer said.

Willow opened the utensil drawer and pulled out a potato peeler, which she placed on the table in front of Sawyer. She then picked up the cucumber and cut both ends off. "Here, you can start by peeling the cucumber. And you may want to take your jacket off."

"Yes, of course." Sawyer removed her jacket and looked around awkwardly for a place to hang it.

"Just drape it over the back of the chair for now. It'll be fine there." Willow assessed her guest. *Probably a spoiled rich kid. My money's on her not knowing how to use the potato peeler.*

Sawyer picked up the potato peeler and the cucumber and looked at both objects hopelessly.

Bingo! "Okay, are you right- or left-handed?" Willow asked.

"Left."

"All right then. Hold the cucumber in your right hand and drag the potato peeler along the length like this." She guided Sawyer's hand down the length of the cucumber, removing the first strip of skin. "Got it?"

"I think so."

"Okay." Willow pulled another knife out of the drawer, along with a small cutting board, and placed them in front of Sawyer. "When you're finished peeling, use this knife to cut the entire thing into slices."

"Got it."

Willow grabbed a tomato and began to slice. "So do you want to tell me what this is all about?"

"I couldn't possibly do it justice in one evening. Do you think we can save this conversation for tomorrow? I'll come back when it's convenient for you."

Willow frowned. "You came all the way out here from Boston just to tell me you want to talk tomorrow?"

"It's rather complicated."

Willow looked at the hack-job that used to be the cucumber. Sawyer's hands were shaking violently. "Okay. Stop. Step away from the cucumber and sit down before you hurt yourself."

Sawyer did as she was told and sat with her hands clasped together on the table. Willow went to the cupboard and pulled down two wineglasses. From the refrigerator, she got a bottle of chilled wine. She pulled the cork, filled both glasses, and placed one in front of Sawyer.

"Here, drink this. It'll calm your nerves."

"Thank you, Ms. McCord."

"I think we're way beyond the Ms. McCord thing, Sawyer. You can call me Willow."

"Thank you, Willow."

Willow went back to making the salads. "I think I've figured out that the brooches were made to be together."

"Yes, that's true."

"Mine was given to me by my grandmother—Jenny McCord. Considering how old the brooches are, I assume you received yours in a similar manner?"

"Yes, from my nana, Melinda Hawksworth."

"Is it possible that our grandmothers knew each other?"

"I have reason to believe they knew of each other, but I doubt they had ever met, or even spoken to one another."

Willow put a generous layer of salad greens on each plate and topped them with sliced cucumbers, tomatoes, radishes, and avocado. "Do you like onions?" she asked.

"Very much, thank you."

"How about garlic?"

"A tad bit, please."

Willow added a few sliced onions and a sprinkle of garlic salt, basil, and pepper to the salads.

"One more question—are you a meat eater or vegetarian?"

"I love meat—well, except for liver," Sawyer said.

"I'm with you on that one, sister. I hate liver, too." Willow piled a generous amount of cooked chicken on each salad and put the remaining ingredients back into the refrigerator. "Okay, we have French, Italian, Ranch, Blue Cheese, and the homemade Asian dressings. What can I get for you?"

"The homemade Asian sounds delightful."

"Asian it is then." Willow grabbed the Mason jar with the Asian dressing and placed it on the table in front of Sawyer. "You'll need to shake it first." Willow took two forks from the utensil drawer and a couple of napkins from the napkin holder and placed one of each beside Sawyer's plate as she poured her dressing. "Here you go."

"Thank you again, Willow. You're most kind."

Willow refilled their wineglasses and poured dressing on her own salad. "I hope you like it."

"I'm sure it will be wonderful," Sawyer said as she waited for Willow before beginning to eat.

Willow motioned to her plate. "Please, eat. You must be hungry. I know I am."

"It has been a long while since lunch. It took some time to find your house."

"So why did you come out here tonight if you didn't intend to talk to me?"

"I wanted to meet you and to introduce myself. I actually underestimated how far your home was from Boston. I thought it was much closer." Sawyer took a bite of her salad. Her eyes grew wide as the rich Asian flavor filled her mouth. "This is really good. You must share your recipe. I'll ask Matilda to make it for me."

"Matilda?"

"My housekeeper."

"Of course."

"Well, she's more like a nanny than anything." Sawyer chuckled. "She's from Germany, and she's been with my family since I was a child. I think I've received more pats on the behind from her than from my parents. She keeps the estate in tip-top shape."

"You live on an estate?"

"It belongs to my parents. Or it did until they were killed in an automobile accident about a year ago."

"I'm sorry to hear that."

"Thank you. I never dreamed I would be moving back home after ten years on my own."

"What do you do?"

"I own a financial advising firm."

"That's a pretty lucrative business."

"It can be, but I make a point of taking on a portion of my caseload pro bono as well. There are a lot of unfortunate people in Britain who suffered terribly through the recent worldwide financial crisis. They deserve representation, but they can't always afford to pay for it."

"You know what I do for work, considering you were waiting for me outside my office this morning… and this afternoon."

"Yes. I must apologize for accosting you like that. I only wanted to introduce myself."

"How did you find me?"

"I hired a private detective."

"How did you even know to look for me? How did you know I had the other half of the brooch?"

"That is the discussion better left for tomorrow."

Willow filled Sawyer's wineglass once more. "Are you feeling better?"

"Yes, very much so. This salad is wonderful. Do you do all your own cooking?"

"Every bit of it. I learned to cook from my mom at a very young age. She's a fantastic cook."

"Your parents are still living then?"

"Yes."

"And they never spoke to you about the brooch?"

"Not a word."

"And your grandmother, Jenny McCord—did she say anything to you?"

"Grammy McCord died when I was relatively young. I was maybe ten years old, but to answer your question—there was never any discussion about the brooch, other than her telling me to take good care of it and to pass it down to my children before I died. How did you know my grandmother's name was Jenny

McCord?"

"That was very irresponsible of her, and of your parents, not to pass on the meaning of the brooch."

"I don't appreciate you talking about my grandmother, or my parents, in that tone."

Sawyer sat back in her chair. "My apologies for offending you, but there is much that you will need to learn about the brooches—and very soon."

Willow sipped her wine as she watched Sawyer eat her salad. "Much to learn, huh? Like what?"

Sawyer finished her salad and placed her fork perfectly centered on her folded napkin. "Tomorrow, Willow. I promise I will tell you everything. That was an excellent dinner. Now if you'll excuse me, I'll take my leave of you this night." Sawyer stood, teetered a bit, and fell back into her chair.

"You're not going anywhere tonight, Sawyer. Hand over your car keys. You can sleep in the guest room."

# Chapter 19

## 1610—North Yorkshire, England

Hadley sat at the foot of the bed with her knees pulled into her chest and her arms wrapped around them. Jenna lay with her back against the headboard.

"What are we going to do, Jenna? If what thou dost say is true… and we fail…"

Jenna leaned forward. "We shall not fail. We cannot fail."

"But the king's men… what if they find out? We shall surely be burned at the stake."

"Have some sense, woman. 'Tisn't like we shall do it in the courtyard of the king's castle. The clan shall do what they can to protect us—all of us. They shall be involved as well. Will there be risk? Aye, 'tis unavoidable, but 'tis a risk we have to take."

Hadley rested her forehead on her knees and began to cry.

Jenna crawled to the foot of the bed and took Hadley into her arms. "Great Goddess, pray don't cry. I won't let anything happen to thee, my love. I promise."

Hadley looked into Jenna's eyes. "And thee? I shall lie down beside thee and die if something happens to thee."

"I will not have that, Hadley. If something doth happen to me, thou dost need to go on. Thou wilt need to see that future generations are prepared."

"How canst thou be so confident, Jenna Hawksworth?"

Jenna lifted Hadley's chin and wiped her tears away. "Because I have known it for some time. I have planned. If the high priest is right, it will not happen for three years hence.

Thou hast time to learn and prepare. Fear not. I will content thee. Go to thy heart and draw on thy love for me. I will not fail thee."

"I would lie to say I am not scared."

"Aye. I am scared as well. Come—lie with me, and we will plan how to survive this unholy mess."

\* \* \*

Jenna pushed the door to Hadley's tailor shop open and walked in. The sound of the bell attached to the top of the door drew Hadley's attention to her. Jenna nodded in Hadley's direction and waited patiently while she finished helping her customer. She browsed through the bolts of cloth displayed near Hadley's workbench.

"I'll be with thee in a moment, blacksmith," Hadley said, smiling at her in a way only Jenna could understand.

"Take your time, Mistress Metcalf. I hurry not."

"Is there anything else thou dost need, Mistress Fagan?" Hadley asked before she rolled her customer's purchases in a scrap of cloth and tied it with twine. She handed the package to her customer. "All right, then. Be sure to come by if thou hast any questions. Good day to thee."

Jenna kept her back to Hadley until the customer left the store. When she heard the door close, she turned around just in time to catch Hadley falling into her arms.

"I missed thee, blacksmith."

"We've only been apart for all of two hours, woman."

"I know, but thou hast been on my mind for every moment of that."

"Aye—and thou hast been on my mind, as well. That's why I stopped by. I need to go out of town for a day or two."

Hadley stepped back and frowned. "Pray tell, why?"

Jenna looked around the shop to assure they were alone before continuing. "I need to see the high priest."

"Whatever for?"

"Thou dost possess the blue feather, and as such, thou hast been invited into the coven, but the high priest needs to officiate over an initiation ceremony. I need to discuss when this shall happen and how."

"Initiation ceremony? I do not like the sound of that."

Jenna grasped Hadley's shoulders. "I promised to prepare thee for what lies ahead. Thou needest to trust me, woman."

"Wouldst thou be gone long, then?"

"No more than two days, I promise."

"Should I not be going with thee?"

"Not this time. Perhaps soon. I will discuss this with the high priest."

Hadley threw herself into Jenna's arms. "When wouldst thou go?"

"Forthright. I will return the day after the morrow."

"I shall miss thee. God speed with thee and blessed be, Jenna Hawksworth."

* * *

"Lord Weller, may I seek your counsel?" Jenna asked.

"Aye. Pray, walk with me," the priest said as he directed Jenna toward the vineyards. They walked side by side for several minutes without talking. "I sense thou art troubled about something, Jenna."

"Aye, Lord Weller, I am. 'Tis about Hadley Metcalf."

"Ah, Mistress Metcalf. She is well?"

"Aye, she is. Lord Weller… I explained to her what lies ahead."

"And?"

"As expected, she is frightened."

"Hast thou explained her role?"

"Not entirely. She understands my role as the chosen one, and she is willing to support me in this quest."

The priest stopped and placed his hand on Jenna's shoulder. "Jenna, we sent thee to her for a very specific reason. Her ancestors have participated in the repression, and she needs to do the same for it to be successful. 'Tis why it was so important for you to give her the brooch. It needs to be in her possession for it to be most powerful."

Jenna nodded. "I understand."

The pair resumed walking.

Jenna spoke again. "She shall need to be initiated into the coven. She needs to be immersed in our teachings. Her ignorance has left her terrified of what lies ahead. Pray tell, when?"

"In a fortnight, at the next Dark Moon. We shall make the preparations."

Jenna took the priest's hand and kissed the back of it.

"Gramercy, Lord Weller."

"Jenna, look at me."

Jenna raised her eyes to meet his gaze.

"Thou art in love with her. Is that not so?"

Jenna grinned slightly. "'Tis true. She is my reason for rising each morning. I would gladly die for her."

"Do not be so foolish as to trade thy life for hers, Jenna Hawksworth. Thy lineage must continue to assure success for future generations. Hers must continue as well. Regardless of how thou dost feel about her, heirs must be produced. Dost thou understand that?"

"Aye. That I do."

# Chapter 20

## 2013—Plymouth, Massachusetts

Sawyer opened her eyes and looked around. Where am I? She lifted her head off the pillow and acknowledged a slight ache in her temples. What happened last night? With a little effort, she threw off the covers and pushed herself into a seated position on the side of the bed. She was in a spacious bedroom, tastefully decorated in a seashore motif... and she had no pants on. What the hell? The last thing she remembered was having dinner in Willow's kitchen and excusing herself to head back to the hotel in Boston. Willow. She's different from what I expected her to be. Independent. Strong willed. This may not be as easy as I thought. She glanced at the digital clock on the bedside table. Ten a.m. Great Goddess! I can't believe I slept so long.

She looked around until she located her trousers folded neatly across the top of a wingback chair in the corner of the room. She pulled them on and slipped her feet into her boots, which were on the floor by the foot of the bed. After making the bed, she went in search of a bathroom. Bathroom chores over, she looked in the mirror. "Great hairdo, Sawyer," she said as she ran the water to wet her hair down and wash her hands.

She stepped out of the bathroom and was met with the aroma of freshly brewed coffee. Following the scent, she walked down a short hallway and encountered what she assumed to be Willow's bedroom, decorated with a feminine touch. Another, smaller room that contained a desk, a file cabinet, and a laptop computer lay off to the side. She walked into the office space and put a finger against the touch pad on the laptop. The screen immediately came to life and displayed a list of websites all with the word "Hecate" in the description. *She's been doing her homework.*

Sawyer left the office and stepped back into the hallway. The stairs to the lower level were directly in front of her. *I don't remember climbing these stairs last night.* She descended the stairs slowly while scanning the pictures of Willow's family that were hung on both sides of the staircase. Some of them were quite old. She gasped when she stopped in front of one particularly old picture. *It's grandmother Richelle! Who is that woman with her? Could it be Maggie McCord?*

Sawyer descended the rest of the stairs quickly and walked through the living room and into the kitchen. Willow was at the counter, making a cup of coffee.

"Good morning," Willow said over her shoulder. "You must have been tired. It's after ten o'clock."

"I'm sorry for that. I generally don't sleep that late. Please accept my apology."

"Are Brits always this polite?" Willow asked.

"I'm sorry. What did you say?"

"You're so damned polite. Chill out a bit. It's okay to sleep in. I'm sure your flight took a lot out of you."

Sawyer nodded. "Indeed, it did."

"Coffee cups are in the cupboard above the coffee maker, and creamer is in the fridge. Help yourself," Willow said. "Are you hungry?"

"Coffee will be fine. I dare say I'm a tad hung over. What happened last night?" Sawyer asked as she prepared a cup of coffee.

"Sorry about that. The wine we drank was from a local vineyard and the homegrown stuff tends to be a little higher in alcohol than you're probably used to."

"I don't remember going to bed last night."

"Well, you originally intended to drive back to Boston. It didn't take much convincing for you to stay the night."

Sawyer took a sip of coffee. "This is really good coffee."

"Thanks. It's also a product of New England—Vermont in fact."

"I woke up this morning partially unclothed."

"That would be my handiwork. It was a bit of a challenge getting your boots off, but the pants came off pretty easily."

Sawyer looked around uncomfortably.

"Whoa. Wait a minute. You can wipe that look right off your face. Nothing happened, I promise you. I don't do drunk girls."

"I'm not familiar with that phrase. What do you mean by 'do'?"

"Are you for real? What do they call it in Britain?"

"Call what?"

"Doing. It means having sex."

Sawyer nearly choked on her coffee. "So that's what it means? In Britain, we would say 'have it off.'"

"Have it off? So you wouldn't 'have it off' with drunk girls."

"Correct."

"For your information, then, I don't have it off with drunk girls."

Sawyer smiled. "You're very entertaining, Willow McCord."

Willow blushed. "I am who I am."

"I may be going out on a limb, but may I surmise from your remark that you prefer the fairer sex?"

"If you're asking if I'm gay, then yes. I totally dig girls."

"Well that complicates things just a bit, but it's not insurmountable."

"And what exactly do you mean by that?"

"Well it does make procreating just a tad more difficult."

"And who exactly am I supposed to procreate with, huh? You?"

Sawyer chuckled and finished her coffee. She retrieved her jacket from the back of the kitchen chair and turned to address Willow. "I'd be honored if you would join me for dinner tonight in Boston. You can even choose the restaurant if you'd like."

Willow leaned her backside against the kitchen counter. "I thought we had some things to discuss."

"We do. Hence, the dinner. I have a business proposition for you that will pay handsomely. But right now, I need to get back to my hotel and take care of a few things. Will I see you later?"

Willow wrote her cell number on a scrap of paper and handed it to Sawyer. "I guess you'll need this to let me know what time dinner is. There are tons of good restaurants in Boston. Just choose one. I'm not picky, except for liver." Willow grinned.

Sawyer couldn't keep the smile from her own lips. "Liver. Yes, I remember." She shoved the phone number into her breast pocket as she headed toward the door. She paused before leaving, "Oh, and, Willow, bring the brooches with you if you would."

"Hey, Sawyer," Willow said as Sawyer opened the front door. "Catch."

Willow tossed the car keys to Sawyer, who grinned once more before leaving.

\* \* \*

Sawyer paced back and forth across her hotel room, her Bluetooth earpiece firmly in place. "Good afternoon, Lord Somers. I'm calling to let you know that I've made contact with Willow McCord."

"Have you discussed your proposal with her yet?" the priest asked.

"Not exactly. She was difficult to pin down. She actually gave me the brush-off earlier in the day, so I made an appearance at her home last evening. She's quite an interesting woman."

"In what way?"

"For starters, she prefers relations with members of her own sex."

"That's certainly a bonus. She should fit in nicely with the clan."

"Yes, I thought so as well, but she's also very independent and strong willed. And she isn't lacking for anything financially. Her home is modest but quite comfortable. It's yet to be seen if she can be enticed by financial gain."

"You do understand what is at stake here, Sawyer. She must be convinced to cooperate."

"I do understand, and yes, I will do my best. In this day and age, participation in the repression is relatively low risk. It could even be looked upon as an adventure, but it's the longer-term commitment that I'm concerned about. She seems to be quite content with her life as it is."

"I assume she still has the brooches?"

"Yes. I've asked her to bring them to dinner tonight."

"The brooches are critical to the repression. If for some reason she refuses to cooperate, you must gain possession of them. We'll deal with the other issue after the repression."

"I understand. I'll do my best."

"Blessed be, Sawyer."

"Blessed be, Lord Somers."

# Chapter 21

## 1610—North Yorkshire, England

Hadley had just finished the repairs on a customer's quilt when a young man entered her shop. He was relatively slim, but tall, and had medium brown hair which he pulled back to the nape of his neck with a piece of leather. "May I help thee, sir?" she said.

"Kind lady, I am looking for work. I'll do anything to earn a hot meal."

"What is thy skill, lad?"

"Farming, smithing—and I have a strong back. Dost thou need anything heavy moved?"

Hadley walked up to the young man and studied his face. He looked familiar to her. "Thou sayest thou canst do smithing? We have a new blacksmith in town—arrived just a few weeks ago. Perchance thou canst find some work there. What's thy name, lad?"

"Caleb. Caleb Hawksworth."

Hadley grabbed the edge of the counter. "Holy mother of God. Hawksworth, thou sayest?"

"Aye, Mistress."

"Art thou from Billingham, perhaps?"

"Indeed I am. Dost thou know of my family?"

"In a sense. I've heard thy sire is a bit of a tyrant."

Caleb looked down and played with the cap he held between his hands. "He is a monster. Near beat my sister to death because of his bigoted religious ways. 'Tis the reason I left home."

"Well, Master Hawksworth, I happen to know where thou canst get a nice hot meal—and a clean bed to boot. Give me a few minutes to close up shop. 'Tis near closing time anyway. Tomorrow, we'll see about getting thee a job."

* * *

"Go on out to the well and wash thyself, then come hither and give me a hand. Thou canst carve the smoked ham while I rinse the vegetables and slice the bread. Take that bar of soap by the basin with thee."

Caleb did as he was told and returned moments later. Hadley handed him a knife. "Here, lad. Cut off a few good slices."

"I can't thank thee enough for thy kindness, Mistress Metcalf," Caleb said. "Dost thou always take as kindly to strangers?"

"Not all strangers. But thou art a special case."

"How so?"

Hadley arranged salad fixings on two plates and turned to address the young man. "Master Hawksworth, canst thou keep a secret… a secret that could end up hurting someone very dear to me, and to thee, if it be broken?"

"Thou art talking in riddles, Mistress."

"I just need to know if thou canst be trusted."

"I will take thy secret to my grave, Mistress Metcalf."

"Put one piece of ham on my plate and the rest on thine, and sit down before I tell thee."

"All right, pray tell."

"I am one with thy sister. We are very much in love."

Caleb jumped to his feet. "Jenna? Jenna is here? I demand thee tell me where!"

Hadley picked up her knife and stuck it into the table. "Thou demandest naught! Sit thy carcass down, young sir. I will not tolerate insolent behavior in my home."

Caleb sat down and bowed his head. "Pray accept my apology, Mistress Metcalf. I… I haven't seen my sister in…"

"Four years. Aye, she told me how thou didst leave after the beating." His gaze met Hadley's. She could see the mist in his eyes.

"Is she well?" he asked.

"That she is."

"Where is she? I must see her."

"Thou wilt see her soon enough. She is on a two-day mission and will return on the morrow."

"Mission? Where?"

"I will let her explain that to thee. In the meantime, thou art my guest and I expect thee to behave like one." Hadley cut three slices of bread and placed two on Caleb's plate and one on hers. She then retrieved a mixture of oil, vinegar, and herbs from the storage room and placed it on the table between them. "Eat thy fill, Caleb Hawksworth, and then we'll talk about where thou wilt sleep."

\* \* \*

Hadley woke the next morning to an odd sound coming from outside her cottage. "What the devil is that?" She cursed as she climbed out of bed. She noticed the sleeping pad and group of blankets lain for Caleb near the fire the night before were neatly folded and stacked on the rocking chair. She threw a shawl over her shoulders and opened the front door. Out in the courtyard was Caleb, chopping wood. He stopped when he saw her.

"I aim to earn my keep, Mistress Metcalf, so I figured I'd split and stack this firewood. I hope I didn't wake thee."

"Not at all. I appreciate your kindness, Master Hawksworth. I will fix us a nice breakfast and call for thee when it's ready."

Hadley closed the door and hurried to dress. "Who would have aimed so near as to think I would be having my darling's brother in my home? At least he appears to be a good lad. 'Twill be quite a shock for Jenna when she returns later this day."

Hadley made a breakfast of fried eggs, ham, and bread with fresh creamy butter. She marveled at the speed at which her young guest ate. She tucked two pieces of fruit into his hand for a mid-morning snack as they left the cottage for the short walk to the shop.

Caleb spent the morning organizing the shelves in the main shop, as well as dusting and repairing worn shelf units. In the afternoon, Hadley assigned him to clean the storage room in the back of the shop, all the while keeping an eye on the road that ran in front of the shop for signs of Jenna's return. All day long she watched, but to no avail. By day's end, the shop was clean and organized and it was time to go home.

Caleb resumed chopping and stacking firewood while Hadley fixed a chicken stew for their dinner. When it was done, she called him in. She ladled stew into two bowls and placed them on the table. Very little was said. They took seats opposite each other, with Caleb's back toward the door, and began to eat.

Hadley cut a slice of bread from the loaf and handed it to Caleb. Instead of taking the bread directly, he reached for the hand offering it to him and held it gently. "She will return anon. I know she will."

Hadley looked into his eyes and saw Jenna there. She put the bread beside his bowl and cupped the side of his face. "Thou hast your sister's kind eyes. Thank thee for all of thy help today."

Just then, the cottage door flew open. "Sweet Hecate! I leave for two days and come back to this? I could see this intimate scene through the window from across the yard. How dare thee, Hadley?"

Hadley rose from her seat and met Jenna in the middle of the room. "Jenna! 'Tis not what thou thinkest."

Jenna pointed to Caleb's back. "Who is this cad thou art breaking bread with?"

Caleb rose to his feet and turned around. "Welcome home, sister."

Jenna was stunned. She held on to Hadley's shoulder for support. "Caleb? Caleb Hawksworth?"

"Aye, but before thou dost start slobbering all over me, thou dost owe thy lady an apology. She's done naught but welcome me into her home and put warm food in my belly."

Jenna looked at Hadley, who at this point had her arm around Jenna's waist. "I... I don't know what to say. I was wrong. Canst thou forgive me?"

"Aye. 'Tis kind of flattering the green-eyed devil got to thee. Now go give thy brother a hug. He's been waiting two days to see thee."

Jenna ran into the circle of her brother's arms and held on to him as tight as she could. Speech was impossible through the tears that filled her eyes and throat. Caleb picked her up, swung her around in a circle, and cried his own share of tears. Finally he placed her on her feet and took a step back.

"Thou hast got so big," Jenna said. "Thou wast only sixteen when thou didst leave home and not much taller than I. Now look at thee. Thou didst break my heart when thou left, little brother."

"I was weak, Jenna. There was naught I could do to stop that bastard. I was ashamed. I had to go."

Jenna hugged him again. "Well, thou art here now. How didst thou find us?"

"By chance, sister. I had no idea thou wast in this town. I stopped at Mistress Hadley's shop, and she was kind enough to give me work, food, and a roof over my head. Of course, she perceived at once that I was thy brother."

"Well, the Hawksworth name did give it away," Hadley said.

"Come hither, woman," Jenna said as she opened her arms to Hadley. She kissed her tenderly on the temple. "Thank the Goddess he found thee. And thanks to thee for taking such good care of him.

I love thee, Hadley Metcalf."

"And I love thee, too, Jenna Hawksworth. Now sit thyself down here and have some stew. Thou must be starving from being on the road all day."

"So tell me, sister, where hast thou been for the past two days?"

"Just outside of Billingham."

"Why wouldst thou go there? Didst thou not have enough of his abuse when thou wast living there?"

"I didn't go to see him, Caleb. I went to the Clan Council."

"Thou art still mixed up with them? That's one of the things that got thee beaten in the first place."

"'Tis true, but he has no power over me anymore. I went to arrange initiation for Hadley."

Caleb looked at Hadley. "And thou hast agreed to this?"

Hadley put her hand on Caleb's arm. "I love Jenna very much and want to support her in any way I can. I won't say I grasp this repression she doth talk about, but to understand her, I need to understand it. I am willing to learn."

"But art thou willing to believe?" Caleb asked.

"I am willing to try," Hadley replied.

# Chapter 22

## 2013—Boston, Massachusetts

When Sawyer returned to the hotel, she had time to remotely resolve three customer issues related to her financial advising business, as well as shower and change into suitable dinner wear before leaving for the restaurant. She arrived at her destination twenty minutes early to assure she got there before Willow. Her heart was in her throat as she struggled with the best way to convince Willow to cooperate with the council's needs.

Sawyer was already seated when Willow arrived promptly at six p.m. She almost didn't recognize her in the black cocktail dress and heels. Her wavy auburn hair fell loosely around her shoulders. Wow. *Now that's a far cry from the scrubs she was wearing earlier today.* Sawyer rose to hold her seat for her. "You look very nice,

Willow."

"Thank you. I don't get a chance to dress up very often. The scrubs get old after a while, you know what I mean?"

"Are you telling me you don't go out much?"

"Almost never. Unfortunately, I don't have a lot of close friends out where I live and the ones I have in the Boston area are mostly straight co-workers. Not a lot in common, I'm afraid."

"Well, I appreciate your willingness to meet me for dinner. Would you like something to drink?"

"I'll have wine. Just one glass. I need to drive home after this."

"Wine it is." Sawyer flagged down the waiter and ordered two glasses of wine.

"So, how did the rest of your day go?" Willow asked.

"Fine. I took care of some business, made a few phone calls, showered, changed, and here I am."

Sawyer could feel Willow assess her attire of black trousers, jacket, and white button-down shirt.

"I take it you like black," Willow said.

"Yes, very much. It looks good on you as well. It complements your red hair."

"I'm pretty limited with this hair color. Pastels are kind of out. Blacks and earth tones as well as teals are good for me."

"Of course."

Willow leaned forward. "So why don't we skip the chitchat and get to the point?"

Just then, the waiter approached the table with their wine. "Are you ready to order?"

Sawyer looked at the waiter. "I'm sorry, we've been busy talking, and we haven't looked at the menu. Could you give us a few minutes?"

"Of course. Take your time."

Sawyer looked at Willow who simply raised her eyebrows and smiled at her. *She's playing with me.* Sawyer picked up the menu and perused the entrée selections. "What do you say we call a truce and get through dinner?"

"Works for me," Willow said. She picked up her wineglass and sipped from it without taking her eyes off Sawyer.

"You might want to look at your menu. The waiter will be back in a moment."

Almost as though on cue, the waiter returned, notepad in hand. "Have you made your decision?"

"Willow?

"I'll have the lobster ravioli and a side salad. Light, creamy Italian dressing on the side, please."

The waiter looked at Sawyer. "And for you, sir?"

Willow nearly choked on her wine, which earned her a scowl from Sawyer.

"Make that two, if you would."

"Thank you," the waiter said as he collected the menus.

Sawyer looked at Willow and struggled to suppress a grin. Willow leaned in again. "How is your wine, sir?" she said.

Despite herself, Sawyer smiled. "It was rather funny, wasn't it?"

"Could I ask you a question, Willow?" Sawyer said around a bite of ravioli.

"Ask away."

"There's a picture hanging in your stairway—a rather old picture, of two women. Do you by chance know who they are?"

"If it's the one I think you're referring to, that's my great-grandmother, Maggie McCord, and her friend Ricky."

"Ricky? What kind of name is that for a woman?"

"It's a nickname. Anyway, my great-grandmother was involved with the USO for the troops during World War I, and she met Ricky in Britain, of all places. They spent a significant amount of time together. If you ask me, I think they were a couple."

"Well here's something you'll find interesting. Ricky is actually Richelle Hawksworth—my great-grandmother. I recognized her picture when I came down the stairs this morning—and I agree with you—I, too, think they were a couple."

"Seriously? It certainly is a small world."

"Actually, it isn't. It's not a coincidence that we're here together today. Our families have been linked for four hundred years."

"By the brooches, I assume?"

"That has something to do with it."

"I think it's time we have that talk."

\* \* \*

Sawyer and Willow strolled side by side along the Boston Harbor Walk. A light breeze marked the summer evening.

"It's a splendid evening for a walk," Sawyer said.

Willow shook an errant lock of hair away from her face. "Yes, it is. Boston harbor is beautiful at this time of year. It'll be dark soon. If we're lucky, the sunset over the ocean will be amazing."

Sawyer shoved her hands deep into her pockets as they strolled. "Willow, have you ever heard of the repression?"

"Repression? With a capital 'R' as in... some famous event? Can't say that I have."

"It's well-known but only in certain circles." Sawyer stopped walking and ran a hand through her short hair. "This is harder than I thought it would be."

Willow turned around to face her. "What's harder?"

Sawyer looked out over the ocean. "There's so much I need to tell you, and I'm struggling with how to do that. A lot of what I need to say will seem surreal to you."

"Surreal?"

"Indeed."

"Why don't you start with how our great-grandmothers knew each other?"

"The repression."

"The repression—of course. So what the hell is the repression?"

"Not a good place to start, I'm afraid. You need some background first."

"Damn it, Sawyer. Stop beating around the bush. Out with it!"

Sawyer walked over to the railing and leaned her forearms on it. Willow joined her, resting her hip against the balusters so she could see Sawyer's face. Sawyer said, "I saw what you were searching for on your computer."

"My computer? What are you talking about?"

"This morning, before coming downstairs, I noticed your laptop open on your desk. I put a finger on the touch pad, and your search results displayed."

"You were snooping in my office? How dare you?"

"I wasn't snooping... at least I didn't intend to. Anyway, I saw that your search results were for Hecate. Could you tell me why you were looking for information on her?"

"I asked the reference librarian at the Boston Community Library for help identifying the brooches, and Hecate's name came up associated with some group called the Blue Feather Coven."

"You took the brooches to the library? I wish you hadn't done that, Willow. Who else did you show them to?"

"My co-worker, Susan, and a couple of jewelers. Why the secrecy?"

"Your Mr. Wilkinson called me about them and offered to enlighten you about their meaning... for money, of course. I told him no. That was something I felt a responsibility to do myself. You mentioned another jeweler."

"Yes. A Mr. Kipling at—"

"Treasured Moments. I know of him. He's been an outspoken foe of the coven for quite some time."

"He was really nervous when I showed the brooches to him—almost afraid."

"He should be afraid. We all should be."

Willow took a step away from the railing. "Look, Sawyer, I'm tired of all these cryptic messages. I want to know why you sent the brooch to me. I want to know how two brooches from different sides of the planet just happen to fit together like they were made to be that way. I want to know why in the middle of the night I had a nightmare about a pentagram burning in my backyard, only to wake up the next morning to find the interlocked brooches had burned an 'H' into my nightstand. I want to know why your great-grandmother's picture is hanging on my goddamned wall. I need answers, Sawyer, and I need them now!"

Sawyer looked over her shoulder at Willow. "The brooches burned a symbol into your nightstand?"

"Yes, they did. Come home with me and I'll show it to you."

Sawyer looked back out over the ocean and sighed. "It's beginning."

"What's beginning?" When Sawyer continued to look out over the ocean, Willow grabbed her arm and swung her around. "Damn it, Sawyer—talk to me!"

"The uprising. The uprising is beginning, and only you and I can stop it just like our ancestors before us, and just like our descendants in years to come."

"What the fuck are you talking about—that picture of our great-grandmothers? What uprising are we stopping, Sawyer—the attack of the killer lesbians? Are you involved in some sort of 'fixing the gays' cult or something? You're gay, Sawyer. A blind man could see it. Get over it!" Willow began to walk away but stopped and turned back to Sawyer. "Oh, and for the record—I don't have any descendants."

"That's why you need to become impregnated. And so do I," Sawyer said.

Willow marched directly up to Sawyer. "Are you out of your fucking mind?"

Sawyer grabbed Willow's arm and looked around. "Please, keep your voice down."

"Are you out of your fucking mind?" Willow said again in a hoarse whisper as she shook her arm free of Sawyer's grasp.

"From your perspective I probably am, but I assure you there is a sane reason for all of this."

# Chapter 23

## 2013—Plymouth, Massachusetts

Willow inserted her key into the front door lock. "I can't believe I let you talk me into allowing you into my house again," she said as Sawyer waited on the porch behind her.

"Willow, if I wanted to hurt you, don't you think I could have done it already?" Sawyer reasoned.

Willow pushed the door open and allowed Sawyer to enter first. She walked in behind and threw her keys and clutch on the table beside the door. "I don't know about you, but I need a stiff drink. Can I get something for you—a beer, maybe?"

"That sounds delightful."

While Willow was in the kitchen, Sawyer quickly opened Willow's clutch and searched through it. "Damn," she whispered under her breath. "They're not here." She closed the clutch and stepped away just before Willow came back.

"Well, at least this will afford us a little more privacy to talk," Willow said as she handed the beer to Sawyer.

"Agreed. I have so much to tell you, but I feel like I need to gain your trust first."

"Good luck with that. Quite frankly, I think you're a little whacked."

"I can't blame you. It is a lot to take in."

Willow took a draw on her beer and set it on the coffee table. "I'm going to run upstairs and change my clothes. Make yourself at home. I'll be back in a few minutes."

"Take your time."

Willow picked up her clutch from the table and took it upstairs with her. She closed the door to her bedroom and leaned against it. *Willow, do you need your head examined?*

*She's obviously a nut case. Who the hell is she to tell me I have to get pregnant? At least I know it won't be by her!* Willow took off her dress and hung it in the closet. She sat on the bed and rolled off her hose. *What to wear? Something appropriate to spend the evening with a lunatic. Let me see...* She settled on a pair of spandex shorts and a T-shirt, along with low ankle socks and running shoes. *I need to be prepared in case I have to run away.* She chuckled to herself. Once dressed, she glanced at herself in the mirror. She turned to walk away, hesitated, and looked once more. *Why do I even care what I look like? It's not like I'm attracted to her or anything... am I?*

Willow halted halfway down the stairs to gaze at the picture of her great-grandmother and Richelle Hawksworth. The two posed side by side in front of an American USO sign with a World War I army tank in the background. They were holding hands and smiling broadly. She took another step downward and stopped in her tracks. Wait a minute, she thought. She went back up a step and peered at the picture more closely. "Well I'll be damned. Sawyer, come look at this," she called.

Sawyer went to the bottom of the stairs and looked up. "What is it?" she asked.

Willow took the picture off the wall and headed back up the stairs to her office. "Come with me."

Sawyer ran up the stairs and followed her into the office in time to see Willow disassemble the frame and remove the photograph. "What are you doing?"

"Give me a minute." Willow opened her scanner and put the photograph on the glass. She then called up the scanner software and copied the picture into her computer while Sawyer watched over her shoulder.

"Here it comes," Willow said. "Just a little tweaking... image sharpening... a little brightness... now let's zoom in. Right there. Do you see what I see?"

"The brooches. They're wearing the brooches."

"Now I can figure out which one is mine," Willow said. "Wait here." She went to her room, retrieved the brooches, and returned to the office. She tipped the brooches toward each other and separated them. "According to the picture, Jenny was wearing this one." Willow indicated the brooch in her right hand. "So that means this one is yours." She handed Sawyer's brooch to her.

"Willow, do something for me if you would," she asked. "I want to lock them back together with you holding one and me holding the other." Sawyer extended her brooch toward Willow.

"Why?" Willow asked.

"Please, humor me."

Willow reached forward and tilted her brooch so that it locked with Sawyer's. The stones came to life, radiating brightly, while a rush of heat and energy shot through her like a bolt of electricity.

"Oh, my God! Did you feel that?" Willow asked.

Sawyer released the brooches and allowed Willow to take possession of them. Her eyes were closed, and her breathing came in halted gasps. "I did. Have they ever done that before when you've locked them together?"

"Never."

"Now I know for sure you are the one."

"What do you mean, I am the one. One what?"

"Just like our great-grandmothers."

"The fact that our grandmothers wore the brooches proves nothing more than they knew each other. The brooches could have been their gifts to each other for all I know."

Sawyer put up her hands to Willow. "You're right. I haven't told you what you need to know... mostly out of fear, to be truthful."

"Fear? You're afraid? I'm the one dealing with the psycho here!"

"I really wish you didn't feel that way."

"How do you expect me to feel? You come waltzing into my life, stalk me, tell me our families have been linked for hundreds of years, throw words around like 'great Goddess' and 'sweet Hecate,' and tell me I have to get pregnant. Give me a break, Sawyer. Doesn't that sound like psycho behavior to you? No, wait a minute, maybe I'm the psycho here, because despite all that, I still let you back into my house."

"All right. You don't want to help? Fine. Give me my

brooch, and I'll be gone," Sawyer said angrily.

"Fine!" Willow shouted. She laid the brooches in her palm and grabbed one to tilt it in on the other. Just as she was doing so, they began to glow once more and grow very, very hot. "God damned son of a bitch!" She dropped the brooches to the carpet.

"What happened?" Sawyer asked.

"They're hot. The bastards burned me."

"Let me see. We need to get some ointment on this before it blisters."

"There's some in the bathroom medicine cabinet."

"Come along then." Sawyer led her to the bathroom. "Sit on the john and let me take care of it."

"The ointment's on the right side of the cabinet, and the bandages are in a basket beneath the sink," Willow said.

Sawyer rummaged quickly through the cabinet and gathered what she needed to doctor Willow's hand. She knelt on one knee in front of Willow and rested Willow's hand on her leg. She carefully spread the burn ointment around the reddened area and wrapped it in gauze. "Tape?" she said.

"Also under the sink," Willow replied.

"I'm so sorry for this. The last thing I wanted was for anyone to get hurt."

"It wasn't your fault."

"Still, I feel responsible. I never should have sent you that brooch."

Willow studied Sawyer as she tended her wound. A pang of guilt ran through her as she realized, despite the odd circumstances, she really hadn't treated Sawyer very well since they met.

"There. That should hold until morning, at which time, you'll probably need to change the bandage."

"Thank you," Willow said.

"Think nothing of it." Sawyer rose to her feet. She put the bandages and tape back into the basket under the sink and opened the medicine cabinet to set the ointment back next to the mouthwash. She closed the door and immediately opened it again.

"That's it!" she exclaimed.

"What's it?"

Sawyer turned to Willow. "Do you have a torch?"

"A torch? What do you need a torch for? Do you plan on burning down the house or something?"

"Damned language barrier. What is it Americans call it? Yes, of course—a flashlight."

"What do you need a flashlight for?"

"Proof."

"Proof?"

"Yes. Trust me, Willow, or at least I hope you will after I show you something."

"Okay. The flashlight's in the junk drawer in the kitchen. Head on down. I'll be right behind you in a minute."

"Junk drawer?"

"Tell me you have a junk drawer in your kitchen. Everyone has a junk drawer... you know that drawer that seems to collect everything imaginable... screws, batteries, matches, photographs, broken cell phones, tools."

"Ah, you mean a gadget drawer. Yes, I had one in my flat."

"Well, it's the drawer right next to the refrigerator. I'll be down in a minute."

As soon as Sawyer cleared the stairway, Willow went to her office to check on the brooches. They were no longer hot to the touch. "Damn things," she said. "I'll need to check before I handle them next time."

"I found the flashlight," Sawyer called from the kitchen.

Willow met her halfway across the living room. "Okay, you have the flashlight. Now what?"

"This will sound a bit odd—"

"Why am I not surprised?"

"Like I said—this will sound a bit odd, but I want you to shine the light inside my mouth and tell me what you see."

"This just keeps getting stranger and stranger." Willow took the flashlight in her good hand. "You're going to have to sit down. You're considerably taller than me."

Sawyer sat down on the edge of the coffee table and opened her mouth. Willow stepped in between her legs and shone the light into Sawyer's mouth, starting with the back of her throat. When she directed the light to Sawyer's right cheek, a chill ran down her spine and she took two steps back. "Oh, my God!"

"Tell me what you saw, Willow."

"Open your mouth again." Willow shone the light on the inside of her right cheek one more time. "Three dark blue lines, side by side."

Sawyer took the flashlight from Willow. "Now open your mouth."

Willow just stood there, a frown on her face.

"Please, Willow. This is important."

Willow opened her mouth, and Sawyer shone the light inside her right cheek. "Three dark blue lines, side by side. The mark of the chosen one."

# Chapter 24

## 1610—North Yorkshire, England

"Here are thy new quarters, Caleb," Jenna said as the pushed open the door to the back room of the blacksmith shop.' "'Tisn't much, but 'tis clean and comfortable."

Caleb walked into the room and looked around. There was a bed on one side of the room, a dresser on the opposite wall, and a wash basin in the corner. A small wood stove sat in another corner.

"'Tis perfect, sister, but the truth is, I have no way to pay for it."

"The room came with the blacksmith job—free of charge. I lived here for the first few weeks I was in town. When Hadley and I became one, I began staying at her cottage. This is thy room now if thou dost want it."

"Aye. I will take it, gratefully. Now all I have to do is find work."

"Thou canst help me out in the forge until thou findest more steady work. It is paying enough to feed thyself at least."

"I appreciate thy kindness. I will be moving my meager belongings from Mistress Hadley's cottage today."

"Hadley is quite taken with thee, little brother. She is grateful for the work thou didst around her place."

"It was the least I could do for good food and a warm bed. She is a good woman, Jenna. Thou wouldst be wise to treat her like a queen."

"Aye. She took me quite by surprise. I did not expect to fall in love with her."

"So thou art taking her to Billingham in a fortnight. Is that really wise?"

"Thou knowest how I feel about the clan, Caleb. I am the chosen one. I do not have a choice in the matter."

"Aye. 'Tis all fine and good to involve thyself, but if things go wrong, how wouldst thou protect Hadley?"

"I will find a way, little brother. I will find a way."

Caleb put his hand on Jenna's shoulder. "Sister, I may not understand thy commitment, or what thou dost feel thy duty is, but I vow to support thee and Hadley. If anything happens to thee, I will see to it that Hadley is taken care of. That is a promise I shall take to my grave."

Jenna hugged her brother tight. "Thank thee, Caleb, and welcome home to thee as well. Thou wilt always have a place with Hadley and me."

* * *

Jenna sat in the wagon with her foot pressing a long, wooden pole against the wheel to prevent the horse from moving forward.

"Hadley, art thou ready to go? We have a long journey ahead of us."

"Stop thy humming, Jenna Hawksworth. I am fixing thee something to eat on our way. Be thankful I am looking out for thee."

Hadley hurried to the wagon.

"Let me give thee a hand," Caleb said. He helped Hadley climb into the wagon and handed her bundle up to her. "Don't be worrying while thou art gone," he added. "I will be keeping an eye on things here."

"I appreciate that, little brother. Don't forget to fill that horseshoe order. Master Wiltshire will be by to collect it the day after the morrow."

"Aye, I won't forget."

"We should be home in three or four days."

"There are preserves and a fresh loaf of bread in the pantry, Caleb. Help thyself to them," Hadley said.

"Be gone with thee. I will be fine. God speed and safe

journey," Caleb replied. "Blessed be."

* * *

Near the end of the first day's journey, Jenna and Hadley stopped at a country inn for the night. They retired to a room after seeing the horse had feed and fresh bedding.

"What will it be like, Jenna?" Hadley asked as she drew lazy circles around the nipple of Jenna's left breast.

"The ceremony?"

"Aye."

"'Tis been four years since my initiation, but I remember it being a bit emotional in a cleansing kind of way." Jenna lifted Hadley's chin so she could look into her eyes. "Art thou afraid, love?"

"Nervous, aye, but I would not call it fear."

"I won't be letting anything bad happen to thee, Hadley. I promise."

"Will I be different after?"

"The initiation is meant to open a person to the teachings of the clan, not to change who they are inside." Jenna took her hand and kissed the palm. "Thou wouldst not be the same woman I fell in love with if thou wast changed."

"But our lives will change, Jenna. Three years hence, they will change."

"And we have those three years to prepare for whatever happens. We are stronger together than each of us alone. We shall be prepared, and we shall succeed, and then we shall have the rest of our lives together." Jenna kissed Hadley on the forehead. "Sleep now, Hadley Metcalf. We have a half-day travel ahead of us on the morrow."

"Blessed be, Jenna."

"Blessed be."

* * *

When Jenna and Hadley arrived at the compound the next afternoon, they were greeted with much fanfare. Hadley was welcomed into the community with open arms. Festivities, games, music, dancing, and an abundance of food were ongoing throughout the day and into the evening. Hadley's outgoing personality drew  people to her as she mingled with men and women alike. Jenna was especially intrigued by the way Hadley interacted with the children, racing them across the yard with her skirt billowing behind her, or holding a newborn infant—and the look of maternal bliss on her face as she cradled them in her arms.

Later in the evening, when the little ones had been put to bed, the adults stoked up the fire and broke out the instruments. They played, drank, and danced into the wee hours of the morning. Jenna stood on the edge of the crowd and watched approvingly as Hadley lifted her skirts and joined the lively dance while other clan members circled around her and clapped. She was seeing a side of Hadley she didn't know existed—one of carefree exuberance. It saddened her that life in North Yorkshire didn't afford her many opportunities to just enjoy herself in the midst of friends.

"She is a beautiful woman, thy Hadley Metcalf. She appears to have taken well with the clan members."

Jenna turned to see who had addressed her. "Lord Weller," she said, bowing slightly. "Aye indeed, she is a beauty. I am a lucky woman to have her."

"We thought she would be a good match for thee—especially when we learned her ancestors participated in the last repression. Hence the reason for sending thee to North Yorkshire. That thou didst fall in love is a bonus."

"A bonus indeed, and I have won the biggest prize of all—her heart."

"Thou hast told her about the repression?"

"Aye. She is fearful, but supportive. As I said, Lord Weller, her fear is rooted in ignorance. We are hopeful these next three years can be a time to prepare and to chase those fears away. She is a strong woman. I have faith in her."

"Hast thou chosen the sire yet?"

Jenna looked nervously at the priest. "Nay, but we have time."

"Don't wait too long, Jenna Hawksworth. She is not as young as thou art."

"Aye. I understand."

* * *

"Heavens above, Jenna... harder... pray... I'm fading... I'm fading! Holy mother!" Hadley screamed as her body arched toward the ceiling.

Jenna increased the intensity of her thrusts until she felt Hadley tighten around her hand. She coordinated her ministrations with the spasms that wracked Hadley's body and drew them out for an extended period of time, until they subsided and Hadley's muscles relaxed. Jenna extracted her hand and crawled up the length of Hadley's body to lie on top of her and to bury her face in Hadley's neck.

Hadley wrapped her arms around Jenna. "By all that is holy, thou dost know how to please a woman."

Jenna didn't respond.

"Jenna?" Hadley lifted Jenna's head. Jenna was crying. Hadley rolled her onto her back and lay on her side facing her. "Why art thou crying?"

Jenna reached up and stroked the side of Hadley's face. "Hadley Metcalf, I love thee with everything that I am."

"That's naught to cry about, blacksmith."

Jenna tried to smile through her tears at Hadley's attempted humor. "I want to give thee everything thou dost want in life, but there's one thing I cannot do."

"I have everything I want—right here. I need naught more."

"I cannot give thee babes, Hadley. I can never give thee babes. I saw how thou wast with the wee ones tonight. The look on thy face was blissful."

Hadley looked hard and long at Jenna. "That is something I came to terms with a long time ago, when I realized 'tis women I prefer. 'Tis naught for thee to fret about."

"The time is near past for thee, Hadley."

"I'm all of thirty years old. Thou wouldst have me all old and grey and near to the grave to harken unto thee."

"Know that my love for thee is strong. If thou dost want a child, we will find a way, I promise."

* * *

The next morning, Hadley sat on the stool in front of the hearth as Jenna ran a soapy cloth across her back. Her eyes were closed, and she moaned with pleasure at the ministrations. At one point, she took Jenna's hand and pulled her around in front to stand between her legs. She wrapped her arms around Jenna, rested her head between her breasts, and ran her fingers up and down Jenna's lower back and bottom. "I love you, Jenna Hawksworth," she said.

Jenna kissed the top of Hadley's head.

Hadley smiled when she felt Jenna shudder.

"Thou art a wicked woman, Hadley Metcalf."

Hadley tried to look insulted. "Me?"

"Thou knowest we have to meet the council for breakfast, yet thou intentionally dost get me worked into a lather."

"Dost thou mean this?" Hadley slipped her fingers into the folds between Jenna's legs.

Jenna's legs immediately buckled. "Sweet Hecate."

Hadley ran her tongue around and into Jenna's navel. "Let me love thee, Jenna," she whispered.

"But… we have to…"

"I will be quick about it. Let me love thee like thou didst love me last night."

Hadley led Jenna back to bed and laid her on her back.

Jenna put forth a half-hearted attempt to stop her. "I will be having to wash again… don't have time for… good Goddess!" Jenna moaned as Hadley took her tender bud between her teeth and swirled her tongue around Jenna's moist folds before plunging two fingers deep inside her.

A short time later, on shaky legs, Jenna quickly washed, dressed, and escorted Hadley to breakfast with the council.

# Chapter 25

## 2013—Plymouth, Massachusetts

"It's just a birthmark, Sawyer. It doesn't mean anything," Willow said as she paced back and forth across her living room.

"A birthmark? What are the chances we would both have the same birthmark? You're a dental hygienist. How many other people have you seen in your career with a mark like that in their mouth?" Sawyer asked.

"The only thing I've seen that is similar is dental tattooing caused by metal crowns, but it's usually only one line… and it's more a mark than a line. But that's not the point."

"What is the point?"

"It could be a coincidence."

"Coincidence is something that happens to two or more people accidentally. Key word here is 'accidentally.' This isn't an accident. It's the same exact mark in the same exact location on two people who live thousands of miles apart. My father had the same mark inside his cheek… and I'm willing to bet my nana did, too."

Willow's eyes opened wide. "Your father? My father has the mark, too."

"I rest my case." Sawyer approached Willow and grasped her upper arms. "Willow, we've been chosen for a very special purpose. In three months, the uprising will happen if we don't do something to stop it. You and I."

Willow broke free of Sawyer's grasp. "There you go again with the uprising. You want so badly for me to believe you and to blindly follow along like a mouse behind the Pied Piper, but you've yet to tell me what the hell is happening. Talk to me, Sawyer."

Sawyer walked a few feet away and ran a hand through her hair before turning back to Willow. "Okay, but you may want to grab another ale. You might need it."

\* \* \*

"Thanks for the shorts and sweatshirt," Sawyer said as Willow built a bonfire in the backyard fire pit.

"I couldn't see that nice designer suit smelling like smoke."

"Did you put the brooches back in their box?" Sawyer asked.

"Yes. Luckily, they didn't burn the rug in the office like they did my bedside table. Why do you think they got hot?"

"My guess is it was Hecate. We were arguing. I assume our bickering made her unhappy."

"Lovely. Not only am I dealing with a lunatic, but with a temperamental Goddess as well. Just my luck."

Several minutes of silence passed as Willow stoked the fire.

"Do you do this often?" Sawyer asked.

"Have a fire?"

"Yes."

"Not as often as I'd like. I used to go camping with my mom and dad when I was a kid, and sitting around the campfire was one of my fondest memories."

"Did you have a good childhood?"

"Yeah, I did. How about you?"

"Mum and Dad loved me, of that I'm sure, but they were so busy with work and social events that we never had time to do things like this. Nana is the one I have my fondest memories of… and of course, Matilda."

Willow poked at the growing fire with a stick. She looked over her shoulder at Sawyer, who sat in a lawn chair nearby. "You said earlier you got your brooch from your nana."

"Yes. It was from her that I learned most about the uprising. From her and the Book of Shadows. That book has been passed down to each generation of Hawksworths for the past four hundred years."

Willow threw a large piece of wood on the fire and stood up. "There, that should just about do it." She returned to her seat and picked up her beer from the folding table she had placed between hers and Sawyer's seats. She watched the striations of light from the fire dance across Sawyer's face as she sat mesmerized by the fire. *She's kind of cute in my Provincetown sweatshirt.*

Sawyer broke out of her trance. She locked gazes with Willow for several long moments during which neither of them spoke. Finally, she broke the silence. "Where should I begin?"

"You said I needed some background information before you explain the uprising to me, so why don't you start with that?"

"Fair enough. Willow, what do you know about Hecate?"

"Nothing actually. That list of websites you saw on my computer was as far as I got in my search before you rang my doorbell yesterday."

"Was it only yesterday? It seems like so much longer than that."

"I know what you mean. What surprises me is how much I've let a psycho like you into my life after just one day." Willow grinned, which caused Sawyer to chuckle.

Sawyer looked back at the fire. "Hecate is one of the Greek goddesses, probably best known as the Goddess of Death and the Underworld."

"She sounds like a real peach."

"It's not as bad as it sounds. Most people equate the underworld with the Christian version of hell, but in Greek mythology it's a place of divine transformation—similar to a cocoon from which a butterfly emerges. Hecate presides over the realm that exists between life and death. The underworld didn't take on a negative connotation until organized religion became polarized and used it to frighten people into behaving the way they wanted them to. The ordinary souls that exist in Hecate's underworld came to be demonized as monsters to be feared."

"I thought Hades was the Greek God of the Underworld."

"Yes. We also have organized religion to blame for that. The patriarchal hierarchy of emerging religions in Greek society demanded a male ruler for the underworld and replaced Hecate with Hades from the Olympian family of gods."

"Well that sucks."

"When Hades became the ruler of the underworld, Hecate was relegated to guardian of the gates of the underworld. Her job was to escort souls on their way to Asphodel Meadows, Tartarus, or Elysium. In her role as Goddess of Death, she was responsible for freeing the spirits of the dead from their earthly bodies so they could begin their journey to the afterlife."

"So what has this got to do with the uprising?" Willow got up and put another piece of wood on the fire.

"I'm getting to that. Now, where was I? Oh yes, Hecate was also known for her ability to see into the future and to be connected to dreams. These visions normally came at night by moonlight. They have been known to be so vivid and powerful that they result in nightmares, night terrors, and even insanity."

"I knew insanity had to enter into this somewhere," Willow joked.

Sawyer sat back and sighed heavily, and Willow could see she had upset her. She reached her hand out and covered Sawyer's. "I'm sorry. This is just a little tough to absorb."

Sawyer turned her hand over, squeezed Willow's fingers for a brief moment, and released her. "That's okay. I know it's hard. And yes, I can see where the uninitiated might see a little insanity in it."

"Sawyer, you mentioned nightmares brought on by the visions. Do they always result in insanity?"

"No. As with anything, too much is never a good thing. In moderation, Hecate's visions act as a sedative of sorts. In excess, they could lead to insanity or death. It's kind of like drinking a couple of ales versus drinking a whole case. The more you drink, the more out of control and dangerous it is. People who experience these intense visions see things they normally wouldn't notice in the daylight. Everything appears distorted. Colors are washed out and things seem surreal."

"Sounds scary."

"To some, perhaps, but in ancient times, being moonstruck

was considered a state of divine inspiration. The belief was that a moonstruck person had greater insight because they were able to push the boundaries of normal reality. Some even believe moonstruck individuals have the ability to walk between the worlds of the dead and the living."

Willow got up from her chair. "Got to pee. Want another beer?"

"Actually, I need to use the loo as well. I'll come with you."

Sawyer and Willow entered the kitchen through the back door.

"I'll use the upstairs bathroom," Willow said. "If you're finished before me, the beer is in the fridge. Grab one for me and one for yourself if you want another." Willow headed for the living room. Moments later, she returned to the kitchen to find Sawyer taking two bottles from the refrigerator.

"You do realize you're not going back to Boston tonight," Willow said as she took the beer offered to her.

"I kind of came to that conclusion when you threw your clothing at me and told me to change," Sawyer replied with a grin on her face.

When they returned to the fire, Willow put yet another chunk of wood on the embers and sat down. She twisted the top off her beer and threw it in the fire. "I have to admit I'm enjoying the mythology lesson."

"To be a true believer, it has to become integrated into your heart, into your morality."

"So, your nana taught all of this to you?"

"Actually, no. What Nana taught me was the basics of witchcraft. The lessons of Hecate are something I sought on my own after I read the family Book of Shadows and realized the extent of my responsibility during the uprising."

"Are you telling me you're a witch?"

"I guess you could say that."

"So, how on earth can you reconcile Greek mythology with medieval witchcraft?"

"They are actually more connected than you might think. Most people associate witches with Medieval England. But there were shamans during European Pre-History and witches as well during the Greek era, that specialized primarily in herbalism."

"The reference librarian told me that early witches were really just women who were good at using herbs to help sick people. She said their healing skills were often considered to be 'powers' of some sort, which of course threatened the Church, and in those days, anyone who threatened the Church was pretty much labeled a witch."

"That's almost correct. Anyone seen as committing 'unnatural acts' was considered doing the work of the devil. That included herbalists, fortune tellers, spell casters, and homosexuals."

"How did homosexuals get thrown in with witches?"

"The Church considered any sexual activity that could not lead to procreation an unnatural act. It was also believed that many of the followers of Hecate were male to female transsexuals called Semnotatoi. These followers were physically changed during a ritual in which the testicles and sometimes the penis were removed."

"Damn. That's some nasty shit."

"Sucked to be a guy in that coven, apparently," Sawyer said.

Willow nudged Sawyer's arm. "Did you just make a joke? And here I was beginning to believe you didn't have a sense of humor."

Sawyer grinned and shook her head.

"So, basically members of Hecate's sect were misfits, outcasts, gay, lesbian, and transgendered individuals," Willow said.

"That pretty much sums it up. Their form of witchcraft was considered illicit, because they had no temples or organized priesthood. Most of the followers practiced their form of herbalism and magic on the fringes of wild places, such as forests."

"When I think of Greek goddesses, what comes to mind are beautiful women wearing togas and gladiator sandals and with their hair all tied up on top of their heads. Halloween witches don't exactly look like that," Willow said.

"I hate to keep blaming the Church for everything distasteful in the Middle Ages, but as the fear grew relative to the perceived power of witchcraft herbalism, they began a campaign to increasingly portray Hecate and all associated with her in a negative way. The Christian Church projected its fears and insecurities on her and turned her into an evil figure, synonymous with the devil. Since Hecate was the goddess of witches, they too were portrayed as the ugly hags we associate with the word 'witch' today. She is a goddess that encourages women and transgendered individuals to be powerful and independent. In that respect, she was a threat to all patriarchal religions."

"Humph! Leave it to men to minimize and demonize her just because she promotes power in women. Geesh!" Willow said.

"My thoughts exactly."

Willow pulled her cell phone out of her pocket and looked at the digital time display. "Holy shit, it's one a.m."

"Maybe we should call it a night," Sawyer said.

"But I still don't know why you're here. I mean... somehow I've become a 'chosen one.' What the hell does that mean?" Willow stood up and began to pace. "What do the brooches have to do with all of this? And you've thrown out the words 'uprising' and 'repression' a few times. I have no clue what they mean. Oh, and this bullshit about having a baby. Give me a break!"

"Please don't take this too lightly, Willow. There's a lot at stake here."

Willow bent down in front of Sawyer and took her by the shoulders. "That's just it. I have no idea what's at stake, but know this. I will not let you leave here until I find out."

# Chapter 26

## 1610—North Yorkshire, England

Hadley clutched Jenna's hand tightly as they approached the clearing where the initiation ritual would take place. They could see a large circle of clan members, also clothed in white robes, standing around a very large bonfire. There was an altar in front of the fire with several implements on it. Hadley was wearing only a long, white, hooded robe, tied in the front. Before joining the others, Jenna took Hadley into her arms and kissed her tenderly. "I will be close by, my love. Try to not be afraid. 'Tis a ritual of acceptance and cleansing. Thou shalt not be harmed. Just open thy mind and let the Goddess enter."

"I would be lying to say I wasn't a bit scared, but I trust thee. I shall call for thee if something happens I cannot handle. Just like we agreed."

"I shall be here for thee, but things shall be fine. My heart is filled with pride for thee. I love thee, Hadley Metcalf.'

"And I thee, Jenna Hawksworth."

Through the corner of her eye, Jenna could see the escorts coming for her.

"The high priest is ready," one of the escorts said.

Hadley and Jenna followed them to the edge of the circle where they stopped and waited. After what seemed like a very long while, a bell was rung three times. On the third ring, the edge of the circle in front of them opened up. Jenna and Hadley stepped to the opening but did not enter.

A high priest stepped forward to face them. "All are welcome to find love and peace within the circle," he said. "No one within the circle shall suffer loneliness. No one within the circle shall be without a friend. No one within the circle shall be without a brother or sister. With open arms, we welcome all."

One of the escorts stepped forward. "Lord Weller, I bring news of someone who has traveled far seeking the peace of the circle. Long has been their journey, but the journey's end is nigh."

"Of whom dost thou speak?" the priest asked.

"I speak of her who stands at the edge of the circle seeking entry," the escort replied.

The priest looked around. "Who hath caused her to come hither?"

"She hath come of her own free will," the escort answered.

"And what doth she seek?" the priest said in a loud clear voice.

"She seeks to become one with the Goddess Hecate and to join with us in our worship of her."

"Who can vouch for this person?" the priest asked.

Jenna spoke clearly. "I, Jenna Hawksworth, the chosen one, vouch for her. I know her to be pure of heart and filled with kindness. I have shown her the ways and have set her feet upon the path. She now has chosen of her own free will to take this step and to bid thee give her entrance into the circle."

The priest lifted his arms out to the sides. "Let her be brought to us."

The two escorts approached the altar and picked up a red, nine-foot-long piece of cord, a bell, a candle, and a blindfold. Together, they walked clockwise around the circle until they reached the place where Jenna and Hadley stood. Hadley dropped her robe to the ground and allowed herself to be blindfolded and her hands bound loosely with the cord. The escorts then turned around and faced the altar and the bell was rung three times.

"Who seeks entrance into this circle?" the priest called out.

"Hadley Metcalf, whose soul is one with the chosen one," Hadley said clearly. "I beg of thee, entrance into the circle."

"Hadley Metcalf, enter our circle."

The two escorts walked toward the priest with Hadley between them, each with a hand under her elbow to guide her in her blindfolded state. They stopped within a few feet of the priest. The bell was rung once more.

"Why dost thou come hither, Hadley Metcalf?"

"To worship the Goddess Hecate and to become one with my brothers and sisters in the circle," she replied.

"What dost thou bring with thee?"

"I bring naught but myself and my heart, naked and unadorned."

The priest turned to the altar, collected the censer and a vial of salted water, and faced Hadley once more. "Hadley Metcalf, I hereby consecrate thee in the name of the Holy Mother Goddess Hecate." The priest circled Hadley with the smoke from the censer while anointing her with the water. He placed the implements back on the altar and turned to Hadley. A bell was rung twice.

"Dost thou wish an end to the life thou hast known so far?" the priest asked.

"I do," Hadley replied.

With an athame, one of the escorts cut a lock of Hadley's hair and placed it on the censer. The other escort then led Hadley around the inside of the circle. "Here is the one who shall join us. Welcome her and bring her joy," he chanted. He then placed Hadley once more in front of the priest. A bell was rung three times.

The priest raised his hands. "Thou must face the ones thou dost see."

Hadley's blindfold was removed, and her eyes immediately sought out Jenna. Jenna smiled and nodded her head slightly. A small smile formed at the corners of Hadley's mouth, assuring Jenna that she was all right.

"I salute the Goddess Hecate and pledge my love and support to her and to my brothers and sisters of the clan," Hadley said.

The priest looked directly at Hadley. "Hadley Metcalf, dost thou know the Wiccan Rede?"

"I do. As it harms none, do what thou wilt."

"Hadley Metcalf, dost thou vow to abide by that Rede?"

"I do."

"Let thy bonds be loosened that thou mayest be reborn."

Hadley held her hands out as the escort untied the cord. The priest picked up the anointing oil from the altar and, with the oil, drew a Celtic cross in a circle on Hadley's forehead, a pentagram over her heart, and an inverted triangle by touching her pubis, right breast, left breast, and pubis again.

"With this sacred oil, I anoint and cleanse thee. From this day forth thou art a member of this circle and one with thy brothers and sisters of the clan. So be it one and all."

A cheer of "so be it" rang from all clan members in attendance.

"Hadley Metcalf, thou art now one of us. 'Tis thy duty to share our knowledge of the Goddess Hecate, and of the arts of healing, divination, magic, and all the mystic arts. This knowledge and these skills shall be learned as thou dost progress."

"I shall do what pleases the Goddess Hecate," Hadley said.

"Be cautious and ever mindful of the Wiccan Rede, Hadley Metcalf. As it harms none, do what thou wilt."

The priest stepped forward and kissed Hadley on both cheeks. Then he raised his hands to the congregation. "'Tis time for celebration."

A loud cheer rose from the crowd as the escorts led Hadley back to where Jenna waited.

Jenna placed Hadley's robe around her shoulders and pulled her in for a loving embrace. Her voice was choked with emotion.

"Never have I been so proud. My life is one step closer to being complete. Thank thee for loving me."

# Chapter 27

## 2013—Plymouth, Massachusetts

Sawyer folded the lawn chairs and carried them to the back porch while Willow pushed the embers around with a stick. Sawyer then returned to the fire to pick up the beer bottles. "Do you have a special place for these?" she asked.

"There's a recycling bin on the back porch."

She carried the bottles to the back porch and properly disposed of them. Once again she returned to the fire to find Willow trying to manipulate a bucket of water with one hand. "Here, let me help with that."

"I can do it myself."

Sawyer grabbed the handle of the bucket. "No, you cannot. You only have the use of one hand, remember?"

Willow stubbornly held on to the handle.

"Why, Willow? Why are you being so stubborn? You know you need help, so let me do it."

Willow still refused to yield the bucket.

"God damn it, Willow. Let go of the fucking bucket!" Sawyer yelled.

Willow finally relinquished it.

"For crying out loud. How is it you can so easily push me to lose my temper? That's twice in the same day."

"Technically, that's twice in two days. It's after midnight, after all."

"I don't believe it. Are you always like this?"

"Like what?"

"A smart-ass. And by the way, that's three curse words

you've made me use in the span of four sentences. I've never met anyone like you in my life. I don't know how you do it, but you make me all crazy inside."

Willow grinned. "Welcome to the human race, Ms. Hawksworth. It's about time you show some emotion. You need to deal with these issues you appear to have on a truly emotional level rather than being so fucking clinical all the time. You can't waltz into someone's life and make life-altering demands of them and not expect emotion. You'll never understand that unless you experience it yourself. Now pour the fucking water on the fire so we can go to bed."

As soon as Sawyer went into the house, she ran upstairs and got her car keys out of her trouser pocket. She passed Willow on the way back down the stairs.

"Where are you going? You really shouldn't be driving after the few beers you had."

"For someone who doesn't want kids, you sure are a mother hen. I'm just getting my bag from the car."

Willow yelled after her as she ran down the remaining stairs, "I never said I didn't want kids."

"The woman is going to drive me mad," Sawyer said under her breath as she retrieved the backpack. On the way back up the driveway, she scooped up a handful of stones and slipped them into her pocket.

She let herself in the front door and locked it. The lower level of the house was already dark. "Did you lock the kitchen door, Willow?" she called up the stairs.

"Yes."

Sawyer ran up the stairs and walked by the open bathroom door on her way to the guest room. Willow was in there trying to remove the old bandage from her burned hand. Sawyer immediately put her bag down and knelt on the floor in front of her. "Let me do that," she said, "and I don't want an argument." To her surprise, when the old gauze was removed, there was no trace of the burn. "That's odd," Sawyer said.

"What is?"

"The burn's gone. Does this hurt?" Sawyer poked at the area that was red and blistery several hours before.

"Not at all. Let me see." Willow held her hand up in the light at various angles. "Wow. You're right." She opened and closed her hand in a fist several times with no discomfort. "How can this be?"

Sawyer stood up. "It's the work of the Goddess."

Willow raised her eyebrows. "The work of the Goddess? Seriously?"

Sawyer picked up her backpack and stepped out of the bathroom. "Do you have a better explanation?"

Willow had no answer.

"Good night, then. Sleep well." Sawyer walked into the guest room and closed the door. "Blessed be, Willow," she whispered under her breath.

Willow lay on her back in bed, staring at the ceiling. Why do I let her get to me? I can't help myself. It's almost like I intentionally bait her. I have to admit I was kind of shocked when she let me have it tonight. It's about time she got the wedgie out of her ass. That actually might be it… she comes across with a superior air. And just when I've convinced myself I don't like her, she gets all tender on me—like when she bandaged my hand earlier today. Willow rolled over and turned the light on then looked again at her hand. She couldn't believe the burn was gone. It had hurt like a bastard when it happened. It was already blistering by the time Sawyer wrapped it. How could it possibly have healed so fast? Could she be right about the Goddess? And what the hell was that lightning bolt that struck when we locked the brooches? It was almost orgasmic. She had never felt such an intense jolt in her life.

As Willow reached over to turn off the light, she heard a low hum coming from the guest room. "What the hell is that?" she whispered to herself. She threw off her covers, shut off the light, and tiptoed down the hall to the guest room. As she approached the room, she could smell something odd. "What the hell?" She sniffed the air. "Smells like incense." She stopped outside the door and realized it was slightly open. A flickering light came from within.

"Goddess Hecate, I bid thee hear my plea."

Willow strained to see Sawyer through the crack in the door. She was sitting on the floor, a lit candle and burning incense in front of her. She pulled something out of her pocket and placed it in a pile on the floor in front of her. It looked like stones. One by one, she placed them in a circle around the base of the candle. She then reached into her backpack and withdrew a small glass jar and put that on the floor in front of the candle.

*What the hell is she doing?* Willow thought.

Sawyer picked up one of the stones, placed it in the jar, and held the lit candle above it. "Candle's flame burning bright. By your flame on this night. Trap all evil, seal it well. In each stone, make it dwell. Into the stone let evil flee, as I will it, so shall it be."

Willow frowned. Trap all evil? *She'd better not be putting a spell on me. What's she doing now?*

Sawyer lifted the candle and allowed a half-dozen drops of wax to drip onto the stone in the jar.

She set the candle back on the floor and reached for another stone. Six more times she repeated the process and the chant until there was a pile of rocks and melted wax in the bottom of the jar. Finally, she screwed a cover onto the jar and put it back down in front of the candle.

"Goddess Hecate, I implore you to trap forever all the evil and negativity of this dwelling in this vessel and to protect all those who reside in this home from future influence."

Willow tiptoed back to her room when it became obvious Sawyer had finished the ritual. She closed her bedroom door and slipped into bed. "She's doing witchcraft in my house. Holy shit! I'm definitely going to hell for consorting with a witch," she whispered into the dark.

Sawyer turned her head quickly toward the bedroom door as she thought she saw some movement. She got up and opened the door to an empty hallway. She narrowed her eyes and walked quietly down the hall to Willow's room. The door was closed, and no evidence of light came from beneath it. It must have been her imagination. She looked at the jar in her hand. *I need to take care of this.*

She crept slowly down the stairs into the kitchen and took a large spoon from the ceramic container by the stove. As quietly as she could, she opened the kitchen door and slipped out. Guided only by the light of the moon, she walked to the very edge of Willow's backyard and dug a small, but deep hole near the fence. She pushed the jar of rocks as deep into the hole as she could and covered it with dirt and leaves, hoping it would be indiscernible to the naked eye. It was imperative they not be found and the jar never opened. Then, just as quietly as she had slipped out, she returned to the kitchen, rinsed the spoon and placed it in the dishwasher, and crept upstairs and into the guest room. Moments later, she lay under the covers in the darkened room. *Willow McCord, I know beyond doubt that you are the one. The Goddess's sign was clear when we joined the brooches tonight. You are the one I was meant to spend the rest of my life with.*

From her bedroom window, Willow had watched her houseguest creep across the back lawn. In the darkness, she couldn't tell what Sawyer was doing. She appeared to squat near the fence for a few moments then rose again and walked back toward the house. "Sawyer, what are you up to?"

# Chapter 28

## 2013—Plymouth, Massachusetts

Willow awoke the next morning to the aroma of bacon cooking. She glanced at the clock—seven-eighteen a.m. *I can't believe she's up so early after our late night.* Suddenly, she bolted upright in bed. "Shit—I'd better go help her. She doesn't even know how to use a potato peeler for Christ's sake." Willow threw off the covers, took care of morning bathroom chores, and headed downstairs.

She stopped dead in the kitchen doorway. "Oh, my," she said. There on the table was the most magnificent breakfast Willow had ever seen.

Sawyer turned around from the stove with a frying pan in her hand. "I hope you don't mind. I foraged around a bit and found what I needed to make English breakfast crepes. Have a seat, and I'll get you a cup of coffee."

Willow stared at her in disbelief. "Who are you, and what did you do with Sawyer?" she asked.

Sawyer laughed. "I'm afraid I might have misled you the other night with the potato peeler incident. I must say I've never used one before. I generally use a knife to peel things, but I assure you I can cook."

"Obviously," Willow said as she approached the table. "This all looks so good."

Sawyer skirted around the table and held her chair out for her. "Lovely pajamas," she said as Willow took her seat. "I'm not complaining, mind you."

Willow looked down at herself and realized she should have at least pulled on a pair of lounge pants, as she sat there in her boy-cut boxer briefs and short T-shirt. She was about to apologize for her state of undress when she noticed what Sawyer was wearing—baggy men's boxers and an oversized T-shirt.

"You're pretty sexy yourself, especially with that frilly apron on," Willow quipped.

Sawyer grinned and placed a cup of coffee in front of her. "Truce?" She offered her hand.

Willow smiled and reached toward Sawyer. "Truce."

Sawyer took her hand and turned it over, palm side up. There was an imprint from the brooches but no blisters or redness. "How does it feel today?"

"Wow. That wasn't there last night. It feels fine, actually."

"The Goddess works in mysterious ways sometimes." Sawyer released her hand and walked back to the stove. "Eat while it's hot. Mine's just about finished."

Sawyer used the spatula to roll the bacon-egg-and-cheese-filled crepe and put it on her plate beside the fried potatoes and fruit slices. She returned the pan to the stove, took off the apron, and sat down.

"This looks wonderful." Willow took a bite. "Oh wow... that's it. I'm holding you prisoner here forever so you can cook for me every day. My God, this is good."

"I'm glad you like it."

They ate in silence for the next few minutes until Willow got up to refill her coffee cup. Sawyer beat her to it. "Here, let me do that," she said.

Willow stood with her hip leaning against the counter while Sawyer refilled her cup. "Thanks." She got the creamer from the refrigerator and brought it to the table.

"So, are you ready for the rest of the discussion?" Sawyer asked as she sat down.

"After breakfast. Maybe we can go for a walk while we talk. It looks like it's going to be a beautiful day."

"That sounds nice. I'd like that."

Willow knocked on the bathroom door.

"I'm in the shower!" Sawyer called out.

"I have some clean clothes for you to put on. I'll leave them by the door in the hall."

"The curtain is drawn. Come in and leave them if you want."

Willow pushed the door open and was met by steam and the odor of shampoo. "I hope you don't mind wearing my underclothes as well. They're clean."

"No problem. It's good that we're relatively close in size."

"I'll put them here on the chair for you."

Sawyer pulled the curtain back so just her face was showing. "Thanks. I appreciate it."

Willow suddenly felt shy about being in the room with a naked Sawyer, albeit behind a shower curtain. "Take your time."

"I'll be done soon."

Willow ran down the stairs and into the bathroom off the kitchen. She looked at herself in the mirror. "What the hell is wrong with me?" she said. "My heart is racing a hundred miles an hour."

While she waited for Sawyer, Willow decided to investigate the area by the fence where she saw her the night before. She put on her running shoes and let herself out the back door. "What a beautiful July morning, it is," she said to no one in particular as she walked across the backyard to the fence line and looked around. She didn't see anything suspicious. Wondering if she was looking in the wrong spot, she walked halfway back to the house and looked up at her bedroom window and then again at the fence line, trying to gauge the exact spot she had seen Sawyer. When she thought she had it right, she walked back to the fence and looked around again but still saw nothing suspicious. "Hmmm. I'm sure this is where she was. I had a clear view from my window." Willow looked again at her bedroom window and gasped. "What the fuck?" There in her bedroom window was the outline of a woman looking down at her—and it wasn't Sawyer.

Willow turned around and ran back toward the house just as Sawyer stepped out onto the back porch.

"Move, please," Willow said urgently as she brushed by her and ran into the house.

"Willow, what is it?" Sawyer followed her through the house and up to the second story. Sawyer arrived at Willow's room just moments behind her and stopped in the doorway. "What's wrong?" she asked.

Willow looked all around the room, including in the closet and under the bed.

Sawyer stepped in and grabbed Willow by the arms. "What is it? Talk to me."

Willow pushed an errant lock of hair behind her ear. "There was a woman in my room. I saw her from the backyard. She was standing right in that window, looking down at me."

"A woman? Describe her to me."

"She wore a cloak clasped at the neck by something shiny."

"What color was her hair?"

"Christ, I don't know. It wasn't blonde, and it wasn't as dark as yours. Somewhere in the middle."

"Was her hair up or down?"

"Down, I think. I'm not really sure. I must have been forty or so feet from the house."

"I wonder if it was the Goddess," Sawyer said softy.

Willow broke free of Sawyer's grasp. "The Goddess? For crying out loud, Sawyer. She was from Greek mythology. There's a reason that word starts with 'myth.' Myths are usually imaginary or false. And even it was the Goddess, how the hell would anyone even know what she looks like? There wasn't any kind of photography around in the time of ancient Greece."

"Have you got a better explanation? It sure as hell wasn't me in that window, and I don't see anyone else here except you—and you, by the way, were out in the yard."

Willow sat on the edge of her bed. "All I know is that it scared the shit out of me. I'm not even sure I'm safe in my own home anymore."

Sawyer knelt in front of Willow and took her hands. "Willow, I can assure you if it was the Goddess, you're not in any danger from her. You are a chosen one and way too important for her to put in harm's way."

"And if it wasn't the Goddess?"

Sawyer sat back on her heels. "If it wasn't the Goddess, we'll have to invoke her name to protect you."

"And, pray tell, how do we do that?"

"When the sun sets, we'll do a summoning prayer spell together."

"You want me to cast a spell? On myself no less?"

"If that wasn't Hecate who appeared in your window, it may be the only way to protect you."

"That's a comforting thought."

\* \* \*

"Where does this path lead?" Sawyer asked as she followed close behind Willow. They had walked about a mile down the paved road by Willow's house before abruptly veering off on a well-worn path that led through the trees.

"To the beach," Willow said. "We're almost there."

True to her word, a break in the trees just a short distance ahead led directly to a sandy beach.

"This is amazing." Sawyer scanned the length of the beach.

"Take your shoes off and carry them, or the sand will get inside them and wear the skin right off your feet."

Sawyer removed her shoes and walked a few feet in the warm sand. "That feels heavenly on my feet."

"Yeah, until you step on a broken clam. Just be careful."

"It's kind of hard to walk in."

"Yes it is. When I need a good workout, I run on the beach. Come on, let's get closer to the water's edge. The sand isn't so yielding there."

Willow and Sawyer ambled side by side down the length of the beach. At one point, Sawyer stopped, picked up a sand crab that had been washed ashore by the tide, and returned it to the edge of the water. "Go on little fella," she said as she coaxed it into moving toward the surf.

Willow felt a rush of warmth fill her as she watched. "So tell me about the uprising," she said as Sawyer rejoined her.

"The uprising. Yes. Well—" Sawyer was interrupted by the ringing of Willow's cell phone.

Willow pulled it out of her pocket and looked at the

incoming call information. "Hold on a sec, it's Mom and Dad. They're apparently home from their cruise." She pushed the answer button on her phone and held it to her ear as they continued to walk.

"Mom. How was your trip?" Willow smiled at Sawyer as she listened for what felt like an interminable amount of time for her mother to rave about their cruise. "It sounds like you had a great time," Willow said. "Me? I'm actually walking on the beach right now. No, I'm not alone. I'm with a friend." Willow spared a glance at Sawyer who smiled at the "friend" reference. "Her name's Sawyer. Yes, it's an unusual name. Her last name? Hawksworth. Sawyer Hawksworth."

Willow took several more steps then stopped. "Mom? Are you still there? Oh, hi, Dad. I thought I lost signal or something. Is Mom okay? She just stopped talking. Sawyer? What about her? I'm not in any danger, Dad. She's pretty scrawny. I think I can take her."

Willow looked at Sawyer and winked. "What's that? What's not a laughing matter? Dad, is there something you're not telling me? All right. Okay, I'll see you in a bit. Bye." Willow slipped her phone back into her pocket. "Sorry about that. It seems they're worried that you might be an axe murderer after all."

"I surmise we're heading back home to meet the parents, so to speak?"

"You surmise correctly, Watson," Willow said as they turned around and headed back the way they came.

# Chapter 29

## 1612—North Yorkshire, England

Hadley stood at the table and kneaded dough in a bowl while Jenna mended the cane webbing on one of the chairs. It was mid-February and the temperature outside was near zero. "If thou dost not mind, Jenna, I need thee to bring in a few more pieces of wood to keep the fire going tonight," Hadley said.

"Aye. I will take care of it right after I finish this chair."

"I hope Caleb hath warmth tonight in his room."

"He has a heating stove, and I helped him stack wood just outside the door yesterday, so he shall be fine."

"I was pleased he found work at the mercantile. I feared the forge would not do enough business in this cold weather to keep both of thee busy," Hadley said.

"Thou art right about that. Work always slows down while the snow blankets the ground. I am thankful 'tis been steady enough to keep the forge running every day, but I'm certainly not turning work away."

"'Twill pick up in the spring."

"Aye. That it will, I am sure."

"I wonder what Caleb doth on a night like this when it's too cold to be out and about."

"He is reading and studying."

"Reading?"

"Aye. He is reading the teachings of the clan for the past year."

"Doth he seek initiation?"

"He hath not said. Methinks he just wants to know more about it to support us, and it doth pass the time."

Both fell silent for several minutes.

"Jenna, didst thou hear about Mrs. Thompson?"

"The midwife?"

"Aye. She was taken away by the king's men today. Folks were in and out of the shop all day talking about it."

Jenna sat back. "She is but a harmless soul. What did they want with her, I wonder?"

"Word is a child she was birthing died, and the mum accused her of casting spells over the wee one."

"Some folk are always looking to blame others for their folly. I shall pray to the Goddess to save the poor woman's soul." Jenna tightened the last strand of cane and tied it off. She stood and placed the chair back under the table. "There, a good job done. Now I will be seeing to the firewood."

Jenna pulled her boots on and donned a heavy coat. She made multiple trips between the woodpile and the hearth until several dozen pieces of firewood were stacked inside, while Hadley put her bread dough into four loaf pans and placed them on the table to rise.

When Jenna was satisfied they had enough wood for the next day or two, she hung up her coat and put her boots by the hearth to warm. She came up behind Hadley and put her cold hands into the low-cut neckline of Hadley's smock.

"Great Goddess, Jenna," she screamed as she backed away, "Thy hands are colder than a witch's tit!"

Jenna continued to advance on her and eventually chased her around the room until she finally caught Hadley and threw her on the bed. Jenna lay on top of her. "I know a nice warm place I could put my hands to stave off the cold."

"I cannot imagine I would be liking that very much, blacksmith."

Jenna put her hands on Hadley's neck. Hadley slapped them away. "Stop that, you scallywag." Jenna rolled off Hadley, laughing.

Hadley turned over to lie on her stomach and propped herself up on her elbows. "Jenna, during my initiation ritual, thou didst say thou wantest a child."

"Aye."

"I was thinking all day about the babe that died when Mrs. Thompson birthed it. I thought about what it would be like to be that babe's mum. When I was a young girl, I dreamed about having babes, but as I grew older and realized I was a lover of women, I pushed those thoughts out of my mind. At the initiation, thou didst say we'd find a way. Didst thou mean that?"

Jenna caressed the side of Hadley's face. "Aye. I meant it. Dost thou want a child?"

"Methinks so. We have been one for eighteen moons now. Methinks 'tis time to have a family."

"Then we shall find a way."

\* \* \*

Jenna dug the pre-made horseshoe out of the coals with the tongs and placed it on the anvil. Ta-ting... ta-ting... ta-ting, sounded the hammer as she flattened the softened metal. She worked the shoe, alternately heating and hammering and checking it against the horse's hoof, until it was just the right shape and flatness. When she was satisfied, she placed it in the bucket of water to cool. "One down, three to go," she said to herself as she put a second shoe in the coals to soften.

"Good morning to thee," Caleb said as he emerged from his room adjoining the forge.

"Good morning, brother. Did I wake thee with all this racket?"

"Nay. I was up and at the basin before I heard any noise. I'm going to the tavern for a cup of coffee and a bite to eat if thou dost care to join me."

"I have work to do. Besides, Hadley made muffins this morning, so I've had my fill."

"How is thy lady?"

"Very well. She was quite chipper this morning. We came to a decision last night that made her pretty happy."

"And what would that be?"

"She wants to have a babe."

Caleb walked over to his sister and placed his hand on her shoulder. "Now, Jenna, thou dost understand how that works, dost thou not?"

Jenna ribbed him with her elbow. "Of course I know how that works."

"Well, I'm thinking thou art missing a key part to make that happen."

Jenna grinned. "I'm well aware of what I'm missing, dear brother."

Caleb warmed his hands in front of the forge. "So how dost thou propose to get her with child?"

Jenna put her tools down and wiped the sweat from her brow. Even in the cold of February, working directly in front of the forge drove her to shirtsleeves. "I honestly don't know. 'Tis the first time in my life I regret being a woman. I would love naught more than for her to have a child with my blood in its veins."

"Thy blood, sister… or Hawksworth blood?"

"Jenna Hawksworth, I am not fornicating with thy brother," Hadley said. "Sorry, Caleb, I mean no disrespect, but I'm not interested in doing that with a man."

"I'm not asking thee to, Hadley," Jenna said. "There's a ritual the coven performs when females who prefer their own kind want children. Caleb will just supply what we need to make that happen."

"'Tis true, Hadley," Caleb said.

"And how art thou going to feel when the child calls thee uncle instead of father, Caleb?"

"I'm not ready for children right now, but thou art and so is my sister. Being uncle sounds like a fine thing to me."

Jenna grasped her shoulders. "Hadley, the child would have Hawksworth blood. I would give anything to be able to do this for thee… for us… but the Goddess knows that's not possible. This is as close as we'll ever get to this child being my own."

"It means that much to thee, blacksmith?"

"It doth," Jenna said.

"All right then. I shall agree to it."

Jenna took Hadley into her arms and held her close. "Every

day you give me more and more reasons to love thee, Hadley Metcalf."

"Hey—what about me? I'm the one making this happen," Caleb joked.

Jenna and Hadley both reached out for Caleb. "Thou art the finest brother a girl could have," Jenna said. "I cannot thank thee enough."

"My pleasure, sister."

"Thy pleasure, indeed!" Hadley teased. "So when should we do this deed?"

"I will pray to the Goddess and consult the clan. My recollection is that the summer solstice is best for this ritual."

"That's five months away. Plenty of time to prepare," Hadley said.

"What art thou going to tell the town folk when it becomes obvious thou art with child, Hadley," Caleb asked.

"I will be telling them naught. 'Tis none of their business. Besides, 'twill remove any suspicion they may have about Jenna and me doing unnatural acts."

"Thou art right about that," Jenna said. "Unless my tongue is loaded, there's no way I could be accused of making you with child."

"Thou art so romantic, Jenna." Hadley shook her head and moaned.

# Chapter 30

## 2013—Plymouth, Massachusetts

"Mom, Dad, come in," Willow said as she opened the door for her parents.

Roger McCord walked a full circle around Willow and checked her out.

"Really, Dad? What did you think you'd find when you got here—that I'd been turned into an old hag with dry frizzy black hair, green skin, and warts on my nose?"

"How long has she been here?" he asked.

"Since Friday. Daddy, she's not what you think she is."

"And what exactly do you think she is, Willow?"

"A spiritualist."

"When I was your age, we called them witches."

"Daddy, witches are simply people who practice the Wicca religion. Since when are you biased about religion?"

"So she hasn't told you about the uprising," he said.

"She was just about to when Mom called me a while ago."

"You might just change your mind about her once you have that information. Where is she?"

"I'm right here, Mr. McCord." Sawyer stepped into the living room from the kitchen. She walked across the room and extended her hand. "I'm happy to meet you. My name is Sawyer Hawksworth."

"I know who you are, and what you want, Ms. Hawksworth." Roger didn't take her hand.

"Roger, where are your manners?" Willow's mother said.

"She's about to put our daughter in danger, Sandy. I have a

right to be concerned about that."

"I'll do everything in my power to keep Willow safe, Mr. McCord," Sawyer said. "I have no intention to expose her to grave danger."

"Their power just might be stronger than yours. Have you thought of that?" he asked.

"That's possible, but their power will not be stronger than mine and Willow's combined."

"I have powers?" Willow asked.

"What makes you so sure?" Roger said to Sawyer, ignoring Willow's question.

"Because she is a chosen one, and so am I. The Goddess will see that we have the power we need to defeat them."

"Them?" Willow asked. "Who is them? Someone had better explain what the hell is going on."

"How do you know you're chosen? Prove it to me," Roger said.

"Mr. McCord, I'm sure you're well aware of the so-called birthmark you have on the inside of your right cheek—three dark blue parallel lines. Well, I have it, too—same mark in the same place—and so does Willow. Legend has it that all the chosen ones over the past four hundred years carried the same mark."

Sandy took her husband's arm. "Roger, maybe you should at least hear her out."

"Before she passed, Willow's grandmother, my mother, Jenny McCord, gave Willow a blue feather brooch. According to the teachings, the other sentry should have one similar to it," Roger said.

Sawyer looked at Willow. "Willow?"

"I'll be right back." Willow ran upstairs. A few moments later, she returned carrying the wooden box Sawyer's brooch was mailed in. "Daddy, not only did Sawyer have the other brooch, but it's a mirror image of mine, and they lock together. Look." Willow took the cover off the box and handed it to her father.

"Well, I'll be," he said.

Willow picked up the interlocked brooches from inside the box. She held them in front of her parents, tilted them toward each other, and they parted into two separate brooches.

Sawyer came up beside Willow and put her hand on the small of her back. "Lock them back together, Willow, and show your father how they glow."

Sawyer's hand on Willow's back felt like fire, shooting warm feelings deep within her. She locked the brooches together, laid them in the palm of her hand, and watched as they glowed brightly.

Sawyer picked them up and looked at them closer. "They are beautiful. More beautiful than either one by itself."

Willow put her hand on Sawyer's shoulder and leaned in, their cheeks nearly touching. She pointed at the brooches. "Look right here, Sawyer. There's an image of a naked woman inscribed on each one, and when you lock the brooches together, they appear entwined in an embrace."

"Good Goddess—I wasn't even aware that image was there. Legend has it that Jenna Hawksworth made these brooches. In fact, she made individual brooches for the Elders of the thirteen clans in the coven."

Roger sat on the couch and covered his face with his hands. Sandy went to sit beside him. He lowered his hands. "I so wanted this to be only legend, a myth," he said. "My mother and grandmother filled me with stories when I was a child. They were fantastic—full of danger and intrigue. It didn't take much to figure out you'd be next in line, Willow. I didn't want you exposed to that kind of danger. My grandmother, Maggie McCord, actually participated in the last repression." Roger looked toward Sawyer. "That would have been with your great-grandmother, Richelle Hawksworth."

"Yes, that's true," Sawyer replied.

"Daddy, did you know the other woman in Maggie's USO picture is Richelle? I remember you calling her Ricky."

"Yes, I've known all along who the woman in the picture was. They were a little more than just chosen ones—relative to their relationship, I mean—despite the fact they were both married to men."

"Yeah, Sawyer and I figured that one out from the picture. I copied it into my computer and blew it up, and we discovered they're wearing these two brooches."

"Mr. McCord, please don't take this the wrong way, but what did you think would happen with the repression if I didn't find Willow? The Metcalf and Hawksworth lines made ancestral vows to pass the teachings down to each new generation. The uprising will happen with or without the participation of the chosen ones. The repression, on the other hand, has a greater chance of success if a chosen one from each line works together to stop the uprising."

"Look," Roger said, "the last generation that participated was two removed from me. The history becomes diluted over time, and before you know it, it becomes more legend than fact. I guess I was hoping it really was just legend."

Sandy stood up and walked to the center of the room. "I've remained silent long enough," she said. "Willow, Roger, I heard about this event from both Jenny and Maggie McCord repeatedly until the days they died. I believe it to be real, and it's the duty of these two families to do whatever possible to stop it from happening. Sawyer, you seem like a lovely girl with a good head on your shoulders, and I know Willow's a very smart and capable woman. It's time to put your heads together and make plans to stop this thing—and Roger, you need to help in any way you can."

"You go, Mom!" Willow said.

"Thank you, Mrs. McCord. I appreciate the vote of confidence," Sawyer said.

"There's just one problem," Willow said. "I still don't know what this thing is."

\* \* \*

"Roger, honey, please go light the grill. Now let me see…" Sandy rummaged     through Willow's refrigerator, verbally checking off things she needed.   "Eggs, mayonnaise, onion, celery, cucumber. Wonderful. If there's macaroni and tuna fish in the cupboard, I'll have what I need to make a pasta salad."

"Mom, what are you doing?"

"We can't tackle something as big as the uprising on an

empty stomach. I'm going to make a salad while you and Sawyer run to the supermarket and pick up burgers hot dogs, sweet sausage, corn on the cob, and maybe some wine."

Sawyer was grinning at Willow ear to ear. "I like your parents. I can see where you got your sassy attitude."

"I heard that, Sawyer Hawksworth," Sandy said from where she had her head buried in the refrigerator.

"Oops! Maybe we should go," Sawyer said.

Roger carried the empty propane tank into the house. "Better get this refilled while you're shopping."

"Outside with that, Roger. What's wrong with you?" Sandy said.

"If you don't mind putting it in the back of my car, that would be great, Daddy."

No sooner had they climbed into the car, when a text came into Willow's phone. She handed it to Sawyer. "It's from Mom. Want to see what it says?"

"Tuna fish. It says tuna fish."

"There's a pen and an old deposit slip in the glove compartment. Maybe we should write down what we need to buy. Ready? Okay, burgers, dogs, sausage, wine, corn, tuna fish, sponge cake, whipped cream, and strawberries."

"Sponge cake, whipped cream, and strawberries weren't on your mother's list."

"They are now."

\* \* \*

Roger and Sawyer sat on one side of the picnic table while Sandy and Willow sat on the other, with Willow sitting opposite Sawyer. Heaps of food covered the table: grilled meats, corn on the cob, salad, rolls, condiments, and a pickle and olive tray.

"Great salad as always, Mom," Willow said. "And, Daddy, the meat is done perfectly. Thank you for cooking."

"Did you remember to slice the strawberries and add sugar?" Sandy asked.

"Sawyer took care of that."

"Thank you, Sawyer. Do you cook much?"

"I make a mean breakfast," she replied.

"I can vouch for that. English crepes, no less!"

Sawyer blushed under the praise.

"Okay," Sandy said, "now that we have all this wonderful food in front of us, none of us should have to get up from the table for a while. So, who would like to start?" She looked at both Roger and Sawyer.

Willow kissed her mother's cheek. "You'll never give up being a teacher, will you, Mom."

"Sorry. Force of habit, I guess."

"I'll start," Sawyer said. "Mr. McCord, please feel free to jump in at any time. Willow, we talked quite a lot last night about the Goddess Hecate. One of the things you'll remember is that she was the sole ruler of the underworld before the patriarchal religions began to rise in ancient Greece and insisted primary gods had to be male. She was replaced by Hades as the primary ruler, and she was more or less demoted to the guardian of the gates of the underworld. With that demotion, came a reduction in power. There are some who believe her name may have been derived from the word 'hekaton,' which means one hundred. Because of her demoted power and authority in the underworld, every one hundred years the energy of the spirits of evil witches who were put to death by burning at the stake, hanging, or water torture joins together and they become strong enough to rise up and attempt to force their way through the gates of the underworld and into the land of the living.

"Legend has it, prior to Hadley Metcalf and Jenna Hawksworth, hoards of these spirits escaped and spread their evil on the world. As a form of revenge, they tainted the minds of the religious leaders and convinced them that countless innocent people, guilty of no more than using herbal medicines to heal the sick, were actually using black magic. These innocent people were labeled witches, and most of them were executed by the authorities.

"Hadley and Jenna belonged to a clan called The Blue Feather Coven, which developed spells and rituals strong enough to repress the uprising. The blue feather brooches were key to those rituals. When used in combination with the rituals—and especially if carried out by descendants of Hadley Metcalf and Jenna Hawksworth—they possess special powers that close the gates of the underworld and prevent the evil from escaping. Just imagine the risk those women took. They lived in a time when even being suspected of being a witch was punishable by death. Being homosexual was also punishable by death. They were both."

"So," Willow said, "let's suspend disbelief for a moment and assume that what you described actually can happen. In today's environment, people wouldn't be executed for being accused of witchcraft. If you use that logic, then the risk of these evil spirits wreaking havoc on the world is pretty low."

"Willow," Roger said, "being accused of witchcraft is just one example of what these evil spirits could do. I mean, what if they somehow managed to control the minds of people who have their fingers hovering over the nuclear bomb strike buttons in various countries? What if they could control the minds of scientists who can develop strains of plague? What if the evil spirits had influence over someone like Hitler, resulting in another Holocaust, or people like the terrorists on 9/11? What if the spirits are responsible for the recent genocide in Syria? I'm not saying that's what happened, but what if these spirits were able to do something like that? Do you see what I mean? In a lot of ways, an uprising could be even more damaging today than it was one hundred, two hundred, or even four hundred years ago because today's technology in the wrong hands could have catastrophic consequences."

"So, we're basically talking about a poltergeist here," Willow said.

"Essentially, yes," Sawyer replied. "Lots of them, all wanting the same thing, and coming out of the underworld to achieve it."

"Okay, so who wants some strawberry shortcake?" Sandy asked.

# Chapter 31

## 2013—Plymouth, Massachusetts

"Bye, Mom and Dad. Love you both." Willow waved as they drove away. She went back into the house and found Sawyer cleaning up the dinner dishes. "You don't need to do that."

"I'm not doing much. We ate on paper plates and with plastic utensils. It's really only cooking implements."

"Well, I appreciate it."

Sawyer rinsed off the spatula Roger had used to flip the burgers and placed it in the dishwasher. "There, finished."

"Do you want a beer?" Willow asked.

"Actually, I'd prefer a glass of wine."

"Wine it is." Willow poured the wine for Sawyer and grabbed a bottle of beer for herself. "Let's go sit on the front porch swing," she said.

"Okay."

Willow sat and held the swing still for Sawyer.

"This is nice," Sawyer said.

"I love it here. It's so peaceful and quiet, and I love how close it is to the ocean. When are you going back to England?"

"I'm not sure. Why do you ask?"

"Because it would be nice to get to know you better and take you around to see the sights—you know, Provincetown, the wineries. I think you might enjoy that."

"I can stay for as long as you need me to," Sawyer said.

"I don't want to take you away from your business."

"Fortunately, a great deal of what I do is done before or after I meet with clients, so it can really be done from anywhere. And if I need to get documents signed, I can always have Catherine fax them or email them to me."

"Catherine?"

"My secretary."

"Well, if you decide to stay longer, there's no need to rent a hotel room. Especially since you haven't used the one you've reserved since you've been here, except for that first night."

"Speaking of which, I need to go check out of the hotel and pick up the rest of my belongings."

"Again, no pressure, but you're welcome to stay here for as long as you want."

"I just might do that. You need to go back to work tomorrow, right?"

"Unfortunately, yes. I'm booked with cleanings through Wednesday. I can see about taking Thursday and Friday off as vacation days though. Maybe we can do a little sight-seeing over a long weekend, if you're planning to stay that long, that is."

"It sounds delightful. I'll spend the first couple of days this week catching up on work things and making plans with the Council of Thirteen to have you initiated."

"Whoa. What do you mean by initiated? And what is the Council of Thirteen?"

"It's a ceremony to welcome you into the coven, and the Council of Thirteen is the ruling body, composed of the leaders of each of the thirteen clans in the coven."

"So... I need to become a witch to participate in this repression?"

"You need to understand the rituals, and it would help if you knew your way around the principles of the coven."

Willow pressed her toe into the floor to increase the momentum of the swing. "When does this uprising begin?"

"At the end of October."

"You mean, like on Halloween?"

"Yes. It actually happens on the night Americans traditionally celebrate Halloween. There's a reason that day is referred to as Samhain, or All Hallows' Eve. It's when the door or gate between the worlds of the living and the dead are the thinnest. Before Hadley and Jenna discovered a way to restrain the evil spirits, they broke free on that evening every one hundred years."

"Does this uprising happen in a physical location, or is it in the spiritual realm?"

"The uprising itself happens in the spiritual realm. The repression ritual is generally done near Billingham, England."

"Billingham? I've never heard of it. Why there?"

"Because that's where the first successful repression was held by Hadley Metcalf and Jenna Hawksworth."

"Does that mean I'll need to go to England for this event?"

"That is precisely what it means."

"I guess I'd better be planning some vacation time from work."

"Do you think you could arrange a leave of absence? You really need to immerse yourself in the teachings of the coven for at least a full month before the uprising."

"You want me to take an entire month off from work? Unlike you, I kind of need to work to pay the bills."

"Not if you allow me to take care of them for you for that month."

"No."

"Why not?"

"Because I can take care of my own damned bills, thank you very much."

"I'll make a deal with you. If you'll have me, I'll spend the next four weeks with you and I will refrain from spending scads of money while I'm here, if you allow me to return the favor by taking care of you for a month."

"That's not quite the same. I won't be paying your mortgage while you're here."

"That's because I don't have a mortgage."

"Bitch."

"Is it a deal, or not?"

"Sawyer, my taking care of a month of room and board is not going to equal your paying for a month of mortgage and utilities."

"Okay, how about I stay for the next two months, then you and I can fly to England together at the beginning of October."

Willow pushed the swing back and forth with her toe as she stared out over the lawn.

"Well?" Sawyer said.

Willow looked at her. "Before I commit, let me see if I can get the entire month of October off. I'll let you know tomorrow."

"Okay. If you can, I'll call Matilda and ask her to pack and mail some clothing to me. I certainly can't be wearing your clothes for the next two months."

They swung back and forth for several minutes in silence. "A penny for your thoughts," Sawyer said.

"What do you know about Hadley and Jenna?"

"Only what's written in the Book of Shadows and what has been handed down through the Blue Feather Coven."

"Tell me about them."

"From all accounts, Jenna joined the coven in her very early twenties. A couple of years later, the high priest began to have dreams or visions he didn't understand, so he asked the Goddess Hecate to provide a sign to help him. When he rose the next morning, there were three dark blue parallel lines on the calf of his leg, almost as though an animal had clawed him. He showed the mark to the members of the coven, and Jenna revealed she had similar marks inside the right cheek in her mouth. The high priest was convinced this was the sign the Goddess intended, the sign that Jenna was the chosen one."

"So how did Hadley come into the picture?"

"Keep in mind that Jenna was relatively young and inexperienced so the high priest set out to find someone to help her—someone who had ties, through ancestors, to previous repression ceremonies. That person turned out to be Hadley."

"The high priest arranged for Jenna and Hadley to meet? That must not have gone over like a fart in church!"

"From what I can tell from the Book of Shadows, Jenna didn't let her know until much later. Hadley wasn't even aware of her family's history with previous repressions."

"Kind of like me, huh?"

"In a way, but I'm more inclined to believe it was because

up until then those ceremonies were largely unsuccessful."

"Anyway, they met and as fate would have it, they fell in love. From all accounts, Hadley was quite a spitfire and she gave Jenna a run for her money. She owned the town tailor shop, and Jenna found work as a blacksmith when she came to town, so they were mostly comfortable financially. And even more so when they decided to live together."

"I thought it was dangerous to be known homosexuals in those times."

"It was, and they were very careful not to be affectionate in public. And when Hadley became pregnant, any suspicions the townsfolk may have had about the two of them vanished, because after all, it would be impossible for Jenna to impregnate Hadley."

"Who was the baby's father?" Willow asked.

"It was important for Jenna, and to the coven, that the child have Hawksworth blood running through its veins, so Jenna's brother, Caleb, provided the means to fertilize Hadley's eggs."

"Hadley had sex with Jenna's brother? Ewww!"

"Not exactly. You see, the coven had developed a way to impregnate lesbian members without them having to have intercourse with a man. The implement was somewhat of a medieval turkey baster, but it had a surprisingly high success rate."

"So what happened with them? I mean, how is it they were so successful suppressing the uprising when no one else had been?"

"I mentioned Jenna was a blacksmith. She's the one who actually crafted and forged the brooches. She made one brooch for each leader of the thirteen clans of the Blue Feather Coven, but the two she made for her and Hadley were the only ones that were mirror images of each other and could lock together. Prior to that, the clan leaders wore actual blue feathers on their lapels. The symbolism of the Mother Goddess was crafted into the brooches, not only in the design but also in what Jenna inscribed on the back."

"Maiden, Warrior, Mother, Crone, 13," Willow said.

"Yes. Hecate is a triple goddess but she's most often represented by the Crone. The triple goddess symbol represents the cycles of a woman's life and reproduction. This could symbolize a cycle of rebirth after the one hundred year uprising. I didn't realize there's a thirteen included in the phrase. That must represent the years the uprising occurs in. The number thirteen has many meanings in witchcraft—some of them positive and some negative."

"I guess I don't understand why a piece of jewelry would make a difference in the success of repression. It was a symbol. Not much different from the real blue feathers they wore."

"It wasn't just a piece of jewelry. It was the sapphires in them, which, by the way, are said to be blessed by Hecate. And the fact that they were able to be locked together. But most of all, when Jenna forged them, she cast a spell on each one."

"She cast a spell while she was forging them?" Willow asked.

"Yes. Each brooch was enchanted such that when the wearer died, their soul could voluntarily reside inside the brooch. As the brooches were passed down from generation to generation and more and more souls were added, they became more and more potent. You can imagine the original fourteen brooches by this day and age have become quite powerful."

"Fourteen? I thought there were thirteen clans."

"There were. Jenna was the representative of her own clan, and she made two interlocking brooches for herself—one of which she gave to Hadley. The remaining brooches were made for the twelve other clans within the coven."

"So there were actually fourteen chosen ones?"

Sawyer stood up. "Wait right here. I have something to show you that will make this easier to understand." She went into the house and returned a few moments later carrying a folded piece of paper. She sat down on the swing next to Willow and spread the paper out on her lap. "Here is our family genealogy," she said. "As you can see, there have been fifteen generations between Hadley and Jenna and us. All of the names at the top of the chart are chosen ones. The ones highlighted are those who participated in the last four repressions." Sawyer pointed to Hadley's and Jenna's names. "When the brooches were crafted, Jenna and Hadley were the only chosen ones. The other twelve leaders were actually chosen by the brooches themselves. Their role was to support the chosen ones during the repression ceremony."

Willow got up from the swing and walked back and forth across the porch. "Okay, this is all sounding pretty crazy. How on earth can a brooch choose a clan leader?"

"Jenna prayed to the Goddess Hecate to help the brooch choose the clan member who was the wisest and strongest of character. Each clan member was given the opportunity to hold the brooch. When the correct clan member held the brooch, it glowed."

"Our brooches were handed down to us by our ancestors. Was that the same for the other clan leaders?"

"No. Unfortunately, strength of character isn't always inherited, so when the current clan leader either died, or became unable to carry out their duties, the Goddess Hecate was once again called upon to help the brooch choose a new clan leader."

"So back to my original question. How can a piece of jewelry, or fourteen pieces of jewelry to be exact, be successful repressing hundreds of years of evil spirits?"

"As I said, each brooch has the spirits of ancestors past residing in them. That includes yours and mine and the other thirteen held by the clan leaders. The combined power of all the souls residing in these fourteen brooches, when put together, especially in the presence of the right chants and spells, will enhance the strength of the Mother Goddess and become quite powerful."

Willow became quiet for long moments.

Sawyer touched her cheek. "Are you okay?"

"Yeah. I'm just wondering why Daddy didn't tell me about this years ago. I would have had so much more time to prepare."

"For the same reason my father didn't tell me. He was afraid for you. Thank the Goddess I had my nana to teach me everything I needed to know. I don't blame him any more than I blame my own father. Willow, you need to understand you could be killed if the repression ceremony doesn't go well."

# Chapter 32

## North Yorkshire, England
## October 31, 1612—All Hallows' Eve

Jenna, Hadley, and Caleb spent two days traveling to Billingham. When they arrived, Jenna insisted Hadley rest while she and Caleb talked to the council and finalized plans for the ceremony on All Hallows' Eve.

"Lord Weller, I present to you, Caleb Hawksworth, who is my brother and the man who will make it possible for Hadley and myself to have this child."

Caleb extended his arm and shook the high priest's hand in a full forearm grasp. "Lord Weller, 'tis my pleasure," Caleb said.

"The whole clan appreciates your willingness to sire this child, Caleb Hawksworth. Future generations depend on it. We are in thy debt."

"Nay, Lord Weller. I do this for my sister and Hadley, They are good people and deserve a family."

"Aye, they are."

"I wish to make a request before the ritual on the morrow," Jenna said.

"What is that, Jenna?" the high priest replied.

"I would like to handfast with Hadley Metcalf and legitimize the conception of this child."

"I see. And is Hadley willing?"

"I haven't talked to her about it yet, but I know she shall agree."

"Thou dost understand knowledge of this can never be

shared?"

"Aye, I am aware it must be kept within the secret of the clan and, of course, my brother here."

The high priest put his hand on Jenna's shoulder. "Then we shall have two reasons to celebrate come the morrow. We shall hold the joining ceremony just before the conception ritual."

"Thank thee, Lord Weller."

Caleb slapped his sister on the back. "Well thou hast better go ask her to marry thee, then."

Jenna quietly entered the room, undressed, and slipped into bed behind Hadley. She spooned herself into Hadley's back and wrapped her hand around her waist to pull her close. "I love thee," she whispered in Hadley's ear.

Hadley moaned and snuggled closer, squeezing the arm Jenna placed around her waist. "I love thee too, blacksmith," she said.

"Wouldst thou handfast with me, Hadley Metcalf?"

Hadley's eyes flew open, and she rolled onto her back to look into Jenna's face. "Jenna Hawksworth, why art thou asking me that question?"

"Because I love thee and because I want to be committed to thee before our child is conceived. What sayeth thee?"

Hadley grinned. "I say I am going to hell for handfasting with a witch!"

\* \* \*

Caleb led Hadley down a path through the trees that ended in a clearing in the forest. The sun shone brightly through the treetops and cast muted shadows on the ground. The entire coven awaited them, including Jenna, who stood with the high priest in the middle of a circle of clan members all clad in white robes. Hadley wore a simple white gown with a square peasant neckline and tied at the waist. A crown of flowers sat upon her head. Jenna wore brown leather trousers and a fresh white shirt tucked into her pants. Black knee-high boots pulled on over her trouser legs completed her dress.

Caleb brought Hadley directly to Jenna, kissed her on the

cheek, and hugged his sister before joining the rest of the clan members in the circle.

Jenna held Hadley's hands and smiled. "Thou art beautiful, Hadley Metcalf."

"I've said it before. Thou trimmest well, blacksmith," Hadley replied, followed by a teasing grin.

The high priest raised his hands to the crowd. "We have come hither to this sacred place to celebrate the joining of Hadley Metcalf and Jenna Hawksworth in a handfasting ceremony. Hadley, hast thou come of thy own free will?"

"Aye," Hadley replied.

"Jenna, hast thou come of thine own free will?"

"That I have."

"Who giveth these two people to each other?" the priest asked.

Caleb stepped forward. "I do. Caleb Hawksworth, brother of Jenna Hawksworth."

The priest turned to the altar set up behind him and picked up a candle. He held the candle before Hadley and Jenna. "Hadley and Jenna, this candle represents thy union. Light it to represent the merging of thy lives and thy passions."

An attendant brought two lit smaller candles to Hadley and Jenna, and together, they lit the wick of the larger candle.

"Hadley Metcalf and Jenna Hawksworth, you have declared your intent to handfast before the assembly of thy brothers and sisters. You must now declare thine intent to the Goddess Hecate. Know that the promises you make today will cross over the years and souls of all that lies ahead. Do you still wish to enter this union?"

Jenna and Hadley answered together, "Aye."

"We seek the blessings of Mother Earth and the virtues of the cardinal directions, East, South, West, and North. Take this censer and cleanse the corners of this sacred place."

Jenna took the censer and Hadley's hand and walked to each cardinal direction of the sacred clearing in cadence with the priest's words. "May the East bless this union with the rising of each sun. May the South bless this union with warmth of hearth and home and the heat of the heart's passion. May the West bless this union with the cleansing of the rain and the passion of the sea. May the North bless this union with a firm foundation on which to build the fertility of the fields and a stable home."

Hadley and Jenna returned to the center of the circle.

"Each of these blessings from the four cardinal directions will help you build a strong, happy and successful union, yet know that they are only tools that you will need to learn to use. Jenna, look into Hadley's eyes. If you cause each other pain, will you both work to cure it?"

"We will," they said together.

"Hadley and Jenna, join thine hands." The priest draped a cord across their joined hands. "Would you both look for the brightness in life and the good in each other?"

"Aye," they answered together.

The priest draped a second cord across their joined hands. "Would you share life's burdens so thine union may grow stronger?" the priest asked.

"'Tis our intention," they answered together.

The priest draped a third cord across their joined hands."Would you share thy dreams and build new hopes?"

"We shall."

The priest draped a fourth cord across their joined hands. "Would you use the heat of anger to temper the strength of this union?"

"Aye."

The priest draped a fifth cord across their joined hands. "Would you honor each other and never give cause to break that honor?"

"We shall."

The priest draped a sixth cord across their joined hands, then reached for the ends and tied all of the cords. "These knots are not formed by the cords but by the strength of thy vows. The length of thine union will be based on you keeping those promises." The priest removed the cords and placed them on the altar. He motioned for Hadley and Jenna to face the clan members.

"In the name of the Goddess Hecate, I proclaim Hadley

Metcalf and Jenna Hawksworth joined for as long as they shall love."

Jenna filled the ritual tub with warm water and added a generous amount of patchouli. She lit incense and used it to cleanse the four corners of the room, starting at East, then South, West, and finally North. She then went to the adjacent room and pushed the door open. "Art thou ready, Hadley?"

Hadley came into the room wearing a white robe with the hood pulled down nearly in front of her face. She walked slowly to the tub where Jenna removed her robe and helped her into the warm water. Jenna knelt beside the tub, and they held their hands up toward each other until their palms were touching. With heads bowed, they called the Goddess Hecate.

"We call on the Triple Goddess—the Maiden, the Mother, and the Crone and ruler of the moon cycles to assist us in our quest. We implore thee to make the vessel of womanhood fertile so that a child can be conceived."

Jenna picked up a long wide plank and placed it across the tub in front of Hadley. From the altar, she lifted a bowl of fresh soil, which she sprinkled in a circle around the tub. Together, they chanted: "Oh Mother Goddess, this is the soil from whence thou dost provide life." Jenna handed a small quilt to Hadley that she had lovingly sewn several months earlier when they made the decision to conceive. Hadley spread it across the plank in front of her. Again, they chanted: "Mother Goddess, this is the wrap that will keep our wee one warm."

"Here thou art, Hadley," Jenna said as she handed the three candles to her wife.

Hadley placed the green candle in the center of the altar, a blue candle to the left of it, and a pink candle to the right of it. They chanted: "Mother Goddess, these are the candles that fire the womb."

Jenna picked up the green candle, oiled it with patchouli, and handed it to Hadley. "Close thine eyes, my love, and imagine the child... see the child. See thyself heavy with child. See thyself holding the child in thine arms."

Hadley began to cry. "She looks like you," she said.

Jenna struggled to hold back her own tears as the emotions threatened to overwhelm her. "Put the candle down now, Hadley, and light the blue candle and then the pink one."

Hadley did as she was told. Jenna picked up the blue candle while Hadley picked up the pink candle, and together, they lit the green one in the middle and chanted: "Sweet Goddess, fill up this womb with baby life. We are strong and we are worthy to lead this baby on its life journey. This child shall know thy name and follow thy ways. Fulfill our desire and make us with child this day. As we will it, so shall it be."

Jenna handed a piece of parchment and a quill to Hadley who wrote down a girl's name. Hadley folded the paper in half without showing it to Jenna. Jenna wrote down a boy's name and folded it in half without showing it to Hadley. She took both pieces of paper and placed them in a small wooden box, which she put in front of the green candle, still on the plank suspended over the water in the tub.

"Art thou ready, love?" Jenna said.

Hadley nodded and accepted Jenna's help out of the tub.

Jenna toweled Hadley down and led her back to the bedroom where she lay on the bed. Several pillows were under her hips, tipping her pelvis up and back. She kissed Hadley tenderly. "I will be right back with the healer and the high priest," she said.

Moments later, after the insemination process was over, the healer and priest left them alone. Jenna slipped into bed beside Hadley and held her close. "I love thee more at this moment than I ever thought I could. Thank thee for doing this."

"I want this as much as thee, Jenna, and now that I am thy wife, this child is truly thine as well. We shall be good mothers. This child shall want for naught."

"Aye."

Hadley squirmed, trying to get comfortable propped up on the pillows.

"Be still with thee," Jenna said. "Thou needest to stay this way for the next hour."

"And what wouldst thou be doing while I'm lying here in this unnatural position?"

"I could rub thy legs and feet."

"Could thee now? That would be heavenly."

For the next hour, Jenna kept her word and rubbed Hadley's feet and calves while they talked and made plans about the baby.

After an hour had passed, Jenna removed the pillows from under Hadley's hips and lay down beside her. She took Hadley into her arms and held her close.

"Wouldst thou make love to me?" Hadley asked.

Jenna rolled Hadley over and lay partially on top of her. "I ache to make love to thee, but I do not want to risk doing something that shall stop the babe from taking hold."

"So thou dost plan to not make love to me until this child is born?" Hadley was incredulous.

"I did not say that. I am not sure I could do that. Thou makest me all crazy with desire just by looking at me. I cannot imagine sharing thy bed and not touching thee for near a year. I just want to wait to see if thou hast thy moon cycle before we make love again. If thou dost not have a moon cycle, we shall know it worked and then I shall make love to thee all night."

"'Twill be a long two weeks!"

# Chapter 33

## 2013—Plymouth, Massachusetts

Willow yawned as the front porch swing swayed back and forth. "God! I'm sorry. I must be more tired than I thought," she said.

"Think nothing of it. It's been a pretty intense few days. I don't blame you for being tired," Sawyer said.

"Has it really only been a few days? It feels so much longer than that."

"I know. It feels that way to me, too."

"All right then. I'm going to hit the hay. Got to work tomorrow. Let me have your glass."

"Why don't you let me take care of that while you secure the windows and doors for the night?" Sawyer said.

Willow relented, handed her empty bottle to Sawyer, and followed her into the house. Sawyer put the wineglass in the dishwasher and the empty beer bottle in the recycle bin on the back porch while Willow locked the front door and made sure all the first-floor windows were secure. Sawyer locked the back door when she came back in.

"All buttoned up?" Sawyer asked.

"Tight as a drum."

"Okay, upstairs with you, woman," Sawyer teased.

Willow headed up the stairs and took a left at the top of the landing toward her room, while Sawyer, who was right behind her, took a right. "Good night, Willow," Sawyer said.

"'Night, Sawyer. Sweet dreams," Willow replied as she closed her door.

"Sweet dreams to you, too," Sawyer whispered under her breath as she closed her own door.

Willow stripped down to her panties and pulled a short tank top over her head. She set her alarm clock for six–thirty a.m. and slipped in between the covers of her bed. She lay on her back and allowed the tension to drain from her body. *God that feels good.* She stared at the ceiling and thought about Sawyer. *I can't believe I offered to let her stay here for the next two months. What is it about her that makes me trust her? Is it because she and Daddy have the same understanding of this uprising thing?* Willow thought back to her father's reaction when he first found out Sawyer was with her. *He sure was upset. I think he was ready to come over and throw her out of the house. It didn't take her long to win him over. Is there really any truth in the uprising thing? It sounds too incredible to be true, but it appears both Sawyer and Daddy think it is. Somehow I don't think he'll be very happy when he finds out I need to go to England for this repression ritual.*

Willow closed her eyes and opened them again, only to find a dark form hovering over her. She was paralyzed into inaction. All she could do was watch as the form floated to the ceiling and disappeared. She bolted upright in bed. "Holy shit!" she exclaimed as she threw the covers off and ran out of her room, straight down the hall to the guest room. She knocked urgently on the door.

"Sawyer, can I come in?"

Sawyer yanked the door open. "Willow, are you all right?"

"She's back."

"Who's back?"

"The ghost. I was in my bed, lying on my back with my eyes closed, and when I opened them, she was hovering over me."

"Wait here." Sawyer ran down the hall to Willow's room. She searched the room thoroughly and returned to the guest room.

Willow was sitting on the edge of the bed. "Willow, what did she look like?"

"Like a black, human form. It didn't have any features, just a human shape. It was inches away from my nose, and it floated up to the ceiling and disappeared."

"Did it say anything?"

"No. Maybe it was just the light playing tricks on me," Willow said.

"That's possible, but considering what you saw earlier in your bedroom window while you were in the yard, I wouldn't put my money on it." Sawyer sat on the bed beside Willow and put her arm around her. "You're shaking."

"Of course I'm shaking. There's some kind of evil spirit haunting me."

"That may not be too far from the truth," Sawyer said.

"Who is she?"

"It's possible a lone spirit has managed to escape the gates of the underworld and is maybe trying to scare you off."

"Well, I'm here to tell you it's working."

"It can't hurt you unless you let it, Willow."

"How the hell can I stop it?"

"Well, for starters, we need to do a protection chant. It will call on the Goddess Hecate to help protect you."

Willow hugged herself. "At this point, I'll try anything."

"Okay." Sawyer picked up her backpack from beside the dresser. From it, she extracted a set of keys, a moon amulet, three small pieces of sapphire, and a silver Celtic cross, as well as a black candle. "Come sit on the floor with me."

Willow sat cross-legged opposite Sawyer. Sawyer set the candle between them, and at the four cardinal directions, she laid the keys, the sapphires, the moon amulet, and the Celtic cross. She positioned her forearms on her knees, palms up. "Place your hands in mine," she said.

Willow rested her forearms on her own knees and put her hands within Sawyer's.

"Now close your eyes and focus on the apparition. Clear everything else from your mind, and think only of what you saw."

Sawyer waited for several minutes before continuing. "Repeat after me. Hecate, mighty Goddess of crossroads, darkness, death, wisdom, and the moon, please come to me."

"Hecate, mighty Goddess of crossroads... darkness, death, wisdom and the moon, please come to me." "Please, Hecate, protect me and help me when I am in danger." Willow repeated the phrase dutifully.

"Treat me as one of your own, and give me all that is needed."

Again, Willow repeated after Sawyer.

Sawyer continued. "Hecate, surround me in your darkness so that I can bring forth my light."

"Hecate, surround me in your darkness so that I can bring forth my light." Willow suddenly squeezed Sawyer's hands, as a light breeze tussled her hair, despite all the windows being closed.

Sawyer held her hands tighter. "Don't be afraid," she whispered. "Goddess Hecate, protect me in my time of need. Protect me from harm and allow my light to shine. My light shines bright before me, as I will it, so shall it be."

Willow said, "Goddess Hecate, protect me in my time of need. Protect me from harm and allow my light to shine. My light shines bright before me, as I will it, so shall it be."

"Pick up each of the symbols, beginning with East, then South, West, North, and place them in front of the candle."

Willow did as told.

"Now blow out the candle."

When the candle was extinguished, Sawyer collected the symbols and the candle and returned them to her backpack.

Willow stood up and sat on the edge of the bed.

"You should be safe now," Sawyer said.

Willow just continued to sit on the edge of the bed.

Sawyer sat down beside her and took her hand. "Willow, you need to trust the Goddess. She will look over you."

"I'd be happier if you would look over me."

"Me?"

"Yeah. I'm afraid to go back into my room. Any chance I can bunk with you?"

When the alarm went off the next morning, Willow reached over to the bedside table and turned it off. Immediately something struck her as being different. *Wait a minute. I'm not in my room.* She looked over her shoulder and saw Sawyer sleeping on her back beside her. Oh yeah—the ghost. She rolled onto her back and fought the urge to return to sleep. She glanced at Sawyer and found herself smiling. *She really is very cute, especially all relaxed and tussled like this.* She closed her eyes again and felt herself drifting off. *Ugh! I've got to get out of bed before I fall asleep.* She pushed the covers off and began to turn onto her side. Suddenly, Sawyer rolled over in her sleep and threw an arm across her midsection. *Whoa! Now how am I going to get out of this without waking her up?* Willow waited a minute or two for Sawyer to settle back in then very carefully took her wrist, lifted her arm up, and pivoted it back. She gently laid it down on Sawyer's hip and sat up on the edge of the bed before she became trapped once more. She stood up and pulled the covers over Sawyer. *Do I dare go back to my room?*

She opened the door to the guest room and turned the light on in the hallway. She slipped out of the room, closed the door, and walked gingerly down the hall toward her own room. Before entering, she reached in to turn the light on and peeked inside. Nothing was unusual or out of place. She made the bed she had vacated in haste the night before and went to the adjoining bathroom to shower and get ready for work. She appeared in the kitchen an hour later, dressed in scrubs and looking for coffee.

Willow dropped a bagel into the toaster and set the coffeepot to brew. She made a mental note to put in for an extended leave at work as she reached into the refrigerator for the cream cheese. When she closed the door and turned around, Sawyer was standing in the kitchen, again in her oversized T-shirt and men's boxer shorts. "Oh. You surprised me," Willow said. "Good morning."

"Good morning," Sawyer said. "The wonderful aroma of coffee woke me."

"I'm sorry. I closed your door so I wouldn't disturb you."

"Trust me, coffee is not a disturbance."

Willow pulled a travel mug and a coffee cup down from the cupboard, filled both, and handed the cup to Sawyer. "I'll get the creamer."

Sawyer held the coffee below her nose and inhaled the

steam while Willow got the creamer and put some in her travel mug. She held it above Sawyer's cup, which she eagerly offered. "Spoons are in the drawer," Willow said as she returned the creamer to the refrigerator.

"How did you sleep last night?" Sawyer asked as she stirred both hers and Willow's coffee.

"I crashed. Like I said last night, I was exhausted. I don't think I moved a muscle all night. I hope I didn't disturb you."

"Not at all. I hardly knew you were there." Sawyer took her first flavorful sip. "Ah—this is good coffee."

"Thanks for letting me bunk with you. That ghost scared the bejesus out of me."

"There's no need to be afraid now. We asked Hecate to protect you last night. Trust that she will."

"I wish I had the same level of conviction that you have, Sawyer, but you've got to understand that, from my perspective, this is just a bunch of mumbo-jumbo."

"That's why it's so important that you come to England early, to immerse yourself in the history and beliefs of the coven and to truly understand what is at risk here. If you're not a believer, it may not work."

"I'll try to have an open mind." Willow looked at the clock on the wall. "Oops… seven-thirty. I should get going."

Sawyer put her coffee cup on the countertop near the coffee maker. "I have several things to do myself today—including checking out of my room. I think I'll go shower."

Willow and Sawyer looked at each other for several long static moments, neither one able to look away. Finally, Willow took a step forward and embraced Sawyer, holding her tight. Sawyer's arms went around Willow's waist, and she pulled her close. A surge of heat and energy passed through Willow. She closed her eyes and whispered, "Thank you for being my protector last night. I really needed that." Willow kissed Sawyer on the cheek and stepped out of her embrace. "I'll see you after work."

Sawyer nodded and watched her go. "It was totally my pleasure, Willow. Truly, it was," Sawyer whispered.

# Chapter 34

## 2013—Boston, Massachusetts

"What do you mean you're staying there for two months? Are you out of your bloody mind?"

Sawyer paced back and forth across Willow's kitchen. "I don't have a choice, Bridgit. Our worse fears were confirmed. The legacy was not passed down to her. She has so much to learn, and I can help her with that. You know what's at stake here."

"Did the little princess freak out when you told her about it?"

"Willow is made of much tougher stuff than you might think. I wouldn't exactly call her a princess."

"There's got to be another way, Sawyer. Send her the historical documents, e-mail her, call her. You don't need to stay there. I insist you come home immediately."

Sawyer stopped in her tracks. "You insist? I don't answer to you, Bridgit."

"That's not fair, Sawyer. I thought I meant something to you."

"I do care for you, but no one tells me what to do."

"Are you sleeping with her?"

"If you're asking if I've had sex with her, the answer is no."

"Sawyer, please come home."

"I can't. Not right now. She's very vulnerable. She's had two apparitions in the past thirty-six hours."

"Apparitions? What do you mean?"

"Twice a form has appeared to her. Once in broad daylight, and the other last night while she lay in bed. We called upon

Hecate for protection together before she went to bed, but considering she's still quite skeptical about all of this, I fear it may not be fully effective. I need to protect her. Surely, you can understand that."

"So what is she going to do when you come home?"

"She will be coming with me."

"What? Over my dead body! Where exactly is she going to stay?"

"With me, at the estate."

"Sweet Goddess. And what about me?"

"What about you?"

"I love you, Sawyer."

"No you don't. You love the idea of my money and status. What you and I have shared thus far has never been about love."

"You will regret this, Sawyer. I vow—you will regret this."

"Don't push me, Bridgit. You can't match me, so don't even try."

* * *

"I cannot allow Willow McCord to threaten my plans," Bridgit mumbled to herself as she lit the black candle and placed it on the floor in front of her. "Considering the apparitions that have been visiting her, she apparently has enemies. I can use that to my advantage." She closed her eyes, made a fist with her hand, and placed it over her heart. She thought deeply about her hatred for Willow and her anger toward Sawyer.

"I, Bridgit Cooper, invoke the spirits who never sleep. I seek the enemy of my enemy to befriend and empower me with hatred and fire. Give me limitless power. Bring me forth the power of destruction so I might strike down your enemies who are also my own. Bring forth this power to me so I may do your bidding. As I will it, so shall it be!"

Bridgit grasped her chest as a searing pain shot through her. She fell to the floor and drew her knees into her chest as convulsions overtook her. Her neck muscles strained against the spasms, and her head hit repeatedly against the floor. Suddenly, the convulsions stopped and she rolled onto her back, eyes closed while her breathing returned to normal. Finally she opened her eyes. "It is done," came a deep voice from within her throat.

\* \* \*

"Willow, are you sure that's wise?" Susan asked. "I mean, she was kind of stalking you. Is it really safe to invite her into your house—for two months, no less?"

"I can't tell you why, Susan, but I trust her. If she wanted to hurt me, she's had plenty of opportunity since last Friday."

"It's the same woman that was waiting outside the office on Friday?"

"Yes."

"She was attractive."

Willow blushed.

Susan grabbed her arm. "Wait a minute here. Don't tell me you're attracted to her."

"Well, like you said, she's very attractive."

"She's a stalker, Wills. Don't you think you're taking a big chance here?"

Willow grinned at the nickname Susan sometimes used for her. "There's a lot more I wish I could tell you, Susan, but I can't right now. You'd probably think I was nuts anyway. If it makes you feel better, my parents have met her and she and my dad have something pretty important in common. He trusts her, and I trust my dad."

"So you've put in for a month's leave of absence?"

"Yes. A month... maybe a bit longer."

"Starting when?"

"Early October. I should be back sometime in November."

"I hope you don't end up regretting this, Willow."

"You've read my mind, Suze... you've read my mind!"

\* \* \*

Sawyer packed the last of her belongings in her suitcase

and placed it by the door of her hotel room. She then made three phone calls. The first was to her secretary to check in on work-related items. There were several documents that needed her signature that Sawyer asked Catherine to fax to the hotel. There were also cases to be reviewed, for which Catherine would send all the critical information by e-mail. The next call was to her maid, Matilda.

"Hi, Matty, this is Sawyer. Yes, I know, I should have called. I apologize. Yes, I know you promised Mom and Dad you'd look after me if anything happened to them, and I appreciate that. I'll try to do better. Matty, I need you to ship a large selection of my fall clothing to Plymouth, Massachusetts, for me. Yes, that's in the United States. I will be staying here for a couple of months." Sawyer grinned as she listened to a lecture from her housekeeper. "Thank you for being concerned about me, Matty. I do appreciate it, but I promise you I will be fine. Yes, two months. I'll be home in early October, and I'll be bringing someone home with me for a visit. Her name is Willow. What's that? Yes, she is very cute. You would approve. No, she's nothing like Bridgit. I thought that would make you happy. Do you have something to write with so I can give you Willow's address?" Sawyer read Willow's address from a piece of paper in her wallet. "Okay, Matty, I promise to check in with you in a few days. I love you, too. Bye."

The final phone call was to the Council of Thirteen. "Lord Somers, it's pretty much as we feared. The legacy wasn't directly passed down to Willow McCord."

"Do you know why?"

"For the same reason my father didn't pass it directly to me. Her father feared for her. I met her parents. Her father is very much a believer, but he hoped the legend was nothing more than that. I believe I've convinced him this is real, and he's willing to help if he can."

"That's good, but it's Willow we need."

"Agreed. Needless to say, she's skeptical, but she's willing to keep an open mind. I'll be staying in her home for the next several weeks. I'll do my best to educate her while I'm here."

"Very good."

"Lord Somers, she has had a couple of visions in the past day and a half... more like apparitions. Is it possible a soul has escaped the underworld?"

"Anything's possible, Sawyer, but it's not likely. There are members of the coven that are very in tune with movement of souls through the gates of the underworld. There has been no call for alarm of late."

"She was quite shaken by the sightings. I don't think they were imagined."

"Keep her safe, Sawyer. She's vital to the repression."

"I understand. Blessed be, Lord Somers."

\* \* \*

Sawyer was waiting for Willow outside her building when she got out of work. "Willow," she called as Willow walked right past where she was talking to Pete.

Willow stopped and looked around at the sound of her name. "Sawyer! Have you been here long?"

"A half hour or so. Pete has been keeping me company."

"Has she been pestering, you, Pete?" Willow asked with mock gruffness.

"This pretty lady can pester me anytime she wants, Miss Willow," Pete said.

"Pete, you're nothing but a big flirt," Willow teased.

Pete stepped in close and whispered in Willow's ear. "I suspect I'm not the one she'd like to be flirting with." He stepped back and winked.

Willow could do nothing but blush.

"Could I interest you in some dinner before we head home?"

Sawyer asked.

"Dressed like this?" Willow asked, referring to her scrubs.

"We don't need to go anywhere fancy. I was in town taking care of the hotel room and thought we could get a bite on the way home."

"Okay. There's a great diner on the Cape I think you'll like. It's about an hour's drive from home, so maybe we should drop your car off. Where are you parked?"

"In the garage just a few spaces down from your car."

"All right then. Let's go."

Willow spared a glance back at Pete as they departed. He grinned and winked at her once more.

"Moby Dick's. That's an interesting name," Sawyer said as they waited in line.

"It's a unique restaurant, but the seafood is to die for. Okay, you need to order from the menu above the desk and then find a place to eat and they'll bring it to you."

"They don't come to your table to take your order?"

"Nope." Willow put her hand on Sawyer's arm. "Let's stand here out of the way while we choose. There's so much on the menu it takes forever for me to make up my mind."

A young woman wearing a skimpy fisherman's outfit approached them. She hugged Willow. "Hey, Willow. It's been awhile since you were here, darlin'. I've missed you. Do you know what you want?"

"Hi, Amy. It's been awhile, that's for sure. I'll take the fried haddock and seasoned fries. Sawyer?"

Amy hip bumped Sawyer. "Sawyer, huh? That's a cool name. What can I get for you, love?"

"I believe I'll have what Willow's having."

"Oh—she's a Brit! That accent must drive you wild, Willow."

"Always the joker, huh, Amy? We'll be at table eight. Oh, and can you bring us a couple of beers and a bucket of shrimp?"

"Sure thing, hon. Go have yourselves a seat."

Willow and Sawyer made their way through the crowded screened-in dining room and sat at table eight. Sawyer looked around. "Is it always this crowded?"

"Yes, in the summertime. Wait until you taste the food, and you'll understand why."

"The waitress is a little over the top, wouldn't you say?"

"Amy? She's harmless."

"I get the impression she's quite fond of you."

"She's not my type, Sawyer, and I'm not even sure she's gay. She's kind of like that with most customers."

Just then Amy delivered their drinks as well as a bucket of shrimp with cocktail sauce and lemon wedges. "Here you go, darlin'," she said to Willow. "The rest of your food will be up in a minute."

"Thanks." Willow took a shrimp out of the bucket, dipped it in cocktail sauce, and sucked it out of the shell surrounding the tail. She pushed the bucket toward Sawyer. "Help yourself."

Sawyer picked up a piece of shrimp and tried to eat it the way Willow did, with little success. She reached over to Willow's dish and picked up the shell she threw down there after eating her shrimp. It was empty. "How did you do that?"

"Pinch a little tail—suck a little head," Willow said.

"I beg your pardon?"

Willow tilted her head back and laughed. "Pinch a little tail—suck a little head. Grab a shrimp, and I'll walk you through it."

Sawyer took a shrimp from the bucket.

"All right," Willow said. "We'll do this without sauce so you can see what's happening. Pick the shrimp up by the tail and put your forefinger and thumb on the shell, then pinch it."

Sawyer squeezed the tail fins instead of the shell.

Willow reached across the table with both hands and positioned the shrimp between Sawyers forefinger and thumb. "Now squeeze. You should feel it release inside the shell."

Sawyer did as instructed. Her eyes opened wide as she felt the shrimp tail nearly slip out of the shell.

"Now, suck it out by the head like this." Willow demonstrated by putting the meaty part of the shrimp in her mouth and sucking it out. "Try it."

"Mmm, that was easy."

"Now dip your next one in sauce before pinching it."

Amy approached the table with their dinners just as Sawyer perfectly maneuvered the next shrimp. "I see you're teaching her how to suck head, Wills."

"Very funny, Amy," Willow said.

"I thought so. Two haddock and fries dinners. Enjoy, ladies,"

Sawyer picked up another shrimp and shook it at Willow. "Why do I get the feeling there's another meaning to the phrase, 'suck head'?"

Willow grinned. "Some things are better left unsaid."

Sawyer ate another shrimp. "Wills, huh? Do many people call you that?"

"My friend Susan does occasionally, and my father, and of course, Amy. It was kind of a nickname when I was a kid."

"I like it."

"Try the haddock," Willow said.

Sawyer broke off a piece and dipped it in the tartar sauce before putting it in her mouth. "This is good. In England, we'd be dipping our fish in malt vinegar. We need to come here more often."

"I thought you'd like it. So, did you get all of your business done today while you were in town?"

"Yes, I did. Catherine faxed a few things for me to sign, and Matilda will be sending me a care package of clothing so I don't have to wear your clothes."

"I don't mind if you're in my pants," Willow said and chuckled.

"Very funny, Wills. I do appreciate your lending them to me. I also talked to the Council of Thirteen today about the apparitions you've seen over the past few days."

"And...?"

"The high priest doesn't think it's an evil soul who escaped from the gates of the underworld. He apparently has a group of followers who are especially sensitive to the comings and goings through the gates, and he feels they would have sensed a disturbance if that had happened."

"Then what could it be? Who could be haunting me?"

"I don't know, and that has me concerned."

# Chapter 35

## 1612—North Yorkshire, England

"Art thou all right?" Jenna said as she stood several feet behind Hadley who leaned over the basin while emptying the contents of her stomach.

Hadley reached toward Jenna and accepted the cloth handed to her. She wiped her mouth and sat in a nearby chair. Sweat adorned her brow. Jenna knelt at her side and tucked a strand of her wild red hair behind her ear. "Is there something I can do for thee?"

"'Tis three days now starting like this. I pray to the Goddess that 'tis not like this the whole nine moons."

Jenna sat back on her heels. "Nine moons? Hadley—dost thou think thou art with child? Dost thou think the conception ceremony worked?"

"I missed my moon cycle a fortnight ago, Jenna. I have no other reason for the sickness."

Jenna held both hands over her mouth while her eyes misted over. "Sweet Hecate." She grabbed Hadley's face between her hands and kissed her soundly.

Hadley pushed her away. "Begone with thee—my mouth is vile. If thou dost want to do something for me, bring water and let me rinse the foulness away."

Jenna ladled a cup of water out of the urn and brought it to Hadley. She waited patiently while Hadley drank then handed the cup back. "Art thou feeling better now?"

"A bit. Hast thou been much around wee ones, Jenna?"

"Nay. I was all of four years old when Caleb was birthed, and mother and father had no brothers or sisters, so there was no other kin around."

"Then we will be leaning on each other for this one. I have not been around wee ones much either."

Jenna knelt in front of Hadley and reached for her hands. "I vow to always be here for thee, Hadley Metcalf. I shall be the best wife and mother I can be."

"I will hold thee to that, Jenna Hawksworth, and I vow the same."

Jenna wrapped her arms around Hadley's mid-section and laid her head on her stomach. "Art thou happy about this, blacksmith?" Hadley asked.

"I am truly blessed. It means more to me than thou wilt ever know."

"So wilt thou be making love to me again, then?"

"By the gods, Jenna, it's been too long," Hadley said as she pulled Jenna's blouse over her head and threw it on the floor. "Been waiting all day for this."

Jenna grinned. "Thou must be feeling better, then," she said as she allowed Hadley to unbutton her trousers.

"It passes quickly after that first bit in the morning. I've missed thy touch, blacksmith. Take me to bed."

Jenna held her trousers up with one hand as she walked Hadley toward the bed with the other. When she reached the edge of the bed, she took Hadley's face between her hands and kissed her, gently at first, but with an increasing sense of urgency. Hadley opened her mouth to allow Jenna's tongue entry. Jenna moved across Hadley's chin and down her neck, nipping gently as she went. Hadley's moans enticed her to go farther as she reached for the hem of Hadley's skirts and pulled them upward over her head. She rained kisses across Hadley's collarbone and into the cleavage between her breasts.

"Jenna, thou makest me crazy. Pray, I need to feel thee."

Hadley pushed Jenna's trousers off her hips and grasped her buttocks.

Jenna's legs nearly buckled as she fought to maintain control of her own desires. She kicked off her trousers and placed one knee on the bed, taking Hadley down onto the mattress with her. She hovered over Hadley and moaned loudly as she felt her erect nipple being sucked into Hadley's mouth. "By the gods," she said as she arched her chest forward.

"I have been needing thee for a long time, Jenna."

Jenna had all she could do to hold herself above Hadley as she felt her other breast being nipped and suckled. Her abdomen constricted, and a wave of desire passed through her. Finally, she took Hadley's wrists, pinned them to the bed above her head, and placed her knee between Hadley's thighs. Hadley gyrated her hips against Jenna's knee, pushing them both nearly to the edge. Jenna's breathing was ragged as she devoured Hadley's mouth and moved again to Hadley's ear.

A deep growl emitted from Hadley's throat as she broke one hand free from Jenna's grasp and guided Jenna's hand to the flood of moisture between her legs. "Now, Jenna," she demanded. Jenna thrust deep into Hadley as Hadley sought out Jenna's moist spot. Nearly at the same time, the floodgates of desire burst and both of them plummeted over the cliff, muscles straining against the waves of contractions as their bodies sought relief. A sheen of sweat coated Jenna's back as she sought to bring fulfillment to Hadley, even in the wake of her own climax. Finally, it was over and Jenna lay like a damp rag on top of Hadley, her face buried in Hadley's neck.

Hadley wrapped her arms around Jenna and closed her eyes. "I love thee, Jenna Hawksworth."

"I love thee back, Hadley Metcalf."

"Blessed be."

# Chapter 36

## 2013—Plymouth, Massachusetts

"That was a wonderful meal, Willow. I thoroughly enjoyed it."

"I thought you might. I'm glad to see things haven't changed much. I haven't been to Moby Dick's in a long time."

"Why not?"

"Dining alone isn't my idea of fun."

"Don't you have friends you regularly spend time with?"

"Not really. There's a large LGBT community in Boston, but I live so far away, it's kind of inconvenient to go all the way home after work and come back into town later in the evening for any kind of date."

"I would think if someone really cared, they would come to you," Sawyer said softly.

Willow smiled. "That's very sweet of you to say."

"I just believe people worth having in your life are worth any inconvenience it may take to keep them there."

"I guess I just haven't met anyone yet that has felt that strongly about me."

They fell silent for several long moments.

"Sawyer, what do you think about these ghosts I've been seeing? I'm more than a little unnerved by them."

"I wish I knew what to think. It's getting late now, but while you're at work tomorrow, I'll cast some nested protection spells on your property. That should help."

"Nested protection spells? What do you mean?"

"Nested—kind of like a bulls-eye," Sawyer said. "I'll start

at the four corners of your property, then at the four corners of the house, and finally in the four corners of your bedroom."

"I see. What about tonight?"

"I would actually like to bunk with you tonight in your room. I'm curious to see if the apparition will return if there's someone else in the room. Is that okay with you?"

"As long as I don't have to be in there alone, I'm very okay with that."

\* \* \*

Willow threw her car keys on the table beside the door and headed straight up the stairs. "I'm going to take a quick shower before bed. I won't be long," she called over her shoulder. "I'll jump in right behind you," Sawyer said.

Sawyer went to the kitchen and helped herself to a glass of milk while she waited for Willow to shower. She stood with her backside leaning against the kitchen cabinet and thought about her host. *You are certainly growing on me, Willow McCord. I came here to offer you a business proposition in exchange for your participation in the repression, and instead, I find myself wanting to protect you. You may not know it, Willow, but your power is strong. I'll help you harness it, and together we will be successful. Life as we know it is about to change, for both of us.*

"Sawyer, the hot water is all yours," Willow called from the second floor.

The sound of Willow's voice broke Sawyer out of her reverie. She finished her milk, rinsed her glass, and headed for the stairs.

It was ten p.m. by the time Willow and Sawyer slipped into Willow's bed and turned off the light. They both lay on their backs, side by side.

"This bed is comfortable," Sawyer said.

"It's the memory foam mattress topper. Relax and you'll feel yourself sink into it."

"You're right," Sawyer replied.

Willow turned her face toward Sawyer. "I know you want me to go to England for the entire month prior to the repression, but can't you teach me all I need to know right here over the next two months?"

"I can give you a very good basis, but exposure to and immersion in the coven is really an important part of this." Sawyer propped herself on her elbows. "Were you denied the leave of absence?"

"No. Quite the contrary. They made it clear that my job would be waiting for me when I returned. They nearly made me promise I was indeed coming back. Susan was a little wigged out about it, but otherwise, I'm good to go."

"Susan is your co-worker, correct?"

"Yes, although there was a time I wished she was more than that."

"I see," Sawyer said.

"Unfortunately, Susan doesn't play with girls, if you know what I mean."

"Ahh. You said there was a time… don't you feel that way about her anymore?"

"There's only so long you can beat a dead horse before it begins to stink. I always knew I was wasting my time pining after her, but it was only recently that I decided to put it behind me and enjoy her friendship."

"Wise move."

"Yeah. Straight girl crushes are non-starters. However, they are safe."

"Do you always choose the safe path?"

"Yes… that is, until I met you."


Sometime around three in the morning, Sawyer was awakened by the sound of something creaking. She sat up in bed and saw a form standing by the tall dresser. Its back was facing her. Slowly, she reached into the backpack she had placed on the floor beside the bed and extracted a pentacle about the diameter of a baseball. She held it in front of her. "By the power of the Goddess, I banish you from this place," she chanted. The form whipped around, screeched, and faded away.

Willow awoke with a start and saw the figure as Sawyer

confronted it. She grabbed Sawyer's arm as the apparition disappeared. "Oh, my God."

Sawyer threw the covers off and sat up on the edge of the bed. She turned on the light on the bedside table. "It was after something." She walked to the tall dresser and saw that the top drawer was partially pulled out. *That must have been the creaking sound I heard.* She finished opening the drawer and looked inside. There lay the box containing the brooches. She picked up the box and returned to the bed. "This is what it was looking for," she said as she handed it to Willow.

"What does it mean?" Willow asked.

"Someone is trying to stop the repression."

"So, it's the brooches they want, and not me?"

"We can't be sure of that. The first apparition you saw—the woman standing in your window—had ample opportunity to take the brooches, but didn't. Willow, you need to keep them on you at all times from now on so that no one, or nothing, can gain access to them. They've been blessed by the Goddess. They are one of your best protections—particularly when clasped together."

"I'm scared, Sawyer."

Sawyer lay back down, pulled Willow with her, and wrapped her arms around her. Willow laid her head on Sawyer's shoulder and draped her arm over Sawyer's waist. Nestled in the hand trapped between her and Sawyer was the box containing the brooches.

Sawyer kissed her on the forehead. "I won't let anything harm you, Willow. I promise."

A rush of heat ran through Willow's chest as the box she held became warm. *What are you doing to me, Sawyer Hawksworth? My life was just fine before you began stalking me four days ago. You've turned my world upside down. Why do you intrigue me so? What is it about you that makes me want to throw caution to the wind? I don't know if what I feel is fear or excitement. What I do know is life will never be the same.*

\* \* \*

"I will place wards around the house and grounds while you're at work today, Willow," Sawyer said as she poured coffee for the two of them.

"Thank you," Willow said when Sawyer handed a cup of coffee to her. "If they're after me because I'm one of the chosen, wouldn't they also be after you?"

"Yes, but it seems whoever is behind this knows I have the means and knowledge to stop them. You, on the other hand, are much more vulnerable. That's one of the reasons you need to immerse yourself in the teachings and practices of the coven."

"I'm beginning to think Daddy was right to worry about you."

"I'm not the one you need to be concerned about. I would never hurt you."

"No, but if you hadn't sent me your brooch, none of this would have happened. Don't you think that maybe, just maybe, the brooches act like a homing signal, especially when they're locked together?"

"That's exactly what's happening. It's a double-edged sword. On one hand, they are a homing mechanism, but on the other, they allow the Goddess to protect you... if you believe."

Willow looked into her coffee cup and tried to control her emotions. Nonetheless, a small quiver entered her voice. "You said you wouldn't let anyone hurt me."

Sawyer put her coffee down on the countertop and took Willow's from her and set it on the table. She then wrapped her arms around Willow and held her close. By instinct, Willow's arms went around Sawyer's waist. Willow began to cry.

"Don't cry. I'll do everything in my power to protect you. Please believe that." Sawyer kissed her on the temple and felt Willow's embrace around her waist tighten. "Are you all right?"

Willow nodded.

"Good." Sawyer tilted her head back so she could look directly at Willow. The fear in her eyes clenched at her heart like a vise. "I'm so sorry. I wish I could spare you this."

Sawyer's gaze locked with Willow's, and by some force, she was drawn to Willow's lips. Her hands rose to cup Willow's face between them. Tentative at first, she allowed her lips to brush across Willow's. She felt Willow pull her closer, fueling her courage to deepen the kiss. Every fiber of her being screamed as the fire consumed her. Finally, her senses returned. She ended the kiss and rested her forehead against Willow's. "I'm sorry. That shouldn't have happened," Sawyer said softly.

"It wouldn't have if I hadn't allowed it," Willow replied.

Sawyer kissed her again, very tenderly, then broke the embrace and stepped back. "If you don't get out of here, I won't be responsible for what might happen next."

"I do have to go to work," Willow replied.

Sawyer nodded and stepped aside to allow Willow to pass. She stood in the front doorway and watched Willow start up her car. She stood there until Willow was long out of sight. "Hawksworth," she said, "you're in big trouble."

# Chapter 37

## 2013—Boston, Massachusetts

"She kissed you? You actually let her kiss you? Willow, you've only known her for what—five days? Are you sure that's wise?" Susan asked as they worked to restock the hygienist stations in the office.

"How long did you know Larry before you let him kiss you?" Willow asked.

"Okay, busted, but he didn't just show up out of the blue one day from halfway around the world. I knew him for quite a while before we hooked up as a couple."

"Are you telling me you may not have fallen in love with him if you hadn't known him before you became involved?"

"Yes. No. I guess I don't know what I'm saying. This just seems really odd. First this Sawyer person shows up and stalks you, then she moves into your house and somehow extracts a commitment out of you to take a month off from work and spend it with her in England, of all places. And now she kisses you, and I suppose you didn't resist?"

"I couldn't resist. She has some kind of power over me, Susan. I wanted her to kiss me, and damn, my toes are still curled up inside my shoes."

"Willow, promise me you'll be careful. I hate to judge people I've never met, but something about this doesn't feel right."

"I'll be careful, Suze. I promise."

\* \* \*

Sawyer searched through Willow's cupboards until she found where the spices were stored. "Ah, that's what I'm looking for." She grabbed a nearly full canister of sea salt. Next, she located a five-gallon bucket in the garage and filled it with water into which she emptied half the container of salt. She stirred it with a large wooden spoon and searched the kitchen drawers until she found a two-cup measure. She carried the bucket of salt water and the measuring cup to the far corner of the property and methodically poured a continuous thin line of water around the four sides of the property while chanting, "Mother of the Earth, mother of fertility, protector of the underworld, Goddess Hecate, guard and protect this house and everything and everyone in it from all evil." Halfway through the ritual, the text alarm on her phone sounded off. Not wanting to break the flow of the spell, Sawyer ignored it and completed the ring of protection around the house.

Next, she took more sea salt and repeated the chant at each window and door as she sprinkled a line of salt across every threshold and sill. Finally, she carried what was left of the sea salt and a large ceramic plate from the kitchen cupboard to the guest room and collected her knapsack, which she took to Willow's room.

She removed a blue candle, a lighter, and a bundle of sage from her bag and sat on the floor. She placed the candle in the middle of the plate and created a circle of salt around it. Then she lit the candle and meditated to create a source of light around herself. Next, she lit the sage and carried it to all four corners of the room beginning with the East, then South, West, and North, waving the sage gently at each corner. When she was satisfied the smoke had adequately saturated each corner, she extinguished the sage and put it inside the circle of salt around the candle. She then sprinkled a pinch of sea salt in each corner of the room in the same order as the sage. Finally, she returned to the candle and sat cross-legged on the floor in front of it.

"Beings of light, far and wide, this spell I cast, you shall abide. With sage and salt and guiding light, I banish all evil from this site. Mother Goddess, I beseech of thee, rid this home

191

and make it free. As I will it, so shall it be." Sawyer then carried the plate containing the lit candle and circle of salt to the dresser where she left it to burn down.

As she descended the stairs to the living room, her text alarm went off a second time. She pulled her phone out of her pocket and opened the text application. She had two incoming messages, both from Bridgit. Sawyer frowned. I wonder what she wants?

She opened the first message. *Sawyer, call me. You cannot stay there for two more months. We have to talk.* "Like hell I will," Sawyer mumbled before opening the second text. Damn it, Sawyer. I don't know what you're up to, but it won't work. Sawyer sighed.

"Bridgit, why don't you just take a hint and leave me alone?"

* * *

"I'm running to pick up lunch," Willow said to Susan. "Do you want anything?"

"Sounds wonderful. I'll call it in. Do you want your usual?"

"Yes. Tell them I'll be there in about twenty minutes."

Willow left her office building and walked two blocks to the parking garage. She climbed three flights of stairs to where her car was parked on the fourth level. She looked around as she exited the stairwell and realized her car was the only one on that level. That was odd, she thought. There was barely an empty parking spot when she got to work just four hours ago. She shrugged and walked across the empty garage. As she got to within six feet of her car, a rust-colored sedan with dark tinted windows came tearing down the ramp from the level above and headed straight for her. She had all she could do to leap onto the hood of her car to avoid being run over.

"What the fuck? Asshole!" Willow screamed. She slid off the hood and brushed the dust from her scrubs. "Son of a bitch! He could have killed me!" She leaned against her car and tried to compose herself. "Fuck! Calm down, Willow. I need to tell

Sawyer about this." She pulled out her cell phone and called her home number. *Hey there! This is Willow. I'm not home at the moment, so leave me a message at the beep. Beep!*

"Sawyer, pick up the phone. This is Willow. Someone just tried to kill me."

"Willow? Where are you?" Sawyer asked.

"I'm in the parking garage. Someone just tried to run me down."

"Why are you in the parking garage?"

"I'm going out to pick up lunch."

"And where are the brooches?"

"Ah… in the car."

"In the car? I told you to keep them on you at all times. They won't afford you much protection if they're in the car."

"Yeah, yeah."

"Damn it, Willow. You need to take this seriously."

"I know… I know."

"Did you see who it was?"

"No. The windows were tinted dark. Sawyer, tell me this isn't another ghost."

"I doubt that ghosts drive cars."

"Then who the hell is trying to kill me? If I find the motherfucker he's dead meat!"

"Willow, get in your car and lock all your doors right now."

Sawyer waited a few moments to give her time to get into the vehicle. "Are they locked?"

"Yes."

"Now go pick up lunch, but try to stay where there are a lot of people. Whoever is doing this won't do anything in front of a lot of witnesses. And for crying out loud, take the brooches with you. When you get back to the parking garage, park in your usual place if you can and stay in the car. I'm on my way to meet you there. I'm going to be sure you make it back to your office safe and sound and then wait for you to get out of work."

"Really? I mean, it just might have been some random lunatic in the parking garage."

"Until we know what's going on, I'm not taking any chances. I will be there waiting for you in the parking garage.

Now, deal with it. If you get there before I do, wait for me. Do not get out of your car. Do you understand?"

Willow didn't answer right away.

"Damn it, Willow. I said do you understand?"

"Yeah, yeah, yeah. You're such a mother hen."

\* \* \*

Sawyer grabbed her cell phone and car keys and ran out the door. She synced her phone with the media system in the car so that her cell phone became a hands-free device. She immediately called England.

"Lord Somers," Sawyer said to the high priest.

"Sawyer, so good to hear from you. How are the preparations coming with Willow?"

"Lord Somers, I can't do this."

"You can't do what?"

Sawyer could hear the caution in the high priest's voice. "I can't put Willow in danger any longer. I won't put her in danger anymore."

"I'm not sure I approve of your tone, Sawyer. You knew there was the possibility of danger for both of you."

"Someone tried to run her down today in the parking garage. And she was visited by another apparition last night. I was witness to it as well. It was trying to get the brooches."

"It appears there's some external force at work here. As I said before, I don't believe it's a soul from the underworld, at least not the incident in the parking garage. You need to determine who, or what, is behind this, Sawyer. Willow must participate in the repression ceremony. We cannot have anything happen to her before then."

"And what about after the repression? What happens to Willow then?"

"She must produce an heir. After that, her fate is up to the Goddess."

"Forgive me, Lord Somers, but it is now I who do not approve of your tone. Willow is not disposable. I will not allow her to be harmed in any way."

"You may not be able to stop it."

"I understand the importance of her role in the repression, but this is non-negotiable."

"Sawyer, are you sleeping with the girl?" the high priest asked coyly.

"We have not had carnal relations," Sawyer said.

"I hear an unspoken 'yet' in your statement. I caution you to not allow feelings you may have for this girl to influence your commitment to the Goddess—or to the coven."

"My commitment runs deep, but I won't allow it to be at the expense of Willow's life."

"So be it. I'll start an investigation within the coven relative to potential assassins. I suggest you do the same on your end. I'll inform you as soon as I know more."

"Thank you, Lord Somers. Blessed be."

* * *

When Sawyer pulled into the parking garage, Willow was already there. As luck would have it, there was one space available next to Willow's car. The rest of the garage was full. Sawyer parked her car and climbed into the front seat next to Willow. She immediately took Willow into her arms. "Are you all right?" she asked.

"Other than having the shit scared out of me, yes."

"Have you been here long?"

"No, I pulled in no more than five minutes before you. I went to pick up lunch for Susan and me. I got something for you as well if you'd like to join us."

"You're going to introduce me to your co-worker?"

"Why not?"

"If you think that's all right."

"Why wouldn't it be? Look, Susan is about the only friend I have. Granted, she's a straight girl and we don't really spend any time together outside of work, but she's a good friend. I think you'll like her."

Sawyer got out of Willow's car and walked around the front to open her door for her. "Do you have the brooches on you?"

"They're right here in my purse."

"Okay then, lead the way."

They walked the two blocks to the dental office, passing Pete's stand along the way.

"Hi ya there, Miss Sawyer. Good to see you again," Pete said.

Sawyer hugged Pete. "The pleasure's all mine, Pete. Are you having a good day?"

"Mighty fine. You take care of that pretty lady now, ya hear?"

"She doesn't make it easy, Pete," Sawyer joked.

"Have yourself a fine day, ladies."

"You too, Pete," they said in unison.

Sawyer held the door open for Willow to enter, and they waited for the elevator in silence. Willow looked at Sawyer. "Are you nervous about meeting Susan?"

"Somewhat."

"Well I have to warn you that she thinks this whole thing is a bit off the wall."

"What whole thing? Did you tell her about the repression?"

"Hell, no—she'd be ordering up a straight jacket for me for sure. No, she thinks this whole 'relationship' with you is moving extraordinarily fast."

"Would you say this is a relationship?" Sawyer asked.

"I can't speak for you Brits, but I generally don't go around kissing people I'm not in a relationship with."

The bell rang for the fourth floor. "Are you ready?" Willow asked.

"As ready as I can be."

Sawyer followed Willow into the dental office and down the hall to the break room.

"You're back! I was wondering if you got lost," Susan said. "And who do we have here?" she asked, looking Sawyer up and down.

"Susan Davis, meet Sawyer Hawksworth," Willow said.

Sawyer extended her hand. "It's nice to make your

acquaintance, Ms. Davis."

Susan looked at Willow as she shook Sawyer's hand. "Ooh. A polite one... and with a sexy accent to boot. It's nice to meet you as well, Sawyer. Call me Susan. Willow has talked a lot about you over the past few days."

"All good, I hope," Sawyer said.

"I recall a comment about curled toes. I'd say that's good. Ow! What was that for, Willow?" Susan rubbed her arm while trying to hide a grin.

"Sawyer was in town taking care of some business when we ran into each other in the sandwich shop, so I invited her along to have lunch with us," Willow said.

Sawyer raised an eyebrow to Willow behind Susan's back.

Willow just smiled sweetly.

"Well, I'm glad you could come. It's nice to put a face to the name," Susan said. "Have a seat."

For the next hour, Sawyer entertained Susan with stories about how her and Willow's great-grandmothers had been good friends who volunteered for the USO together, and how as a child, she was intrigued with the person who was Maggie McCord. Sawyer explained that her curiosity got the best of her when she learned Maggie had a great-granddaughter close to her own age, so she decided to investigate and thus found Willow.

Willow raised an eyebrow to Sawyer behind Susan's back at her ability to manufacture her own tall tail. Sawyer just smiled.

"So how do the brooches figure in?" Susan asked.

"Actually," Sawyer said, "that's what prompted my search. You see the brooches belonged to our great-grandmothers. Mine was passed down to me, and I was curious to see whether Maggie passed hers down to Willow."

"Willow showed them to me. They're beautiful."

"Yes they are."

"I hate to break up the fun, kiddos, but we need to get back to work," Willow said.

"Yes, I'm afraid I'm overstaying my welcome," Sawyer said.

"If you will excuse me, ladies," she said shaking hands

with Susan again.

"I'll walk you to the elevator," Willow said. She turned around to look at Susan just before she walked out of the office and grinned as she saw Susan mouth the words, "I like her."

# Chapter 38

## 1613—North Yorkshire, England

Hadley walked arm in arm toward the tailor shop with Jenna. At six months, her protruding abdomen was overly large and cumbersome.

"How art thou feeling, this morn?" Jenna asked.

"Like a cow. Great Goddess, I do not know how I can go three more months. I will be as big as a house by then."

"Methinks thou art beautiful, Hadley."

"Well, thou mayest be the only one who thinks that. The town folk are looking at me odd."

"Odd, how?"

"Mrs. Williamson and Mrs. Thomas were talking about me in the shop yester morn like I'm deaf or something. They were guessing who the sire of the babe is and saying less than kind words about a woman with child but no husband."

"Doth that bother thee, Hadley?"

"Aye. More that I want it to. I am a good person, Jenna— kind and generous. 'Tis hurting to hear things said about me."

"They are ignorant gossips. Pay them no mind. The people who love thee know how kind thou art. The rest of them be damned."

"Caleb was in the shop when they spoke ill of me. He wanted to tell them he was the sire, just to keep them quiet. I forbid him to. He is a nice young man who needs not the reputation of making a lass with child, then not caring for the mother and babe."

Jenna squeezed Hadley's hand. "Thou art a fine woman. Don't let them make thee feel anything but."

Hadley stopped walking and looked at Jenna. "I fear for the

child."

Jenna frowned. "Fear, how?"

"In the eyes of the town, the babe will be a bastard. Thou knowest how bastards are treated by bigoted folk."

Anger filled Jenna's eyes. "Damn them all. To punish a wee one for a deed not of their own making is sinful. May they all rot in the fires of Tartarus."

"Cool thine ire, Jenna. 'Twill do no good for thee, nor the babe."

They began slowly walking again toward the tailor shop.

"Jenna," Hadley said. "I have been thinking a lot about the life we will give the little one."

"Aye? And what is thy thought?"

"I want to leave this town. Leave it all behind."

Jenna stopped and took Hadley by the shoulders. "Art thou serious, woman?"

"Aye, 'tis so."

"Why wouldst thou be wanting to do such a thing?"

"For the reasons I already said. The town folk shall be unkind to our child, and I shall never be able to hold my head up with pride because they will be thinking I am a wanton woman. My business already suffereth for it."

"'Tis really?"

"Aye. Since the babe began showing in my belly, business has dropped off."

"Where shall we go? What shall we do?"

"We can live in the community of the coven. Thou sayest thyself they need a blacksmith, and there is never an end to clothes that need mending or sewn."

"Dost thou really want to do this?"

"Our baby would be loved in the coven. It would be accepted. It would be chosen, and we have skills to share with the others. What sayest thou?"

"I say I will be going to Billingham on the morrow to discuss it with the high priest."

Jenna knocked on the door of the blacksmith boarding

room with no response. "Caleb, art thou sleeping in there?" Still no response. "Where is that boy?" Jenna mumbled to herself as she walked across the common toward Hadley's house.

"Sister," Caleb called from across the square.

"Caleb Hawksworth, where in Tartarus hast thou been?"

"At the tavern having me some dinner." Caleb placed his hand on Jenna's shoulder. "Thou dost look concerned, sister. What is bothering thee?"

"I need thee to look in on Hadley for the next few days. I will be taking a trip to Billingham."

"Why art thou going there?"

"Hadley wants to move into the community of the coven, so I shall discuss this with the high priest."

"Thou art serious, sister? Methinks that is a wonderful idea. I didn't want to be making thee angry, but the town folk haven't been treating thy woman well. A woman with child and no husband is marked."

"So Hadley tells me."

"If thou and Hadley go to the coven, then I will be going as well."

"But thou hast a good job here, Caleb."

"'Tis only a job. 'Tis not my family. I can find work in the town nearest the coven, or perchance in the coven itself. It concerns me not."

"So wouldst thou keep an eye on Hadley while I am gone?"

"Thou canst count on me, sister."

* * *

"Lord Weller, thank thee for an audience. I have an important matter to discuss with thee."

The high priest put his hand on Jenna's shoulder. "How is Hadley, and the wee one?"

"That doth be just what I need to talk to thee about."

"They are well?" he asked, a tinge of concern in his voice.

"They are well."

"Good. So what is it thou needest to say?"

"Hadley fears for the child. She fears 'twill be marked as a bastard."

"She is right to be concerned. 'Tis true some folk punish the babe for what they see as sins of the parents."

"Lord Weller, Hadley wants to sell everything and live in the community of the coven."

The high priest smiled broadly. "She is a smart woman. And it seems she also is a fortune teller. The council discussed this very thing but a day ago."

"'Tis so?"

"Aye. The community of the coven shall welcome all into our family, and by right of sire, thy brother Caleb is welcome as well."

Jenna clasped forearms with the high priest. "Lord Weller, we shall earn our way. My blacksmith skills are in need in the coven, and Hadley is an amazing seamstress."

"'Tis a good match, Jenna Hawksworth. The child should be near six months by now, 'tis so?"

"Aye."

"Then the move must happen anon before it becomes difficult for Hadley to travel for two days."

"It shall be done, Lord Weller. Thou hast my gratitude."

"Blessed be, Jenna."

\* \* \*

"Is there room on the wagon for the bed?" Hadley asked.

"We'll make room, sister," Caleb said. "But I thought thou wouldst be leaving the furnishings to the new owner."

"All but the bed. I was fortunate to get a handsome price for the lot of it."

Jenna came out of the house carrying a basket of clothing. "Methinks that's the last of it."

Caleb jumped down from the wagon. "We will be taking the bed, sister. Back inside with thee to give me a hand with it."

A half hour later, the bed was strapped down on top of the pile of other personal effects in the wagon: Hadley's bolts of cloth and seamstress tools, Jenna's blacksmith tools, clothing for all three of them, the bed, larder supplies, firewood, and the baby cradle Caleb was crafting by hand. There was barely enough room for Caleb to squeeze into the wagon while Jenna and Hadley rode on the seat. A curious group of onlookers gathered to watch them leave.

"Go back to your lives, good people, and remember us fondly," Jenna said.

A few hundred paces down the road, Caleb spoke up. "How canst thou be treating them so kindly when they are ornery with Hadley?"

"The Goddess teaches forgiveness, Caleb. Thou wouldst be wise to learn the ways of the clan if thou wilt be living in the coven."

Caleb nodded his head. "Aye. I just may do that."

\* \* \*

"Jenna. Jenna, wake with thee. Be quick about it."

Jenna shot up in bed. "What is it, Hadley? Art thou all right?"

"The bed is wet."

"Thou hast had an accident?"

"Methinks not. Quick, light the candle."

Hadley pushed the covers away as soon as the candle was lit. She was lying in a puddle of bloody mucous. Jenna was visibly shaken by the sight of so much blood.

"Sweet Hecate, Hadley! I need to get help."

"Be quick with thee," Hadley said. "By the gods," she added as a cramp doubled her over.

Jenna barely had time to pull her trousers on before she ran out the door and across the common area toward the midwife's quarters. She banged loudly on the door. "Lizabet! Lizabet, comest thou quickly!"

An elderly woman opened the door a crack to see who was making all the ruckus.

"Lizabet, Hadley needs help. She is bleeding."

"Calm thyself, blacksmith. Thou wilt do her no good with thy panic." Lizabet reached for her robe. "'Tis early for the babe to come. She is only eight months. Get Lord Weller. We shall need prayers to the Goddess to help her through this. Come back to thy quarters as soon as thou canst. I shall be with her when thou returnest."

Jenna returned to their quarters about fifteen minutes later with the high priest in tow. She ran to the bed and fell to her knees. She picked up Hadley's hand just as a contraction tore through her.

"Ahhh, make it stop," Hadley screamed.

"Thou art doing fine, Hadley. Thou hast a ways to go yet. Don't wear thyself out," Lizabet said.

"What is happening?" Jenna asked.

"The baby is coming," the midwife replied.

"'Tis too soon."

"Babes come when they are ready. Blacksmith, come over here and help me with the purification water."

Jenna leaned in and kissed Hadley on the forehead. "I will be right back." Jenna joined the midwife by the table.

"Didst thou get the things on the list I gave thee?" Lizabet asked.

"Yes."

"Well, go get them, girl. They won't walk over here by themselves."

Jenna ran to the chest by the fireplace and pulled out a burlap bag that she carried back to the table. Just then, Hadley screamed as another contraction hit her. Jenna immediately went to her side.

"Blacksmith. I need thee over here. She will be fine."

Jenna reluctantly returned to the table.

"Put the herbs onto the table and bring the basin over here. Thou needest to warm some water over the fire."

Jenna handed the basin to Lizabet. She returned to the fireplace, poured some water from the urn into a metal pan, and placed it directly on top of the coals. She looked nervously back at Hadley while she waited for the water to warm. Lizabet sorted the herbs on the table, reciting each herb by name, "Verbena, olive, rue, rosemary, oak, pine, acacia, rose, carnation, thyme, basil, jasmine, and mistletoe. Very good." She reached into her bag for a mortar and pestle and ground the herbs into a fine powder. "Is the water warm yet, Jenna?" she asked.

Jenna stuck her little finger into the water. "Aye. Not hot, but warm."

"Ahhh. Goddess, pray take this child from my womb," Hadley cried as she clutched the bed sheets.

"Bring the water to the table, Jenna, and pour the herbs into it while I see to Hadley," Lizabet said. "Lord Weller, pray grant thy blessings on this child. 'Twill be with us anon."

"Aye," the priest said as he approached the bed. Lizabet lifted the sheet to assess how far the labor had progressed.

"Sweet Goddess," the high priest said when he realized there were three tiny arms extending from Hadley's vagina. He stepped back, fear evident on his face.

"What is it?" Jenna said as she carried the water to the bed."Holy Mother Goddess," Jenna whispered. She looked across the expanse of stomach to Hadley's face.

"Jenna, tell me. What is the matter? Ahhh!" Hadley slammed her head into the pillow once more, her face red from enduring the pain.

Jenna handed the basin of water to the midwife and went to Hadley's side. She wiped the sweat from Hadley's brow. "'Twill be over anon. I promise."

"This one doth be birthing chest first. Jenna, thou needest to hold her down. I have to push the wee one back in and turn it around. 'Twill be painful for her."

Jenna sat on the bed beside Hadley and took her into her arms. "Hold on to me, love."

"What's wrong with the babe? Tell me," Hadley said. "By the gods!" she suddenly screamed as she arched her back and pressed into Jenna. She grit her teeth and dug her nails into Jenna's arm as a low-pitched growl emitted from deep within her.

"I've got thee, love." Jenna held her close while the midwife manipulated the position of the baby inside the birth canal.

"Nearly there, Hadley," Lizabet said. "That's it. The head is out."

Jenna leaned forward over Hadley's stomach for a better

view just in time to see the child slip out of the birth canal into Lizabet's arms. "Sweet Hecate," she whispered.

"'Tis a boy," Lizabet said as she held the infant high enough for Hadley to see.

Hadley began to cry. "A boy? We have a son, Jenna," she choked out between her tears. "He hath red hair like his mama," Jenna said. "He is a beautiful lad."

Lizabet tied and cut the umbilical cord then soaked a cloth in the herb water and washed the afterbirth from the baby's face.

Jenna got off the bed and walked to the foot next to where the little boy lay. She looked him over. "Lizabet, he hath two arms."

"Of course he hath two arms. What didst thou expect?"

"I… I saw three." Jenna looked to the priest who stood in the corner. "Lord Weller?"

"Aye, I saw it, too," the high priest replied.

Just then, Hadley screamed as another contraction tore through her.

"What's happening?" Jenna asked, her voice panic stricken.

"The next one is birthing," Lizabet said.

"Next one?"

"Aye. Where didst thou think the other arm came from?"

"Twins?"

"Twins," Lizabet said.

Jenna returned to Hadley's side. "Hadley, there are two babes. Thou art birthing twins!"

Hadley grabbed the front of Jenna's shirt and yanked her close. "I don't care what they are—just get them out!"

# Chapter 39

## 2013—Boston, Massachusetts

Willow stepped onto the sidewalk and looked around for Sawyer, who was nowhere to be seen. After a few minutes, she fished the brooches out of her purse and held them tightly in her hand while she headed toward the parking garage. She walked one of the two blocks between her office and the garage when she suddenly found herself swung around by the elbow.

"Didn't I say I'd be here after you got off work?" Sawyer said gruffly.

Willow yanked her arm loose. "You weren't there. I waited for a few minutes, and when you didn't show, I decided to go. I wasn't going to wait all day."

"What time do you get out of work, Willow?"

"Five o'clock. Why?"

Sawyer pulled up her sleeve and showed Willow her watch. "And what time is it now?"

Willow looked at Sawyer's watch. "Four fifty-five."

"Exactly. Would it have been so hard to wait five or ten minutes? If I say I'm going to be somewhere, I'll be there. Remember that next time."

Willow turned and walked toward the parking garage.

Sawyer hurried to catch up with her. "What's wrong now?"

"I don't need to be lectured. In case you haven't noticed, I'm a big girl. I don't need a babysitter."

Sawyer placed her right hand on her hip and ran her left hand through her hair. "Look, I'm sorry, but I was worried about you."

"Yeah, I know. I'm important to the repression. Whatever."

Sawyer grasped her shoulder. "You're important to me."

"Would that still be true without the uprising?"

"Yes."

"But you haven't known me for very long."

"I have known *of* you all of my life."

Willow's eyes brimmed with moisture as an overpowering sense of emotion filled her.

Sawyer took her arm. "Come on. Let's go home."

Sawyer pulled into the driveway behind Willow and got out of her own car to open Willow's door for her while she collected her purse and jacket. Just then, another text came into her phone.

"Thank you." Willow climbed out of the car. "Someone just texted you," she said on their way to the house. She noticed the line of salt across the front doorway. "What the hell?"

"You'll see that at all external access points—doors and windows. I initiated a protection ritual that will hopefully keep the apparitions away."

"I remember. The nested spells you talked about earlier."

"Exactly."

Willow opened her mouth to speak but changed her mind and entered the house. Sawyer touched her arm.

"What were you going to say?"

Willow dropped her purse on the coffee table and kicked off her shoes. "I don't know. This all seems so unreal. I mean, what if the spells are nothing but words? What if they have no influence at all?"

"They will indeed be useless if you don't believe. After what you've seen and experienced in these past few days, why are you still skeptical?"

"It's hard to explain. The apparitions, I believe are real. I saw them with my own eyes. The incident in the parking garage today could have been a total coincidence. If there's something dark and sinister after me... after us, I have a hard time believing a few words and rituals will stop them."

"You need to trust me, Willow. Your life may depend on it."

"And what exactly does that mean?"

"I spoke with the high priest today. There's not much he can do from England to prevent anything from harming you. That task will fall on me. He'll begin an investigation to find the source of these apparitions, but he doesn't hold out much hope."

"So he thinks there's a specific individual responsible for sending these demons to me? Is that what you're saying?"

"Anything is possible."

"And he expects you to protect me?"

"Yes."

"What if they're stronger than you?"

"If I can't protect you, then I will die trying."

Willow walked up to Sawyer and stopped within a few inches of her. "Listen to yourself. Do you know how crazy you sound?"

"Is your father crazy? He collaborated with me on everything. Do you trust him?"

"Of course I trust him. He's my father."

"Then why don't you trust me?"

Willow sat down on the couch and covered her face with her hands. "I don't know what to think. All I know is that since you came into my life, everything has gone to shit. Everything has turned upside down."

Sawyer sat on the coffee table in front of Willow. She reached forward and took Willow's hands in her own. "I'm sorry, Willow. Believe me when I say I wish things could be different. I didn't ask for this any more than you did. But like it or not, this has fallen on our shoulders. I for one want to put this behind us so we can go on with our lives."

"So that we can go on with *our* lives? As in you and I—together?"

Sawyer's gaze locked with Willow's. "If you'll have me."

Willow's eye misted over once more, and tears spilled onto her cheeks. Sawyer knelt on the floor in front of Willow and pulled her in close.

"It breaks my heart to see you cry," Sawyer said softly into her ear.

Willow pulled back and rested her forehead on Sawyer's. "I'm sorry. I'm such a baby sometimes."

"It's all right."

Willow sat back and wiped the tears from her cheeks. "Are you hungry?" she asked.

"Not especially."

"It's too early for bed, what do you want to do?"

"Who says it's too early for bed?"

"My room or yours?"

"Yours. I want to see if the protection spell is working."

"Okay."

Sawyer rose to her feet and held her hand out. Willow slipped her hand inside Sawyer's, and together, they walked up the stairs to Willow's room. Willow stopped as soon as she crossed the threshold. "What's that smell?"

"Sage. I used it to purify the corners of the room. Do you find it distasteful?"

"No, not at all. In fact, it smells nice."

"There's some left on the plate over there." Sawyer pointed to the plate on the dresser that contained the remains of the candle she had lit earlier in the day. "Do you want me to light it?"

"Please."

Sawyer lit the sage, placed it on top of the melted wax on the plate, and turned back to Willow. She stood in front of her and ran her fingers down the outside of Willow's right arm. "You are so beautiful," she whispered.

Willow shivered as Sawyer's touch sent a burning sensation down her spine. Their gazes locked.

Sawyer placed her right hand on Willow's cheek and very lightly brushed her lips against Willow's. She closed her eyes and inhaled Willow's scent. "Do you have any idea what you do to me?"

"I'm pretty sure I know, but tell me anyway," Willow said.

"Better yet, show me."

Sawyer took Willow's face between her hands and kissed her passionately, her tongue fighting for dominance and space. Willow pulled Sawyer's shirttail out of the back of her pants and worked to unbutton the front.

"Damned buttons." Willow broke the kiss and began pulling the button-up shirt over Sawyer's head. "Off with this."

Sawyer helped her remove the shirt, which Willow discarded on the floor. She then pulled Willow's scrub top over her head. "Sweet goddess, you are so beautiful," Sawyer said as she ran her hands across Willow's collarbones and down her arms. Willow unhooked Sawyer's belt and pants and pulled down the zipper. She slid her hands into the back of Sawyer's boxers and rested her forehead on the space between Sawyer's breasts as she gently squeezed her buttocks. "I need to feel you."

Sawyer took Willow by the shoulders and sat her on the bed, then she pushed on her shoulders until she was lying on her back with her feet still on the floor. Sawyer made short work of Willow's scrubs pants, which joined the other clothing in a rapidly growing pile on the floor.

Willow sat up and grabbed Sawyer's waistband. She pulled her in to stand between her legs, her face even with Sawyer's navel, which she immediately invaded with her tongue.

Sawyer placed shaking hands behind Willow's head. "By the gods, Willow," she moaned.

Willow slipped her hands into Sawyer's boxers once more and pushed them downward, along with the trousers, all the while trailing her tongue from Sawyer's navel to the top of her dark tangle.

Willow looked up and held Sawyer's gaze as she slipped one finger between the folds of Sawyer's womanhood. Willow's desire grew as she watched Sawyer's eyes roll back under hooded lids and heard her moan in pleasure.

Sawyer stepped back out of easy reach of Willow's wandering fingers. "Not too fast," she said as she removed her sports bra and threw it on the floor. "Lay back."

Willow lay lengthwise on the bed while Sawyer knelt on the bed between her knees. She reached down and slipped Willow's panties off her buttocks and down her thighs, bending her knees into her chest in order to remove them completely. She then reached under Willow and unsnapped her bra, which quickly joined the other clothing on the floor. Sawyer sat back on her heels and closed her eyes for several long moments.

"What are you doing?" Willow asked.

"I am thanking the Goddess for bringing you into my life. I am truly blessed."

"Come here," Willow said.

Sawyer slowly lowered herself onto Willow, breast to breast, as she lay between Willow's open legs. She propped herself up on her elbows, positioned on each side of Willow. Once again, she claimed Willow's mouth in a passionate kiss. Willow raked her nails down Sawyer's back, inflaming both of them even more. Sawyer pressed herself into Willow's core. "Sweet Goddess, I want you," she said.

"What's stopping you?" Willow pushed Sawyer downward.

Sawyer placed one knee on the bed and slowly slid down the front of Willow. She stopped at her breasts and took each erect bud into her mouth, one at a time, nipping gently until small whimpers escaped Willow's lips. She ran her tongue along the tender skin of Willow's hip and followed the crease of her leg.

Willow pushed Sawyer's head toward her heated center and lifted her pelvis in invitation.

"Patience," Sawyer said as she slipped her hands under Willow's cheeks and squeezed gently.

"Now, Sawyer. I need you now."

Sawyer blew a stream of warm air across Willows damp curls.

"Oh God," Willow moaned.

With two fingers, Sawyer parted the curls and traced the outer layers of folds with her tongue.

Willow spasmed.

Sawyer took the swollen bud between her teeth and gently sucked while at the same time she inserted two fingers deep into her.

Willow's hips came off the bed as she pushed herself closer to Sawyer. "Oh, my God!" she screamed. "Harder. God... Sawyer, more, please."

Sawyer added another finger and drove deep into her over and over. Soon, Willow stiffened and clenched around her fingers. Sawyer turned her hand palm up and massaged the front of Willow's vagina. Wave after wave of spasms wracked Willow's body until suddenly she fell still and sank into the bed. Sawyer carefully extracted her hand. She crawled back up Willow's body and lay partially on top of her, with her head buried in Willow's neck.

"Good God, Sawyer. No one has ever made me feel like that before. Thank you."

"My pleasure."

Willow worked her way out from under Sawyer. "Come here," she said as she patted the center of the bed. Sawyer rolled over until she was on her back facing Willow.

"My turn," Willow said.

"I assure you," Sawyer said, "this won't take long. I could hardly hold it back when you climaxed."

Willow reached between Sawyer's legs. "My God, you're drenched."

"Your fault," Sawyer said.

"Guilty as charged."

Sawyer's body arched as Willow's fingers teased her sensitive folds. She reached down and grasped Willow's wrist to still her hand.

Willow looked at the mask of concentration on Sawyer's face. "You're that close, huh?"

Sawyer just nodded and clenched her jaw.

Willow got to her knees and lowered herself between Sawyer's legs. "I guess we need to take care of that sooner rather than later." In one swift movement, Willow drove three fingers into Sawyer while running her tongue over the swollen bud and damp folds.

Sawyer completely lost all control. Her whole body convulsed with orgasmic spasms. "By the Gods, Willow! Ahh! Harder."

Willow came to her knees in order to increase the force and velocity of her thrusts. "Let it go," Willow whispered. "That's it, love. Give it all to me." She slowed the cadence of her thrusts as the spasms abated, finally falling still. She could feel Sawyer's muscles pulse around her fingers for several minutes. Finally, she removed her hand and looked at Sawyer. She was crying. Willow lay beside Sawyer and took her into her arms. "What's wrong? Talk to me."

Sawyer touched the side of Willow's face. "Nothing's wrong. In fact, everything's just perfect. I love you, Willow McCord. I always have and I always will."

# Chapter 40

## 2013—Plymouth, Massachusetts

Willow woke in the middle of the night with a heavy weight on her abdomen and legs. Sawyer was curled up in a ball by her side, with her head resting on Willow's stomach and her arm draped across her thighs. Willow ran her fingers through Sawyer's hair, gently rousing her from sleep. "Hey... got to pee."

Sawyer rolled onto her back. "Sorry."

"Nothing to be sorry about. I just need to use the bathroom. I'll be right back." Willow took care of business and returned to bed to find Sawyer lying with her back to her. She slipped in between the sheets and spooned behind her. Closing her eyes, she savored the sensation of her nakedness pressed up against Sawyer's back. "You feel so good," she whispered.

Sawyer rolled away and pulled Willow on top of her. Willow rested her head beneath Sawyer's chin while Sawyer gently ran her fingernails up and down Willow's back.

With a low moan, Willow said, "Oh, my God... that's orgasmic."

Sawyer kissed the top of her head. "What time is it?"

"Early. Still several hours before I have to get up for work."

"Hmmm. I could lay like this forever."

"You won't hear me complain." Willow lifted her head and kissed Sawyer on the cheek. "Go back to sleep."

Sawyer continued to caress Willow's back.

Willow propped herself up on her forearms. "Are you all right?" she asked.

"Yeah. I'm just thinking."

"Want to share?"

"I'm worried about what will happen after the uprising."

"What do you mean?"

"Well, you'll need to come back to the States, and me—I have the estate in Newcastle to consider."

"Sawyer, this is all so new. Why don't we take it one day at a time and not worry about the future until it gets here?"

Sawyer smiled and tucked a lock of auburn hair behind Willow's ear. "You might be right."

"I know I am. Now clear your mind and try to sleep."

Sawyer awoke the next morning alone in Willow's bed. The bathroom door was slightly ajar, and she could hear the shower running. Time to get up. She rose, made the bed, and padded naked down the hall to the guest bathroom. She turned on the shower and stepped into the warm spray. She made quick work of washing her hair then lathered the cloth to wash her face and body. As she passed the cloth between her legs, she felt a slight tenderness there. She smiled. *That was the most amazing lovemaking*, she thought. She closed her eyes and allowed the warm water to run over her body. *Goddess help me, Willow, but I am totally in love with you. I can only hope you'll feel the same about me someday.*

Willow set the coffeepot to brew and put six link sausages in the microwave. She beat four eggs with diced onions and peppers and a dash of milk. She could hear the shower running in the guest bathroom above the kitchen and was trying to time breakfast to coincide with Sawyer's appearance in the kitchen. She dropped four slices of bread in the toaster and turned on the heat under the small frying pan, into which she tossed two pats of butter. Ten minutes later, the eggs were cooked, sausage warmed, toast buttered, and coffee brewed—just as Sawyer descended the stairs into the living room. Willow carried their plates to the table as Sawyer entered the kitchen.

"Wow, you look nice," Willow said as she took in the formal business attire Sawyer was wearing. "Plans today?"

"Lots, but first…" Sawyer walked around the table and took Willow into her arms for a warm embrace. "Good morning," she said.

Willow leaned back a bit to look at Sawyer but maintained her arms around Sawyer's waist. "Good morning to you. How did you sleep?"

"After that workout you gave me, I slept like a baby. That is, until your bladder woke me up in the middle of the night."

"Sorry about that. I kind of don't have any control over Mother Nature." Willow stepped out of her embrace. "Sit. Eat your breakfast while it's still hot."

"Mmm, it smells wonderful. Thank you." Sawyer sat down and took a bite of the scrambled eggs. "This is really good."

"Thank you." Willow filled two coffee cups, carried them to the table, and fetched the creamer from the refrigerator. "Here you go." She placed the creamer within Sawyer's reach and sat down. "So where are you off to today, dressed all formal?"

"I thought, since I'll be here for the next two months, and since I insist on seeing you safely to work, that I would rent some offices near your building to work out of until we go back to England. I scouted them out yesterday after I left you and Susan. I have an appointment at nine a.m. with the property manager to discuss the rental."

"Sawyer, you really don't need to escort me to work and back every day."

"Maybe not, but I'll feel better if I do. We can ride together most days, I think."

"If you insist."

"I do. So, today is Wednesday. You're planning to take the next two days off, right?"

"Yes. I thought we could tour some wineries and maybe visit Provincetown. We might even want to rent a room in P-Town for the next few nights. You'll love it there."

"I'm looking forward to it."

"Oh, look at the time. It's nearly eight o'clock. We'll have to get going if you want to make your nine a.m. meeting."

Sawyer ate the last of her sausage and carried hers and Willow's plates to the sink where she rinsed them and put them in the dishwasher. "Okay, let's go."

* * *

"I think the offices will suit my needs, Ms. Anderson," Sawyer said as she shook the property manager's hand.

"Wonderful. So if you'll sign right here, I'll give you the keys and be on my way."

Sawyer signed the lease agreement and handed it back to her. "There you go."

Ms. Anderson extended her hand to Sawyer. "Enjoy the offices. And here's my business card if you have any questions."

"Thank you, Ms. Anderson. Have a nice day."

Sawyer saw Ms. Anderson to the elevator and returned to the offices to plan a layout for furniture she would lease. She took her phone out of her pocket to search for office furniture rentals, when the e-mail alert sounded. She also noticed the text message that had come in the previous evening right after she and Willow arrived home. She opened the text message first. *You will regret ignoring me, Sawyer. Don't mess with me. I don't play nice. You have no idea what you're dealing with.* Sawyer frowned. "I warned you not to challenge me, Bridgit" she muttered. "You can't win that battle."

She deleted the text message and opened her email. There was one new message, also from Bridgit, with the subject line, "I warned you." In it, was a JPEG attachment which Sawyer opened. "What the devil?" It was a picture of Willow's car in the parking garage.

Sawyer met Willow on the sidewalk outside her office building after work. "How was your day?" Sawyer asked. She took Willow's hand and they walked toward the parking garage.

"Busy. Two emergency dental procedures and a shitload of scheduled cleanings. I'm looking forward to the next four days off. How did the meeting with the property manager go?"

"Great. Do you want to see my new offices?"

"Sure." They walked to the crosswalk and down one block. "Here it is." Sawyer opened the door to the office building.

"You weren't kidding when you said it was close to my building."

They waited for the elevator, and when it opened on the third floor, Sawyer once again took Willow's hand and led her to the end of the hallway. She fished a key out of her pocket and unlocked the door. "After you," she said. They walked through a moderately sized reception area and entered a door at the far end.

"A corner office. This is really nice." The two external walls of the room were floor-to-ceiling windows.

Sawyer slipped her hands into her pockets and walked around. "I can make this work. I've already asked Catherine to send my files on the next express flight."

"Will you hire a receptionist?"

"Probably not. This is only supposed to be for a couple of months, after all. I'll use the reception area as a waiting room if I need to."

Willow walked up to Sawyer and put her arms around her waist. Sawyer's hands naturally rested on Willow's shoulders. "With you so close, maybe we can have lunch together now and then."

Sawyer kissed her. "That sounds like a wonderful idea." She looked at her watch. "It's getting late. Did you want to head into P-Town tonight?"

"We might as well. P-Town is only about an hour and a half from the house. Let's see—it's just after five, so if we pack as soon as we get home and head out by maybe six-thirty, we'll be there around eight... just in time to check into the Crown and Anchor and hit the beach to watch the sunset."

"Sounds like a plan. I'm looking forward to having you all to myself for four days." And being able to keep an eye on you."

An hour later, Sawyer and Willow pulled into the driveway of Willow's home. On the porch was a large box.

"That must be my clothing." Sawyer climbed out of the car and went to check it out. "Yes, that's exactly what it is," she said after reading the return address on the box label. She waited for Willow to unlock the door then dragged the box inside. "Phew, this is heavy. Matilda must have packed a year's worth of clothing in here."

"Let me give you a hand carrying that upstairs," Willow said.

Within a half hour, Sawyer and Willow packed clothing appropriate for a four-day summer outing on Cape Cod, loaded their luggage into the car, and pulled out of the driveway.

"We're off," Willow said. "I hope you like the Cape. It's very beautiful there this time of year."

Sawyer placed her hand on Willow's thigh. "I'm sure I'll love it, especially since I'll be sharing it with you." She squeezed

Willow's leg. "Do you have the brooches?"

"Yes, Mommy, they're in my bag."

Sawyer lowered her gaze to their lap and grinned. "I'm sorry. I just need to keep you safe. I would be devastated if something happened to you."

Willow placed her hand on top of Sawyer's. "Sweetie, chill out. I was only kidding. You really need to learn how to relax."

Sawyer looked out the side window. "That's hard to do."

"I'll tell you what. You try to relax and not think too much about the uprising thing for the next few days, and I'll try real hard to take this voodoo stuff more seriously. Okay?"

"It's not voodoo, Willow," Sawyer said solemnly.

Willow switched on her directional and abruptly pulled off the road. She threw the transmission into park and faced Sawyer. "It was a joke, for crying out loud! Look, Sawyer, I'm not going to spend the next four days walking on egg shells around you. This weekend is supposed to be fun. If you can't make an effort to relax and not be so damned uptight and serious all the time, we might as well turn around and go back home. Your choice."

Sawyer studied her clasped hands in her lap for several long moments before she finally looked at Willow. She nodded her head. "I'll need your help. Quite frankly, I don't know how to relax."

"Let me guess. You spent your entire childhood being an overachiever, trying to impress your parents and trying to be as independent and self-sufficient as possible. How close am I?"

"You're spot on. I'm sorry."

Willow reached across and took Sawyer's chin in her hand. "Look at me. We're going to kayak, swim, whale watch, dance, shop, watch the sunset, hike, drink wine, and eat our way up and down Commercial Street until we fall into bed exhausted every night. You are going to have fun this weekend if it kills you—understand?"

Sawyer grinned. "I'd rather not be exhausted when we fall into bed, if you know what I mean."

Willow smiled. "Now yer talkin'," she said. She leaned in and kissed Sawyer tenderly then shifted the car into drive and pulled back onto the highway.

An hour later, Willow drove slowly down Bradford Street and took a right-hand turn onto Winslow. She drove up the hill and parked in the lot behind the Pilgrim Monument. Sawyer got out of the car and looked in amazement at the tall structure lit by flood lights. "It looks like a very tall medieval watchtower."

Willow opened the trunk and pulled out their luggage. She placed Sawyer's bag and knapsack next to her and extracted the handle on the roller bag. "Here you go." Her gaze followed Sawyer's. "That's the Pilgrim Monument and Provincetown Museum. It commemorates the history of the Mayflower pilgrims. You can go inside and climb to the top. The view is beautiful from up there. We can do that tomorrow if you'd like."

Sawyer consciously pushed the anxiety she was feeling to the recesses of her mind. She smiled at Willow. "Sounds like fun."

Willow slipped her arms into her backpack and pulled the handle up on her own roller bag. "We've got a bit of a walk to the Crown and Anchor. Unfortunately, a lack of parking is one of the few inconveniences in Provincetown. The good news is that we shouldn't need to use the car at all over the next few days. Everything is pretty much within walking distance of our hotel."

Sawyer shifted her backpack into position on her back. "I don't mind the walk." She offered her free hand to Willow, and they set out down the hill toward Commercial Street, towing their bags behind them.

When they reached the bottom of Winslow, Willow directed Sawyer down Gosnold, a narrow side street that emptied out on Commercial Street just a few dozen yards from the Crown and Anchor. They checked into the hotel and found themselves in a second-story room on the ocean side of the facility, with a sliding glass door and balcony.

Sawyer dropped her knapsack on the bed and slid the door open. Immediately, the sound of squawking seagulls and the dull roar of the rolling tide flooded the room. A gentle breeze blew the curtains inward. She stepped onto the balcony and held onto the railing. She closed her eyes and inhaled deeply. *Relax. Willow is right. You're too uptight. You've got her full attention for the next four days. Don't blow it.*

Willow stepped onto the balcony and draped her arm around Sawyer's waist. Beautiful, isn't it?"

"It's calm and relaxing."

"Yes it is. What do you say we take a walk on the beach while the sun sets then maybe grab a late dinner?"

"Okay. But do me a favor?"

"Let me guess," Willow said. "Bring the brooches, right?"

"Am I that transparent?"

"Like glass."

# Chapter 41

## 1613—Billingham, England

Jenna and Hadley sat side by side with their backs propped against the headboard, knees up, and babes resting in the crooks of their elbows. "Thou art beautiful, baby girl," Jenna said to the tiny infant in her arms. "Lachina. I like the name, Hadley. Thou hast chosen well."

"It means 'warrior,' I want our daughter to be strong and independent, so she needs a strong name," Hadley replied.

"She has red hair, just like thee and her twin brother Ewain." Sawyer reached over, kissed the little boy in Hadley's arms, and rested her head on Hadley's shoulder. Gramercy, Hadley. Thou hast made my life complete."

"The babes have my hair color, but they both have the Hawksworth nose and yes. 'Tis good that thou and Caleb lookest so much alike. Speaking of Caleb, he hath yet to see his niece and nephew."

"I spoke to him right after the birthing. The midwife forbade him entrance. She said thou needest thy rest after birthing twins."

"So he knoweth the babes are two?"

"Aye. He hugged me two times, once for each babe. Oh, and he said to deliver this to thee." Jenna kissed Hadley. "Of course, 'twas a hug he sent, but my arms are a little tied up right now."

"He is a kind and generous man, thy brother."

"That he is. Speaking of Caleb, I am getting the idea he is sweet on the baker's daughter, Maura Jennings."

"Maura Jennings, thou sayest? A pretty one she is with that long butter-colored hair. Is she returning his favors?"

"He gaveth her some flowers two days past, and she was smiling ear to ear, so 'tis true, I'd say."

A knock came upon the door. "Who is it?" Hadley called out.

"Lord Weller."

Jenna placed Lachina in the crook of Hadley's free arm and got up to welcome the high priest into the room. "Lord Weller, pray come in," she said.

The high priest walked across the room and looked at the children in Hadley's arms. "The coven hath been blessed with the birth of twins." He looked at Jenna. "Are they chosen ones?" he asked.

Jenna was caught off-guard by the high priest's questions. "I... I know not."

Lord Weller took Ewain out of Hadley's arms and held him close to the candle. "Look into the babe's mouth, Jenna, and tell me what you see."

Jenna teased her son's mouth open and looked inside. "He has the mark."

The high priest returned the little boy to Hadley's arms and took Lachina from her. Again, Jenna looked into her mouth. She glanced at Hadley and then at the high priest. "She, too, has the mark."

Lord Weller handed the baby girl over to Jenna. "Hadley was a good choice for thee, Jenna. Blood from her ancestors floweth through these wee ones—the same ancestors who fought to keep evil in the underworld one hundred years ago. Thou hast proven thyself loyal by accepting the coven's choice for thee. As of this day forth, thou wilt be known as the leader of this clan."

Jenna looked at Hadley and immediately knew she was in trouble. She turned back to the high priest. "Lord Weller, such an honor thou bestowest on me."

"Wear the mantle well, Jenna. Many lives depend on it." With that, the high priest left.

"Jenna Hawksworth, thou currish brazen-faced devil-monk—thou hast some explaining to do," Hadley said.

Jenna returned Lachina once more to Hadley's arms and knelt on the floor beside the bed. She could feel Hadley's glare bore through her soul.

"I am waiting, blacksmith," Hadley said sternly.

"I will not lie to thee. The clan sent me to North Yorkshire in search of thee. I was sent to woo thee and convince thee to be part of the repression."

"Ahh! Of all the roguish, lily-livered things thou couldst do! So is this life naught but a lie? Is this all trickery, Jenna Hawksworth?"

Jenna reached for Hadley's arm and felt her flinch.

"Touch me again, blacksmith, and I will rip thine arm off and beat thee with it. No wonder thou wast in such a hurry to give me thy brooch after such a short courtship. Thou art a lying cad."

Jenna pulled her hand back quickly. "Hadley, when first I saw thee in thy tailor shop, thoughts of trickery were far from my mind. The moment I saw thy face, I was lost forever. It mattered not what the clan wanted of me. It mattered only that thou heldest my heart in thy hands, even if thou knewest it not."

"Lord Weller spoke of my ancestors at the last repression. What doth he mean?" Hadley asked.

"Hadley, thou art chosen by the clan on account of thy ancestors taking part in the last repression. It was the hope of the high priest that thou hadst knowledge of the deed. I told them thou knewest naught of it, but it was too late to turn back. My heart was thine."

"Jenna Hawksworth, thou hast allowed me to marry thee and birth thy children, yet still thou hast kept this secret from me. Who but a churlish idle-headed cad would do that? Thou hast better have a good reason for this, woman."

"The reason mattereth not. Thou stolest my heart. I strive to make thee happy and to share my life with thee with or without the blessing of the coven. I came to thee for the wrong reasons, but I stay with thee for the right ones. I love thee, Hadley Metcalf. I love thee as much as one being can love another. I implore thee to believe me and forgive this lowly blacksmith for her deception."

"Trust cometh not easy, Jenna. I trusted thee and thou hast

deceived me."

"'Tis true. I cannot undo what has been done. What will it take for thee to give me another chance? I want not to lose thee or the babes. I shall do anything."

"Anything?"

"Aye," Jenna said, her voice quivering.

"Wouldst thou leave the clan?"

Jenna looked Hadley straight in the eyes. "For thee, I would leave the clan. Is that what thou wantest, Hadley?"

"Nay. I do not. I know what the clan means to thee, Jenna, and what thou dost mean to the clan. I ask not that thou leavest, but thy willingness to do so has proven thy love for me."

Jenna bowed her head. "So thou forgivest me then?"

"Thou art lucky I love thee, blacksmith. I forgive thee, but if thou wantest to keep thy arse out of the fire, thou needest not keep secrets from me. If thou deceivest me again, there will be no forgiveness. Art thou clear on that?"

Jenna nodded solemnly. "Aye."

"Good. Now take thy son. He hath a gift for thee in his nappy."

\* \* \*

"Lord Weller, may I seek thy counsel?" Jenna said as she caught up with the priest.

"What is on thy mind, Jenna?"

"Hadley. Sire, she kneweth not of the clan choosing her for me. She was quite distraught when thou didst leave last night."

Lord Weller clasped his hands behind him as he walked. "I see. And why didst thou fail to tell her, Jenna?"

"I was afraid to lose her. She was a non-believer when first I laid eyes on her."

"I regret if my words caused thee grief, but Hadley doth need to know her place in the clan and accept the clan's teachings."

"I ask thy forgiveness, sire, but the clan doth not teach deception, and thus Hadley doth not have to accept that."

"She must accept that thy position as leader doth sometimes require deception."

"I will deceive the enemies of the Goddess, but I will not be deceiving Hadley. She deserveth better than that. If thou seest fit to remove the mantle of leader from my shoulders because I respect my wife, then so be it."

Lord Weller stopped and crossed his arms in front of him.

Jenna stood her ground, hands on her hips.

"Jenna Hawksworth," the high priest said. "Nary have I met a woman like thee. I like that thou speakest thy mind, and I like that thou standest up for what thou dost love. Thou shalt keep the mantle. Thou wilt make a good leader." He started to walk away then stopped. "The Council of Thirteen will want to meet the newborn chosen ones. Thou must hold the naming ceremony forthright."

Jenna quietly slipped into the cottage, took off her boots, and tiptoed her way across the kitchen to the adjoining bedroom. She was surprised to see Hadley still awake, sitting up in bed and hand sewing a quilt. "Thou dost not sleep," Jenna said as she sat on the edge of the bed and tucked a lock of Hadley's hair behind her ear.

"The babes have just quieted down. Thy daughter was a fussy one this night."

Jenna walked over to the cradles placed side by side just a few feet from the bed and knelt on the floor beside the babes. She placed one delicate kiss on each of their cheeks and then sat back on her heels. "Gifts from the Goddess, thou art," she whispered.

Jenna stood and began to remove her clothing. "I spoke to Lord Weller this night," she said. "I told him I will not deceive thee ever again. I offered to give back the mantle of leadership."

Hadley put her sewing in her lap. "And hath he accepted it?"

"Nay."

"He is a wise man. Loyalty and honesty are good traits for a leader."

Jenna slipped into bed beside Hadley and took her sewing from her. She placed it in the basket beside the bed and blew out the candle. "Come hither, love. Let me hold thee while thou sleepest this night."

Hadley rolled into Jenna's embrace and placed her head on her shoulder. "Gramercy, Jenna Hawksworth," she said.

"For what?" Jenna asked.

"For thy loyalty… for thy honesty… and for loving me."

"I do love thee… and I love the babes, who need a naming ceremony, by and by."

"Aye. 'Tis been on my mind," Hadley said.

"How long afore the cords fall off?"

"The midwife says a fortnight or so."

"Aye, then plan we must."

\* \* \*

"Jenna and Hadley, enter the circle and be one with the coven," the high priest said.

Jenna and Hadley walked side by side toward the circle, Ewain tucked into Jenna's arms and Lachina in Hadley's. The circle opened to admit them as they approached. They walked directly to the altar in the middle of the circle where the high priest and Caleb waited for them. They stopped in front of the priest.

The priest raised his hands out to the sides. "Friends, family, come closer to share in the Goddess's blessing for the wee ones."

The circle around the altar closed in.

"Goddess, accept our prayers in the names of these infants." He looked at Jenna and Hadley. "What say you?"

"We dedicate and bind our lives to the children. We swear an oath to the Goddess to protect them, love them, and teach them to be kind, gentle, and compassionate."

The priest once more raised his hands. "Under this blue sky and gentle breeze, all here gather to bless thy children. New lives have become part of our world." The priest approached Hadley and, with blessed oil, drew a pentagram on Lachina's forehead. "We welcome this child into our hearts and lives and bless her with the name, Lachina." He faced Jenna and again, with blessed oil, drew a pentagram on Ewain's forehead. "We welcome this child into our hearts and bless him with the name, Ewain."

The high priest returned the oil to the altar and faced Jenna and Hadley once more. "Have you appointed a guardian for the babes?"

"We have. We appoint Caleb Hawksworth, uncle to the babes, to protect them, love them, and teach them to be kind and compassionate in our stead if we are unable to do so ourselves."

The priest turned to Caleb. "Caleb Hawksworth, dost thou accept this responsibility?"

"I shall die for them if I must, Lord Weller. Hawksworth blood flows through them. They are my family and I am theirs."

"Dost thou understand thy role as guardian?"

"Aye. 'Tis to love and nurture, guide and counsel. 'Tis to help them make wise choices. 'Tis to be a father when needed and to be there when called upon."

"Pray, place the babes on the altar," the high priest said.

Hadley and Jenna placed the infants side by side and folded back their blankets. The high priest held his hands above them.

"Pray the Goddess doth keep these babes pure and free from negative forces. That they always have good fortune, good health, joy and love, in their hearts." Once again, the high priest picked up the blessed oil. With it, he drew a pentagram on Lachina's chest. "Thou art known to the Goddess as Lachina. Dost thou never dishonor thy name. We beseech thee in the name of the Goddess." He then drew a pentagram on Ewain's chest. "Thou art known to the Goddess as Ewain. Dost thou never dishonor thy name. We beseech thee in the name of the Goddess."

The high priest wrapped the blankets around the babies and handed them back to Hadley and Jenna. He turned to the circle of clan members. "Come, welcome these babes into our family."

One by one, coven members touched the children's heads and said their names followed by 'I honor thee.' When everyone had a chance to welcome the children, Hadley and Jenna approached the altar and held the babes high above their heads.

The priest faced the crowd. He tilted his head back and closed his eyes. "Great Goddess, look upon these innocents and protect them with thy love. Blessed be—for they are the chosen ones."

# Chapter 42

## 2013—Provincetown, Massachusetts

Willow and Sawyer sat across from each other on the back porch of Bayside Betty's Restaurant. Dusk was approaching, and the sky over the ocean was tinged with orange. Willow held her glass of wine up to Sawyer. "A toast. To four days of sun, fun, food, and wine."

"Hear, hear." Sawyer touched her glass to Willow's. She took a sip and put her glass beside her plate. "This was a great idea, Wills. Dinner and the sunset at the same time."

"Well, it's getting late, so killing two birds with one stone sounded like a good idea. How's your Chicken Parm?"

"Wonderful. I'm finding I quite enjoy American food."

"This town is loaded with good restaurants. There's so much I want you to try while we're here. You will absolutely cream over the Portuguese bakery. The pasties are to die for, and the fried bread dough is out of this world. We'll do breakfast there tomorrow morning."

Sawyer placed her elbows on the table and sipped her wine. She smiled. "Do you often 'cream' over pastries, Wills?"

Willow put a bite of her shrimp scampi into her mouth—all except for one strand of angel hair pasta, which she sucked into her mouth seductively and licked her lips, all the while maintaining eye contact with Sawyer. "Any excuse to cream is a good thing," she said.

Sawyer sipped her wine again. "I quite agree."

The waitress approached their table. "I see you ladies are just about finished. Do you care for dessert?"

Sawyer looked at the waitress then back at Willow. "No, I have something sweet in mind for later."

Willow couldn't stop the smile from forming on her lips.

"Okay then," the waitress said quickly. "I'll get your check."

Sawyer shoved her hands deep into the pockets of her jacket while Willow hooked her hand through the crook of Sawyer's arm.

"That was a great dinner, Sawyer, but we agreed you weren't going to spend a lot of money over the next two months," Willow said.

"That doesn't apply to road trips."

"Do you always make up the rules as you go?"

"When it suits me."

Willow took Sawyer's hand and pulled her into an alley between two buildings. "Come on. Let's walk the beach for the rest of the way so we can catch what's left of the sunset."

The alley emptied out onto the sandy beach where they both removed their shoes and walked in the soft sand toward their hotel.

"This feels amazing," Sawyer said. "It's still warm from the sun."

"I loved seeing that look on your face," Willow said as they strolled along.

"What look?"

They stopped and faced each other. "That mischievous look you gave me in the restaurant when you said in that sexy British accent, 'I have something sweet in mind for later.' Damn—talk about creaming my jeans!"

"Really?"

Willow took Sawyer's hand and slipped it into the front of her shorts and panties. Her hand easily slid between the wet folds.

"See?"

Sawyer felt like someone took her legs right out from under her as she fought to stand. "By the gods, Wills. You're so wet."

Willow put her hand over Sawyer's on the outside of her shorts and pressed. Sawyer squeezed. "Oh God." Willow placed her forehead on Sawyer's chest just below her chin. She reached between Sawyer's legs and felt the heat through Sawyer's clothing.

In spite of Willow's protests, Sawyer extracted her hand. "Come on," she said as she took Willow's hand and quickly covered the remaining distance over the sand to their hotel. As soon as they were in their room, Sawyer threw her shoes on the floor and pressed Willow up against the door. "Good Goddess, you make me wild with want," Sawyer said before devouring Willow's mouth.

"Wild is good," Willow said. "Don't hold back."

It took very little time to divest themselves of clothing as they moved across the room and fell onto the bed. Sawyer was overwhelmed with desire as she aggressively took Willow, nipping her breasts and plunging deep into her.

Willow fueled the fury by moaning loudly and arching her pelvis to match Sawyer's thrusts. "Oh, my God, Sawyer. I need more… harder, please."

Just before climaxing, Willow stopped Sawyer and pushed her onto her back on the bed.

"No, Willow, you're almost there," Sawyer said.

"I want us to come together." Willow treated Sawyer to the same aggressive lovemaking she had been privy to. "Don't hold back, Sawyer. I want to hear you. Tell me what you want."

Sawyer restrained herself. "I can't, Wills. I can't."

Willow sucked Sawyer's swollen bud into her mouth and flicked it with the end of her tongue. Sawyer arched high into the air.

"By the Gods, Willow."

Willow turned around and lay on top of Sawyer so they could please each other. She plunged her fingers back into Sawyer and once again sucked on her swollen bud as Sawyer did the same.

Almost instantly, the dam broke. "Don't stop, Sawyer. Ah… God… Yes!" Willow moaned as spasms consumed her. Even in the throes of orgasm, she realized Sawyer was once again holding back.

"Damn it, Sawyer, trust me. Please let go."

"Sweet Mother Goddess!" Sawyer screamed loudly as she

totally lost control of her body's reaction to Willow's lovemaking, riding wave after wave of spasms.

Sawyer's reaction was so intense, Willow climaxed a second time, finally turning around and falling limp on the bed beside Sawyer. She lay her head in the crook of Sawyer's shoulder and drew lazy circles around Sawyer's nipples as secondary spasms continued to roll through Sawyer's abdomen.

Sawyer looked at her through hooded eyes, barely able to keep them open. "I love you, Willow McCord. Blessed be."

Willow smiled and watched Sawyer close her eyes and almost instantly fall to sleep. She reached down and pulled the sheet over both of them then lay her head down.

"The feeling is mutual, darling," she whispered before drifting off to sleep.

* * *

Sawyer lifted her head off the pillow and looked around. She was alone. "Willow?"

"Right here." Willow appeared in the bathroom doorway holding a toothbrush in her hand. "Just getting ready to brush my teeth." She picked up a pillow from a nearby chair and threw it at Sawyer. "Get your butt in gear if you want freshly baked pasties and bread dough for breakfast. They go fast."

Sawyer threw the covers off and hurried to the bathroom. Willow waited for her in the doorway. "You're very sexy, you know," Willow said.

"That's a word I would use for you—not me."

"Let's just say if you don't put some clothes on soon, I may opt to skip breakfast and eat you instead."

Sawyer circled around her and embraced her from behind, nibbling on her neck. "Hmmm. You took the thoughts right out of my mind."

Just then, Willow's stomach rumbled. "Uh-oh, the beast is growling."

"I guess I'd better jump in the shower then."

Twenty minutes later, Sawyer and Willow shared a booth at

the Portuguese bakery while enjoying coffee and eating malassadas, covered in butter, powdered sugar, and cinnamon.

"This is amazing," Sawyer said. "Is it really just bread dough?"

"It's kind of a cross between a funnel cake and a churro."

"Do they serve pastries all day?"

"Yes, but they also have a wonderful vegetable soup and meat-stuffed turnovers."

"If you don't mind, I'd like to come back tomorrow morning."

Willow wiped powdered sugar from the corner of Sawyer's mouth and followed it with a kiss. "We can come here every morning if you'd like. The rabanada is to die for."

"What's that?"

"It's the Portuguese version of French toast."

Sawyer took another bite of her malassada. "This is heavenly. If I lived in this town, I'd weigh three hundred pounds."

"Not to worry, I have plans for today that will work off the calories you're consuming right now."

"You mean we're going back to our room?" Sawyer asked as her eyebrows bounced up and down on her forehead.

"You are incorrigible. No, I was actually thinking we'd do the Pilgrim Monument this morning then maybe a guided bike tour on the National Seashore… oh, and I think there's a dune tour and sunset beach fire tonight. You do know how to ride a bike, right?"

"Sounds like fun, and yes, I know how to ride a bike. On the way to dinner last night, I saw advertisements posted for something called 'Girl Splash.'"

"Is that this week? Cool! We couldn't have timed that better. It's basically several days of nonstop partying, dancing, comedy shows, and activities specifically for lesbians. We should check out the box office at the Crown and Anchor and get tickets to some of the shows."

Sawyer drank the last of her coffee. "Let's do it."

Over the next two days, Willow played tour guide, engaging Sawyer in so many activities, they fell into bed each evening exhausted. In two days, they crammed in a hike up the Pilgrim Monument; a bike tour of the National Seashore; a rowdy sunset beach fire, complete with loud music and a Congo line of tipsy lesbians dancing around the bonfire; and a whale watch and sensual dancing at the popular nightclub, The Pied. On Saturday morning, dawn found them wrapped around each other, with Sawyer's leg draped over Willow's thigh and her arm holding her waist hostage.

Willow fought off the nagging sensation of her bladder screaming at her for as long as she possibly could, but she was finally forced into action. She nudged Sawyer.

"Sweetie. Sawyer. Sweetie, I need to get up."

"Hmmm."

Willow shifted her weight until she managed to roll out from under Sawyer's appendages.

"Nooo," Sawyer said and moaned as she tried to regain her hold on Willow.

"Got to pee. I'll be right back."

Sawyer lifted the sheet for Willow when she returned to bed and wrapped herself around her once more. "I want to spend the rest of the weekend right here… just like this," she said.

"And miss the fried bread dough?"

Sawyer opened her eyes. "You've got a point there. What time is it?"

Willow glanced at the clock. "It's only six am."

"What's on the agenda for today?"

"There's a pool party sometime around noon, and we have tickets to a comedy show tonight at eight. I thought maybe we could do some shopping as well."

"Pool party? I didn't bring a swimming costume."

"Swimming costume? Is that what the Brits call it? We call it a bathing suit."

"But you're not really bathing. You're swimming."

"Yeah, yeah, whatever. I guess we'll have to do our shopping this morning then."

"Right now? I doubt the stores are open yet."

"Whine, whine, whine," Willow said.

Sawyer grinned.

"Okay, we can sleep for a couple more hours, but we'll need to get up early enough to hit the bakery before all the good stuff is gone."

Sawyer pulled Willow closer. "Sounds like a good plan to me."

By nine a.m., Willow and Sawyer were enjoying rabanadas at the Portuguese bakery. Willow said, "There's a shop just down a bit from the Governor Bradford that sells bathing suits, and across the street from the Governor Bradford is a leather store. You look very yummy in black, so I thought you might want to browse through that store as well."

"I look yummy in black, do I?"

"Oh, yeah! That was the first thing I noticed about you when you were stalking me."

"I wasn't stalking you."

"I think when you follow someone around who doesn't know you, that qualifies as stalking."

"Hmm. Then I guess I was. Sorry about that."

"Don't be sorry. I'm not."

Sawyer smiled. "You're quite an outspoken person, Willow McCord. I like that about you."

"I believe in letting people know what I think and where they stand with me. No surprises that way."

"I quite agree. I just can't bring myself to do it."

"I've been trying to figure out if your reserved style is just you, or if all Brits are like that."

Sawyer chuckled. "I would say it's more me than a cultural thing. We have some very fun-loving, outspoken people in my country. I, on the other hand, was raised to be quiet and contemplative. I'm a thinker and a planner."

"That can be a good thing, but it could also be a problem."

"How so?"

"I dated a woman once who would never tell me what was on her mind. There were days when she was so moody and silent that I wondered what I did to offend her. I prefer someone to be forthcoming and open with their thoughts."

"I'm afraid I'm more like your ex than I'd like to admit. I've been making an effort this week though."

Willow grinned. "That you have. Has it been so hard?"

"Not really, but then I think a lot of that is the company I'm in. You make it very easy for me to let loose and have fun. I feel safe with you. I appreciate that."

"Well as long as you're here, the only one you need to worry about jumping your bones is me… as often as I possibly can."

"Is 'jumping your bones' another Americanism?"

Willow tilted her head back and laughed out loud. "You are very funny. Jumping your bones means taking you to bed."

"Really? Well, you can jump my bones anytime you'd like."

"I will take you up on that offer."

Nearly three hours later Willow and Sawyer returned to their room and deposited their purchases on the bed. "Holy shit. Look at all the stuff we bought," Willow said.

"I couldn't resist the leather dusters," Sawyer replied.

"I'm glad they had one short enough on me to not the drag the ground."

"I really like the blown glass figurines you bought at Womencrafts."

"I do, too. I love that store. They have such a nice selection of books and artwork. I make a point of stopping in there every time I'm in town."

"Maybe we should take our purchases to the car, so we won't have so much to carry when we leave tomorrow," Sawyer suggested.

"That sounds like a good idea. Maybe we can do that after the pool party. Speaking of which, why don't you put on your new bathing suit so I can see how sexy you are in it."

"There's that word again."

"Well, you are sexy."

"As you would say… yeah, yeah, yeah, whatever!" Sawyer joked as she grabbed her suit and went to the bathroom.

While Sawyer was changing, Willow browsed through the books they purchased at Womencrafts bookstore then re-bagged everything to be taken to the car later in the day. She rummaged through her suitcase for her bathing suit and put it on. Sawyer came out of the bathroom wearing a navy blue one-piece suit with white piping. The legs were high-cut and the neckline plunged into her cleavage.

"Wow! You look hot," Willow said. "Turn around."

Sawyer did as told and modeled the bathing suit for Willow.

"I really like the sports-bra straps in the back. Nothing worse than diving into a pool and having your straps fall down your arms. Damn. Sexy is an understatement."

"I'm glad you approve."

"How does it feel?"

"A bit scant. But comfortable."

"It was a good choice, although the two-piece you tried on looked good on you as well."

"I'm afraid I don't have the curves to pull off a bikini like you do," Sawyer said as she pulled Willow toward her. "You look fantastic."

"Thank you. Are you ready to go?"

"Yes, but you're not."

"What do you mean?"

"Where are the brooches? You need to have them on you, Willow."

"I can't wear them in the pool, Sawyer. And besides, there isn't exactly a lot of real estate to pin them to on this bikini."

"I'd feel better if you at least had them with you."

"Ahh! The things I do for you." Willow broke free of Sawyer's embrace. She retrieved the brooches from the top of the dresser and slipped them into the fanny pack containing some cash and their room key. "There. Are you happy?"

"Yes. Thank you for indulging me."

"You're welcome. Now let's go join the fun."

Willow and Sawyer spent the next few hours swimming and getting to know several other women who had also joined the party at the hotel pool. At one point near the end of the party, they were sunning themselves side by side on lounge chairs with their towels and fanny pack on the deck in a pile between their chairs.

"I'm going in for a dip," Sawyer said. "This sun is hot."

"That sounds like a good idea."

The two ladies dove into the pool and swam across to the other side where they surfaced. "That feels wonderful," Sawyer said.

"Race you to the other side." Willow gave her a quick grin.

"You're on. On three. One… two… three."

They dove under the water and began to swim toward the opposite side of the pool. Sawyer, being the better swimmer, arrived first and hoisted herself out of the water and onto the deck. She turned around to look at Willow and immediately realized something was wrong. Willow was near the edge of the pool and was struggling to surface—almost as though she was hitting up against a glass ceiling.

"Great Goddess!" Sawyer ran back to their lounge chairs and grabbed the fanny pack. She fumbled with the zipper and finally opened it enough to grab the brooches from within. They were glowing. She ran back to the pool and thrust the hand holding the brooches into the water. Willow immediately broke through the surface, gasping for breath and coughing up water.

"Help me," Sawyer said to the other women around the pool who ran toward her. She slipped the brooches inside the cleavage of her suit and grabbed one of Willow's arms as one of their new acquaintances grabbed the other. Together, they pulled her onto the deck.

"Are you all right?" Sawyer asked.

"Maybe we should call an ambulance," their friend said.

Willow held up her hand. "No. No. I'm okay. Just swallowed a little water."

Sawyer looked up at their new friend. "Thank you. I think she'll be all right." She went back to their lounge chairs and picked up one of the towels, which she draped over Willow's shoulders.

"Come on, love. I think we've had enough swimming for

one day. Let's go back to our room."

Back in their room, Sawyer paced back and forth while Willow sat on the bed.

"What happened back there?" Willow said in a voice made raspy from choking on the pool water.

"The brooches were too far away from you to offer protection. Damn it! I need to find out who, or what, is behind this. This is obviously an attempt to stop the repression." She halted in front of Willow and knelt on the floor between her legs. She took Willow's hands in hers. "Willow, you need to learn how to protect yourself. We can't put off your training any longer. It appears whatever is behind this will stop at nothing to get to you. Maybe we should go home today instead of tomorrow."

"No. I'm not going to let this change our plans. We can't be living our lives looking over our shoulders all the time. I'll just need to make sure the brooches are on me at all times."

"How are you feeling?"

"Raspy, and my chest feels tight, probably from struggling to breathe. But otherwise I'm okay."

"Look, I'm going to jump in the shower, then I'll run out and purchase a chain for the brooches so you can wear them around your neck."

"Why don't we shower together and both run out for the chain? That way we can get an early dinner and go directly to the comedy show."

"Are you sure you're up to going out?"

Willow took Sawyer's face between her palms. "I'll be damned if I'm going to let some evil spirit... or force... or whatever you want to call it, ruin our weekend. I'm sure. I'll go start the shower."

Sawyer began stripping her clothes off when a text came into her phone. "Damn it, Bridgit, can't you just leave me alone?" she said as she opened the text and read it. *Tip of the day: To drown your troubles, you must not let them surface.*

Sawyer opened the door to their room and allowed Willow to enter before her. She closed and securely locked it behind them.

Willow walked to the center of the room and turned around. "Aren't you glad we went out? That show was damned funny."

Sawyer walked into the circle of Willow's arms and wrapped her own arms around Willow's waist. "Yes. I enjoyed the show, but I couldn't help but be on edge waiting for something else to happen."

"I'm wearing the brooches, Sawyer. You said yourself they'll protect me."

"I know, and they will. But the thought of something happening to you... the thought of losing you..." Sawyer shuddered in Willow's arms.

Willow put her hands on Sawyer's chest and pushed her back. "Are you crying?" Sawyer tried to hide her tears with her hand, but Willow pushed it away. "Sweetie, I promise not to take any more chances than necessary. Please don't cry."

"I will die if something happens to you, Willow. I can't bear to lose you."

"Sweetheart, look at me." Willow lifted Sawyer's chin until their eyes met. "I'm not in a hurry to check out of this world any sooner than necessary. I have too much to live for. We both do. I will be careful."

Sawyer wiped her tears and trailed the back of her hand down the side of Willow's face and across her shoulder. "Thank you."

"I have such intense feelings churning in my chest right now, Sawyer. Feelings I've never felt before. I don't know if it's fear, or desire, or sympathy, or something else... whatever. What I do know is it's breaking my heart to see you like this."

"I'm sorry," Sawyer said as she tried to break away.

Willow held on tighter. "No. Never apologize for feeling."

Their gazes held for several long moments, sparks of desire and need passing between them. "Let me love you," Sawyer whispered.

It was well into the wee hours of the morning before they both drifted off to sleep, naked and entwined in each other arms.

# Chapter 43

## 1613—Billingham, England

Jenna paced back and forth across the room while Hadley sat naked on the bed with her back against the headboard. "Jenna Hawksworth, come to bed."

Jenna stopped. "Dost thou expect me to come to thee like that? Thou art naked, Hadley. Thou surely knowest how to torture a soul."

"So 'tis torture now, making love to me?"

Jenna fell on her knees beside the bed. "Hadley, I want naught more than to make love to thee. I dream of thy taste and touch. I think often of how soft thou art inside. It drives me mad, but thou just gavest birth. I fear to hurt thee."

"Blacksmith, 'tis been two moons since the babes birthed. I need to feel thee inside me again. Wouldst thou have me lie beside thee in this bed yet another night with such need?"

"The need is mine as well."

Hadley lifted Jenna's hand from the bed and placed it between her legs. "Feel what thou dost to me with only a look, blacksmith."

Jenna closed her eyes and caught her breath. "By the gods, Hadley."

Hadley pushed Jenna's hand deeper, causing a moan to escape her own lips.

Jenna retracted her hand and immediately began to pull her clothing off, letting it lie where it fell. She climbed onto the bed and knelt near Hadley's feet. In one swift movement, she grabbed Hadley's ankles, pulled her down into a prone position, and lay directly on her between Hadley's legs. She gyrated her hips, grinding herself against Hadley.

"That is more to my liking, blacksmith," Hadley said. "'Tis been too long."

Jenna buried her tongue deep into Hadley's mouth as it fought with Hadley's for dominance. Deep guttural moans from Hadley spurred her on. She moved to Hadley's neck, struggling to hold back her aggressiveness as she nipped, leaving marks that would surely bruise later.

"Thou makest me wild with need, Hadley. I want to be inside thee. I want to hear thee scream my name."

"I feel thy need. Why dost thou take so long? Take me, Jenna. I need thee inside me."

Jenna propped herself on one knee and reached between Hadley's legs. She drove three fingers deep into her. Hadley arched upward and screamed, "Sweet Goddess!"

"Lift thy knee, Hadley." Jenna straddled Hadley's leg and rubbed herself up and down with each thrust. Her thrusts into Hadley increased as her own ardor rose. Before long, they were both balancing on the precipice.

"By the gods, Jenna. I am there. Please let me go," Hadley begged.

"Aye. I shall fall with thee. Let it go, my love. Now... let it go."

Jenna threw her head back. She strained to hold on until she felt Hadley begin to spasm, then she ceased all pretense of control as she fell over the edge with her. They clung to each other as spasms wracked their bodies for several minutes, their moans and cries prolonging the sweet torture. Finally, all was still and Jenna collapsed on the bed beside Hadley.

"Blessed be, Hadley Metcalf," Jenna whispered.

Within moments, both of them were fast asleep.

\* \* \*

"Art thou ready to go, Hadley?" Jenna asked.

"Aye, just as soon as I change Ewain's nappy. Here is Lachina's sling. Put it around thy shoulder."

Jenna hung the sling around her neck and put her right arm

through the opening, then she picked her daughter up from the bed and tucked her inside it. "There, little Mistress Lachina. All snug and warm."

"There thou goest, Master Hawksworth, nice clean nappies," Hadley said to the little boy before handing him to Jenna. "Go see thy mama while mum puts on thy sling."

Jenna helped settle Ewain into the sling once Hadley had it positioned across her chest. "Great Goddess, having wee ones is a lot of work."

"Aye. Now art thou ready?"

Jenna and Hadley walked through the Billingham market place looking for food stores and quilting supplies. Jenna pulled a small wheeled basket behind them for their wares. After bargaining for and purchasing all the items on their list, Hadley tucked a cloth over their goods in the basket. Lachina stirred and whimpered.

"The babes are hungry," Hadley said. "Best we head home so they can take nourishment."

"How is the little man faring?" Jenna asked.

"Still sleeping, but I fear not for long."

"Aye. We must go then."

Jenna took the handle of the basket and turned toward home, Hadley by her side, when a man stepped into her path. He stood before them with his arms folded across his chest. Jenna stopped short and stared. A momentary wave of fear gripped her insides.

Hadley looked at the man, then at Jenna, and noted the fear on her wife's face. She placed her hand on Jenna's arm. "Jenna, who is this man?"

Jenna answered without taking her eyes off him. "He is my sire."

Hadley gasped.

"Jenna Hawksworth," the man said. "Thou wast told never to return. What sayest thee?"

"Jenna, pray walk away. Thou dost not have to answer him."

"Silence woman, or thou wilt find thyself on the ground," the man said.

Jenna stepped forward. "Thou shalt not touch her, Thomas Hawksworth."

He walked in a circle around Jenna and Hadley. "Thomas Hawksworth, is it? Hast thou no respect, girl? I am thy pa. I deserve to be treated as such."

"Thou deservest naught. Thou art a heartless bastard."

He raised his hand to strike Jenna but found it shopped short by a firm grasp on his wrist.

"I think not, sire," Caleb said. "I ran in shame the last time thou didst beat her. I will not allow it to happen again."

Hadley took Jenna's hand and pulled her a few feet away.

"Thank the Goddess thou art here, Caleb," she said.

Hawksworth shook himself free of Caleb's grasp. "Caleb Hawksworth. Why dost thou defend this wagtail?"

Caleb took a step toward his father. "Jenna Hawksworth is no wagtail. She is a good, respectable woman and a better person than thou wilt ever be."

Hawksworth raised his hand to strike his son and again found his wrist held fast. "Do not do it, old man."

Just then, Lachina began to cry. Hawksworth narrowed his eyes at Jenna. Caleb followed the direction of his gaze. "That is thy grandchild, as is the babe Hadley holds. Take a good look, old man. 'Tis the last time thou wilt ever see them." Caleb pushed his father away and turned to Jenna and Hadley. "I shall escort thee home."

Hawksworth shook his fist at their retreating backs. "Take thy bastards and go. Thou wilt rue the day thou camest back to Billingham, Jenna Hawksworth. I will see to it."

\* \* \*

Jenna paced back and forth as Hadley nursed the children. Caleb sat across the room and listened to her rant. " What man raiseth his hand to a wee babe, for surely his blow would cause me to fall. Ahh! I am so angry with him... and with myself."

"Why art thou angry with thyself? Thou didst naught wrong," Caleb said.

Jenna stopped in front of Caleb. "I was a coward, Caleb. I did not stand him down. He might have hurt the babes, and I did naught to stop him."

"Thou couldst do naught with a wee babe at thy chest. Do not be angry with thyself."

"How didst thou know to find us, Caleb?" Jenna asked.

"Thou shalt think me mad."

"I shall harken without judgment."

"A voice in my head told me to find thee in the market place."

"A woman's voice perchance?" Hadley said from across the room.

"Aye."

"'Twas the Goddess, Caleb, and she sent thee to save us."

# Chapter 44

## 2013—Plymouth, Massachusetts

On Monday morning, Sawyer left Willow at the door of her office building and walked the extra block to her own office. She spent the better part of the morning taking care of business-related emails that had come in over the four-day weekend she and Willow had spent in Provincetown. Just before noon, she placed a call to England.

"Lord Somers, this is Sawyer Hawksworth."

"Sawyer. It's so good to hear from you."

"Lord Somers, I'm calling to see if any headway has been made to identify those responsible for the paranormal attacks against Willow McCord."

"Very little, I'm afraid. Has something else happened since we last spoke?"

"Yes. Willow was almost drowned two days ago. She was blocked from surfacing while in a swimming pool."

"I see. Since you're not calling to tell me she has passed, it must mean she survived."

"Yes, but only because I had the presence of mind to use the brooches to break the spell. Lord Somers, I would like you to investigate Bridgit Cooper's potential role in this."

"Bridgit Cooper? Do you mean the woman you were having a relationship with before you went to the States?"

"Yes. She has sent a few disturbing text messages and an e-mail to me over the past couple of days. I have reason to believe she is behind the attack on Willow in the parking garage and in the near-drowning in a pool."

"What motive would she have for doing that?"

"Revenge, maybe? I don't know, but I would appreciate you investigating her."

"Sawyer, maybe it would be wise for you and Willow to come to England sooner than planned."

"I'm afraid that isn't possible. She's unable to take leave from her job until the beginning of October."

"How do you plan to keep her safe in the meantime?"

"She's wearing the brooches on a chain around her neck, and I'm escorting her to work and back on a daily basis."

"I see. Have you spoken with her yet about conceiving?"
Sawyer hesitated.

"Sawyer?"

"Ah, forgive me, Lord Somers. No, I haven't broached that subject with her since I first mentioned it nearly two weeks ago."

"You know how important that is."

"I do, but for the uninitiated, it's a rather sensitive subject. I mean, we're talking about a life-long commitment on her part to raise a child specifically to pass this legacy on to. She barely understands her own role in the process, and quite frankly, if the repression doesn't go well, I don't know how willing she'll be to expose her child to it."

"Don't fail us, Sawyer. It's your duty to carry this out."

"I'll do what is within my influence to do. I can do no more than that."

Sawyer hung up the phone and immediately dialed Bridgit. Her phone went to voicemail after several rings. "Bridgit, this is Sawyer. I don't know what you're trying to do, but if you're behind these attacks on Willow, you will live to regret it. Don't mess with me, and don't mess with Willow. I will destroy you if something happens to her, and you know I can do it."

\* \* \*

Lord Somers hung up the phone and folded his arms across his chest. "I specifically told you not to contact her. Why are you disobeying my orders?"

"She owes me. I was so close to gaining control of her

fortune before Willow McCord came along. Imagine what the coven could do with Sawyer's personal riches."

"Her fortune may be beyond our reach at this point due to your thirst for revenge. You will obey me from this point on, is that clear?"

"Yes, Lord Somers."

Bridgit turned and walked away from the priest. An evil grin spread across her face as the conversation inside her head waged on. *I will get my hands on Sawyer's fortune yet—just as soon as we get rid of Willow McCord. Yes... the spawn of the devil will hang, and I will have my revenge.*

\* \* \*

Sawyer visited with Pete while she waited for Willow to get out of work.

"Hey there, Miss Sawyer. How are you doing today?" Pete asked.

"I've had better days, but all in all, I'm doing okay. How is your day going?"

"Couldn't ask for a finer day," Pete said. "Weather's been good, and business is booming."

Sawyer scanned the headlines of the papers on display in Pete's booth. She picked up the paper and reached into her pocket. "What do I owe you for this one?"

"That'll be one dollar fifty cents."

Sawyer paid Pete, folded the newspaper, and put it under her arm.

"Thank you kindly," he said.

Just then, Willow stepped out of her building and onto the sidewalk. "Sorry I'm late. We had a late emergency call in."

"No problem. I had the most marvelous company while I was waiting."

Willow knit her brows together and looked at Pete. "Pete, have you been sweet-talking my girl?"

"Now would I do that to you, Miss Willow? Besides, what would Miss Sawyer want with an old coot like me when she has

you? Now get on out of here, you're wrecking my business."
Pete winked as he accepted a hug from each of the ladies.

"See you tomorrow, Pete," Willow said as they walked
toward the parking garage.

Sawyer glanced at Willow. "Your girl?"

"Well, aren't you?"

"I don't know. Am I?"

"Do you want to be?"

Sawyer stopped Willow by placing a hand on her arm.
"You already know how I feel about you. I've been pretty
honest about that."

"Yes you have." Willow moved again toward the parking
garage. When she saw Sawyer wasn't following her, she turned
and went back. Sawyer gave her a quizzical look. "What?"
Willow asked.

"And you? How do you feel?"

Willow stepped into Sawyer's personal space and kissed
her directly on the mouth. "How do you think I feel?"

"I'm not much of a 'fill in the blanks' kind of girl. If you
leave it to me, I may answer in a way you don't agree with."

"Don't be so sure of that, Sawyer. Now, let's go home so I
can make dinner. I'm starving."

"I spoke to Lord Somers today," Sawyer said as she drove
toward Willow's home.

"Lord Somers. He's the high priest in your coven, right?"

"Yes. He still has no leads on what's behind these
paranormal attacks on you."

"So they're now paranormal attacks? Whatever happened
to apparitions?"

"Apparitions are harmless. What happened to you in that
pool was meant to kill you. No, there's something else going on
here. These are not simply visitations. Anyway, we need to
begin your training immediately, tonight in fact. The sooner you
become familiar with the teachings of the coven, the sooner
you'll know how to casts spells and carry out rituals to protect
yourself."

"I will tell you one thing," Willow said. "I'm beginning to
believe more and more that this is real rather than the mumbo-

jumbo I originally thought it was. When I tried to break the surface of the water in that pool, it was like hitting my head on a windowpane. I just couldn't break through. At least not until you stuck the brooches into the water."

"I'm sorry that it's taken attempts against your life for you to begin believing, but I am glad it's helped you to open your mind and accept things that seem so surreal on the surface."

Sawyer pulled into Willow's driveway and turned off the ignition. Willow threw open the door and climbed out. "I'll get the mail," Sawyer said as she opened her door. "If you want to get dinner started, I'll be there in a minute or two to help."

"Tomato-mozzarella salad sound okay to you?" Willow called over her shoulder as she walked toward the house.

"Sounds great." Sawyer tucked the paper she bought from Pete under her arm and crossed the street to the mailbox opposite the driveway. She retrieved several envelopes, including one addressed to her with no return address. She pondered who it could be from as she headed toward the house. She stopped on the porch and opened the envelope, from which she withdrew a single piece of paper. She read it aloud. "Red rose, thick with thorns. Tattered skin, sliced and torn. Tear my heart out from my chest. No compassion for the rest. Left hand path will beat you down, since you are not honor bound. Rue the day your betrayal rang, 'twill cause you and all yours pain." Sawyer frowned and read the poem again. "What the hell?"

The front door opened. "There you are. I thought you got lost on your way to the mailbox," Willow said.

"Sorry. I became distracted." Sawyer handed the letter to Willow. "Take a look at this, and tell me what you think."

Willow carried the letter into the kitchen with Sawyer following close behind. She sat at the table and read it out loud while Sawyer looked over her shoulder. Willow picked up the envelope and looked at both sides of it.

"No return address," Sawyer said. "I already looked."

"You really pissed someone off. Do you have any idea who sent it?"

"I'm afraid I do."

"I would venture to guess it's from an old girlfriend."

"In her mind, maybe."

Willow got up and pulled another sharp knife and cutting board out of the drawer. She placed them in front of Sawyer. "Okay, I want to hear all the juicy details while you help me make the salads."

Twenty minutes later, Willow and Sawyer sat on adjacent sides of the kitchen table, each with a hearty salad, dinner rolls, and a glass of wine in front of them. "So was Bridgit your girlfriend or not?" Willow asked around a bite of salad.

"It was a complicated relationship. In her mind, we were a couple, but I knew from the start she was only after wealth and status, so I never committed myself to her."

"But you slept with her?"

Sawyer squirmed under Willow's scrutiny. "Technically, yes."

"Look, Sawyer, either you did or you didn't have sex with her. Which is it?"

"I did."

"Was she any good?"

"Oh for crying out loud, Willow. Do you really need to know that?"

"Only if she was better than me."

"Well she wasn't. It was all about satisfying her. She was quite the diva, I must say. You, on the other hand, are warm and tender and more concerned about meeting my needs than your own. Never in a million years did I feel with her what I feel with you."

"That's good. So what do you think she meant by the letter?"

"At first glance, I would say she just intended to make me feel guilty about being here with you, but the second part of the poem is foreboding."

"What do you mean?"

"Look at what it says here: 'Left hand path will beat you down, since you are not honor bound. Rue the day your betrayal rang, 'twill cause you and all yours pain.' The words 'left hand path' usually refer to black magic."

"Bridgit is a witch?"

"Yes, and based on this note and other communications I've received from her this week, I assume she's turned from the light."

"What kind of communications?"

"Veiled threats—just like in the letter, although some of them were directed at you as well as me."

"What are the chances we'll run into this woman when we go to England in two months?"

"Pretty good, I'm afraid."

"Well then, let's get those lessons started so I can whip up some hocus pocus on her ass when we get there!"

# Chapter 45

## 2013—Plymouth, Massachusetts

Willow and Sawyer sat on the rug in the middle of the living room, an array of documents scattered on the floor between them and a half-empty bottle of wine on the coffee table nearby. A fire was burning in the fireplace, and the lights were dimmed.

"Wait… wait… wait. Are you telling me they actually tied those poor women up and threw them in the water and if they floated, they were convicted of being witches and hanged?" Willow asked.

"That's exactly what happened," Sawyer replied.

"So let me get this straight. If they float, they're hanged, and if they don't float, they drown and they're dead anyway."

"In a nutshell, yes."

"Holy shit!"

"The sad thing is that most of these women were simply midwives, or herbalists. They were harmless. Their skills at healing the sick were twisted by organized religion as being supernatural powers of some sort, most likely granted to them by Satan himself. Like the teachings of the Blue Feather Coven, they dedicated their lives to helping others. The clerics couldn't tolerate anything that shifted power from them to anything or anyone else. One way to prevent that was to kill those perceived as powerful."

Willow picked up the bottle of wine from the coffee table and refilled their glasses. "So, what about burning at the stake? I mean, that's what we think of first, relative to the witch hunts."

"Actually, there wasn't much of that done in England. There was some, granted, but most of it took place in Scotland

and other places in Europe. There were fire tests though. Women accused of being witches were required to either walk on hot coals, or carry red hot irons in their bare hands for a distance of about three feet. If they still had open wounds after three days, they were convicted of being witches and hanged. Funny thing is, if you could bribe the right corrupt cleric, they could be convinced the wounds were healed even if they weren't."

"The bastards. Someone ought to stick a hot poker up their asses and see if they heal in three days."

"So you can understand why Jenna and Hadley had to be so careful. Being found out could cost them their lives, and the risk was doubled if one was a homosexual. The coven was a way to afford protection for people who practiced white magic. Outwardly, they appeared simply to be a group of people who lived in communes."

"Wait a minute. I'm confused. So the coven isn't a place then. It's kind of a group or club, kind of like a family. Is that right?"

"Exactly. Coven members don't necessarily have to live together. Today, that rarely happens, but in the 1600s in England, it was almost a necessity in order to afford protection for the group."

"I've heard you talk about your high priest."

"Lord Somers?"

"Yes. Is he the president of the coven?"

Sawyer chuckled. "In a way. There is usually a couple, most often a man and a woman, who lead the coven. They're referred to as the high priest and high priestess. They have pretty much absolute power over the running of the coven, who is initiated, and so on."

"So how does one become a witch?"

"It's not so much how to become a witch, but how to find the witch within your soul. It's a choice you need to make for yourself. If you choose to be a witch, you're basically deciding to put your life on a spiritual path that embraces life and the Goddess Hecate. It isn't a decision to take lightly. You can't just turn it on and off at will. It becomes a life-altering decision, and it will affect the way you look at everything around you. It's amazingly empowering."

"It all seems so overwhelming. I don't know where to start," Willow said.

"Where to start and how quickly you transform really depends on you. If you're the kind of person that completely throws herself into something, then the transformation may happen sooner than if you approach it cautiously. So, I think the best place to start is within your heart and soul."

"We have so little time before the uprising."

"That's true. I'll help you learn the rituals and spells as soon as possible, but equally as important is to get yourself into a psychological frame of mind in order to accept the Goddess. She will give you the strength to deal with the uprising."

Willow signed heavily. "Sawyer, I have to admit I'm not keen on changing my entire focus in life toward being a witch. I kind of like the way my life is."

"Willow, I know witches who allow the craft to consume them. Their very identity is tied to being a witch. I also know witches who practice the craft only when it suits them and otherwise live very ordinary lives. I firmly believe that anything in excess is not good for you... even if by itself, it's something good. I'm not asking you to become consumed by witchcraft. What I am asking you to do is to become aware of your potential and your place in the universe and to use it to promote goodness in the world. How involved you become is totally up to you."

"So, what about you? Where do you fall on the spectrum of involvement?"

"Me? I usually start each day with a prayer to the Goddess to give me strength, wisdom, and guidance throughout the day, and I try to do something each day in her name that will improve the world around me. Most evenings, I light a candle to the Goddess to thank her for her support throughout the day. It's kind of like bedtime prayers in Christianity."

"And you do spells. I've been witness to one or two of them."

"Yes, I do spells and rituals when needed. What you've

seen me do while I've been here is pretty much an exception. I've done more spells this past week than I normally do in a month. My day-to-day life is relatively boring compared to this."

"Will you teach me how to cast all those magic spells you hear about witches doing?"

"One thing you need to understand is that witches are not magicians. Learning how to do spells is not about suddenly having amazing powers. It's about learning how to use your inner strength and spirituality to harness the energy of the moon and earth. You'll need to learn the basic Wicca chants, circle principles, energy principles, and coven etiquette before you become initiated. I'll help you learn all that."

"So I'll need to be initiated into the coven to be a witch?"

"Yes and no. You don't need to be initiated into anything to be a witch, but you'll need to be initiated into the coven to be a Wiccan."

"Can't you just do that for me here?"

"We need permission from the high priest and priestess, but if you're nervous about it, we can do a practice initiation so you can see what it'll be like."

"I'd like that."

"Okay then, let me run upstairs to get my backpack. There are a few things in there I'll need."

"Great. That gives me a chance to go pee and to fetch another bottle of wine."

When Willow returned to the living room, Sawyer was already back and removing several items from her backpack including a bell, a bottle of scented oil, incense, a censer, a lighter, a length of cord, and a blindfold.

Willow opened the new bottle of wine and refilled their glasses. She added another log to the fire and sat down on the rug facing Sawyer. She took a long draw on her wine and put her glass on the coffee table.

"Off with your clothes," Sawyer said.

"What?"

"The first part of the ritual is done with the initiate naked."

"Seriously? And exactly who will be at this ceremony in October?"

"Most of the coven members."

"Do you really expect me to get naked in front of a room full of strangers?"

"Actually, it will be outside."

"At night, I hope!"

"Yes, at night, with a bonfire for atmosphere," Sawyer said, grinning at Willow's discomfort.

"Damn, woman, what I do for you!" Willow stood again and took off all of her clothes.

"You can sit," Sawyer said, motioning to the rug in front of her.

"No freakin' way. If I'm getting naked, you're getting naked, too."

"I won't be naked at the ceremony," Sawyer said.

"All the more reason for you to be naked now."

"If you insist." Sawyer climbed to her feet and stripped off all her clothes.

"Now that's what I'm talkin' about," Willow said as they both sat down facing each other.

"Okay, the initiation starts with you being led blindfolded into the circle." Sawyer picked up the blindfold and tied it securely around Willow's eyes.

"You're not going to do anything funky, are you?"

"No."

"Damn."

"Stop your cursing. It's bad karma."

"Oops."

"Once you're in the circle, the high priest will say something like, 'Everyone is welcome within the circle to find love and peace. No one in the circle will be lonely or without a friend. No one in the circle will be without a brother or sister. All are welcome.' You will then be introduced by the escort who led you into the circle, and the high priest and priestess will alternately ask you questions about why you are there and if you came of your own free will. Don't worry about any of that right now. I'll help you rehearse your answers."

"And all of this is done with me standing there naked."

"Yes."

"Sweet Hecate!" Willow joked.

"They will then ask who is sponsoring your initiation. I will answer that question. After that, they will bind your hands together with a nine-foot length of cord."

"Bondage, too! Woo-hoo! You didn't tell me this was going to be kinky."

"Very funny, Willow. Now hold out your hands."

Willow held out her hands and allowed Sawyer to tie the cord around them.

"Once the cord is wrapped around your hands, the priest will again ask you to identify yourself and the reason you're there. You'll tell the priest who you are and that you are there naked and unadorned."

"It will be pretty obvious to the casual onlooker than I'll be naked and unadorned," Willow said.

"Hush! He will then anoint you with salted water like so."

Sawyer took her scented oil and rubbed a liberal amount over Willow's chest. She lit a cone of incense and placed it in the censer on the coffee table. "Then the priest will take some incense and circle it around you. Can you smell it?"

"Yes. It smells good."

"At this point, you'll hear a bell ring." Sawyer gently shook the bell. "The priest or priestess will then ask if you are ready to give up your old ways and learn the ways of the Goddess. You of course will say yes. The escort will cut a lock of your hair and put it in the censer, and again the bell will ring three times. Finally, your blindfold will be removed and you will face the coven members. In all your glory, I might add."

"Don't remind me."

Sawyer did not remove the blindfold.

"You will then pledge your love and support to the coven and to the Goddess, after which the priest will ask you to recite the Wiccan Rede."

"Which is?" Willow asked.

"As it harms none, do what thou wilt."

"As it harms none, do what thou wilt," Willow repeated. "I like that."

"At this point, the cord is removed from your wrists and the high priestess will draw a Celtic cross in a circle on your forehead with the anointing oil, like this. " Sawyer drew the Celtic cross on Willow's forehead. "Then she will draw an inverted triangle on your torso in this order... from your pubis to your right breast, from your right breast to the left breast, and from your left breast to your pubis."

Willow moaned as Sawyer's fingers traced the triangle in oil on her bare skin.

"The priestess will say something like 'with this sacred oil, I cleanse thee. You are now a member of this circle and one with your brothers and sisters of the coven. So be it, one and all.' Finally, the priestess will kiss you on both cheeks and call for a celebration. That's pretty much it."

"Then can I put on a robe or something?"

"Yes, of course." Sawyer picked up her wine and took a drink. "This wine is good."

"Ah...did you forget something?" Willow said.

Sawyer took another sip. "I don't think so."

"I'm still standing here in front of the coven, naked, bound, and blindfolded."

"Oh, I didn't forget. That was on purpose," Sawyer said.

"On purpose?"

"Yes. I'm not a stupid woman. I have you right where I want you... naked, bound, blindfolded, and covered in oil—all in front of a cozy fire with incense burning in the background and a good bottle of wine at hand. What more could a girl ask for?"

"Sweet Hecate!" Willow said as she allowed Sawyer to push her onto her back in front of the fire.

# Chapter 46

## 1613—Billingham, England

Hadley was hanging clothes on the line outside their cottage when a lone rider galloped rapidly into the compound on a horse frothing with exhaustion. He fell off his horse just a few feet from Hadley.

"Quick, my lady, I need to see the high priest," he said, his breath short and rapid.

About a dozen community members ran toward the man from several points across the common, including Jenna, still dressed in her blacksmith apron. "Hadley, pray get the man some water." She turned to the gentleman. "What is it, kind sir?" Jenna asked.

"I… I need to see the high priest. Grave danger awaits. Many deaths in Lancashire," he said.

Jenna grabbed a young lad out of the crowd by the scruff of the neck. "Jonathan, see to this poor man's horse," she said.

"Aye,' the boy said, taking the reins out of the man's hands.

"Please, take me to the high priest. I come from the coven at Malkin Tower."

"Pray tell, what hath happened?"

Just then, Hadley returned with a glass of water. "Drink, sire," she said.

The man drank the entire contents of the glass without pause and handed it back to Hadley. "Gramercy, Mistress."

Jenna extended her hand and helped the man to his feet. "Come hither. I shall take thee to Lord Weller."

"Wait here," Jenna said to the man as she entered the quarters of Lord Weller. Moments later, she exited. "Lord Weller will see thee now." Jenna allowed the man to enter but held her hand up to the dozen or so clan members who followed her and their guest to Lord Weller's chambers. "He doth request only our visitor and one escort. I shall take him in." Jenna entered behind the man and directed him to a small room at the far side of the great room where he stood before the high priest.

"What is thy name, kind sir?" Lord Weller asked.

'Michael Donnelley," the man replied. "Michael Donnelley from the Pendle area of Lancashire."

"Michael Donnelley, what is the urgency that brings thee to Billingham?"

Donnelley fell to his knees in front of the priest. He held his hat in his hand, his head bent low. "My lord, a fortnight ago, two score citizens were imprisoned for witchcraft in Lancashire."

"Sweet Goddess," said Lord Weller. "Pray tell, how?"

"'Tis said a peddler named John Law haggled with a poor young mistress named Alizon Device near Colne. During the encounter, he fell into a fit that left him with his head drawn awry and a hideous look upon his face. He had not speech to make himself heard, and his arm and leg on one side were unable to move. Mistress Device was arrested and confessed to bewitching the poor man. Magistrate Roger Nowell was summoned, and Mistress Device accused her grandmum of leading her astray."

"Her grandmum? What is the woman's name?" Lord Weller asked.

"Demdike. She is well known in the Lancashire area for charms, cures, magic, and curses. Magistrate Nowell questioned her and her daughter—and Demdike's rival Old Chattox and her daughter Anne. All were arrested and thrown into the Lancashire jail."

"When did this happen?"

"Five moons ago."

"Michael Donnelley—thou hast mentioned two score arrested. Pray tell, who be the others?"

"Not long after the women were arrested, Mistress Device's younger brother and sister told the magistrate there was a great meeting of witches at Demdike's house at Malkin Tower. The town folk say the meeting was to discuss the fate of the women arrested and the fear of more arrests, but the children told the magistrate the witches planned to blow up Lancaster Castle and free the witches."

"Who was at the meeting that night?"

"'Tis told they were family members and neighbors and a high bred woman named Alice Nutter."

"Sounds like a lowly group of common folk. Why would a well-bred woman be in their midst?" Jenna asked.

"'Tis not known. Mistress Nutter was known to be a Catholic. Thou knowest how the Puritans feel about them. She was rounded up along with all the others at the meeting, named by the children, and thrown in the dungeon where they sat four moons. One of them died in the dungeon. The trial was held near seven days ago. It took but two days to try them. Ten were hanged, eight were let go, and one sentenced to stand in the pillory."

Lord Weller rose, walked a few feet away, and turned to face Donnelley once more. "Why didst thou ride all this way to deliver this news, Michael Donnelley?"

"Lord Sneddon of the Malkin Tower Coven bid me leave, Lord Weller. He fears the Puritans do seek out more of our kind. The uprising will be two moons hence and may draw Puritan forces. Lord Sneddon sends word of caution and secrecy for the repression."

Lord Weller turned to Jenna. "See that this man has food and a warm bed and is paid handsomely for his trouble, then return to me. Blessed be, Michael Donnelley."

"Aye, sire." Jenna led the man out of Lord Weller's quarters and escorted him to the inn. A short time later, she returned.

"Pray, sit," Lord Weller said. "Summon the Council of Thirteen to meet at the next moon three days hence. The repression must not be discovered. We must call on the Goddess for help."

* * *

Jenna returned to her quarters that evening with a heavy heart, a fact not missed by Hadley as soon as she entered the house. "What is the problem, Jenna?"

Jenna knelt at the side of each cradle and kissed her children tenderly on the forehead. She took Hadley in an embrace and held her close.

"Thou art shaking, blacksmith. Pray tell, what is wrong?"

"The rider brought distressing news. Ten of our brethren in the Malkin Tower Coven were hanged for witchcraft two days ago."

"Sweet Goddess, save their souls," Hadley said. "Who did this heinous act?"

"From all accounts, the Puritans, and 'tis told they seek others."

"Jenna—the babes… they must not be harmed."

"Aye."

"What shalt thou do?"

"We must cloak the repression in a veil of secrecy. If found out, many will die and evil will escape the gates of Tartarus."

# Chapter 47

## 2013—Plymouth, Massachusetts

Sawyer sat in a tub full of hot water, leaning against the back wall, with Willow sitting between her legs. Willow's back rested against Sawyer's chest. Both were drinking white zinfandel wine. A half-empty wine bottle sat on the floor outside the tub, just within Willow's reach.

"I kind of knew when I was in third grade," Willow said. "My first crush was on Candy Johnson. She was amazingly beautiful to my eight-year-old mind."

"Eight years old, were you?" Sawyer said. "I was much older than that."

"How old?"

"I was in secondary school before I realized it."

"Secondary school? As in high school?"

"Tenth grade to be exact."

"That would be a sophomore in high school in the US. So you were what? Fourteen?"

"Something like that."

"You had no idea before then," Willow stated rather than asked.

"Well, I knew I didn't like boys, but it didn't occur to me I could like girls. It wasn't something I was exposed to as a child."

"You make it sound like something contagious," Willow joked.

Sawyer chuckled. "I've never met anyone like you before, Willow."

"What do you mean?"

"From the top of your curly red head to the tips of your toes, you're unique."

"Unique can be good."

"I quite agree. Seriously though, you speak your mind without fear of retribution and without apology. You're adventurous and fun loving and totally uninhibited. I wish I was more like you."

"How so?"

"Take tonight, for example. I've never shared a tub with a romantic interest. It would never cross my mind to do so."

Willow tilted her head back on Sawyer's chest so she could see her face. "I thought the bondage situation I found myself in earlier tonight was pretty original. And quite enjoyable, I might add."

Sawyer grinned. "I honestly don't know where that came from. All of a sudden I found myself in a situation I couldn't resist. I mean, there you were, totally naked, blindfolded, and tied up. I couldn't help but take advantage. You didn't seem to mind."

Willow continued to look at Sawyer over her shoulder. "Mind? Hell, no! I enjoyed every minute of it. I'm proud of you for thinking of it. By the way, blush becomes you."

"Stop it. You're embarrassing me. I don't know how to explain the effect you have on me. You make me look at life differently. You make me believe I can have the best of both worlds—success, status, money, as well as love, happiness, and fun. I grew up basically believing they were mutually exclusive."

"The way I look at it is this—if you have love, happiness, and fun, you are automatically successful. Money is nice, too, but as long as your needs are being met, you only need so much. My richness comes from the people I surround myself with, not from the balance in my bank account."

Sawyer scooped up handfuls of warm water and poured them over Willow's chest and shoulders.

"That feels nice," Willow said. "You've got exactly two hours to stop that."

"It's getting kind of late. You have to work tomorrow,

right?"

"Yes. What time is it anyway?"

Sawyer picked her phone up off the floor beside the tub. "Nearly eleven."

"Ugh! I really do need to get to bed. Six o'clock comes early."

Sawyer wrapped her arms around Willow and kissed the side of her head. "Thank you for tonight. This is the most enjoyable evening I've had in a long time."

"You're welcome. Unfortunately, all good things come to an end." Willow pushed the button drain release with her foot, and the water level immediately began to lower. She climbed to her feet and stood between Sawyer's legs while she reached for her towel. She stepped out of the tub, and Sawyer followed close behind.

"Here, let me dry your back." Sawyer wiped the moisture from Willow's back with her own towel. Willow returned the favor, hung her towel on the rack, and reached for her toothbrush. Sawyer followed suit as they stood side by side brushing their teeth.

"Look at us," Sawyer said. "We look like an old married couple."

Willow grinned. "Do you want to be the husband or the wife?"

"I'll be the husband. Unlike you, I'm not girly enough to be the wife."

Willow rinsed her mouth, put her toothbrush away, and waited while Sawyer did the same. "Okay then, husband, take me to bed," she said giggling.

"Is this where I'm supposed to scratch my balls and fart?" Sawyer asked, trying hard to sound serious.

Willow roared with laughter. "That was funny. See, you do have a sense of humor when you let yourself relax."

"Yes. It's easier than I thought it would be."

Sawyer reached for the bathroom door and pulled it open. Willow screamed at the top of her lungs. Standing in the doorway was the woman Willow had seen in her window from the backyard. Willow's hand immediately flew to her throat, and she realized she wasn't wearing the brooches. She had taken them off before climbing into the bathtub with Sawyer.

Sawyer stood in front of Willow. "Where are the brooches, Willow?"

"On the edge of the sink."

Sawyer quickly looked behind her and grabbed them by the chain. She held them up toward the apparition and shouted "Begone!" The brooches glowed, but the apparition remained.

"Why isn't it working?" Willow peeked out from behind Sawyer.

"Because this one isn't evil." Sawyer lowered the brooches.

"Who are you?" Willow asked.

"'Tis right. I am not evil. Child, I am thy grandmother, thirteen generations past." The apparition looked at Sawyer. "And thine, too, Sawyer Hawksworth."

Sawyer's eyes grew wide.

Willow stepped out from behind Sawyer and walked directly up to the apparition. Although seemingly flesh and blood, when Willow reached out to touch the woman, her hand encountered only air. The hair on her arm stood on end as a surge of energy passed through it.

"Hadley?"

"Aye, child."

Sawyer grabbed one of the robes hanging behind the bathroom door and held it out for Willow. "Here, put this on," she said and took another for herself.

Willow never took her eyes off Hadley as she closed the front of the robe and tied the belt. "Why are you here?" she asked.

"I sensed thine unrest, child. I sensed thy doubt."

"About the repression?"

Hadley nodded. "Aye, and the Goddess. When Jenna Hawksworth first came to me, my doubts were strong. I thought she was a crazy woman and consorting with a witch could mean death for us both. Fear closed my mind."

"How did you get over it?"

"I trusted the love Jenna had for me, and I trusted the Goddess." Hadley looked at Sawyer. "Sawyer Hawksworth, thou wearest thy love for Willow on thy face, in thy words, and in thine actions. Thy love will make her strong. Thy love will make you both powerful."

"I love Willow with all my heart," Sawyer said. "I would die for her."

"Much like my Jenna, thou art. Thy grandmother Jenna put herself in peril to save my life and those of our babes."

"How did you get here? How is this even possible?" Willow asked as she pulled her robe tighter around her.

"The brooches," Hadley replied.

Sawyer looked at the brooches in her hand. "What do you mean?"

"I shall tell you all you need to know, but I fear I keep you from much-needed sleep. I shall return again on the morrow."

"No, don't go," Willow said.

"Fear not, I shall return. I have much knowledge to impart. Pleasant dreams, my children, and blessed be to you both."

In an instant, Hadley was gone. Willow and Sawyer looked at each other. "Oh, my God," Willow said as tears formed in her eyes. The intensity of emotion she felt was overwhelming.

Sawyer took her into her arms, her own body trembling from shock. "I know. I know," she said. "Come on, let's go to bed."

* * *

Sawyer met Willow outside her office building when she got off work. She took Willow into her arms and held her close. "How was work today?"

"The day dragged on forever. Not that we were any busier than usual, it's just that I have a lot on my mind and it was hard to concentrate."

"Same here. I'm anxious for Hadley to return. I never dreamed we'd have an opportunity to talk to her or Jenna directly."

They headed toward the parking garage. "Do you have any idea how crazy this sounds?" Willow asked.

"Even I have to admit you're right about that."

They were silent for the next few minutes. "Would you really die for me?" Willow asked.

Sawyer touched her arm, stopping them both. "I would. I've never felt this way about anyone in my life."

Willow's eyes filled with tears. She leaned in and kissed Sawyer on the lips. "Thank you," she said and began walking again toward the garage.

Willow unlocked the front door and pushed it open with her hip. "I'll start dinner. How about you make a fire in the fireplace? It will be nice to have a conversation with Hadley somewhere else besides the bathroom while we were wearing our birthday suits."

"I can do that."

"Parmesan chicken and a veggie sound okay to you?"

"It sounds wonderful. May I help with something?"

"No, just start the fire. I've got everything covered in here," Willow called from the kitchen.

Sawyer arranged a teepee of kindling over crumpled newspaper in the firebox and lit the paper. As she watched the fire grow and slowly ignite the kindling, she heard a repetitious pounding coming from the kitchen. "What the devil is that?" she said under her breath and went to investigate. "What are you doing?" she asked as she entered the kitchen and saw Willow pounding two chicken breasts with a flat-sided mallet.

"Killing the chicken breasts. They tried to get up and run away." She laughed hysterically at the look on Sawyer's face. "I'm tenderizing them, silly. How's the fire?"

Sawyer glanced back toward the living room. "The kindling was just starting when I heard you beating our dinner up. It should be ready for more substantial pieces of wood by now." She returned to the living room to tend the fire.

Willow turned on the oven and prepared the dinner. Afterward, she joined Sawyer in the living room.

"Nice fire," she said, and knelt down next to Sawyer in front of it. "Dinner should be ready in about fifteen minutes."

They stared at the flames for several minutes, neither one speaking. Finally, Sawyer broke the silence.

"Hadley said you felt fear. Is that true?"

"Fear is just one of several emotions I'm feeling. Anxiety, trepidation, and maybe even a little anger being a few of the others."

"I understand the anxiety and trepidation, but anger? Have I done something to anger you?"

Willow turned to Sawyer. "Sweetheart, you've been a little insistent perhaps, with some pretty wild demands I might add, but otherwise you've been nothing but kind and considerate. No, I'm not angry with you."

"Then why?"

"I'm angry with the situation. I didn't ask for this. When I think about what might happen if we fail… it's overwhelming."

"We won't fail. We can't fail."

"I hope you're right."

Sawyer trailed the tip of her index finger down the side of Willow's face. "We will get through this, Wills. I promise you. We will get through this."

After dinner, Willow and Sawyer retreated to the living room, each with a cup of tea. Sawyer put two additional pieces of wood on the fire.

"Before I forget," Sawyer said, "thank you for dinner. The chicken was wonderful."

"I'm glad you liked it. That's a recipe I got from my good friend Donna, who lives a couple of hours from here. I jokingly call them Donna's Breasts. They're quite succulent, wouldn't you agree?"

"Indeed. You must tell your friend I quite enjoyed nibbling on her breasts."

"I'll do that." Willow stared at the fire for several minutes.

"Sawyer, Hadley said something about Jenna putting her life in peril to save her and their children. Do you have any idea what she meant by that?"

"Documented history is pretty sketchy, but I believe the king's men found out about the repression ritual and arrested several coven members, including Jenna. Legend has it Jenna allowed herself to be arrested to give Hadley time to escape with the babies."

Willow stared at the fire once more through the veil of tears in her eyes. "Were they burned at the stake?" she asked softly.

"No. Most of the captured were hanged. Some were subjected to water torture and subsequently died."

Willow looked at Sawyer. "Was Jenna among them?"

Sawyer looked back at the fire and didn't answer.

Willow bowed her head and allowed the tears to flow down her cheeks. "My God. How could someone do that to another human being? Those poor babies. Hadley must have been beside herself with grief."

"Aye, I was."

"Hadley!" Willow exclaimed. "You came back."

"I said as much last eve, child. A body is only as good as its word."

Sawyer rose from her position by the fireplace and joined Willow on the couch. "Please, sit," she said.

Hadley sat in the chair opposite the couch. "So, where were we last eve?"

"I asked how it was possible that you're here," Willow said.

"Aye. I remember. As thou knowest, Sawyer, when Jenna forged the brooches, she cast a spell on each that allowed the spirits of the chosen to inhabit them. Alone, each brooch holds the spirits of the owner's ancestors. When the brooches are joined, all the ancestors are free to work together. And only when they are joined is any spirit allowed to walk in the land of the living."

"So the joined brooches act as a gate to the land of the living?" Willow asked.

"Aye. 'Tis been since the last repression that the spirit of a chosen one has walked among you."

"Why?" Willow asked.

"Because the brooches have been apart since Maggie and Richelle had them," Sawyer answered for Hadley. "As long as the brooches remain apart, the spirits of our ancestors are trapped inside them."

"'Tis true in part, Sawyer," Hadley said. "The spirits of the chosen ones are free to move in the spiritual realm but not in the living one unless the brooches are joined. This time is called 'The Time of The Joining.' The brooches have been joined for the lifetimes of five generations, all of whom committed their lives to each other. Hadley Metcalf and Jenna Hawksworth, Machara MacDonald and Rowena Hawksworth, Keeley McVicker and Maeve Hawksworth, Maggie McCord and Richelle Hawksworth, and now you, Willow McCord and Sawyer Hawksworth. During these lifetimes, the brooches have been joined, only to be separated when passed down to their descendents."

"Are you saying all of our ancestors who participated in the repression rituals were lesbian couples?" Willow asked.

"Aye. The power of love is immense. The strength of a spell is greater when supported by the passion between those who cast it."

Willow rose and paced back and forth across the room, unconsciously playing with the brooches hanging around her neck. "Why didn't my father tell me any of this? So much is at stake here. What if Sawyer hadn't found me?"

"Fear not, child. The Goddess would have found a way to put thee and Sawyer together to join the brooches and allow me to do what thy sire did not. 'Tis my duty as a teacher spirit to impart what I know."

"Teacher spirit?" Sawyer asked.

"Aye. The spirits of the chosen ones are either teachers or spirit hunters. Those among us who are teachers impart ancient wisdom to chosen ones to assure that the knowledge and power are passed down to those who will fight the uprising. Those among us who doth not teach, use The Time of The Joining to seek out and destroy evil that walks in the land of the living. My Jenna is a spirit hunter. You may not know it, but Jenna has watched over both of you all your lives."

"Are you saying there have been evil spirits after us since we've been born?" Willow asked.

"Aye, 'tis true. One spirit in particular seeks revenge on all descendants of Jenna and me. Jenna hath been watching over all of you since she committed her soul to the brooch."

Willow turned to Sawyer. "Did you know about all of this?"

"Not all of it. It appears I have some learning to do myself."

"That thou dost, my girl," Hadley said. "'Tis nearly three moons to the uprising. I have much knowledge to impart to both of you afore then."

# Chapter 48

## 2013—Plymouth, Massachusetts

Sawyer hefted Willow's suitcase into the trunk of her car. "Is that the last of it?"

"I think so," Willow said. "Are you sure you want to leave your clothes here? We haven't really talked about whether you're coming back."

Sawyer grabbed Willow around the waist and pressed her up against the car. "Do you want me to come back?" she asked.

"Well, I've kind of gotten used to having you around. These two months have flown by so fast."

"Yes they have. Of course, having Hadley pop in and out all the time made it go by even faster."

"I'll say. She's such a big help though. I feel a lot more comfortable going to England now than I did two months ago."

"I wonder if feistiness is a hereditary trait?" Sawyer asked.

"Why?"

"Because your personality and hers are so similar, it's almost scary. I'll bet she gave Jenna a run for her money."

"Are you saying I'm difficult to handle, Ms. Hawksworth?"

"Those are your words, not mine, Ms. McCord."

Willow looked at her watch. "We'd better hit the road. Our flight leaves in three hours, and it'll take half that time just to get to the airport."

"Is your father going to meet us there?" Sawyer climbed into the passenger seat.

"Yes. Mom is actually looking forward to some time by herself while he's gone." Willow closed the driver's door and hooked her seatbelt. "Buckle up."

Sawyer grabbed her seatbelt. "I'm glad he's going. He is, after all, one of the chosen. His presence there will only add power to the repression."

"I think he really wants to go to keep an eye on me. He and mom are both worried I'm going to be blown up or something during this thing."

"He loves you. Be happy he wants to go. I wish my father was still here to participate."

"Thank you for inviting him to stay at the estate."

"I wouldn't have it any other way. He's your father. He's part of you, so by default, he's part of me."

"I'm kind of sad these two months are over. Who'd have thought when you showed up on my doorstep that we would become as close as we are. It's like I've known you all my life."

"I'm a firm believer in destiny, Willow. When something is meant to be, the forces around us find a way to make it happen. It feels so familiar because we've been linked through this legacy even before we were born."

"So you believe we were meant to be together... to be a couple?"

"I do. The Goddess wouldn't have put us together otherwise."

Willow frowned at Sawyer. "Okay, that's where I draw the line. I think people fall in love because they're compatible and their souls touch in a unique and loving way—not because the Goddess planned it even before we were born."

Sawyer grinned. "Are you saying you're in love with me?"

"I'm saying I don't think we were born specifically to be together."

"But we are together. How do you explain that? It's like the brooches. When I sent mine to you, you knew it wasn't a coincidence that two pieces of jewelry a half a world apart could possibly fit together. Like it or not, we are like the brooches. We fit together. You just need to admit it to yourself."

Willow pulled off the road and put the car into park. She threw her hands up. "Okay. Okay. You win. I love you. Is that what you want to hear? I love you. You have wormed your way into my heart, and I can't imagine my life without you anymore. Damn you, Sawyer Hawksworth." Willow folded her arms across her chest and pouted.

Sawyer touched her arm. "I guess this means I'm coming back."

\* \* \*

"Daddy, there's your bag coming around the carousel right now," Willow said.

"I see it." Roger grabbed his bag from the moving belt and carried it to where Sawyer and Willow waited. "I don't know about you girls, but I'm beat. Ten hours in an airplane is not my idea of fun."

"We'll be home soon. My place is only ten miles from here," Sawyer said. "There's the exit. Follow me."

"Should I hail a taxi?" Roger asked.

"That won't be necessary. Ian will be here to collect us."

The trio exited the airport terminal to find a limousine waiting for them at the curb.

"Nice!" Roger said.

Willow grabbed Sawyer's arm and held her back for a moment. "Is this for real? Is this really yours?"

"No, Willow. This is really ours. Yours and mine."

"Holy shit!"

"Welcome home, Ms. Hawksworth," the driver said as he held the door.

"Thank you, Ian. I'm pleased to introduce Mr. Roger McCord and Ms. Willow McCord," Sawyer said.

Roger and Willow both extended their hands. After a moment's hesitation and a slight nod from Sawyer, Ian accepted their greeting and shook their hands. "It's so nice to meet you, Ian," Willow said.

"The pleasure is all mine. Please, have a seat. I will take care of your bags."

Twenty minutes later, the limo pulled up to an elaborate brick archway with a gate across the entrance. Ian punched a number into the keypad mounted on a pedestal near the edge of the drive, and the gate swung open. A full mile later, the manor came into view.

"Sweet Goddess," Willow said under her breath. "It's massive."

"This is your home, Sawyer?" Roger asked.

"It's where my parents lived. My father built up the estate over many years. It's now a successfully producing farm. The excess produce is taken to the local farmer's market. Whatever doesn't sell, as well as the proceeds from what does sell, goes to a food bank in town. I'm looking forward to showing you around."

Ian pulled the car up to the front entrance and held the door open for everyone to exit.

"Let me give you a hand with our luggage," Roger offered.

"That isn't necessary, sir. I'll take care of it."

Just then, the front door opened and a robust older woman came running out. "It's so good to have you home again, bumpkin!" she said as she enveloped Sawyer in a hug.

"It's good to be home again, Matty," Sawyer replied.

"Let me take a look at you." Matilda circled Sawyer, poking and prodding her. "Someone has been feeding you well, although you look a little knackered."

"We just sat on an airplane for ten hours," Sawyer said. "So, yes, I'm a little tired." Sawyer glanced at Willow and rolled her eyes.

Willow grinned from ear to ear. When Sawyer finally broke free of Matilda, she took Willow's arm and pushed her in front of her. "Matty, I'd like you to meet Willow McCord."

Matilda put her hands on her hips. "So this is the Yank that has stolen your heart."

Willow raised her eyebrows and looked at Sawyer.

"You're right, bumpkin. She is a pretty one. Come here and give Matty a hug."

Willow found herself buried in the woman's arms. She looked over Matilda's shoulder and mouthed the word "help" to Sawyer, who simply grinned.

"One more introduction, Matty. This is Roger McCord, Willow's father."

Roger stepped forward, took Matilda's hand and kissed the back of it while bowing. "It is so nice to make your acquaintance, Ms. Matilda."

"Oh, this one has manners," Matilda said. "It is nice to make your acquaintance as well, Mr. McCord."

"Please, come inside." Sawyer led the procession into the building.

"This is an amazing home, Sawyer," Roger said.

"There'll be plenty of time for a tour tomorrow, but considering it's already seven p.m., I vote we have a late dinner and retire for the night. Is that okay with everyone?" Sawyer looked around at several nodding heads.

Ian stepped forward. "If you wish, I'll show Mr. McCord to his room so he can freshen up before dinner."

"That would be great, Ian. Thank you."

"I'll tell cook to begin setting the table," Matilda said. She hugged Sawyer again. "Welcome home, bumpkin."

Sawyer took Willow's hand and led her toward the grand staircase in the middle of the room. "I'll show you to our rooms."

"Okay, bumpkin."

Sawyer hip-checked her.

"We're all the way to the end of the hall," Sawyer said.

"How many people live here?" Willow asked.

"Just me and a staff of about twenty. The staff's quarters are on a lower level."

"It's a lot of house for so few people."

"I know. It really needs to be lived in by a family. Here we are." Sawyer pushed open the door to her chambers.

Willow stepped into an elaborate sitting room, complete with an ornate desk, floor-to-ceiling bookcases, and a large-screen television. "You sleep in a living room?"

"No, this is just the sitting room. The bedroom and bathroom suite is beyond that door over there. I spend most of my time in this room when I'm home."

Willow walked to the door and opened it. The room

spanned nearly the entire width of the house. The furnishings included a king-size four-poster bed, oversized ornate Victorian dressers, and another sitting area with two couches, two oversized chairs, and several tables. "Damn. My entire house would fit in this space." On the back wall was another door that led to a very large bathroom with Jacuzzi tub and separate shower. Both rooms had windows that started about knee high and extended almost to the ceiling. Willow turned to Sawyer. "This is crazy. I feel like a pauper after you spent the last ten weeks in my meager home."

Sawyer took her hand and led her back into the bedroom. "You need to understand that this was my parents' home. Before I moved back here after they died, I lived in a relatively modest high-rise flat in London that was actually smaller than your house."

"But you grew up here, right?"

"Yes. In fact, this has been my bedroom since I was a child."

"This was a kid's bedroom? Geesh. I can imagine what the master bedroom looks like."

"It actually takes up the entire upper story. It's more of a flat than a bedroom."

"Go figure."

"I sense a bit of discomfort in you."

Willow looked around. "Sawyer, this is all really nice, but it's just not me. I'm a pretty simple girl."

"You can't envision yourself living here?"

"I don't know. Maybe, but it would be a huge adjustment. For starters, I'd have a really hard time bossing the servants around."

"To be honest with you, I do, too. I don't like it at all, and I try to avoid it. You see how Matty is with me. I wouldn't dream of bossing her around. She'd whack me a good one if I even tried."

"I like her, especially when she calls you 'bumpkin.'"

"Ugh! That was her childhood nickname for me."

"It's obvious how much she loves you."

"Yes. She's been with my family since before I was born. I spent more time on her knee and following her around the estate than I spent with my own parents."

Willow wrapped her arms around Sawyer's waist. "I'm glad you had her in your life. It sounds like you needed her."

Sawyer lowered her head and kissed Willow. "Yes, I did." She kissed her again... and again.

"Aren't we supposed to be freshening up for dinner or something?" Willow said between kisses.

"Something like that." Sawyer kissed her yet again.

"Sweetie, my dad is probably downstairs by now. Maybe we should save this for dessert."

It was nearly ten p.m. by the time Sawyer and Willow said goodnight and went upstairs with strict orders not to disturb them in the morning. Sawyer went directly to the bathroom and began to fill the Jacuzzi with warm water. She threw in a handful of eucalyptus bath salts, which instantly filled the air with an evergreen aroma. As soon as the tub was filled above the level of the jets, Sawyer and Willow climbed in.

"This is heavenly," Willow said as the warm water churned around her.

"Come here. Let me wash your hair." Sawyer removed the spray nozzle. She sat behind Willow and massaged the shampoo through her hair.

"That feels so good," Willow said. "You're going to put me to sleep."

"Tilt your head back so I can rinse."

Willow shifted toward the end of the Jacuzzi and partially lay back while Sawyer rinsed her hair. In this position, one of the jets was spraying a powerful stream of water at her abdomen. She lifted her head and looked at the jet.

"Hey, I'm not finished rinsing your hair," Sawyer said.

"Sorry. Hurry it up. I have a surprise for you when you're finished."

"What kind of surprise?"

"You'll see."

Sawyer finished rinsing and replaced the nozzle in its holder. "All rinsed. So what's my surprise?"

"Switch places with me," Willow said. She sat with her back against the tub and her knees up. "Now lie back against my legs and let me support your back and head."

"I don't exactly have a lot of room down here."

"You will once you put your legs up on the edge of the tub."

Sawyer looked back at Willow. "What exactly are you going to do to me?"

"Trust me. Put your legs up on the edge of the tub and lean back on my legs."

Sawyer did as she was instructed, and immediately, the jet in front of her delivered a very powerful stream of water directly between her legs. "Sweet Hecate!" She bolted upright, only to be held down by Willow's hands on her shoulders.

"It's okay. Just lie there and enjoy it," Willow said. "Trust me."

Sawyer relaxed against Willow's legs as her body became accustomed to the jet stream of water pummeling her most vulnerable parts. Before long, Willow felt her begin to gyrate as her head pressed harder against Willow's knees. Willow whispered in her ear. "Imagine the water is my tongue, swirling around your folds."

Sawyer moaned and shifted her pelvis higher.

"That's it, my love. I'm sucking your bud in and out of my mouth."

Sawyer whimpered.

Willow reached forward and pinched Sawyer's nipples. "Imagine my fingers slipping inside of you."

"Sweet Goddess," Sawyer rasped as her body began to stiffen.

Willow pinched harder. "That's it, Sawyer. Let it go. Give yourself to me. I want all of you."

Sawyer suddenly arched upward. "Willow! I'm coming. Dear, sweet Goddess, I'm coming."

Willow shifted her legs so that Sawyer's pelvis was completely aligned with the jet stream. The steady pummeling of water prolonged Sawyer's orgasm for several minutes until she fell limp against Willow's legs. Willow slowly lowered her knees into the water and pulled Sawyer up to lie on her chest.

She could feel Sawyer's entire body vibrate with relief.

"Sweet Goddess," Sawyer whispered. "I will never look at a Jacuzzi the same again."

# Chapter 49

## 1613—Billingham, England

Lord Weller stood at the head of the table and looked at the thirteen people seated before him. All were dressed in dark brown robes with oversized hoods, and all wore blue feather brooches pinned to their chests. "Brethren," he said. "You are aware of the deaths of your brothers and sisters in Lancashire, caused by the clerics afeared of our knowledge and truths. Beware, their murderous ways hath just begun. The uprising is in one moon hence. Failure to carry out the repression shall bring doom and carnage to the world. You cannot risk discovery. You cannot allow persecution to sway you from your duty. Harken to my words. Let no man nor woman speak of the repression from this day forth lest in the presence of clansmen. You must all take care to protect the secret of your mission. Under pangs of death, you must succeed, and you must be prepared to sacrifice your own life for the good of the whole."

Jenna stood. "As the chosen one, I call on you, brethren, to pray to the Goddess for guidance, that she might shield and protect us from persecution so you can carry out your mission. You must find a secret and secluded place to stop the uprising. You must ask the Goddess for help in this venture."

A chorus of "ayes" rang out amongst those present.

Jenna extended her hand and pointed to everyone in the room with a sweeping motion. "All of you need to set up guards around your compounds. Not to kill, for killing is not the way of the Goddess—but to be aware of approaching trespassers. Set up guard posts far from your compounds, manned with the fastest runners to forewarn the others. All tools of the craft must be hidden from view. Bury your athames, bollines, pentacles, censers, incense, chalices, bells, and cards deep within the ground. Bury your Books of Shadows as well. They must not fall into the wrong hands. Last, wear not the blue feather brooch unless present at this assembly. Decorate your homes with images of Christianity, bibles and idols. Perchance the clerics or the king's men enter your compounds, they must find only common folk living common lives and worshiping the same God as they. When the danger hath passed, and the clerics are duly satisfied of our commonality, we shall return to our lives honoring the Goddess."

The room was silent as Jenna walked completely around the long rectangular table. When she reached the point where she had started, she turned to the table once more. "The Goddess knows what you must do. You must deceive the heretics to protect the innocent. The clerics cannot see inside your hearts, for that truly is where the Goddess lives... not in your homes adorned with symbols of her, but inside each of you. It matters not, that your homes shall be void of her trappings. It matters only that your heart be full of her. Do I have your word that you shall do this thing?"

In turn, each clan leader stood and put their hand on the blue feather brooch pinned to their chest. Each said in a clear and loud voice, "Aye. In the name of the Goddess, I shall carry out your wishes."

Lord Weller stepped forward and addressed the council. "I shall notify all members of this commune to take action immediately. Go now back to your homes and do the same. Blessed be to all of you."

As the council members filed out of the room, Lord Weller took Jenna aside. "Spread the word to all households and bring to me the twelve most able-bodied amongst them. We shall place sentries on the four roads leading into the village, for surely a league of king's men shall ride in on horseback. They shall guard in shifts so as to avoid errors made due to fatigue."

"As you wish, Lord Weller," Jenna said as she took her leave.

\* \* \*

Jenna returned to her and Hadley's cottage and took Hadley into her arms. "I love thee, Hadley Metcalf."

Hadley pushed Jenna back a bit. "Thou art shaking like a leaf again. What is thy trouble?"

"The Council of Thirteen just left. They have been instructed to remove all signs of the craft from their villages, and we must do the same."

"Remove all signs? For what reason?"

Before Jenna could answer, there was a knock on the door. "Sister, 'tis Caleb. May I gain entry?"

Jenna opened the door. "Pray do. I need to talk to thee anyway, brother."

Caleb came into the room. A young woman came in behind him. "Jenna, Hadley, this is Maura Jennings. I intend to betroth myself to her."

Hadley took Maura's hands in hers. "Dost thou, now?" She looked at Jenna. "Thy brother has a keen eye for beautiful women." Then to Maura, she added, "Thou hast chosen well, sister. Caleb is a good man."

Maura blushed.

Jenna hugged Caleb. "We are happy for you both, brother. I just wish the time was happier to hear this news."

"That is why we are here, sister. There is a stir among the citizens. Dost thou know the cause?" Caleb asked.

"Aye. The rider that came into the village yesterday brought news that ten of our brethren in the Malkin Tower Coven were hanged for witchcraft. We fear the clerics' assassins ride in search of others. We must take actions to protect our own."

"Sweet Goddess. I volunteer to help in any way I can, sister."

"Aye, I thought thou wouldst. When thou didst knock on the door, I was telling Hadley we need to remove all signs of the craft from the village. They need to be buried or hidden in a safe place that shall not be discovered by the clerics or their guard. They need to be replaced with Christian relics so that if the bastards visit our village, they see only commoners who worship the same God as they. We must protect what is ours—especially the children," Jenna said as she glanced at the twins sleeping nearby in their cradles.

Hadley immediately set into action. She carried a woven basket around the cottage and filled it with artifacts of the craft.

Jenna put her hand on Caleb's shoulder. "Brother, I need for thee to do something else for the clan."

"Anything, Jenna."

"We will be posting lookouts on the four roads leading into the village. We need strong men and women, fast runners, to alert the village when strangers approach."

"I will be one of those lookouts, sister. I can run like the wind."

"Aye, I remember losing to thee on many occasions in thy youth. I knew I could count on thee. Much is at stake here. We must secure the village so that no one amongst us falls victim to the murderous wrath of the clerics. And we must assure the repression is carried out in secret. No one must speak of it aloud to anyone. Now go and cleanse thy quarters of coven relics." Jenna looked at Maura. "Mistress Jennings, go inform thy family to do the same."

Hadley put the basket of relics she had collected on the table and wrapped her arms around Jenna. "I fear for us. I fear for the babes."

Jenna held Hadley close and rested her cheek on Hadley's head. "Aye. I fear as well. I will do what I can to keep thee and the babes safe. I will die for thee if necessary."

Hadley squeezed her hard. "Do not sayest that. I do not want to go on in this life without thee."

\* \* \*

For the next few weeks, life settled down into a quiet routine in the commune. Very few visitors came to the village, and those who did were simply in search of a good meal or a warm bed as they passed through. The Council of Thirteen met on a weekly basis to decide on a secure location for the repression ritual and to assure all preparations were underway to make the proper offerings to the Goddess. The site chosen for the ritual was approximately three kilometers from the village in a secluded part of the forest. The atmosphere around the village was heavy with anticipation and nervous tension, escalated by the inability to discuss the plans openly.

Near the end of the third week before the ritual, Caleb was on guard duty on the west side of the village when he spotted a lone traveler very far off in the distance. Since the traveler looked somehow familiar to him, rather than run to warn the village, he waited until the man was close enough to identify. "Sweet Goddess, 'tis the devil himself, Thomas Hawksworth," he whispered under his breath.

Caleb slowly made his way to the side of the road and hid behind a tree very near to where Hawksworth would pass. As soon as Hawksworth was slightly beyond him, Caleb crept out from behind the tree and hit him over the head with a tree branch. Hawksworth fell to the ground unconscious. "I don't know what the devil thou art up to, sire, but I am surely not taking a chance thou shalt betray us." He hefted his father onto his shoulders and carried him toward the village.

Jenna was hammering out the buckle on a horse's bridle when a young boy ran into the forge.

"Mistress Jenna, Mistress Jenna. Come quick."

Jenna put her tools down and knelt on one knee in front of the child. "What is it, lad?"

"Master Caleb captured a bad man."

Jenna looked up into the common area and saw Caleb walking across the square with an unconscious man across his shoulders. Several young boys followed behind. She ran out to meet him. "Caleb, who is this?"

"Thomas Hawksworth. I found him approaching the village on the west road."

"Our sire?"

"Aye. We need to lock him up afore he comes to."

The small boys were making a racket and poking the man with sticks. "Begone with you or I will be tanning all your hides," Jenna shouted, causing them to run off. "Come, Caleb.

We shall lock him in the wild horse bay."

Caleb followed Jenna to the stables and into the bay they used to confine wild horses until they were broken. The bay was made up of iron bars on three sides and was sometimes used as a makeshift jail for rabble-rousers who needed to sleep off the ingestion of too much mead.

"Put him there on the hay," Jenna said.

"Should we tie him up?" Caleb asked.

"Nay. He hath done naught to break our laws, but I will lock the cell, for I trust him not." Jenna latched the cell with a large padlock and turned back to Caleb. "Go find Ethan and send him to guard thy post on the west road. Then come back and stand guard over this devil. I will wait for thee to return."

Minutes after Caleb left, Hawksworth began to rouse from unconsciousness. He pushed himself into a seated position in the hay and grabbed his head. "Where is the coward that hitteth me from behind?" he said.

"The coward thou dost refer to is a brave young man named Caleb Hawksworth," Jenna said.

Hawksworth squinted his eyes at his jailor. "Art thou Jenna Hawksworth?" he asked.

"Aye. What business dost thou have in our village?"

"Open the door, Jenna." "I think not. Answer the question. What business dost thou have in our village?"

Hawksworth looked away. "Thy mum has fallen ill."

Jenna didn't say anything.

After several moments of tense discomfort, Hawksworth lunged at the bars, causing Jenna to take one step back. Just then, Caleb reentered the stable.

"Thy mum has fallen ill, I tell thee." Hawksworth still did not meet his daughter's eyes.

Jenna's face distorted into a sneer. She picked up a piece of wood by the stove and hit the bars with it, just above where his knuckles were. "Thou lying piece of filth!" she yelled.

"Jenna!" Caleb said. "If what he says is true..."

Unknown to Jenna and Caleb, Hadley had heard the racket

from across the square where she had been sweeping the walk in front of their cabin, and she ran to investigate. She stood in the doorway as the scene unfolded.

"'Tis not true, Caleb, and even if it was, she would be better off leaving this world than living with the likes of him. Thy sire is a foul-mouthed liar. He cannot even look his daughter in the eye, he lies so." Jenna approached the bars once more. "Tell him, Thomas Hawksworth," Jenna screamed. "Tell him how thou didst lie to me all those years. Tell him how thou madest me believe I was put on this earth by thy God to be raped and beaten. Tell him!"

Caleb's eyes grew wide. He lunged at his father, reached between the bars, and grasped him around the neck. "Thou filthy bastard," he yelled as Hawksworth gasped for breath.

"Caleb—no!" Hadley yelled as she ran forward and struggled to pry Caleb's hands from his father's neck. "The Goddess would not want thee to kill the man. He is not worth damning thy soul to Tartarus for."

Caleb released him. He spat in Hawksworth's face and turned his attention to Jenna who sat curled up on the floor in the corner. He pulled her to her feet and enveloped her in an embrace.

Hadley stood in front of the jail bars and stared Hawksworth down. "May thy soul burn in the eternal fires of Tartarus," she said vehemently and turned to walk away.

"You will fail... like all the others afore you—you will fail."

Hadley stopped and turned around to look at him once more.

"I was a chosen one, too," he said, "but lucky enough to escape the clutches of the devil Goddess. I saw the errors of my ways. The Church saved me... just like I tried to save thee, Jenna."

Jenna broke free of her brother's arms and walked toward the bars, only to be intercepted by Hadley. "By raping me and beating me whenever the mood struck thee? I hope thou dost die a long and painful death, old man."

Hadley had her arm around Jenna's waist. "Let it go, Jenna. The Goddess will give him just due. Come home with me. Thy babes need their mama."

"Go to thy devil spawn," Thomas said and spat on the floor.

Caleb lunged toward the bars once more and punched his father square in the jaw. Thomas fell to the ground in a heap.

Hadley looked at him, then at Caleb. "Serves him right. Best to bind him, Caleb."

Caleb nodded. "Aye. I will take care of it."

"Jenna, thou toldest me not of thy sire's indiscretions on thy person."

Jenna sat on the edge of the bed, her face in her hands. She flared up in anger, rose to her feet, and paced across the room.

"Ahhh! I should have killed the man when I had the chance."

"Thou dost not mean that, Jenna. Thy anger is well placed, but thou dost not mean that."

Jenna fell to her knees in front of the babes' cradles. She covered her face with her hands, sat back on her heels, and began to cry. "Hadley, if ever anyone puts a hand on Lachina in a way not invited, I will see fit to kill them. How can a man do that to his own child? How can he sit there and justify it with his God?"

"'Tis true Thomas Hawksworth is not fit to walk the earth with the likes of my Jenna, but I will not have thee soil thy soul for him. Trouble is, what to do with him? We cannot keep him locked up forever."

# Chapter 50

## 2013—Newcastle upon Tyne, England

Sawyer and Willow appeared downstairs for a late breakfast around ten a.m.

"Good morning, sleepyheads," Roger said. "Late night?"

"Good morning, Daddy," Willow replied as she kissed her father on the cheek. "Someone got really relaxed in the Jacuzzi last night, and we didn't get to bed until late."

"Fall asleep, did you?" Matilda asked.

"Something like that," Sawyer said, her face a deep crimson.

"Have you had breakfast yet, Mr. McCord?" she added, quickly changing the subject.

"Hours ago. Matty here has been showing me around. Your home is amazing. I spent some time talking with Jonathan, your farm manager, and we went over a few ideas to enhance yield."

"Thank you, Mr. McCord. I had no idea you knew about farming."

"Daddy is a biochemist. He worked for thirty years for a company that, among other things, optimized fertilizer effectiveness."

Roger put his arm around Sawyer. "Isn't it about time you call me Roger?"

"I'd like that. Please feel free to roam about at will, Roger. Willow and I have more lessons to tend to, just as soon as we have coffee. Maybe we can have a late lunch on the veranda."

"Sorry, I've got a lunch date already with Jonathan. Matty offered to throw together a picnic lunch for us to enjoy while we tour the fields."

Sawyer looked at Matilda with raised eyebrows. A slight

blush rose on Matilda's cheeks.

Willow saw the look and grinned. "Don't worry, Daddy's a big flirt, but he's harmless," she said under her breath. "Mom gets on him all the time about the way he acts around her lady friends."

"May I fix you breakfast, girls?" Matilda asked.

"I think coffee and maybe a scone is fine for me," Sawyer said.

"Make that two," Willow added.

Matilda warmed two scones in the time it took Sawyer to fix mugs of coffee and then placed all of it on a tray with raspberry jam and creamy butter. Sawyer picked up the tray. "We'll be working in Father's study today if you need anything, Matty."

Matilda and Roger watched the girls walk away.

"Beautiful lady, your daughter is," Matilda said.

"Yes. She looks like her mother. I've grown quite fond of Sawyer as well over the two months she's lived with Willow."

"Sawyer has a glow about her I haven't seen before. Perhaps your Willow has something to do with that?"

"I believe you may be right."

Sawyer sat on the floor in front of the fireplace in her father's study, her legs splayed far apart. Willow sat between her legs, with her back to her. Very little space separated the two women. Willow's hands were folded in prayer while Sawyer's arms wrapped around her, sandwiching Willow's hands between hers.

"Now close your eyes and concentrate, Willow. Let the Goddess enter you. Feel her spirit. We can't begin the chant until we feel her enter us."

A voice came from across the room. "Jenna taught me to call forth the Goddess by imagining a fading."

Willow's eye flew open. "Hadley!"

Sawyer lowered her hands and placed them on her knees.

"Hadley, it's good to see you. So what exactly do you mean

by a fading?"

"Now, ladies, I have been discreet about the timing of my visits, but surely thou hast each taken pleasure in the other."

"Oh, my God," Willow said, turning fifteen shades of red.

Sawyer cleared her throat. "Ah, yes."

"So what dost thou call it today when thou reachest the peak? In my day, it was a fading."

"Oh… you mean an orgasm," Willow said.

"A rose by any other name, I suppose," Hadley replied.

"So, Jenna taught you to imagine an orgasm to call the Goddess?" Sawyer asked.

"Jenna believed thy mind needs to be open and vulnerable to call forth the Goddess. For her, she was at her most vulnerable when we were making love. Now mind thee, calling forth the Goddess while thou art making love is something I do not recommend, but if thou canst put thyself in that state of mind, thou wilt be more open to receiving her. Go on with thee. Try it."

Willow clasped her hands together once more and closed her eyes. Sawyer assumed her previous position with her arms around Willow and her hands sandwiching Willow's. Within moments, Willow inhaled deeply and tilted her head back, resting it on Sawyer's shoulder. Their breathing increased, and they chanted together.

"Mother Goddess, we call on thee to enter our bodies and commune with our spirits. Be one with us now as we fulfill our destiny to work magic for the good of all. As we will it, so shall it be."

Willow gasped as the brooches around her neck glowed with a blinding brightness. She felt herself melt into Sawyer as their power combined into a single force. The intensity of emotion was overwhelming, and tears she couldn't contain ran down her face. Finally, the glow faded and her breathing returned to normal.

Sawyer wrapped her hands around Willow's waist and pulled her closer. Her breath came in halted pants. "I could feel your mind. Our hearts were one."

"I know," Willow whispered. "I could feel everything you felt. It was almost too intense to bear."

"I love you, Willow."

"I love you, Sawyer."

Hadley smiled and left them.

\* \* \*

"Are you ready?" Sawyer asked Willow.

"As ready as I'll ever be, I suppose."

"Are you nervous?"

"A little."

"Well, if it's any consolation, I am, too. Not that we need his approval, but he'll be overseeing the repression ritual so it's important that we're on the same page with him."

"What exactly will happen during this ritual, anyway?"

"I don't know. I thought we could discuss it with Hadley, although I would expect a lot to change in four hundred years."

They met Willow's father in the vestibule. "You ladies look wonderful tonight," he said. "Do you have any idea what this meeting is all about?"

"We were just discussing that very thing," Sawyer said. "Lord Somers requested it. I assume it is to meet you both and possibly even discuss the repression ritual."

"After you, ladies," Roger said as he held the door open. They headed for the car.

"Wow, I'm in the wrong line of business," Willow said as Ian pulled into the driveway of Lord Somers's residence. "What else does this guy do besides being a coven leader?"

"Nothing, really."

"Judging by the size of this house, it looks like a pretty lucrative business to me," Roger added.

"It's not supposed to be a business," Sawyer said in his defense.

"It just so happens several of the coven members are comfortable financially. Let's just say there are perks to being a third level adept in a coven."

A butler let them into a house and escorted them to a sitting room. "Lord Somers will be with you in a moment," he said.

Fifteen minutes later, Willow looked at her watch. "Well that's pretty rude. In my world the host is not only on time, but he greets his guests at the door. I have to admit I'm not feeling the love here, Sawyer."

"I'm afraid I have to agree with you on the rudeness factor, Willow. It's not like him to keep his guests waiting. My apologies," Sawyer said.

Willow walked up to Sawyer, wrapped her arms around her waist, and kissed her tenderly on the lips. "Don't apologize for him. You've done nothing wrong." Willow kissed her again.

"Ahem," came the sound of a female voice from behind them.

Willow swung around.

"Bridgit," Sawyer said, surprise evident in her voice.

"Sawyer. Care to introduce me to your… friends?" Bridgit said as she walked in a circle around the group, like a tiger sizing up its prey.

"Bridgit, this is Roger McCord. Roger, meet Bridgit Cooper."

"It's nice to meet you, Mr. McCord."

"Likewise, Ms. Cooper," Roger said. He frowned at Sawyer over Bridgit's head.

Bridgit turned and stood directly in front of Willow, who still had her right arm around Sawyer's waist. "And you are…?" Bridgit asked.

"This is Willow McCord," Sawyer said.

Willow removed her arm from Sawyer's waist and extended her hand to Bridgit. "I'm delighted to finally meet you," Willow said in a sickly sweet voice. "I've heard so much about you. And I must say, you write very eloquent letters. Let me see if I can remember—ah yes, 'Red rose, thick with thorns. Tattered skin, sliced and torn.' A little dark but very well written."

Bridgit looked at Sawyer and raised her eyebrows, the muscles in her jaw visibly clenching.

Sawyer placed her arm on Willow's waist and squeezed.

Willow simply smiled sweetly.

"My apologies," Lord Somers said from the doorway. "An

important call came in from The Council of Thirteen. I fear it demanded more of my time than I expected. I trust you have made the introductions, Sawyer."

"Yes, Lord Somers, although I was someone put off guard by it. Nonetheless, may I introduce you to Mr. Roger McCord, Willow's father."

Lord Somers shook his hand. "I assume you are a chosen one?"

"Yes, sir, I am."

"It's good to have you here. Your presence will add strength to the ritual." He turned to Willow. "You must be Willow."

"Willow McCord. Nice to make your acquaintance," she said as she firmly shook his hand.

"I trust Sawyer has told you of your role in the repression?"

"More or less. There's still much to learn, but with Sawyer's skill and knowledge… as well as a little help from other sources, I'm sure I'll be more than ready by the end of the month."

"You do realize this is a life-long commitment?"

Willow reached back and took Sawyer's hand in her own. "I'm prepared for that."

Sawyer smiled as she caught Willow's meaning.

Lord Somers turned to Bridgit. "Bridgit, you have my gratitude for playing hostess while I was tied up. I appreciate your willingness to stay, since I know you have another engagement to get to."

Sawyer could have sworn she saw a flash of anger cross Bridgit's face at the dismissal.

"Ah, yes, Lord Somers. I really must run. It was a pleasure."

Bridgit looked at Sawyer, momentarily narrowed her eyes, and took her leave.

"I didn't expect her to be here," Sawyer said to Lord Somers. "Especially since I asked you to investigate her relative to the attacks on Willow."

"Attacks?" Roger asked.

"Nothing to worry about, Daddy," Willow said. "Do you really think she's behind it, Sawyer?"

"She e-mailed a picture of your car in the parking garage with the words 'I warned you' in the subject line. She sent it after you were almost run down."

"You were almost run down in the parking garage?" Roger said. "That doesn't sound like nothing to worry about."

"Do you think she's also responsible for the pool incident in P-Town?"

"Let me show you the text she sent to me right after that happened. Here it is: 'Tip of the day: To drown your troubles, you must not let them surface.' Do I think she could have done it? Yes."

"I spoke to Bridgit about your suspicions, Sawyer. She denied any knowledge of it," Lord Somers said.

"You spoke to her about it? Of course she'll deny it. Look, I'd appreciate it if you'd tell her to keep her distance, especially where Willow's concerned."

Lord Somers took a step forward and stopped a few inches from Sawyer. "I'll tell you exactly what you told me a short time ago. I'll do what is within my influence to do. I can do no more than that."

* * *

"I don't like him, Sawyer. He gives me the creeps," Willow said on the ride home.

"I have to agree with Willow," Roger added. "I felt a very strong undercurrent of guilt or secrecy about him. He made me uncomfortable as well."

"I can't disagree with either of you. I've seen a side of Lord Somers that I didn't know existed until today. I find myself wondering how much of an influence Bridgit is on him."

"Forgive me for saying this," Roger said, "but I sensed something between you two that I can only describe as lover's betrayal. Tell me to mind my own business if you'd like, but she was pretty passive aggressive."

"Do you really think Bridgit is responsible for these threats against me?" Willow asked.

Sawyer rubbed her hands over her face. "I don't know what to think. Is she capable? Yes, but I have no way to prove it. All I can say is that it appears she has turned from the light. She's a jealous and possessive woman. I only hope she hasn't used that negative emotion to conjure up something she can't handle."

"Willow, I suggest you avoid being alone with her while we're here," Roger said.

"I agree with your father," Sawyer added.

"You know, I am bigger than her. I can probably kick her ass."

"If all she had in her arsenal was her own physical strength," Sawyer said, "I would agree with you, but she's been practicing the craft for a while. She has you beat hands-down in that respect."

"I wanted to slap that smug look off her face," Willow said.

Sawyer chuckled. "I think you did a pretty effective job of that several times during the conversation, my love."

"Whatever do you mean?" Willow batted her eyes and said sweetly.

# Chapter 51

## 1613—Billingham, England

Jenna and Caleb stood at the far end of the stables, debating the fate of Thomas Hawksworth. Hawksworth was lying on a pile of hay inside his cell, seemingly asleep.

"What shall we do with him, Jenna?" Caleb said in a hushed voice. "If we release him, he shall go to the clerics."

"What wouldst thou have me do with him, Caleb—kill him? Thou knowest we cannot do that."

"He would see us hang if he had his way."

"Aye, thou speakest the truth, but if we kill him, we are no better than he."

"So do we just keep him here, locked in this cell, sister?"

"We have no choice for now. We will deal with him after the repression."

"That is five days hence. Even if we release him after the repression, he shall go to the clerics."

"Aye, that is why we must not give the clerics a reason to doubt our 'Christian' faith."

"I say we kill him," Caleb said insistently. "After what the bastard did to thee, methinks thou wouldst want that as well."

Jenna grabbed the front of his blouse. "I said nay. I shall not have murder on thy soul for the likes of Thomas Hawksworth. Thou art a better man than that. Dost thou want thy life with Maura to begin with such a mark on thy soul? Besides, if something happens to me at the uprising, I need thee to care for Hadley and the babes. Thou canst not do that if thou art rotting in the king's dungeon for killing thine own sire."

"I see thy wisdom, sister, but I like it not."

"Aye. I like it even less. Now come, we have preparations

to make in the clearing. Hadley shall bring the bastard his dinner."

Thomas Hawksworth opened his eyes into slits and watched his son and daughter leave the stables. *You shall hang from the gallows for your sins against the Church, you unholy devil... and your bitch and demon spawn will hang right beside you. I shall see to it.* When he was sure they were gone, he sat up and pushed the hay away from the one wall of the jail that was not metal bars. With his bound hands, he resumed digging the hole he had started in the dirt floor at the base of the wall.

Near dusk, Hadley carried a plate of meat and a chunk of bread to the stables. Hawksworth was sitting with his back against the wooden wall when she entered. His hands, arms, and clothing were covered in dirt. She put the food down within reach and turned to leave but then stopped and walked back toward the cell.

"I want thee to know that despite thine efforts, Jenna is a good, decent human being. Thy God will judge thee harshly for what thou hast done to her."

"My God will judge Jenna for her sinful ways, not me."

"Thy God means nothing to Jenna and hence has no power over her."

"I tried to save Jenna from the clutches of that deviant coven. I tried to teach her how a woman should obey a man and how to take care of his needs. 'Tis a woman's duty to do so."

"'Tis not the duty of a daughter to spread her legs for her sire. Thou shalt surely go to the devil for violating thy child. Someone should shove a hot poker up thine arse and let thee die a slow death."

"Hold thy tongue, woman."

"I shall not. Thou art a sick bastard, Thomas Hawksworth. Thou dost not even deserve to share the same name with thy daughter—nor thy son."

"Thou shalt go to hell for thy sodomitic ways, whore, and Jenna will burneth right beside thee."

"Then I shall die happy with the woman I love beside me."

"And I shall die happy as well," Jenna said from behind her.

Hadley ran to Jenna and wrapped her arms around her waist. "Thank the Goddess thou art back."

Jenna kissed the top of Hadley's head. "Aye. Go on home. I will be there anon." She waited until Hadley had left before she spoke to Hawksworth. "The council shall meet on the day after the morrow to discuss thy fate. Thou hadst better hope they are in a charitable mood."

"Go to the devil."

"I am afraid the devil is too busy guiding thee to pay me any heed." Jenna walked to the door then turned around. "Oh, just so thou knowest—I am fond of Hadley's hot poker idea as well. But if it was my decision, I would cut thy member off and stuff it down thy throat before shoving the hot poker up thine ass. Then thou wouldst know how I felt when thou didst rape and sodomize me all those years."

Jenna closed the door to the stable and walked the few yards to her cottage. When she entered, she found Hadley kneading dough like she was beating the devil out of it. She walked up behind her and wrapped her arms around her waist. "What did the dough do to deserve such a beating?" she asked.

Hadley stopped and took a deep breath. "I had to take my anger out on something. That man maketh me want to do ungodly acts to his person. Jenna, how didst thou manage to live in the same house with that devil?"

"Easy, it was not. I spent a lot of time just staying out of his way. He was a tyrant to all of us, especially my mum."

"Especially you. Did thy mum know what he was doing to thee?"

"I told her not, but I think she knew. She could do naught to stop him. When she tried to stand him down, he would beat her until she could not walk."

"The man doth not deserve to breathe the same air thou dost."

Jenna turned Hadley around in her arms and kissed her tenderly. "Dost thou think the dough has been punished long enough to let it rise? If so, I know another way to use all that feistiness thou hast built up."

"Dost thou, now? Pray tell."

"First, I take off thy skirts like this." Jenna lifted Hadley's dress and pulled it off over her head.

"Careful for the breasts, love. A wee tender they are from feeding the babes."

Jenna bent down and softly kissed each one of Hadley's breasts. "What I wouldn't give to be a babe right now... to suckle at thy breast and trap those beautiful nipples between my teeth."

Hadley began to squirm. "Ah, Jenna—thou wouldst be telling me how to use up my nervous energy?"

"Aye, I would. Second, I untie thy corset like this."

Hadley moaned when the corset fell away. "Good Goddess, that feels good."

"Third, I push down thy bloomers and run my hands—"

"Fourth," Hadley interrupted, "I take off thy clothes." Hadley made short work of Jenna's blouse, trousers, and underclothes.

"Fifth," Jenna said, "I take my lady to bed and make her call out my name as she tumbles over the cliff to Elysium." Jenna lay Hadley on the bed and straddled her right thigh while she supported herself with her left arm. She kissed her passionately, shoving her tongue deep into her mouth while her right hand slid between Hadley's wet folds.

"Ahh, that feels so good," Hadley moaned between kisses.

Jenna ran her fingers back and forth over Hadley's pleasure point until she felt Hadley begin to arch toward her hand. Her fingers sought out the warmth of Hadley's body as she drove three fingers deep inside her. Hadley pressed her head back into the pillow, her neck straining against the rising passion in her abdomen.

"Sweet Goddess, Jenna. Thou makest me wild, woman. Ahh!"

Hadley moaned again as Jenna increased her thrusts. Soon, Hadley set up a motion of counterthrusts through which her desire grew exponentially. Suddenly, she arched her pelvis high above the bed and paused for the briefest of moments before she crashed down again in a series of spasms. When the spasms subsided, Jenna removed her hand and lay on top of Hadley, kissing her tenderly. "I love thee, Hadley Metcalf."

Hadley opened her eyes and looked directly at Jenna. "No more than I love thee." Hadley slipped her leg in between Jenna's, and before Jenna knew it, she was lying on her back with Hadley hovering over her. Hadley left of trail of nips and kisses from Jenna's ear, down her throat, across her collarbone, and between her breasts. She teased Jenna's nipples with her tongue then sucked them into her mouth, nipping on them until Jenna whimpered. The trail of nips and kisses began again in earnest as Hadley drew circles around Jenna's navel with her tongue then moved downward to the triangle of hair between Jenna's legs. Hadley looked up, her gaze meeting Jenna's eyes. "Spread thy legs for me, love," she said seductively, causing a spasm to ripple through Jenna's abdomen.

"By the gods, Hadley, I need thee," Jenna said.

Hadley took Jenna's bud between her teeth and flicked her tongue over it until she felt Jenna begin to quiver.

"Now, Hadley. Pray... now."

Hadley inserted two fingers into Jenna and curled them upward, rubbing them against the ribbed patch of tissue inside her. Jenna's hips began to gyrate, and she tried to push herself harder onto Hadley's hand.

"Hadley, I'm burning up inside. I need more. Pray—harder."

Hadley added another finger and drove hard into Jenna. "Yes. Sweet Goddess, yes," Jenna screamed as the floodgates opened and she fell over the edge.

It was several minutes before Hadley crawled back up and lay beside Jenna. Jenna could barely keep her eyes open. "How is thine energy, Hadley?"

"What energy?"

* * *

Jenna woke up with a start in the middle of the night, awakened by an unusual noise. She climbed out of bed, checked on the children, and found them fast asleep in their cradles. She looked around in the darkness but saw nothing out of place. When she turned to go back to bed, a shadow suddenly ran toward her and pushed her down to the floor. Then it ran directly at the door and disappeared.

"What the devil is all that noise?" Hadley said as she sat up in bed. "Jenna Hawksworth, what art thou doing on the floor?"

Jenna crawled to the bed and, with shaky hands, lit the candle on the bedside table.

"What is it, Jenna?"

"Shhh." Jenna carried the candle around the room, exposing every crevice. She then carried it out into the great room and looked around. There was no one there, and nothing was out of place. She made sure the doors and windows were secure and went back into the bedroom.

"What is it?" Hadley asked.

"I heard a noise. Something came at me from across the room and hit me right here," she said, pointing to her stomach. "It knocked the wind out of me. Then it just disappeared."

"Thou felt it hit thee?"

"It knocked me down, Hadley. Thou didst see me on the floor."

"Aye. What could it be?"

"I know not. I shall discuss it with Lord Weller in the morning."

"Come back to bed with thee, then."

Hadley and Jenna were awakened the next morning by the sound of the babes crying. "Aye, I hear thee," Hadley said. "Mum's coming." She put her feet on the floor and grabbed her robe at the foot of the bed. She took a step toward the cradles. They were gone.

"Sweet Hecate." She ran back to the bed to wake Jenna. "Jenna… Jenna, wake up. The babes are gone."

Jenna was out of bed like a bolt. "Gone? Gone where?" She looked frantically around the room. "I heard them cry, not a moment ago."

"As did I," Hadley said. "Wait, I hear it again."

They both looked toward the closed door to the great room. "Great Goddess." Jenna threw open the door and ran into the other room. There, in the middle of the floor, were the two cradles with the babes securely tucked into them. They each grabbed a child and hurried to the bedroom. They placed them on the bed and immediately stripped them of their clothing.

"Ewain is unharmed," Jenna said as she inspected the little boy.

"Lachina is unharmed as well," Hadley said.

"How... how did they get into the other room? Who did this?" Hadley asked.

"I know not. The babes were sleeping sound when I checked on them in the middle of the night," Jenna said.

"Wait here." She went to check the windows and doors once more. "All is secure out there," she said on her return, "and but for the cradles, all is well." She looked around the room once more.

"Wait—the passage behind the bookcase." She pulled the bookcase away from the wall and carried the candle into the narrow passageway that led to the alley behind the cottage. She came back a moment later. "The door leading to the alley is locked from inside.

No one hath gained entry from there."

Hadley said, "Help me to bathe the babes. After they eat their fill, we must pay a visit to Lord Weller."

"'Tis but four days to the uprising," Lord Weller said. "'Tis possible restless spirits are responsible for the odd behaviour last eve. You need to cast a protection spell on your quarters."

"But thou hadst us bury all our tools," Hadley said. "We can't do a proper spell without our tools."

A sudden knock drew their attention to the door. "Come hither," the high priest said.

Several villagers entered. "Lord Weller, a moment with thee if thou wouldst."

"Pray tell the reason for this early morning visit."

"Last night... noises... furniture moved... voices," came a variety of complaints.

Jenna rose and faced the group. "Good citizens, was anyone injured, or things broken during this activity?"

A chorus of no's rang out.

"Hadley and I also had a visitor who came to us twice in the night. During the first visit, it knocked me down to the floor. During the second visit, it moved our babes into the great room without our knowledge. We are scared but unharmed."

"What could it be? It is the devil himself," came the comments from the crowd.

"Good citizens," Lord Weller said, "the Goddess shall protect you. Keep her in your hearts. The spirits are restless and pushing against the gates of the underworld. In four days hence, we shall beat them back and lock them away for another one hundred years. These things that happened most surely are the work of these restless souls."

\* \* \*

Jenna sat silently at the table as Lord Weller addressed The Council of Thirteen.

"Council members, we have a man locked in the stable who hath threatened our community. He hath vowed to report us to the clerics and to see us all hanged from the gallows. 'Tis the sire of one of us."

A low murmur rang from the group as all eyed each other questioningly.

"We are faced with a decision. Do we kill this man, or do we release him and risk that he doth carry out his threat? Know that he hath broken no laws. His crime thus far hath only been to threaten our well-being. Do we compromise our morals by killing this man, or do we put all of us in peril by letting him go? If we kill him, are we any better than our aggressors?"

A tense silence hung over the assembly for a long moment, until one of the council members spoke. "We cannot risk exposure at this late date. We cannot delay the repression. If it doesn't happen in three days hence, a horrible evil will walk the earth."

"I say we hold him captive until after the repression," another one suggested.

"And what then?" Lord Weller said. "If we release him after the repression, he shall still reporteth us to the clerics."

"We shall never be free from those who wish us harm," a third member said. "Do we kill all who oppose us? Killing is not the answer."

Jenna stood. "I wish to speak."

Just then, a young man broke into the assembly.

"Samuel, hast thou no respect?" Lord Weller said.

"The prisoner... he hath escaped."

Jenna threw on her riding cloak and strapped a sword around her waist. "I need a horse," she yelled as she walked across the common.

"Jenna Hawksworth, where art thou going?" Hadley said as she ran after her. "With a weapon, no less."

"That bastard escaped. He is my responsibility. I have to find him."

Hadley swung her around by the arm. "He is not thy responsibility. Thou cannot leave. The repression is just three days hence."

"There shall be no repression if the king's men hang us all. He must be stopped."

Caleb ran across the square. "Then let me go, sister. Hadley is right. Thou art needed here for the repression. No telling how long it might take to find the dog."

"Harken to thy brother's words, Jenna," Hadley said.

Jenna fought with herself and then handed the sword to Caleb. "Do what thou hast to find him, Caleb. Take the north road. 'Tis the shortest distance from here to the castle."

"Aye." Caleb turned to walk toward the stable.

"Wait," Hadley said. She fished a bag of coins from her satchel. "Take this in case thou needest food and lodging."

"I cannot take thy money, Hadley."

"Thou art making it possible for Jenna to stay. Now take it, afore I tan thy hide."

Caleb grinned and took the coins. "My mum taught me never to argue with a lady. I am in thy debt, sister."

"Godspeed, Caleb," Jenna said. She grasped his forearm in a firm shake then hugged him tight. "Be safe," she whispered.

"Blessed be."

# Chapter 52

## 2013—Newcastle upon Tyne, England

"Sawyer, wait up." Willow spurred her horse into a gallop. Sawyer stopped and turned around in the saddle to look at Willow approaching. "Step it up. We're almost there."

"How much farther?"

"Do you see that line of trees over there? That's where the ceremony will take place."

"Oh, joy. I can't wait to parade around naked in front of a bunch of strangers."

"Bridgit will be there. She's not a stranger."

"Oh yeah. I'm especially excited about being naked in front of her."

"She doesn't hold a candle to you, you know."

Willow blushed. "I'm glad you think so."

Sawyer leaned over in her saddle and kissed Willow. "I not only think so, I know so."

"Race you to the trees?" Willow kicked her horse into gear. "Hey, no fair!" Sawyer yelled as she followed suit.

Willow arrived at the tree line just moments before Sawyer. She dismounted and let the reins fall so the horse could graze unhindered. Sawyer did the same, and they walked through the trees, hand in hand, into a clearing.

"Wow, this is bigger than I thought it would be. Do you always hold coven rituals on your land?" Willow asked.

"The larger gatherings are held here. Most of the coven members live in the city, so there's not a lot of room for them to host large rituals."

They walked around the clearing still holding hands. "I can't believe we've been here for two weeks already. It seems like yesterday we drove through the gates of the estate for the first time," Willow said.

"I know. Part of me is sad about that."

"Why so?"

"Because after the repression, we have some decisions to make. I can't just walk away from the estate, Willow. A lot of people depend on it for their livelihood."

Willow nodded. "I know."

"But on the other hand, I can't ask you to give up your home either. I grew quite fond of the Cape myself during the two months I was there. It's a relatively simple life compared to the pressures of running the estate."

Willow wrapped her arms around Sawyer's waist and rested her head beneath her chin. "Who says we have to give up either?

Why can't we live in both places? I mean, your job is pretty portable."

"But yours isn't. You'd have to give it up."

"That wouldn't be such a hardship. I'd miss Susan, but I'd make that sacrifice to be with you. We could always get together with her when we're in the States. Of course, that would mean I'd be a kept woman," Willow joked.

"Not if you married me."

Willow lifted her head from Sawyer's chest and looked at her. "Did you just propose to me?"

Sawyer raised her eyebrows. "I believe I did."

"You realize we've only known each other for three months."

"But I've loved you for much longer than that."

"Say aye to the woman afore she taketh the offer back, Willow McCord," Hadley said from behind them.

Willow looked at Hadley and smiled, then she looked back at Sawyer. "Aye," she said.

Sawyer kissed her and rested her forehead on Willow's. "Thank you. You've made me a very happy woman."

"A happy woman indeed, lass," Hadley said as she hugged them both.

Willow stepped back. "Hadley, I can feel you. You're not a spirit anymore!"

"Nay, lass, I still am a spirit. It takes a lot of energy to appear afore you, but when the energy is high, the effort is less, and when it is as high as it is right now between the two of you, it opens the portal to the living world and allows me to walk among the living as one of you—for a short time, anyway."

"Come, walk with us." Sawyer took Willow's hand and offered the crook of her other elbow to Hadley, who accepted it.

"Hadley, why do you always come alone? Isn't Jenna with you?" Willow asked.

"Jenna is with me in Elysium, but right now she is hunting the evil that haunts you two. Jenna is a spirit hunter, and the Goddess hath sent her to fight for you."

Willow looked at Sawyer. Her eyes grew wide. "So there is an evil spirit at play here."

Hadley nodded. "There indeed is an evil force, Willow, a spirit on a crusade of vengeance and self-righteousness. 'Tis seeking revenge on the descendents of Hadley Metcalf and Jenna Hawksworth and intent on killing the two of you. Wear the brooches that Jenna made. They will protect you."

"When will we see Jenna?"

"Jenna will be at the repression, as will I, among others."

As dusk approached, Willow and Sawyer bade goodbye to Hadley and mounted their horses for the ride back to the stables. They were trotting side by side at a steady pace, when all of a sudden, Willow's horse reared up and kicked the air in front of it. "Whoa, girl, settle down." Willow held tight to the reins. The horse pranced around nervously.

"Are you all right?" Sawyer asked.

"Something spooked her. I think she's all right now." Willow prodded her horse to move forward, but it reared up again. "What the hell?" Willow struggled to hold on as the horse continued to rear.

Sawyer tried to coax her own horse into getting closer, so she could help calm Willow's mount. But it refused to obey her. "Damn it!" Sawyer shouted.

"Fuck!" Willow's mount suddenly took off on a dead run

across the field.

Sawyer did her best to follow, but her mount refused to budge. All she could do was sit and helplessly watch as Willow's horse abruptly stopped and threw her over its head to the ground. As soon as Willow hit the ground, Sawyer's horse responded to her commands and she galloped as fast as she could across the field to where Willow lay in a heap.

Sawyer jumped off her horse as it came to a stop. "Willow," she shouted. "Sweet Goddess, help her." She fell to her knees beside Willow. Her left arm was at an unnatural angle, and she was unconscious. Sawyer grabbed her cell phone and called the estate.

"Matty. Matty, this is Sawyer. Send Jonathan to the east field immediately. Willow is hurt. She was thrown from her horse. We need help. Yes, an ambulance would be good. Okay, bye."

"Goddess, help me," she said as she held her hands over Willow's forehead and closed her eyes. "Broken flesh, piercing pain, I call upon our Lady again. Heal her wounds, and heal them well, so in her pain no longer dwells. Goddess, I do call on thee. As I will it, so shall it be." She focused her energy on Willow and rocked back and forth. "Please don't take her from me," Sawyer whimpered as the tears rolled down her face.

Suddenly the brooches around Willow's neck began to glow.

Willow moaned and opened her eyes into slits. "What happened?"

Sawyer closed her eyes and lowered her head to Willow's chest. "Thank the Goddess you're alive," she whispered.

"What happened?" Willow said again.

"Shhh, don't talk. Help is on the way."

Willow tried to lift her head. "Ahh, that hurts."

Sawyer brushed the hair from Willow's forehead. "Sweetheart, I know it hurts. Don't move, or you'll only make it worse." Sawyer's attention was drawn to the Land Rover tearing across the field, followed closely by a flashing red light. "Help is here, sweetie."

Willow's father was out of the Land Rover almost before it stopped. He ran directly to her and dropped to his knees. "I felt it when she fell," he said. "I knew something was wrong."

"Daddy," Willow said in a weak voice.

"Hey, sweet pea," he said. "The paramedics are here. They'll take good care of you."

"Excuse me. Give us some room," the ambulance crew said as they assessed Willow's condition.

Roger took Sawyer aside. "What happened?" he asked.

"Something spooked her horse. It reared up a couple of times and took off across the field. She would have been fine, but the horse suddenly came to a stop and threw her."

"She's calling for you, Miss," one of the paramedics said to Sawyer.

Sawyer immediately went to Willow's side. "I'm here, love. I'm here."

"If we could have you stand aside for a moment, we need to get her onto the stretcher," the paramedic said.

Sawyer stood aside as they rolled Willow to one side to slip a backboard under her. Her heart broke as Willow cried out in pain during the process.

"On three… one, two, three." The paramedics hefted the backboard off the ground and onto the stretcher. They belted her in and rolled her to the ambulance.

"I'm riding with her," Sawyer told the ambulance crew.

"Roger, if you drive the Land Rover back, I'll take care of the horses," Jonathan said.

* * *

Roger and Sawyer sat in the emergency room waiting area while doctors tended to Willow. Sawyer got up and walked to the window, her hands deep inside her pockets. Roger joined her and put his arm around her shoulder. "She'll be all right, Sawyer. I know she will."

Sawyer fought back the tears as she nodded. "I asked her to marry me, Roger."

"I hope she said yes."

"She did."

"Well then, I guess you should start calling me Dad."

Sawyer sobbed lightly and placed her head on Roger's shoulder.

"Are you Willow McCord's family?" a person said from behind them.

Sawyer and Roger turned around. Sawyer wiped the tears from her cheeks.

"Yes we are."

"Ms. McCord is a lucky girl. It appears she broke her fall with her left hand. If she had fallen on her head, she could have broken her neck, and the outcome would have been very different. We did full spine X-rays, and luckily, they came out clean."

Sawyer smiled through her tears. "Do you mean she'll be all right?"

"She'll be in a bit of pain for a while. Like I said, she broke her fall with her left hand, resulting in fractures of both the radius and ulna. We've set them for now, but she may need surgery at a later date to reinforce the breaks with pins or plates. We'll decide on the next course of action once the swelling is gone. And she has a concussion, so you'll need to watch her for the next twenty-four to forty-eight hours for signs of nausea, confusion, or blurred vision. She'll have one nasty headache for a while, but she'll be fine. Apart from that, she's bound to be sore and quite bruised, but nothing's life threatening."

Roger shook the doctor's hand. "Thank you, Doctor. When can we see her?"

"They're setting her arm in a cast right now. Once it hardens, she'll be able to go home with you." The doctor pulled a prescription pad out of his pocket and scribbled on it. "You'll need to fill this prescription for painkillers. I recommend starting her on two as soon as you get home then one every four hours as needed. There's a pharmacy on the next floor down."

"I'll get this filled right now." Roger shook the doctor's hand once more. "I can't thank you enough."

"Well, like I said, she's a lucky girl. Someone was looking out for her."

"May I stay with her while they cast her arm?" Sawyer asked.

"I don't see why not. Come with me."

The doctor led Sawyer through the emergency room and into one of the treatment rooms where Willow was sitting up with her arm resting on a table beside the bed. Two technicians were busy wrapping fiberglass gauze around a cotton sleeve that encased her arm and halfway up her bicep. She smiled and reached her good arm out to Sawyer as she crossed the room.

Sawyer stopped short and stared at Willow's neck. "Where are the brooches?"

"They took them off to do x-rays."

"We need to find them immediately," Sawyer said in a panicked voice. She went back into the emergency room reception area. "I need to know where Willow McCord's personal effects are."

The receptionist looked at her with a blank stare.

"Look, it's critical that we find them as soon as possible. Willow isn't protected without them."

"Maybe that nurse can help you." The receptionist pointed to the nurse that had just exited Willow's treatment room.

Sawyer intercepted her. "Maybe you can help me. Someone removed a pair of brooches from Willow McCord's neck to take x-rays. It's imperative we find them immediately."

The nurse looked at her clipboard. "Willow McCord. You mean the lady who was thrown from her horse."

"Yes. Please, do you know where the brooches are?"

"I do. Come with me."

The nurse led Sawyer back into Willow's room and lifted a yellow envelope from the countertop. "Here you go. Her ring and watch are in there, too."

"Thank you." Sawyer took the envelope directly to Willow.

"It's about time you came back. Geesh, you're more worried about the brooches than you are about me," Willow said.

Sawyer dumped the contents of the envelope onto Willow's lap. "Not true," she said. "If I wasn't concerned about you, I wouldn't care so much about the brooches." Sawyer picked up the brooches and put them around Willow's neck. They immediately began to glow.

"What is it?" Willow asked when she saw the look of surprise on Sawyer's face.

"They're glowing."

Willow reached up to touch them with her good hand. "And they're warm."

Sawyer leaned down and kissed Willow on the cheek. "It must be the Goddess is nearby."

"Okay, Ms. McCord," the technician said, "your cocoon is finished. You will need to be careful not to straighten your arm for a few hours until it's completely hardened."

"Cocoon?"

"Yes. Your arm will be completely transformed once the cast is removed, like a caterpillar into a butterfly. It'll be all skinny and hairy looking."

"Thank you for sharing that. I'm so looking forward to it," Willow joked with the technician.

"May I take her home now?" Sawyer said.

"As soon as the doctor checks her out. He'll be back in a few minutes."

Sawyer waited for the technician to leave, then she sat on the edge of Willow's bed. She picked up Willow's good hand and kissed the palm. She ran her hand up and down the cast on Willow's arm. "It's warm and very orange."

"It matches my hair."

"Leave it to you to use a cast as a fashion statement."

"Very funny."

"How are you feeling?"

"My head hurts, and my arm aches, but they gave me some pretty good stuff to dull the pain. I'm not looking forward to it wearing off."

"Roger has gone to fill a prescription for painkillers."

"That's good."

"I told him about the proposal."

"Really? What did he say?"

"He said, 'Well then, I guess you should start calling me Dad.'"

"Daddy is a good man."

"That he is. You scared the living daylights out of me," Sawyer said.

"What happened out there?"

"Your horse reared up, twice in fact, and took off running. The next thing I knew, she stopped dead and threw you over her head."

"I remember her rearing. Any idea what spooked her?"

"I'm thinking more along the lines of who rather than what. I mean, my horse refused to move while all this was happening—almost as though something was holding it back."

"But I was wearing the brooches," Willow said.

"Yes, but the horse wasn't."

"Do you think it was Bridgit?"

"That's just what I intend to find out."

Sawyer used her key to unlock Bridgit's door and let herself in. She walked into the room and looked around. Bridgit was nowhere to be seen. As she turned to leave, she heard a sound come from the bedroom. She walked over to the door and kicked it in.

"Sweet Mother Goddess!" Sawyer exclaimed as she saw Bridgit, naked and mounted on Lord Somers. She was wearing a dog collar and gag and wore nipple clips attached to a battery pack while he wore a leather harness, spiked collar, and cock ring and was wielding a riding crop, which judging from the red marks on Bridgit's backside, he had used liberally.

Bridgit scurried off Lord Somers, exposing his erect penis to Sawyer before he hastily pulled the covers over himself.

"I'm going to puke," Sawyer said.

"How dare you barge in here like this?" Bridgit screamed at her.

Sawyer got into her face. "You tried to kill Willow today for fuck's sake! Here's a newsflash for you, bitch. She survived."

Bridgit rolled her head around on her shoulders and sneered at Sawyer. "Silence woman, or thou wilt find thyself on the ground."

"What did you just say to me?" Sawyer asked.

Bridgit shook her head as though to clear it. She looked at Sawyer with a confused expression on her face. "What was it you said?"

"I said you tried to kill Willow today, but she survived."

"I… I don't know what you're talking about."

"Like hell you don't. You failed miserably, Bridgit, but let me warn you. Keep your evil, nasty spells away from her, or you will feel my wrath. Do you understand?"

Sawyer turned to Lord Somers. "You should know better, Your Holiness. Does the council know you're screwing her? Do they know about your fetish? I suggest you keep her in line, if you get my meaning." Sawyer took Bridgit's key out of her pocket and threw it at her. "I won't be needing this anymore." Sawyer turned to go.

"Sawyer," Lord Somers said, stopping her in her tracks.

Sawyer turned around.

"This changes nothing. I expect you to carry on like none of this happened."

Sawyer pointed at him. "Fuck you. No. Better yet, fuck her."

Sawyer left the apartment and slammed the door behind her.

# Chapter 53

## 2013—Newcastle upon Tyne, England

"She was porking the priest? Oh, my!" Willow said.

Sawyer paced back and forth in front of the bed in their room where Willow was sitting, propped up with several pillows. "I have never been so shocked in my life. That's the last thing I expected to see when I kicked the door in."

"You actually kicked the door in? You go, girl!"

"I'll have to wash my eyes out with soap tonight. I'm surprised it didn't blind me. Ugh!"

Willow sat among the pillows and grinned. "I love you."

Sawyer crawled onto the bed beside Willow and stroked her face. "I love you, too. Why are you grinning?"

"I'm thinking back to three months ago, when we met. You were pretty much a stuffed shirt. Now look at you... going off all Rambo-like on Bridgit's ass. I kind of like this side of you."

"Yeah, well I think you're a bad influence on me."

Willow grabbed the front of Sawyer's shirt and drew her near. "Admit it. You kind of like the freedom and power that speaking your mind gives you."

"Busted."

"I am so looking forward to spending the rest of my life with you."

"Why wait? What do you say we get married this weekend?"

"This weekend? Is same-sex marriage even legal here?"

"As luck would have it, legislation was passed allowing same-sex marriage this past July. We couldn't have timed it better."

"But we have no time to plan anything. I mean, there's the

initiation ceremony next Sunday and the repression the Thursday after that. Geesh, I feel like I need an event planner."

Sawyer took the phone out of her pocket and used the search engine to find the next available flight out of Boston. "It's only Monday. We'll get your mom on the next plane out of Boston."

Sawyer showed the flight details to Willow. "According to this, she'll be here tomorrow evening, and we'll let her and Matty plan the whole thing. I'm betting they can pull it off."

"Ya think?"

"I think."

"Okay, Ms. Impulsive, let's call her," Willow said.

Willow put the call on speakerphone and waited patiently for her mother to answer. "Hi, Mom."

"Willow. How are you feeling, honey? When your father called me last night to tell me about your accident I was so worried for you."

"I'm okay. Broken arm and a bump on the head. It could have been worse. I'll be fine."

"I wish I could be there to help take care of you."

Willow glanced at Sawyer and grinned. "Hey, Mom, just so you know, you're on speakerphone and Sawyer is with me."

"Oh! Hi, Sawyer. Are you taking care of my little girl for me?"

"I'm doing my best, Sandy. You said you wish you could be here... are you serious about that?"

"Yes, of course. What mother wouldn't want to be there when their child is hurt?"

"Well, there's a plane ticket waiting for you at Logan. It leaves at one p.m. your time."

"Are you serious? Heavens, I need to pack!"

"Well pack something nice, Mom, like you were going to a wedding," Willow said.

"A wedding? Don't tell me—"

"Yes, and we'd like your help planning it," Sawyer said.

"We're targeting this coming Saturday."

"Oh, my goodness. That's only four days away. Young

people are so impulsive these days. I need to pack. Got to go. Can't wait to see you."

"We'll pick you up at the airport," Willow said.

"All right, dear. I'll see you in a few hours."

Sawyer hung up the phone and pressed the Purchase button on the airline reservation website. "I think she's more excited than we are. She'll be here around dinnertime tomorrow. Should we go tell Roger?"

"Nah, let's surprise him with it in the morning. It's getting late. I just want to snuggle with my honey bun and get some sleep. That is, if I can figure out how to not clobber you with this monstrosity on my arm."

"Let me get you some meds before we turn in. You're due for another dose. Hopefully it will allow you to sleep more comfortably."

\* \* \*

"Good morning, Daddy," Willow said as she entered the kitchen. She kissed him on the cheek and hugged Matty good morning as well.

"How are you feeling, Willie-girl?" Matty asked.

Willow looked at Sawyer with raised eyebrows. Sawyer grinned.

"I'm afraid I kept Sawyer up half the night. Between my arm and head aching and not being able to get comfortable with this rock on my arm, it was hard to sleep. My body feels like I got caught in a cattle stampede, but other than that, the pain meds are doing the job. I could do without this sling though. It's a real pain in the neck, literally."

Willow sat down beside her father and rested her face on his arm. He looked at her. "Out with it, Willow. I know that look. You used it on me a hundred times as a kid."

"Only a hundred?"

"Come on, what's on your mind?"

Sawyer put a cup of coffee in front of Willow. "Here you go, Willie-girl," she said.

"Thank you, bumpkin."

Sawyer grinned and went to help Matilda make breakfast.

"We've kind of got a surprise for you," Willow said to her father.

"Kind of? Out with it, Wills."

"Mom's on her way to England."

"Your mother? Your mother is on her way to England?"

"Yes. We called her last night. We've decided to get married this weekend and figured Matty could use some help planning the wedding on such short notice. She'll be here around dinnertime."

Matilda's eyes grew wide. "Do you really want me to plan your wedding, bumpkin?" she said to Sawyer.

Sawyer hugged her. "Matty, I spent more time with you growing up than I did with my own mother. You're like a mum to me, and I love you very much. Of course I want you to help. You will love Sandy. We have total confidence that, between the two of you, we can pull off a small get-together on Saturday."

Matilda wiped the tears from her eyes and took Sawyer into her arms. "I love you, too, bumpkin. I'm honored to help Willie-girl's mum plan your wedding."

"Mom, over here!" Willow waved her good hand above her head.

"Willow!" Sandy made her way through the crowd, hugged her daughter, and fussed over her broken arm. "Shouldn't you be in bed?"

"It's a broken arm."

"And a concussion," Sandy said.

"Yeah, yeah, yeah."

Sandy hugged Sawyer. "Hi, sweetie. So what brought this on so fast? Did Willow strong-arm you into it? No pun intended, dear."

"Mom!" Willow complained.

"Actually, I asked her," Sawyer said.

"Well, I couldn't be happier. Welcome to the family, darling."

"Thanks, Sandy."

"Welcome to England, sweetheart," Roger said as he hugged his wife. "You will absolutely love Sawyer's home. Did you know it's a working farm? I've been helping her farm manager, Jonathan, improve planting cycles and pesticide schedules. In fact, just the other day…"

While Roger rambled on, Sandy shot a pained expression at Willow and Sawyer, who just laughed and followed them out of the terminal.

Roger accompanied Sandy to their room and gave her a brief tour of the house before they joined the girls in the kitchen.

"What a beautiful home you have, Sawyer," Sandy said.

"It's Willow's home as well now, and yours whenever you're here," Sawyer replied.

"Oh, my. I guess we won't be seeing much of you after the wedding then."

"We're still working that out, Mom. I don't plan to give up my home on the Cape," Willow said.

"Nor do I want her to," Sawyer added. "I'm kind of fond of that home myself. We would like to spend a lot of time in both places, and of course, you're both welcome to join us here whenever you want. But enough of that for now. I want to introduce you to Matilda Gunther. Matty, this is Willow's mother, Sandy."

Matilda extended her hand to Sandy.

"We'll have none of that." Sandy batted her hand away and opened her arms. "Families greet each other with hugs, not handshakes." She embraced Matilda warmly. "It's so nice to meet you."

Matilda looked at Sawyer and grinned as she hugged Sandy back. "The pleasure is mine, Mrs. McCord."

"Mrs. McCord was my mother-in-law. Call me Sandy."

"Okay, Sandy. So what about these girls of ours, dropping this bomb on us like that?"

"Kids today!" Sandy said. "But I'm up for the challenge. How about you?"

"Matty doesn't walk away from any challenge," Matilda said. "How about I make us a pot of tea and a few crumpets, and we'll start making phone calls?"

"Only if you let me help."

\* \* \*

Sandy and Matilda sequestered themselves in the staff office, scheduling a justice of the peace, ordering flowers and a cake, and arranging catering. A small gathering of family and staff would attend the wedding, which was planned to be held in the courtyard at the estate.

Early in the week, they took time out of their busy schedules to drag Willow and Sawyer shopping for wedding outfits.

"For the record, I have a perfectly fine suit in my closet," Sawyer said.

"Nonsense. You need something new to start your life with Willow," Matilda said.

"Really, Matty?"

"No argument, Sawyer. You put us in charge of this thing, so suck it up and do as I say."

"You're rubbing off on her, Sandy," Sawyer teased.

"Deal with it, dear," Sandy replied.

"I need some help here, Willow," Sawyer said.

"Like Matty said, suck it up. I for one like to shop. Let's go!" Willow replied.

"Ahh! Looks like I'm outnumbered."

While Matilda and Sandy worked to organize the wedding, Willow and Sawyer prepared for the coven initiation ceremony that would be held the day after the nuptials. For hours, Willow rehearsed the lines she would have to recite and practiced various chants and spells.

After one particularly late practice session with the tarot cards, Willow slipped them back into their box and put the deck on her bedside table. She looked over at Sawyer, who had fallen asleep about an hour earlier. She kissed her cheek, pulled the covers up over her, and slipped out of bed to go to the bathroom. She padded across the room and pushed the bathroom door open. As she passed over the threshold, a chill ran down her spine.

"Geesh! What the hell was that?" she said. She walked back and forth across the threshold again but felt no temperature deviation at all. "That's odd." She glanced at Sawyer and momentarily considered waking her but decided against it. Bathroom chores over, she returned to bed and snuggled up against Sawyer's back. *Must be my imagination*, she thought as she drifted off to sleep.

Willow awoke the next morning and looked at the clock. Nine a.m. "Holy shit! I never sleep this late." She rolled onto her back and looked at the ceiling. For the first time, she noticed the ornate carvings in the crown molding that ran around the room. Suddenly, she heard giggling coming from outside the room, followed by the sounds of footsteps moving down the hall. *Must be Mom and Matty*. When the sounds abated, she looked back at the ceiling and immediately noticed a dark red stain forming above their bed. What the hell? Is the roof leaking? She got out of bed and went to the window. She pulled back the heavy drapes and was met with abundant sunshine. It wasn't raining. "That's odd." She went back to the bed and looked at the ceiling again. The stain was gone. Was she losing her mind? Just then, the door to their room opened and Sawyer entered, carrying a tray of breakfast foods.

"Good, you're awake." She put the tray down on the bedside table and took Willow into her arms. "Good morning, love. You slept late."

"I did," Willow said and looked at the ceiling again.

Sawyer looked up to see what held Willow's interest. "What do you see? Looks like an ordinary ceiling to me."

"There was a dark red blotch on it just a few moments ago."

Sawyer looked again. "Really? Are you sure it's not your head injury making you see things?"

"Sawyer, I saw it."

"Okay, okay. Come sit on the bed and have some breakfast."

Both ladies climbed onto the bed and sat cross-legged,

facing each other.

"I heard Mom and Matty laughing in the hallway a few minutes ago. They seem to be getting along quite well."

"How long ago was this?"

"Maybe five or ten minutes. Just before the red blotch appeared on the ceiling."

"Willow, they've been gone for the last hour and a half. They went to pick up the flowers and cake."

"Who else is in the house besides you?"

"No one, not even the housekeeping staff. Your dad left a couple of hours ago with Jonathan. I've been by myself downstairs all morning."

Willow's brow knit in a frown. "I heard two female voices giggling in the hall, and I heard footsteps. It was pretty loud. I did not imagine it."

Sawyer put her hand on Willow's knee. "Wills, has anything else odd happened?"

"Now that you mention it, yes. I got up to pee before turning in last night, and when I crossed the threshold into the bathroom, this awful chill ran down my spine, like a blast of cold air. I've been in the bathroom since, and it hasn't happened again."

"Damn," Sawyer said under her breath.

"What? What is it?"

"It sounds like poltergeist activity, restless spirits, most likely those trying to escape the underworld."

"But the uprising is more than a week away."

"The uprising is when their cumulative power is strong enough to break out, but that doesn't prevent individual spirits from trying to escape on their own."

"Are they dangerous?"

"They've been known to cause harm, but from what you've said, this spirit is more or less teasing you."

"I've always had a pretty good sense of humor, but this is pushing things a little too far," Willow said.

"Just make sure you wear the brooches. The Goddess will protect you. All this will be over after the repression ritual next week."

"I will. I can't believe we're getting married tomorrow."

"I know. This week has gone by so fast."

"You aren't getting cold feet are you?"

"No, my answer stands. My feet are quite warm, and you can take that literally or figuratively. I am very much looking forward to marrying you tomorrow."

"The initiation is on Sunday."

"Yes, Sunday evening."

"I guess that means no honeymoon."

"Oh, we'll have a honeymoon, but not until after the repression ceremony."

"That's coming up pretty fast. October thirty-first is next Thursday. We have a busy few days ahead of us… the wedding tomorrow, my initiation the day after, then the repression on the fourth day after that."

"It appears your dance card is quite full, Ms. McCord."

"You said Bridgit was going to be at my initiation. Who else will be there?"

"The Council of Thirteen and other coven members."

"So Daddy won't be there then."

"No, he won't. It's pretty much limited to members of the coven."

"Thank the Goddess for that! I wasn't cherishing the idea of being naked in front of my father."

# Chapter 54

## 1613—Billingham, England

Thomas Hawksworth heard galloping in the distance and hid himself behind a tree a few yards off the road. Several hours had passed since he escaped the prison his daughter had thrown him into, and he was sure she would be out looking for him. The galloping grew louder, and he kept himself hidden, sparing glances at the trail every few minutes to see who was approaching. In his haste to hide, he dropped his bag on the road. He didn't dare retrieve it, in the event he would be seen, so he sat back and hoped the approaching traveler wouldn't notice it. The galloping Hawksworth heard was not one, but two travelers, dressed in full regalia of the cleric's guard—knights of the church. They approached Thomas' hiding place at a full gallop and flew by, but they soon stopped and turned around.

They trotted back and halted near the bag. One man dismounted and picked it up. From it, he retrieved a chalice with a pentagram inscribed on it. He turned it over and found the words "Blue Feather Coven" inscribed on the bottom. "McInnes, come hither and look at this," the man said.

The second knight dismounted and took the object. "'Tis a coven relic," he said. "We will take this to the priest."

"Nay, wait." Hawksworth rushed out from behind his tree.

"'Tis mine… I mean, I found it. Ah… If truth be known, I stole it."

"Seize him," McInnes said.

The guard drew his sword and held the tip of it to Hawksworth chest. "Who art thou, beggar?"

"Thomas Hawksworth. I come from the Blue Feather Coven."

"I thought as much. Tie him up. The beggar will walk to the castle on a tether behind my horse."

"Nay, sires. I am a servant of the Church. I beseech you, heed my words."

"Aye, the church of the devil," McInnes said. "Now move."

Unknown to Hawksworth and the knights of the church, an observer was perched behind a barrier of rocks in a crag high above the road, watching the scene below. "Great Goddess, I plead the king not take kindly to Thomas Hawksworth," Caleb said.

\* \* \*

"In with thee, dog." The guard threw Hawksworth into a cell and slammed the door shut.

"Thou knowest not what thou art doing. I am not what thou thinkest. I demand to see Father Kipling," Hawksworth said.

"Thou dost demand naught. Thou hadst implements of the devil in thy possession. Be silent with thee or I will be cutting out thy tongue. 'Tis soon enough thy neck will see the end of a rope."

For the next twenty-four hours, three changes of guard fell victim to Hawksworth's pleas. Finally, he was brought before the magistrate.

"Thomas Hawksworth, thou art charged with witchcraft. What dost thou say in thy defense?"

"I am innocent, magistrate. I am a servant of the Church. I was held prisoner for three days by the Blue Feather Clan."

"How camest thou to be amongst the clan?" the magistrate asked.

"My daughter, Jenna Hawksworth, is a chosen one, and a member of the clan. I went to free her from their spell."

"A chosen one? Pray tell, what is a chosen one?"

"A duty is passed down to each new generation by the Goddess Hecate. When that generation falls at one hundred years, they are chosen to open the gates of Hell to allow evil spirits to escape. Jenna is one of the chosen. The one hundred year coming of the chosen ones is nigh."

"The duty is passed down, thou sayest? Must be thou art a chosen one as well then?"

"Aye, 'tis true, but I denounced the teachings of the clan long ago. As I said, I am a servant of the Church."

"Art thou to have me believe that evil is lurking at the gates of Hell as we speak and will escape by the hands of the chosen ones?"

"Aye, 'tis the teaching of the Blue Feather Clan." Thomas looked around the room and realized there were several clerics present. "The clan would have you believe the chosen ones are gods, the only ones able to release these demons to the world."

A stir rose from the galleries.

"Dost thou understand thou dost condemn thy daughter to death with thy words?" the magistrate said.

"Aye, better she die at the hands of the Church, than do the will of the devil himself."

"And thou knowest where this clan is?" the magistrate asked.

"Aye. I can lead thy men to their village. 'Tis but a day's ride from here."

The magistrate stood and informed the court. "At first light, a contingent of guards will take Mr. Hawksworth and ride to the village of the Blue Feather Clan. If the clan is not found, Mr. Hawksworth shall be executed immediately. If found, bring Jenna Hawksworth to me."

\* \* \*

Caleb visited the local tavern and ordered a tankard of mead. He sat at the bar and listened to the conversation around him.

"… said he comes from the Blue Feather Clan."

"Not a very smart chap to tell the magistrate he consorts with witches."

"Word is his daughter is the leader of the witches."

"His daughter?"

"Aye. What kind of man condemns his own daughter to death?"

"A man trying to save his own life, I tell thee."

"If thou dost ask me, the Church is afraid of anything that challenges their power."

"Be hush with thy words, or thou wilt be accused of witchcraft thyself, kind sir."

"Word is, they ride tomorrow to find the clan, and they are taking him with them."

Caleb finished his mead and quietly left the tavern. With Hawksworth in prison, he could do nothing to stop him, so he mounted his horse and rode toward Billingham.

\* \* \*

Caleb arrived in Billingham at dusk on the day of the uprising, just as Hadley, Jenna, and the Council of Thirteen were preparing to depart for the clearing. Jenna had arranged a makeshift bed for the babes in the back of a wagon, with a straw base and several layers of warm, soft blankets for comfort.

"Jenna, I bring word of thy father."

"Pray tell," Jenna said, taking him aside.

"He hath been imprisoned in the king's dungeon, arrested and accused of witchcraft."

"Thou speakest the truth?"

"Aye. He had on his person the chalice of someone in the clan."

"Then our worries are over?"

"Nay. He is working with the clerics. He convinced them of his innocence. They ride toward our village this day."

"Caleb, notify the villagers. No one shall speak of the uprising. No one shall betray the work of the Goddess. They must hide all implements of the craft. The clerics must not find reason to accuse anyone. Come to me in the clearing at the completion of thy task.

As the Goddess wills it, so shall it be."

"Aye, sister, I shall do this thing."

Jenna ran across the common in search of Hadley. "Hadley

Metcalf, where art thou?" she yelled.

"Jenna Hawksworth, calm thyself. I am here."

Jenna grabbed Hadley by the shoulders. "Caleb brings news. The king's men are on their way to the village. We must go to the clearing at once. Ready the babes."

\* \* \*

"Search every house," the captain of the guard commanded. "I want Jenna Hawksworth."

The king's guard entered each home and forced the villagers into the common where they were held by burly guards who wielded swords and spears. The captain sat high on his horse in front of them. He called forth one of his guards. "Bring Hawksworth to me."

Thomas Hawksworth, still in irons, was dragged in front of the crowd. Several murmurs were heard rising from the villagers as they recognized him. "Who among these is Jenna Hawksworth?" the captain said.

Thomas scanned the crowd for several minutes. "She doth not be amongst them."

The captain leaned down close to Hawksworth. "Be very sure, old man. The magistrate will not look kindly on thee if thou betrayest him."

Hawksworth looked at the crowd once more. "Nay. She is not amongst them, and many of the villagers are not here as well. 'Tis mostly women and children and old men."

The captain sat erect in his saddle and walked his horse back and forth in front of the villagers. "Who among you knows of Jenna Hawksworth, and where are the other members of the village?" No one responded. "Very well. Burn the village."

The villagers stood by, many of them crying and screaming out in horror as flames lit up the night sky. While the village around them burned, the captain once more pranced on his horse in front of them. "I ask again. Who among you knows of Jenna Hawksworth?"

Again, none of the villagers responded.

"So be it." He rode his horse into the crowd and grabbed a child from the arms of one of the women. He rode back to the front of the crowd and held the infant above the ground by the arm. He removed his sword from its sheath and held it at the ready to strike.

"No!" the mother screamed from the crowd. "I know of Jenna Hawksworth. Please harm not my babe."

The captain dropped the child to the ground, nearly trampling the infant under the hooves of his horse. "Bring the woman to me," he said, "and shut that child up, or surely it will see the point of my sword."

One of the guards grabbed the mother of the child out of crowd as well as an older girl who stood with the woman. He pushed the girl to her knees in front of the wailing child on the ground. "Take care of the bastard," he commanded and led the mother to the captain.

The captain leaned down in the saddle. "What is thy name, woman?"

"Martha Crocker."

"Tell me, Martha Crocker, what dost thou know of Jenna Hawksworth?"

"Jenna Hawksworth is the chosen one."

# Chapter 55

## 2013—Newcastle upon Tyne, England

Bridgit sat in her bedroom with the drapes drawn tight. She turned the light down low and sat in the middle of the floor with a black candle in front of her. She lit the candle and removed a cloth doll from the drawer of her bedside table. She closed her eyes.

"Lord of the Underworld, hear my voice." She held the doll above the candle. "Behold my enemy. What is inflicted on this effigy will be inflicted on them. For what pain my  enemy has inflicted on me, so shall be inflicted on them."

\* \* \*

Willow and Sawyer dressed for the wedding in their room. "You look beautiful, my love," Sawyer said as she stood behind Willow in the mirror and clasped the brooches around Willow's neck. She placed a gentle kiss on her shoulder.

"If you do that again, we may not make the ceremony," Willow said.

"Are you ready?"

"Just about. Why don't you go on ahead? I'll be there in a minute or two."

Willow went into the bathroom and unzipped her cosmetics bag. She pulled out eye shadow, eye-liner, mascara, and blush and began to apply her makeup. Ten minutes later, she tucked the cosmetics back into her bag and took a final look at herself in the mirror.

"You are amazingly beautiful," Sawyer said from the doorway of the bathroom.

Willow turned around quickly, a brilliant smile on her face. "I could do without the cast. It was a bitch finding a dress that went with it."

"Ah, but it goes with your hair," Sawyer said and laughed. "Come, the justice of the peace is here."

Willow took one step toward the door when suddenly it slammed shut in Sawyer's face. "Holy shit!" she screamed. She heard pounding on the door and a muffled voice from the other side.

"Willow! Willow, are you all right?"

"What happened?" Willow asked. She reached for the doorknob and quickly released it. "Damn! The doorknob is hot."

"I can't open it from this side either. It's locked," Sawyer shouted.

"Sawyer, I'm scared."

"Use the hand towel on the knob."

"It won't turn." Suddenly, the lights inside the bathroom went out. "Great. The lights just turned off and they won't come back on. Damn! Now they're flashing on and off."

"Willow, remember your lessons. Hold the brooches in your hand and pray to the Goddess."

Willow screamed.

"Willow! What happened?"

"The lights are out again and someone is touching me... pulling my hair."

"The brooches, Willow. Use the brooches."

Willow pressed her back against the door and grasped the brooches in her right hand. She closed her eyes and concentrated. "By the Goddess's ray, on this October day, I call thee to bring your light... to bring your might. By the power of three I conjure thee to chase away evil surrounding me. As I will it, so shall it be." Willow repeated the phrase three times when suddenly, the brooches began to glow. The hair pulling stopped, and the lights came back on.

"Willow, what's happening? Talk to me," Sawyer yelled through the door.

"It stopped. It stopped." Willow turned around and touched the doorknob. It was cool and turned at will. She moved aside, pulled the door open, and stepped into Sawyer's arms.

"Great Goddess," Sawyer whispered. "You're all right."

"Now do you believe I wasn't hearing things yesterday morning?"

Sawyer took Willow into her arms. "You're shaking. Are you sure you're all right?"

"I'm fine, just shaken up a bit."

"If Bridgit is behind this, I'll…"

They heard a knock on the door.

"Are you gals ready yet?" Roger asked.

"Yes," Willow said. "We're ready. We just had a bit of a problem with a ghost, that's all," she joked.

"A ghost?"

"I'll tell you about it later, Daddy. Right now I have a hot date to keep."

\* \* \*

Bridgit blew out the candle and collected the bits of hair she had torn out of the doll. She looked at the charred spot on the doll's right hand to assure herself it had not ignited. A low, rumble emitted from the depths of Bridgit's being as she took glee in her torture. "Heed my warning, Willow McCord."

\* \* \*

Willow and Sawyer faced each other in front of the justice of the peace. Matilda stood next to Sawyer while Sandy stood next to Willow. Roger positioned himself beside the JP, facing Willow, Sawyer, and the guests. He held six long cords. About a dozen of the staff gathered around them to witness the joining.

Willow met her father's gaze and realized his eyes were open very wide in surprise. She leaned forward. "Daddy, what is it?"

Roger motioned with his head to look behind her. She

turned slightly and glanced over her shoulder. "Oh, my," she said softly.

"What is it, Willow?" Sawyer looked to see what had both Roger's and Willow's attention. "Sweet Hecate," she said.

"Mom... Maggie," Roger whispered.

"Jenny," Willow said.

Sawyer's eyes filled with tears. "Father... Nana."

In addition to the staff, there in the gathering were more than two-dozen spectators dressed in period garb from modern day to medieval times. Hadley and Jenna were among them, as well as Richelle Hawksworth, Maggie McCord, Jenny McCord, Melinda Hawksworth, William Hawksworth, and all of the chosen ones since Hadley and Jenna.

"Willow," Sawyer said. "The brooches are glowing."

"What are you all looking at?" Sandy asked as she turned around.

"The guests," Willow said.

"Yes, dear. Sawyer tells me the housekeeping staff is more like family. I'm so glad they were able to come."

Willow looked at Sawyer. "She can't see them."

"But your dad can. Only the chosen ones can see."

Willow fought tears. "My heart is so full of emotion right now."

Matilda leaned forward to look at Willow and Sawyer. "No crying until after the ceremony, girls. You'll get me going, and then we'll have a mess on our hands."

"Are we ready?" the JP asked.

"Yes, please begin," Sawyer said.

The JP continued. "Willow and Sawyer have asked to combine traditional wedding vows with a handfasting ceremony that was part of their ancestral heritage. Welcome, one and all, as we celebrate the joining of these two women. Willow, you've chosen to speak first."

Willow's voice was choked with emotion. "Sawyer, I come here of my own free will. Promises I make to you today will cross over the years and souls of all that lies ahead. I seek the blessings of Mother Earth and the virtues of the cardinal directions, East, South, West, and North."

"Willow, I come here of my own free will. Promises I

make to you today will cross over the years and souls of all that lies ahead. I seek the blessings of Mother Earth and the virtues of the cardinal directions, East, South, West, and North," Sawyer repeated.

Roger handed them two small candles and lit each one.

"This candle represents our union. We light it to represent the merging of our lives and our passions," they said together and tipped both candles toward the common wick of a larger candle on the table beside Roger.

The JP raised his hands. "Who gives these two people to each other?"

Roger, Sandy, and Matilda said together, "We do."

"Willow and Sawyer, please face each other and join hands."

A bit awkwardly due to Willow's cast, they joined right hand to right and left hand to left.

The JP continued. "Let us begin. Willow and Sawyer, when you cause each other pain, will you seek to cure it?"

"We will." They held out their joined hands for Roger to drape a cord over.

"Will you both look for the brightness in life and the positive in each other?"

"Yes," they answered together.

Roger draped a second cord across their joined hands.

"Will you share life's burdens with each other so your union may grow stronger?"

"That is our intention."

A third cord was draped across their hands.

"Will you share your dreams and build new hopes?"

"We will."

Roger draped a fourth cord across their hands.

"Will you use the heat of anger to temper the strength of this union?"

"I do anger well. My hair is red for a reason," Willow joked, causing the guests to laugh out loud.

"Willow!" Sawyer said.

"Oops, sorry. Yes, we will use the heat of anger to temper

the strength of our union."

"What she said," Sawyer added.

A fifth cord was draped across their joined hands.

"Will you honor each other and never give cause to break that honor?"

"We will."

Roger draped a sixth cord across their joined hands, then he reached for the ends and tied all of the cords.

The JP addressed Willow and Sawyer. "These knots are not formed by the cords but by the strength of your vows. The length of your union will be based on the promises you've made to each other today." He turned to Willow. "Willow, do you take Sawyer to be your wife, to have and to hold, to love and honor, and treat with reverent respect?"

Willow smiled. "I do—with all my heart."

"Sawyer, do you take Willow to be your wife, to have and to hold, to love and honor, and treat with reverent respect?"

"For as long as my heart beats, I do," Sawyer said.

"Then, let it be known, in the presence of all friends and family gathered here today that from this day forward, Willow McCord and Sawyer Hawksworth shall be joined in marriage. Congratulations, ladies. Brides, you may kiss."

\* \* \*

Much later in the evening, after the guests were gone, and after helping to put the courtyard in order, Willow and Sawyer hugged Matilda, Sandy, and Roger and bid them goodnight.

Sawyer entered the bedroom behind Willow, closed the door, and leaned against it. "This has been the most amazing day of my life."

"And mine as well," Willow said. "I got all choked up when I saw the ancestors there."

Sawyer walked toward Willow and wrapped her arms around Willow's waist. "The Goddess made that possible."

Their gazes locked and neither spoke for several moments.

Finally, Willow brushed Sawyer's lips with her own. "My wife," she whispered. "I like the sound of that."

"Me, too. I want to make love to you, Willow. I want to

feel your passion. I want to taste your essence. My heart's overflowing with love for you. I want to know this is real. I need to know this is forever."

Willow frowned. "Are you okay, sweetheart?"

Sawyer nodded. "Yes. I... I'm not used to this intensity of emotion. You bewitch me. You make me feel things in a way alien to my being. What I feel for you and how I feel when I'm with you, scares me sometimes. I fear it's all a dream and I'll wake up one morning and you'll have never been part of my life."

Willow poked Sawyer's chest with her index finger. "Hear this, Sawyer Hawksworth, and hear this good because I will say it just once. You are the air I breathe. You are essential to my being. I cannot live without you. You are stuck with me forever, like it or not. Never hold back, Sawyer. Never hold back from me or from yourself. Don't go through life half alive. I want to experience all of you, good and bad, and I want to feel it at an intensity that scares me sometimes. If you're never scared, then you aren't truly living. Have I made myself clear?"

Sawyer grinned and nodded. "Okay then, wife. Take me to bed and make me scream."

Willow and Sawyer lay exhausted on the bed. Willow was on her back with her long hair splayed over the pillow, and Sawyer was lying partially on her side with her leg and arm draped over Willow.

"Damn. You wore me out," Willow said.

"Be careful what you ask for," Sawyer joked.

"Hell no—I got just what I wanted."

A sudden rumbling caused them both to tense. "Did you feel that?" Willow asked.

Sawyer sat up. "I did."

The rumbling began again, only this time the bed shook violently. Willow grabbed Sawyer's arm. "Holy shit! Is that an earthquake?"

Just then, the heavy drapes blew out into the room, despite the fact the windows were closed.

Sawyer looked at Willow. "Willow, where are the brooches?"

Willow reached for her throat. The brooches weren't there.

"I… I took them off and put them on the table."

"Reach over and grab them," Sawyer said. The bed shook even more violently, to the point that one or more legs lifted from the floor.

Willow reached for the brooches on the bedside table just as the bed collided with it and knocked the brooches onto the floor. The bed began to levitate higher. Three pictures fell from the walls and crashed to the floor.

"Sawyer, I'm jumping off the bed."

"No, Willow, you might get hurt."

"What else can we do? Levitate here forever?"

As soon as Willow put her legs over the side of the mattress, the bed abruptly fell back to the floor with a thud.

"Off the bed, now!" Sawyer said.

Willow slipped off the bed and took three steps away while Sawyer ran around to her side. Sawyer grabbed her hand only to have it snatched away from her as some force picked Willow up and threw her against the wall.

"No!" Sawyer shouted. She scooped the brooches up from the floor and thrust them toward Willow. "By the power of the Goddess, evil force be gone from this place. As I will it, so shall it be!"

The drapes immediately stilled. Sawyer ran to Willow, who sat on the floor in a heap. "Sweetheart, are you okay?"

"Knocked… knocked the wind out of me," she said, gasping for breath.

Sawyer immediately put the brooches back around Willow's neck and grabbed her shoulders. "Do not take these off again, at least not until after the repression, do you understand me?" she said sternly.

Willow's eyes were wide and filled with moisture.

A sudden pounding on the door startled them. "Willow, Sawyer, are you all right?"

"It's Daddy," Willow said.

Sawyer ran to the bathroom and grabbed their robes. She handed one to Willow, slipped her own on, and answered the door.

"Come in, Roger."

"What the hell is going on up here? We heard some banging followed by a very loud thud that shook the house. Are you two okay?"

"We are now," Sawyer said. "We've had some poltergeist activity over the past couple of days. It started out pretty tame, but this one was rough. I have no idea who's behind this."

"My money's on Bridgit," Roger said. "I had a very bad feeling about her when we met."

"If she's responsible for this, she's pushed me just about as far as she can without retaliation. I won't tolerate her putting Willow's life in danger."

Roger walked into the room and wrapped his arms around Willow. "Are you okay, honey?"

Willow nodded but couldn't stop the tears from rolling down her cheeks.

"Maybe I should stay in here tonight. I'll sleep in the chair."

"No, Daddy, we'll be all right."

"Are you sure?"

"Yes. Go to bed. We'll see you in the morning."

"Sawyer, come to bed," Willow said.

"I'm just going to sit right here and make sure you're safe. Get some sleep. Your initiation is tomorrow. You'll need to be fresh for that."

"If you're staying up all night, then I am, too."

Sawyer ran her hand through her hair. "Please don't argue with me."

"Don't *you* argue with *me*. Look, Sawyer, I'm willing to overlook you talking my head off earlier tonight, because I know you were worried about me. But don't think for a minute I'm going to kowtow to you… or anyone else for that matter."

Sawyer lowered her chin to her chest. "I'm sorry I was so firm with you earlier. I was scared… more scared that I've ever been in my life."

"I know, and as much as it pissed me off, I understand why you did it. Now, depriving yourself of sleep is not going to help either one of us. Please come to bed."

Sawyer took off her robe and slipped into bed beside Willow. She spooned herself against her wife and held her close. "Blessed be.

I love you, Willow McCord."

"And I love you, Sawyer Hawksworth."

Within moments, both were fast asleep.

* * *

The initiation ceremony the next day went off without a hitch. As uneasy as Willow was about appearing before the entire coven in the nude, she exuded a sense of confidence that belied the nervousness she felt inside. Lord Somers presided over the ceremony and acted as though nothing was amiss. Bridgit was also there. She kept her physical distance from Willow and Sawyer but didn't hesitate to send hateful looks and vibes toward them. When the ceremony concluded, Sawyer caught Bridgit alone and pushed her roughly against a wall.

"I warned you about casting spells on Willow. You could have killed her last night."

Bridgit looked at her defiantly, a smug sneer on her face. "I don't know what you're talking about."

"You don't know what I'm talking about? Really?" Sawyer said sarcastically. "The levitating bed and blowing curtains? I taught you those tricks, remember? Don't you dare deny it."

"Was your little girlfriend afraid?"

"Here's a newsflash for you, Bridgit. She's not my girlfriend, she's my wife. We got married yesterday."

Bridgit looked like she'd been slapped, then she quickly recovered. She closed her eyes and rolled her head around on her shoulders, finally looking at Sawyer with venom in her eyes. Her whole demeanor changed, including her voice. "I see. You will regret betraying me, Sawyer. If you think levitating a bed was traumatic for her, you haven't seen anything yet."

# Chapter 56

## The Uprising

"It's nearly dusk, Sawyer. Shouldn't we be heading to the clearing?"

"Soon." Sawyer fell silent.

Willow approached her and touched the side of her face. "Something's wrong. What is it?"

Sawyer took Willow's hand and kissed the palm. "You know me so well."

"Sweetie, we promised to be honest with each other, so tell me what's bothering you."

"I'm worried about you. I'm worried about what Bridgit might do. Her last words to me at your initiation were pretty threatening."

"She wouldn't dare do something in front of the entire coven, would she?"

"I would hope not, but who knows what her state of mind really is?"

"I have the brooches to protect me, love."

"Yes, except they must be separated before the ceremony begins. They are less powerful alone than they are together."

"I'll be fine."

"I hope so. If anything happens to you, I don't know how I would find the will to go on living."

\* \* \*

Jenna stood and looked at the raging fire in the middle of the clearing, Lord Weller at her right and Hadley at her left.

"'Tis time," she said softly. She raised her hands and called out in a loud voice, "'Tis time, brethren. 'Tis time to push back the evil waiting to break free at the gates of the underworld. 'Tis time to show your love and devotion to the Mother Goddess Hecate who seeks your help banishing those who would do evil in the world. Gather around, brethren. Take your places in the circle of life."

The air was electric with excitement and power as the Council of Thirteen formed the innermost circle, followed by concentric circles of clan members, all dressed in white cloaks with oversized hoods. All members of the inner circle wore the blue feather brooch pinned to their cloaks. The wind began to blow, bending the tree branches precariously close to the circle and kicking up leaves and dust.

"Brethren, you wear the color of pureness, of goodness, and of light. Cleanse your souls of negativity and fill yourselves with love for the Goddess and your fellow man," Jenna said.

\* \* \*

Sawyer and Willow took their places in the inner circle, which was rounded out by the Council of Thirteen and Lord Somers. Willow was on Sawyer's right, and Lord Somers was on her left. Other members of the coven, including Bridgit, formed concentric circles around them. All were wearing white robes with oversized white hoods. All those in the inner circle wore the blue feather brooch pinned to their cloaks. The flickering glow of the bonfire in the center of the clearing reflected in strobe-light fashion around them.

Sawyer reached for Willow's hand. "Don't leave my side. I need to know you're close."

"I'm right here, love."

The wind began to howl, and the robes snapped at the legs of the clan members as they were blown around. Clouds swirled in a circular motion above them. Sawyer raised her hands. "Brethren, it is time to call upon the Goddess Hecate and to assist her in pushing back those who wish to break free of Tartarus and wreak havoc on the land of the living. They have grown strong over these last one hundred years, and like our ancestors before us, it is our duty to protect the earth from their evil by sealing the gates of the underworld. It is time to pledge your allegiance to Hecate."

A loud roar of approval rang through the crowd as all members voiced their support for the task at hand.

"Goddess Hecate, trust in your servants and show us the way."

\* \* \*

Jenna raised her hands once more and closed her eyes. "Goddess Hecate, show thy followers the gate thou hast so valiantly protected, so that we may gain power from thy trust and fight the evil that threatens to break through." Jenna's hood was blown off, and she looked upward at the angry dark clouds above them. A tree branch broke off and fell to the ground within a few feet of the circle.

A bolt of lightning lit up the night sky. The winds increased in speed and clouds swirled above their heads. "Followers of Hecate, hold strong in your faith. Waver not from your mission," Jenna said in a loud and clear voice.

\* \* \*

The swirling clouds and deafening wind were upstaged only by the display of lightning that lit up the sky. Sawyer looked around the circle and sensed unease and trepidation. "Mother Goddess," she said in a loud voice, "Give us the strength to carry out this mission. Know that we are mere mortals, weak and scared, but firm in our resolve to stop the evil that waits at your door."

A loud crash of thunder caused several in the group to jump as sheets of rain fell from the sky. "Hold fast!" Sawyer shouted above the storm. Suddenly, and without warning, a burst of light lit up the sky and hovered over the gathering.

"Sweet Hecate," Sawyer said.

\* \* \*

Jenna looked at the bright orb of light that hovered over their gathering. The rain plastered her hair against her face. "The Mother Goddess shows us the way, brethren. Fear not. Bask in the light of her goodness. Each of you, remove thy brooch, beginning in the east, and hold it aloft in offering to the Goddess."

Each member of the inner circle removed his or her brooch and, one by one, held it high above their heads, sapphires facing the orb.

\* \* \*

"Remove your brooches—all of you," Sawyer said. "Beginning in the east, hold it high and call upon the spirits of your ancestors, of those who came before us… of those whose spirits reside within the brooch. Call upon their power to assist in the destruction of evil that lurks at the gate of our Goddess." A bolt of lightning, followed by a deafening crash of thunder, shook the ground.

One by one, the Council of Thirteen raised their brooches and verbally called forth their ancestors. Upon doing so, a bright beam shot from their brooch, directly into the orb of light. Beside them appeared the spirits of those who came before them. A new beam was added as each in the circle summoned their power. The progression moved around the circle, creating a cone of luminance above them as the clan leaders in turn added the strength of their ancestors to the ritual.

As the progression came to Lord Somers at Sawyer's left, he held his brooch high, but no brightness came from it.

"Call upon your ancestors," Sawyer shouted.

"I have. It isn't working!"

\* \* \*

Jenna watched each bright beam bridge the distance between the coven leaders and the orb of light hovering over them. With each new beam, the orb became brighter. By the time the progression reached full circle with Jenna and Hadley, a cone of luminance hung over them and it was impossible to look at the powerful orb. Jenna reached her free hand out to Hadley and interlaced her fingers with hers, then raised her brooch toward Hadley, who did the same. The brooches slipped together and locked, emitting two beams of light extending into the orb.

* * *

"Willow, raise your brooch," Sawyer said.

"But Lord Somers—"

"We'll have to do this without him."

Sawyer placed her arm around Willow and raised her brooch towards her. "May the spirits of all before me join in our quest to defeat the evil that intends to do harm in the land of the living."

Sawyer called each by name as loudly as she could over the rumbling thunder and waited for Willow to do the same. The brooches slipped together and locked, and two beams of light bridged the distance between them and the orb. A surge of power ran through them as the orb grew larger and larger and brightened in intensity. The cone of luminance lit up the entire area, creating a surreal tableau of more than two hundred people in silhouette. The ground around them rumbled as Willow began to levitate a short distance above the earth.

"Willow!" Sawyer looked around frantically and located Bridgit in the row behind them. Bridgit's brow was furrowed, and her eyes were rolled into the back of her head. Only the whites were evident. A deep, guttural growl emitted from her throat. She reached inside her sleeve, withdrew an athame, and threw it at Willow. Sawyer jumped in front of Willow to shield her. The knife penetrated deep within Sawyer's chest. She sank to the ground, and blood ran from her mouth.

"Sawyer… No!" Willow cried as she continued to levitate.

The orb, still connected to the rays of light emitting from the brooches, descended toward the ground. A powerful explosion occurred upon impact. A hole opened in the earth, and a vortex of writhing dark forms clawed their way out of the hole. Willow grasped the joined brooches in her hand and thrust them toward the hole.

"By the power of the Goddess Hecate, I call upon our ancestors to close the fissure and heal Mother Earth. Trap the evilness deep within her bowels."

Jenna appeared beside Bridgit and grasped her by the throat. Bridgit's feet nearly came off the ground as Jenna lifted her.

"Thomas Hawksworth, in the name of the Goddess, I, Jenna Hawksworth, spirit hunter, command thee to leave the body of this woman and descend into the depths of Tartarus."

Bridgit's body convulsed as a dark form seeped from her mouth and was sucked into the vortex. Jenna released her and Bridget slunk to the ground in a heap.

A tornado-like whirlpool formed above the hole as the rumbling increased. Tree limbs danced wildly to and fro as loose branches, leaves, and dirt were sucked into the funnel swirling above the hole. The dark forms rising from the underworld were caught up in the whirlwind, reaching out and trying to escape as they circled around.

The funnel slowly sank into the hole. Everything caught up in it disappeared as the earth around the hole slowly closed and sealed it shut. Jenna, Hadley, and all the ancestors faded away. The Earth trembled as it sealed. The shaking knocked everyone off their feet, and a deathly silence ensued.

Willow dropped to the ground with a thud and scrambled over to Sawyer. She held Sawyer's head in her lap. "Come on, baby. Open your eyes. Don't leave me, Sawyer. Please don't leave me."

\* \* \*

The king's guards rode through the forest toward the bright light in the sky ahead of them. Thomas Hawksworth held on for dear life to the back of another guard, upon whose horse he was riding.

Jenna and Hadley were thrown backward as were all other members of the inner circle when the fissure sealed. One by one, they rose to their feet. Jenna immediately helped Hadley up and led her to the edge of the forest where Caleb and Maura were waiting with the children.

"Thou must take the wee ones and go, right quickly. The king's men will be here anon. Thou must save them. I fear I won't escape this time. Pray do as I say. The babes cannot be harmed."

"But they have nothing on thee, Jenna."

"They know who we are, Hadley. Thou knowest they won't rest until we are all dead. After the massacre in Lancashire, no one is safe."

The thunder of hooves could be heard in the distance. "Great Goddess, they are near. Thou must go."

Jenna removed Hadley's white cloak and wrapped a long, dark hooded cloak around her. She clasped it closed with Hadley's blue feather brooch.

Hadley reached for Jenna's arm. "Jenna, where shall I go? What shall I do?"

"Go to the clan in Scotland. They will care for thee."

"I won't leave thee. I cannot. Pray don't make me go."

Jenna took Hadley's face between her hands. "If I can, I will join thee in a fortnight. If not by then, know that I love thee. Forever, thou wilt live in my heart."

"Come with us, pray."

Jenna kissed Hadley tenderly and touched her forehead to hers. "I cannot. The babes must be saved. Thou knowest how important that is. Thou knowest what is at stake here. I will give thee time to escape. I must lead them away—at any cost."

"Nay!"

"Aye. The Mother Goddess will protect thee on thy journey. Go with thee, now. Caleb shall see to thine escape. I will hold them at bay for as long as I can."

With tears in her eyes, Hadley climbed into the back of the wagon and pulled the blanket over her and the babes.

"Wait. Take these." Jenna retrieved a book, a bag of coins,

and something else from the pouch around her neck and pressed them into Hadley's hand. "The Book of Shadows cannot be found. 'Twould mean the end of the family. Pass these on to the children. Future generations shall need them. Now go."

Hadley reached for her one last time. "I love thee, Jenna. I always shall. Pray come to us. Pray."

"I shall try, my love." Jenna kissed the babes' foreheads. "Be good for thy mum, and know I will always love thee." She looked once more into Hadley's eyes. "God speed, Hadley Metcalf. We shall be together again—if not in this life, then in the Summerlands. Blessed be." Jenna nodded to Caleb and ran back toward the clearing.

Hadley felt the jolt of the wagon as it surged forward. She could hear loud voices in the distance.

"Halt! By decree of the king, thou art to be taken into the custody of the court."

"By what charge?" Hadley heard Jenna demand.

"Witchcraft."

Hadley lay beside the babes and pulled the blanket over them. She stifled a sob as she clutched the Book of Shadows close to her chest. "May the Goddess be with thee, my love," she whispered.

She wrapped the cloak tighter around her and realized, still clutched in her hand, was the object Jenna gave to her for the babes. She opened her hand and revealed Jenna's blue feather brooch, the sister to her own that clasped the cloak she wore. She slipped the brooch into the pocket of her cloak and kept it clasped in her hand. She rode silently into the night with tears in her eyes and fear in her heart.

\* \* \*

Jenna was brought before the magistrate two days later. A collar was around her neck, and her feet and hands were in chains.

"Jenna Hawksworth, thou hast been accused of witchcraft. What say thee in thy defense?"

"I have naught to say, my lord."

"Thy sire, Thomas Hawksworth hath filed claims of thy

guilt, not only of witchcraft, but also of lying with thine own kind. What say thee in thy defense?"

"I have naught to say, my lord."

"Thy village hath been burned and many of thy clan members have been hanged at the gallows. A similar fate awaits thee if thou hast no defense."

"My defense is that I love all my brethren. I forgive those who persecute me. I give to the needy and help the sick. I treat all with dignity and respect. If those are crimes, then I am guilty."

"Thou dost not admit to witchcraft?"

"I admit to naught, my lord. I am but a common blacksmith."

"Then we shall allow God to pass judgment on thee." The magistrate picked up his quill and wrote instructions on a piece of parchment that he passed to the bailiff. "Jenna Hawksworth, thou shalt be subjected to the ordeal by water. Water giveth life. Water giveth purity through baptism. Thou wilt be bound wrist to ankle and thrown into the lake. If thou dost float, 'twill be a sign that thou dost reject baptism, proving thy guilt. If thou dost sink, the water accepts thee and thou art innocent. Judgment to be passed two days hence."

\* \* \*

Jenna was thrown back in the dungeon to await her trial by water. She passed her time praying to the Mother Goddess for redemption and salvation. "Mother Goddess hear my prayer, I place my life within thy care. Slow my body, take my breath, make me seem as still as death. When from the water, I am drawn, let me wake to see the dawn. Let me sleep, long and well. Wake me when I hear the bell. Mother Goddess, hear my plea. As thou will it, so shall it be."

Two days later, Jenna was led in a procession to the edge of the lake. Her wrists were bound to her ankles, and she was rowed to the middle of the lake in a small boat and thrown into the water.

During the ordeal, a small group of people gathered on the embankment, far from the crowd of onlookers. They chanted repeatedly in low tones. "Goddess of death, most gracious Goddess. Healer, ender of sorrow, reliever of pain, receive our sister Jenna. May she become a star in your night sky cauldron and be brewed back to life. God of grain. God of seed, show our sister Jenna the long road through the maze to the place of return."

The crowd of onlookers waited impatiently as Jenna sank and did not rise. Finally, she was hoisted back up and into the boat, limp and motionless. When the boat was rowed to shore, one member from the group of chanters stepped forward to claim her body. He placed her lifeless body over his shoulder and walked away.

# Chapter 57

## 1613—Edinburgh, Scotland

Three days after the repression, Hadley reached Edinburgh, Scotland, to a coven led by one of the Council of Thirteen. She rode to the village and was stopped at the entry gate by a coven guard.

"State thy purpose in this village," he said.

"I am Hadley Metcalf, wife of Jenna Hawksworth of the Blue Feather Coven in Billingham, England. I come seeking shelter for myself and my babes."

The guard's eyes grew wide with excitement. "Hadley Metcalf—wife of the chosen one?"

"Aye."

"Come with me."

The guard led Hadley's wagon through the streets of the village to the stable. Hadley gathered the babes in her arms and followed him to the quarters of High Priest Fraser. Fraser greeted her warmly.

"Hadley Metcalf, it warms my soul to see thee and the babes escaped the clutches of the king's men. I barely escaped myself and arrived home just this morn."

"Jenna sent the babes and me away as soon as the uprising was over. Hast thou word of her?"

"Nay, only that she was arrested. I have no news of her since."

Hadley struggled to maintain her composure.

"We shall pray to the Goddess that she be safe. In the meantime, thou art welcome here. Thou shalt be given food and shelter."

"I am a tailor, Lord Fraser. I will be earning my keep."

"Yes, of course." The priest turned to his servant. "Show Mistress Metcalf to the guest room. We will find suitable quarters for her on the morrow. Blessed be, Hadley Metcalf."

\* \* \*

For several days, Hadley relied on the kindness of the Fraser coven for food, shelter, and enough material to make herself a second smock and clothing for the babes, which she insisted on paying for by bartering her sewing skills. On the fourth day in the coven, she was summoned to the quarters of Lord Fraser.

"Pray, come in and sit down, Mistress Metcalf," the priest said.

Hadley sat and studied the man's face as he paced back and forth across the room. "Thou hast bad news?" she said.

Lord Fraser stopped pacing and faced Hadley. He bowed his head.

"Out with it," Hadley said impatiently. "'Tis about Jenna, is it not?"

The priest nodded. "Word is she was drowned during an ordeal by water."

Hadley began to cry and covered her face with her hands. Loud wrenching sobs escaped her throat as she rocked back and forth. "Jenna. My kind, sweet, Jenna," she cried. "What have they done to thee?"

Lord Fraser pulled a chair up beside Hadley and sat down. He put his arm around her shoulder and pulled her into his embrace.

"She is with the Goddess, Mistress. She is where no one will ever harm her again. Thou shalt see her in the Summerlands."

Hadley was beside herself with grief for several minutes as she cried out her anguish. Finally, she composed herself. She stood and took a handkerchief from her pocket to blow her nose. "Lord Fraser, forgivest thou my hysterics. I need to tend my babes and to think about how I shall provide for them."

"Mistress Metcalf, take time to grieve. The community shall see to thy welfare until thou art able to care for thyself."

"I need not thy charity, Lord Fraser."

"'Tis not charity, Mistress. 'Tis our duty to care for a chosen one who has risked her life for the Goddess."

"I appreciate thy kindness, Lord Fraser. I must go care for my babes. Good day to thee."

\* \* \*

Hadley moved through life in a haze. She kept herself busy by taking in tailoring jobs to earn a living for herself and her children, stopping only to feed the babes and sleep for four hours each night. She barely had time to think of how her life had changed… to think of how the person she loved with all her heart was torn from her, never to be seen again.

Lord Fraser stopped in to see her on a regular basis, urging her to take better care of herself. "Hadley Metcalf," he said, "If thou dost continue the way thou art, thy babes will lose both their mothers. Thou needest to eat. Thou needest to sleep."

Hadley looked up from her sewing. "I have lost my reason for living, my lord."

Lord Fraser stood and slammed his fist into the table. The loud noise startled the babes, and they began to cry. He pointed to them. "They are thy reason for living. They deserve more than thou art giving them. Get a hold of thyself, woman, before thou dost lose them, too." Lord Fraser stomped out of the cottage, leaving Hadley to contemplate her situation.

\* \* \*

Caleb carried Jenna's body into the woods and laid it on a bed of hay prepared specifically for her. He knelt beside his sister and wept openly. Maura knelt beside him and wept into her hands.

Lord Weller and other members of the coven circled around her. Lord Weller placed his hand on Caleb's shoulder.

"Her fate is in the hands of the Goddess."

"Her fate is already sealed," Caleb said angrily. "She is dead—canst thou not see that? Where was thy Goddess when those bastards were drowning her?"

"The Goddess has not abandoned her, Caleb. She merely is sleeping."

Caleb sprang to his feet and faced the priest. "Art thou mad, man? Look at her. She hath not breath in her body. Her heart beateth not."

"Trust in the Goddess." Lord Weller motioned for the coven members to gather more closely around Jenna's body. They held hands in a continuous circle around Jenna and chanted, beginning in a low cadence and repeating it three times at increasing volumes.

"Goddess of death, most gracious Goddess. Healer, ender of sorrow, reliever of pain, receive our sister Jenna. May she become a star in your night sky cauldron and be brewed back to life. God of grain. God of seed, show our sister Jenna the long road through the maze to the place of return."

After the third repetition, Lord Weller raised his hand. "As the Goddess wills it, so let it be." He removed a small bell from the bag around his shoulder and rang it three times.

Suddenly, Jenna stirred.

\* \* \*

Lord Weller moved Jenna into the stable of the burned-out village and set up twenty-four-hour shifts staffed with coven members who continued to chant and pray to the Goddess for her soul. Three days earlier, she had stirred, but had not opened her eyes, nor responded to commands. Her breathing was uneven and slow. Caleb and Maura rarely left her side—even sleeping on the ground beside her. They fed her water periodically throughout the day, and Caleb talked incessantly to her about their childhood and about how much she had to live for.

"When thou wakest, sister, I will escort thee to Scotland to be with thy wife and babes. All thou needest do is wake up. Thou hast many who love thee and need thee. Come back to us."

Jenna opened her eyes. "Brother?" she said.

Caleb began to sob. "I am here."

"Had… Hadley?"

"She is with High Priest Fraser's coven in Scotland—just like thou didst want."

"And the babes?"

"Aye, and the babes."

"Need to see them."

"As soon as thou art strong enough, I shall take thee there myself."

\* \* \*

A week had passed after Jenna opened her eyes before she was able to sit up and consume solid foods. Little by little, her strength grew until at the end of three weeks, she was walking slowly across the barn while holding on to Caleb's arm. "Thou art getting stronger, sister. Soon we will leave for Edinburgh."

\* \* \*

Three days after Lord Fraser stormed out of Hadley's cottage, she paid him a visit. She had bathed and taken the time to comb her hair and don the new smock she had made for herself. She waited in his sitting room for him to appear.

"Mistress Metcalf," he said as he entered the room.

Hadley rose from her seat and smoothed her skirts.

"'Tis good to see thee up and about and taking better care of thyself."

"Lord Fraser, I come to apologize to thee for not appreciating thy concern. Thou hast said it right—I was feeling sorry for myself and neglecting the babes. I simply wanted to stop and thank thee for all thou hast done for me since I came to this village."

Lord Fraser walked across the room and took Hadley's hands in his own. "Apology accepted, Mistress Metcalf. Now go home and fix a hearty meal for thyself. Thou hast grown thin with thy worry and grief."

"Aye. Gramercy, Lord Fraser. Blessed be."

Hadley stepped outside, put on her bonnet, and tied it below her chin. She took two steps toward the common when she heard her name being called.

"Hadley! Hadley Metcalf! Sister!"

Hadley swung around in the direction of the voice and nearly fell to the ground as her legs threatened to buckle beneath her. Coming toward her were Caleb and Maura. Between them, they were supporting a thin and gaunt person."

Hadley took several tentative steps forward. "Caleb? Caleb is that you?" she said. Soon she began to run toward them, but stopped several yards later when she realized who the third person was. "Jenna? Jenna! Great Goddess, Jenna!" she said. Again, she began not run, not caring that her bonnet had blown off.

Hadley threw her arms around Jenna. Tears flowed freely as she kissed Jenna's face over and over. "Jenna, I thought I had lost thee. I thought they killed thee. Thank the Goddess, thou art alive."

"They almost succeeded, Hadley," Jenna said in a hoarse voice. Hadley stepped back and looked at her wife. She started crying once more. "What did they do to thee, my love?"

"Jenna's been sleeping for nigh on two weeks," Caleb said. "Took another three to be strong enough to travel. She needs good home cooking to fatten her back up."

"It looks like thou canst use a little fattening thyself, Hadley," Jenna said.

"I wanted to die when I heard what they did to thee. I thought they had killed thee. The babes were the only reason I could get out of bed in the morn."

"The babes. How are they?" Jenna said, tears forming in her eyes.

"Come home, Jenna. Come see them. They miss their mama."

Jenna completely lost control of her emotions and fell into Hadley's arms crying.

"Welcome home, my love. Welcome home." She looked at

Caleb and saw tears in his eyes as well. "Caleb, Maura, thank you for bringing my wife back to me."

# Epilogue

"Matty, don't be mean to Garret," Willow called out to the little girl as she dumped a bucket of water on her eighteen-month-old brother who immediately began to cry. Willow grabbed a towel from the beach bag and walked to the edge of the water to collect her son.

"Garret is a crybaby," Matty said.

Willow knelt in front of her daughter. "Sweetie, you cry just as hard when Garret is mean to you. You're three years old now, and you need to protect your baby brother—not be mean to him."

"He threw sand at me," Matty said and pouted.

"Did you do that?" Willow asked her son.

Uncaring of the consequences, he nodded.

"Well maybe we should go home if you two can't be nice to each other."

"No!" both children wailed.

"All right then. No more fighting. Come on, Garret, you need another dose of sunscreen."

Willow took her son to the blanket and liberally coated his chest, back, face, and arms with sunscreen and sent him off to play once more with his sister. She smiled as the red-headed little boy's attempt to run through the sand resulted in him toppling onto his hands and knees as his feet sunk into the sand. *You are so like me, little man, she thought. You run headlong into something without a care in the world. I never thought in a million years I'd have two small children at this stage in my life. It's the hardest thing I've ever done, but I wouldn't trade this for anything.*

Willow looked at her daughter, who was busy building a sandcastle with her bucket. *Matilda Hawksworth-McCord, master manipulator. My raven-haired beauty. Everything is a negotiation with you... bedtime, treats, even the clothes you wear. You remind me so much of*—Willow's thoughts were interrupted by a voice from behind her.

"Sorry I'm late, love. My last client just wouldn't stop talking, and the traffic in Boston moved at a turtle's pace." Sawyer sat down on the blanket beside Willow and draped one arm around her shoulders. She kissed her tenderly. "How have the kids been?"

"Fighting as usual. As much as I don't approve of hitting, Garret just needs to put Matty in her place. She's quite bossy."

"Just like her mama," Sawyer said, grinning.

"I was thinking, just like her mum," Willow said.

"Mum!" Matty screamed from the shoreline. "Mum is here!"

Both children charged Sawyer, and soon the blanket was a mass of bodies and sand. Sawyer flipped them onto their backs and administered tickle torture to their bellies until they squirmed out from under her and ran down the beach with Sawyer right on their heels, pretending they could outrun her.

As she watched her family frolic on the beach, Willow's heart overflowed with love and joy. She closed her eyes and inhaled deeply, thinking back to that fateful day nearly four years earlier when Sawyer risked her life to save her. She vividly remembered Sawyer diving in front of her to block the knife Bridgit had thrown at her. She remembered Jenna Hawksworth appearing to reclaim the spirit of Thomas Hawksworth, who had possessed Bridgit's body. But most vividly, she remembered holding Sawyer's head in her lap as blood spilled from her mouth and life drained from her body.

As luck would have it, one of the Council of Thirteen was a trained physician and worked to stem the flow of blood while they waited for an ambulance to arrive. Willow refused to leave Sawyer's side during the whole ordeal. By the time the EMTs took over, Sawyer's pulse was very low. Every second counted to get her to the hospital before she bled out. It took nearly an entire week after being admitted before her condition was upgraded from critical to stable. It was the most horrific week of Willow's life. She thanked the Goddess daily for help from her mother, father, and Matilda. They had kept her emotionally sane as they all waited on pins and needles for Sawyer's condition to improve.

Secondary on everyone's mind was the repression. The ritual had successfully closed the portal and sealed the gates of the underworld, taking the evil spirit of Thomas Hawksworth with it. Bridgit was confined to the psychiatric ward of the hospital for many months and then suddenly disappeared. That was three years ago. The brooches remained joined and stored in the wooden box Sawyer originally had mailed her brooch to Willow in. They were always close by and traveled with them between the US and England. They had learned that possession of them made numerous visits from Hadley and Jenna and other ancestral chosen ones possible.

Several months passed before Sawyer was strong enough to travel. They returned to the US, with Matilda in tow, to relax and spend time on the Cape. Before Sawyer and Willow departed England, the Council of Thirteen called Lord Somers before them and questioned why his brooch did not emit the beam of light during the uprising. They forced him to hold the brooch before them. When he did so, it did not glow, indicating the brooch no longer considered him worthy as leader of his clan. He offered no explanation as he meekly removed his robe and surrendered it, as well as the brooch, to the council. They promptly offered his position to Sawyer. Willow was surprised and more than a little pleased when Sawyer respectfully declined. She cited, as her reason, the desire to focus on building a life with Willow in both the US and England.

During her recuperation at their home on the Cape, Sawyer and Willow discussed having a family. Willow thought back to that conversation as they sat on the front porch swing, drinking wine.

"Wills, I've been thinking about our future," Sawyer said.

"That makes two of us. In fact, that's all I've been thinking about since you were injured," Willow admitted.

"I love you, Willow. I love you more than life itself. If I

had never met you, I would have gone through life not knowing what I was missing. I have never experienced such intense emotion in my life as I have since I met you. I realize now I was only half alive and I have you to thank for bringing such fulfillment to my life. There's only one thing I can think of that would enhance our lives even more," Sawyer said.

Willow placed her index finger across Sawyer's lips to silence her. "I know," she said. "I've been thinking the very same thing. Let's have a baby."

Sawyer's eyes filled with moisture. "Thank you, Willow. I'll carry it if you'd like."

"I'll tell you what—we each need to produce an heir to pass the legacy on to, right?"

"Yes."

"So to give you more time to heal, I'll go first. In a couple of years, we'll talk about a child that you can carry. And if I'm going to have a baby, I want it to be your baby."

"Ah, Willow… have you forgotten that I don't have the right equipment to make that happen?"

"No, but technology does. We'll have your fertilized egg implanted in my uterus, and when it comes time for you to carry, we'll implant my egg in you. Of course, we'll need a frozen pop, but we can make sure it's the same donor so our kids are biological siblings."

Sawyer narrowed her eyes. "Just how long have you been thinking about this?"

"Since I almost lost you a few months ago."

Willow broke from her reverie and gazed at Sawyer and Matty working side by side to build a sand castle, as Garret dug a hole nearby. Matty was the image of her mother, right down to the swarthy skin, dark hair, and blue eyes. Garret on the other hand was fair-skinned, red-haired, and green-eyed, just like her.

*I am truly blessed.* Willow thought.

Sawyer looked up and made eye contact with Willow. Willow smiled and watched as Sawyer said something to Matty, rose to her feet, and walked toward her. She stopped at the edge of the blanket and extended her hand to Willow. "Come play," she said.

Willow placed her hand in Sawyer's and they walked together toward the rest of their lives.

Photo Credit: Brad Fowler, Song of Myself Photography

See her author page at www.karendbadger.com

# About the Author

Karen D. Badger is the author of On A Wing And A Prayer, Yesterday Once More (a 2009 Golden Crown Literary Award winner for Speculative Fiction), In A Family Way, Unchained Memories, Happy Campers, Collective Identity Sweet Angel and Relative-ly Speaking (Books I, II, III, IV, V and VI of the Commitment Series), The Blue Feather, All My Tomorrows (sequel to the 2009 award winning Yesterday Once More) and her latest novel, 1140 Rue Royale...all released by Badger Bliss Books, which Karen co-owns with her wife Barbara Sawyer (aka, "Bliss').

Born and raised in Vermont, Karen is the second of five children raised by a fiercely independent mother, who remains one of her best friends to this day. Karen earned her B.A. in 1978 in Theater and in Elementary Education, and in 1994, earned a B.S. in mathematics. In addition to her novels, Karen is the author of many technical papers on photomask manufacturing, which she has presented at numerous semiconductor industry conferences, and is the holder if several technical patents. Karen is currently in her 38th year as a Principle Member of the Technical Staff with a prominent Semiconductor manufacturer in Vermont.

Karen and her wife, Barb (a retired Lt. Col., US Air Force) live in the beautiful state of Vermont—home of Ben and Jerry's. They spend their spare time with family as well as doing home improvement projects on both their homes in Vermont and New Mexico. They also enjoy camping, kayaking, motorcycling and singing Karaoke.

Please visit Karen's author website at www.karendbadger.com, or the Badger Bliss Books website at www.badgerblissbooks.com. Also like us on Facebook!

# TITLES BY KAREN D. BADGER

www.badgerblissbooks.com

### *On A Wing and A Prayer*
First edition published by Blue Feather Books, Sept, 2005
Second edition published by Badger Bliss Books – Sept, 2014
Third edition published by Badger Bliss Books – August, 2016
ISBN 13: 978-1-945761-01-0, ISBN 10: 1-945761-01-6

### *Yesterday Once More*
First edition published by Blue Feather Books, July, 2008
Second edition published by Badger Bliss Books – Sept, 2014
Third edition published by Badger Bliss Books – August, 2016
ISBN 13: 978-1-945761-02-7, ISBN 10: 1-945761-02-4
2009 Golden Crown Literary Society Award - Speculative Fiction

### *In A Family Way – Book One of the Commitment Series*
First edition published by Blue Feather Books, March, 2010
Second edition published by Badger Bliss Books – Sept, 2014
Third edition published by Badger Bliss Books – August, 2016
ISBN 13: 978-1-945761-05-8, ISBN 10: 1-945761-05-9

### *Unchained Memories – Book Two of the Commitment Series*
First edition published by Blue Feather Books, Oct, 2011
Second edition published by Badger Bliss Books – Sept, 2014
Third edition published by Badger Bliss Books – August, 2016
ISBN 13: 978-1-945761-06-5, ISBN 10: 1-945761-06-7

### *Happy Campers - Book Three of the Commitment Series*
First edition published by Blue Feather Books, Sept, 2013
Second edition published by Badger Bliss Books – Sept, 2014
Third edition published by Badger Bliss Books – August, 2016
ISBN 13: 978-1-945761-07-2, ISBN 10: 1-945761-07-5

### *The Blue Feather*
First edition published by Blue Feather Books, July, 2014
Second edition published by Badger Bliss Books – Sept, 2014
Third edition published by Badger Bliss Books – August, 2016
ISBN 13: 978-1-945761-04-1, ISBN 10: 1-945761-04-0

*Collective Identity – Book Four of the Commitment Series*
First edition published by Badger Bliss Books – January, 2015
Second edition published by Badger Bliss Books – August, 2016
ISBN 13: 978-1-945761-08-9, ISBN 10: 1-945761-08-3

*All My Tomorrows – Sequel to Yesterday Once More*
First edition published by Badger Bliss Books – May, 2015 Second
edition published by Badger Bliss Books – August, 2016
ISBN 13: 978-1-945761-03-4, ISBN 10: 1-945761-03-2

*Sweet Angel – Book Five of the Commitment Series*
First edition published by Badger Bliss Books – June, 2015 Second
edition published by Badger Bliss Books – August, 2016
ISBN 13: 978-1-945761-09-6, ISBN 10: 1-945-761-09-1

*Relative-ly Speaking – Book Six of the Commitment Series*
First edition published by Badger Bliss Books – March, 2016
Second edition published by Badger Bliss Books – August, 2016
ISBN 13: 978-1-945761-10-2, ISBN 10: 1-945-761-10-5

*1140 Rue Royale*
First edition published by Badger Bliss Books – Sept, 2016
ISBN 13: 978-1-945761-00-3, ISBN 10: 1-945761-00-8

www.ingramcontent.com/pod-product-compliance
Lightning Source LLC
Chambersburg PA
CBHW051444260626
47162CB00001B/237